THE SCENT OF LIGH

THE PROWLER
1989

In the early Cold War years, Iceland is a pawn in a giant geopolitical chess game. Our young narrator is struggling to navigate the politics and her complicated family, and to find a voice for herself at a time when Icelandic children were told to be silent. A prowler is lurking in the streets of Reykjavík, and this prowler – who may be us, the reader – offers a path to speaking the unspoken.

ZERO HOUR
1991

When the narrator's father, a celebrated geophysicist, falls seriously ill, the diagnosis is an inoperable brain tumour. And so the countdown to zero begins. *Zero Hour* traces the course of the father's illness and final moments, his dignified death a testament to the human spirit. In the shrinking of time and distance between generations, the narrator confronts the reality and grief of absolute endings.

THE SUBSTANCE OF FORGETTING
1992

In the tradition of Anaïs Nin and Marguerite Duras, *The Substance of Forgetting* creates intensely poetic moments of being. Between these moments, in the silences between words, lovers find and lose each other, and the narrator moves to a lush valley in central B.C., awakening to the idiosyncrasies of its seasons and the possibilities of contentment and transcendence.

THE ROSE GARDEN: READING MARCEL PROUST
1996

The narrator is on an academic exchange in Germany wherein all that happens are things that are not supposed to happen, and her life has become a curious mix of reality and fiction. Combining the genres of fiction, memoir, the familiar essay, and theoretical speculation, *The Rose Garden* defies rules of style and genre and provokes the question of what meaning literary works have in our lives.

NIGHT TRAIN TO NYKØBING
1998

A woman in love boards a train, not knowing if the lover she leaves behind will ever be with her again. *Night Train to Nykøbing* is a transformative tale that articulates the dense codes of love, the passion of waiting, and the terrifying intensity of a life on the edge of abandonment. But it also is a story of return to a country, to a culture, to a language, and finally to a heart that has wandered through the desert of time.

THE
SCENT
OF
LIGHT

KRISTJANA GUNNARS

INTRODUCTION BY
KAZIM ALI

COACH HOUSE BOOKS, TORONTO

first edition

Published with the generous assistance of the Canada Council for the Arts and the Ontario Arts Council. Coach House Books also acknowledges the support of the Government of Canada through the Canada Book Fund.

LIBRARY AND ARCHIVES CANADA CATALOGUING IN PUBLICATION

Title: The scent of light / Kristjana Gunnars ; introduction by Kazim Ali.
Other titles: Novellas. Selections
Names: Gunnars, Kristjana, author. | Ali, Kazim, writer of introduction.
Identifiers: Canadiana (print) 20210353236 | Canadiana (ebook) 20210353244 | ISBN 9781552454381 (softcover) | ISBN 9781770567078 (PDF) | ISBN 9781770567061 (EPUB)
Subjects: LCGFT: Novellas.
Classification: LCC PS8563.U574 S6 2022 | DDC C813/.54—dc23

The Scent of Light is available as an ebook: ISBN 978 1 77056 706 1 (EPUB), ISBN 978 1 77056 707 8 (PDF)

TABLE OF CONTENTS

INTRODUCTION
by Kazim Ali

From the late 1980s to the late 1990s, Kristjana Gunnars published five transgeneric books comprised of a dynamic blend of fiction, autobiography, literary theory, and philosophy. Elusive and poetic, these books ranged in setting from the urban spaces of Denmark to remote towns in Iceland and across the northern part of the North American continent from the prairies to the ocean; they also shift between style and literary genre. They were reviewed as novels, as memoirs, as literary criticism, and sometimes reviewers didn't know what category they belonged in. Rigorous yet passionate, informed by writers like Kierkegaard, Nin, Proust, and Duras as much as by the stark and beautiful landscapes of Gunnars' world, these books have been treasured by a devoted readership and lauded by critics and writers alike.

What is it about the number five structurally? Besides the classic dramatic structure, in fiction we have the five novels of Nin's *Cities of the Interior*, Fanny Howe's collection *Radical Love*, Durrell's *Avignon Quintet*, and even what I see as a five-work cycle of books and films in Duras's oeuvre, all based on a single moment – a woman driven mad by the betrayal of her lover – and all made between 1964 and 1975: the novels *The Ravishing of Lol Stein*, *The Vice-Consul*, and *L'Amour*, and the films *India Song* and *La Femme du Gange*.

Howe's and Nin's cycles also both travel over the same incidents, with the same characters, though geographical shifts – in Howe's case from New England (the 'deep north,' Howe calls it) to the California-Mexico border, and in Nin's case from Paris to New York to Mexico as well. In all these works a woman travels through landscapes both external and internal, borne by the poetry of language, a supporting cast that feels more like figures in a dream than real people, and narrative deeply informed by psychoanalysis, in Nin's and Duras's case, and non-dualist Christian and Eastern theologies in Howe's. It's important to say that, unlike Nin (but like Duras and Howe), Gunnars did not necessarily compose these five books *as* a cycle, and any connection between them was not made by publishers as they were being published, but by Gunnars herself. And of course, if the reader has anything to say about it (and of course we do), they can be read that way. They unfold that way.

Gunnars' work differs importantly from these structurally antecedent works in that her short books do not settle at all comfortably into a sole genre: though nominally written under the sign of fiction and in the form of the short novel, they are as equally inflected with autobiography, poetry, theory, and philosophy, shifting seamlessly between them in a swirl, often from paragraph to paragraph. Only one volume – the third of the five, unintentionally or not at centre – has anything close to a traditional chapter structure. The others are made of small fragmented sections that unfold, chapterless, across the entire book. Only in the case of the first volume, *The Prowler*, are these fragments numbered; in the others they are marked, in their original publication, by various glyphs: a fleuron in *The Rose Garden*, a diamond-like glyph in *Night Train to Nykøbing*, and a half-tone horizontal bar in *Zero Hour* (these marks have been standardized in the current edition). 'Writing narratives in fragmented form is not such a new idea,' says Gunnars. 'Ovid's *Metamorphosis* is fragmentary' (*Kristjana Gunnars: Essays on the Work*, 38). She claims that the fragments of *The Prowler*, for example, were essential to tell 'a very dislocated and disconnected story' (*KG*, 39). 'Fragmentation is an obvious experience of migration,' she further comments (*KG*, 40). Jabès, one of her own cited forebears and influences, felt that the fragment was vital to tell of lived experience precisely because the space between the fragments is writing that actually happened (Jabès, qtd in *KG*, 77).

Gunnars' cycle further deviates from previous examples in that a stark realism is married seamlessly to extremely stylized poetic narratives. The cities and landscapes of the Canadian West – Winnipeg, Regina, the Albertan mountains, and the Sunshine Coast – provide vital geographic context for the deeply examined inner lives of the characters. These novels don't really have *plots* so much as they have *situations*. The protagonists – most often women resembling Gunnars herself – contend with various significant moments in a life, telling of girlhood and liberation, of the death of a parent and the loss of a lover, and finally some attempt at reconciliation, with both one's self and what one has lost. The landscapes of Iceland and the Canadian West which dominate these books are rugged, beautiful, and can be treacherous to one who does not know them well. There's always a contrast to the safe and familiar landscapes of the small towns and cities where the narrators live and the wider (and wilder) world around them. The young girl in *The Prowler* is always wet and cold and hungry. This feeling of a desperation for nourishment repeats itself throughout the books, whether it is for actual food, for love, or for fulfillment.

But there is a 'five-act'-ness about the assemblage. Nin's books, as critic Sharon Spencer points out, work more spatially—there's only the lightest sense of a chronological order in which they take place, and Nin herself suggested that a reader could enter at any point. Howe's novels double back on themselves both chronologically and spatially, and they were not written (or published) in the order they now appear together as a cycle. Duras's opus shifted not only between literary genres, but also in mode itself, transitioning into film.

In Gunnars' case, these five works have a chronology, taking the main character from childhood to late middle age and through stages of discovery in her own life, from wonder to sensual pleasure to the sadnesses and regret and particular disappointments that accompany any life well lived. There is also a circular movement through space throughout the cycle from Iceland to Canada, across the continent (including the US American Pacific Northwest) and then back to Europe. One also never gets the sense in these books that they are being told as they are – would the genre be called 'autofiction'? 'Autotheory'? 'Theoretical fiction'? None of these terms seems adequate applied to Gunnars – her style seems to emerge not from a desire for cleverness or an intellectual or aesthetic commitment, but because the stories could not be told any other way.

This remarkable multi-genre approach allows the writer to understand the fact that she too is a flawed participant in the creation of the literary text. As she writes in *The Prowler*, 'The text desires to be true. It knows

that what is written is not exactly true, so the desire goes unsatisfied. //
The story repeats the attempt at telling itself. The text tells all other texts:
there is only one of me' (48 [all page numbers for the five novellas refer to
this edition]). Of course there *isn't*. The complex act of trying to discern
the truth in one's own writing seems to almost *require* repetition. The
'prowler' of the title is an actual prowler haunting the protagonist's Icelandic
hometown, but it is also the adult writer herself, looking back on childhood,
on experience, and trying to synthesize life into literature. This 'stranger
at the door' (Gunnars uses the phrase as the title of her book on writers
and writing) might be the writer herself, who does not know her own text
as she writes it, but may also be the reader entering the text. Throughout
the books, strangers *do* appear at the doors of the narrators themselves,
providing moments of mystery and alarm within the texts themselves.

'The story is always somewhere else,' she concedes. 'I imagine a book
that pretends to tell an official story. In the margins there is another story. It
is incidental, it has little bearing on the official story, but that is where the
real story is' (38). This may put us in the mind of Chimamanda Ngozi
Adichie's 'danger of a single story,' seeming to make the case for fiction that
leans into multivalence, polyvocality, and fracture. Here, however, the books
themselves are very tightly unified around a single situation or theme. In
fact, this is one reason she makes a case for 'short books': 'The truth is always
beyond us, and instead of packing our lives with words, we can draw back
and we can say much less, but make each word count more.' Of course,
writing a 'short book' also lets the writer off the hook in a thrilling way:
without the pressure to be exhaustive (to exhaust!), a writer achieves a certain
kind of freedom with language, with structure, with narrative arc. 'The short
book has in common with poetry that it can be read more than once,' Gunnars
points out, 'and, in fact, is meant to be read again. Unlike the very long novel,
which can only be very long if each word is not too intense, the short book
does not need to be "consumed" as a consumer item' (*Stranger*, 85).

The struggle of the writer to transform or transmute life into literature in a
meaningful way may be why in each book there is a fluidity of time (the
story as it happens, but also the narrator writing the story) as well as place

(Denmark/Iceland, Winnipeg/Portland, BC Interior and Coast, Trier/ Hamburg, and Denmark/Saskatoon/Calgary). The shifts in time and space are required by the core structure of each book: a writer is writing a book. She writes the book and she tells about what it was like to write the book. In the later volume *Night Train to Nykøbing*, Gunnars explains, 'Whenever I look at my watch in British Columbia, I calculate what time it is in Oslo, Norway. What time it is in Copenhagen, Denmark. I live in more than one time zone … I am going to work and coming home from work at the same time' (272). The creation of the narrative by the writer is part of the 'plot' (if there can be said to be one) itself, and the relationship between the writer and her text is fraught indeed: 'The writer cannot escape repression' Gunnars writes. 'The text is the writer's prison.//The words will not take the writer into themselves. The author is therefore locked out of the book' (*Prowler*, 95). This tension, exacerbated eventually by the presence of the *reader*, will continue.

Zero Hour opens with the declaration of such tension: 'To write you this I have come to the Gateway to the West' (89). It's a startling opening, a poetic deviation from what in a more standard grammar and prose might read, 'I came to Winnipeg to write this to you.' It begins, rather, with the verb, compresses the pronouns together, and uses a more myth-building syntax to announce arrival in a more mythic place. Further, this mythic naming becomes ironic because she has come to the 'Gateway to the West' *from* further west: she is driving to Winnipeg from Portland, Oregon by way of Saskatchewan. She has come to write of the death of her father. She says, 'I have heard of *ground zero* writing. I imagine it as a writing in which the author does not know what to do' (89). While attempting to write of the death of her father (a 'bomb' she says, comparable only to the birth of her son), she comes to a strange city in a car whose odometer has spun out of control and can no longer tell her how far she has travelled.

The 'ground zero' invokes this placeless place, a place without knowledge, but also language without progenitor, invoking Roland Barthes' *Writing Degree Zero*. Agreeing with Barthes, who sought a language new and free of 'bondage' (Barthes, 82), Gunnars says, 'The fact is that language becomes tainted with usage. People use words carelessly. Advertising manipulates the meaning of words. Images fall on us from everywhere, disassociating us from our knowledge and experience' (*Stranger*, 11). For this reason, not only must the *language* be new, the book, the way it unfolds, the way a story is told, ought also to be new, fresh, unexpected. It is, of course, *another* argument for the short book: in that brevity, the shock of experience can better be experienced, like a plunge into a cold pool. The difficulty of the new may be impossible to achieve properly in a longer book: 'A regular novel of more than two hundred pages would suffer the chaos of this type of story, told honestly and fearlessly' (*Stranger*, 87).

The shock of the new can be told in a short book better because the reader can experience it quickly and then return to it, then return to it again. Gunnars quotes Barthes himself near the close of *Zero Hour*: 'Literature itself is never anything but a single text: the one text is not an (inductive) access to a Model, but an entrance into a network with a thousand entrances' (Barthes, qtd in *Zero Hour*, 129). *Zero Hour* might easily be read as a memoir – the events described are events that happened; the father described in the book has Gunnars' father's name, Gunnar Bödvarsson, and his career as a geothermal scientist and professor who engineered the system that heats the Icelandic capital – but it is written in the structure of a novel, long before such books of memoir and nonfiction were being commonly written. It uses characterization and the narrative tension intrinsic to good fiction throughout the narrative, including in its dramatic closing: as if acknowledging the actual power of writing in the real world, at the close of the narrative two things happen simultaneously: in homage to the haywire of the odometer, all the clocks in the house stop, and then, at the threshold of the door of the house in Winnipeg, in a burst of music at the end of the book about the death of the father, another of the metaphorical 'strangers' appears.

As Gunnars moves from a childhood in Denmark and Iceland to the pain of losing a parent and negotiating the terrain of recounting such losses, there is a pause in the centre of the quintet, a lull in the beautiful Okanagan Valley, surrounded by fruit-laden trees, along a peaceful lake. In fact, if there's a drama in *The Substance of Forgetting*, it's the drama of how to handle the fruit. The trees are overrich and the protagonist cannot pick the fruit fast enough: it falls to the ground and rots, making the paths and roads dangerous. In one case an old beautiful tree cracks and breaks under the weight of unpicked fruit and must be chopped up and carted away.

Duras is an obvious totem in these books that all look back at an irrevocably gone past, but with something more incisive than mere nostalgia. *The Lover* famously begins with the aged and ruined ('ravaged' in Barbara Bray's English, 'devastée' in Duras's French) face of the author, while *The Substance of Forgetting* opens with beauty: '"You are beautiful, madame." I would like to begin with that. *You are beautiful madame.* Just like that' (148). The book recounts the story of the protagonist and her Quebecois separatist lover in a summer house in the fruit-heavy valley. Unlike Duras, the book is not haunted by death and loss, but by the heavy perfume of late summer: 'How peaceful it is to see. I thought of all the years we wanted to say things and there was no language for them. Even if we had the language, we would not have known how to use it' (153). The protagonist (can we call her Gunnars? For convenience's sake? It seems inaccurate) knows that 'Jules' in the book is not Jules, but there is no other way for her to recount the relationship, and yet she worries because even though she is writing of love, she is well aware of the vexed relationship between a writer and writing, between an author and her book. 'I was thinking that the author of the text no longer remembers what was reality and what was dream,' she writes. 'What was lived and what written. If I write what I have lived I too will think it is just a story. I will forget where the story came from' (158).

The relationship between landscape and character is also foregrounded in this book. At the centre of a cycle in which all the characters are always travelling from one place to another (whether in space or time) here two Canadians (one an immigrant from Iceland and the other a separatist from Quebec) linger in the locus of the valley and in the moment of one summer. One of their curious rendezvous points is the physical manifestation of both the condition of travel and the material construction of the nation of Canada: the railroad tracks that run from coast to coast of the continent and through their small town. They lie on the tracks and hold one another. As Gunnars is always aware that the story could have been told differently, that another story could have happened, she muses, 'If he had kissed me on the railroad track we would have forgotten ourselves in the moment. We would not have heard the train rolling out of the fog. We would not have seen the headlights' (174).

It's not a drama Nin would be concerned with, so embedded in one another are dream and life in her fiction. In fact, Nin's interest was alchemical, precisely that dissolution of individual experiences into some kind of collective unconscious where transmutation could occur. Gunnars lives by the cold light of day. 'For better or for worse this is where I live,' she says. 'The breathing space they sometimes call a tourist trap. The place we would like to be trapped in but never have time. The vacation spot. The carnival where Ferris wheels roll and whistles blow and laughter can be heard ringing among the bells' (167). This moment of pause, of stillness at the centre of a life and at the centre of a cycle of novels – the author herself was perhaps unaware, but the *reader* has come to know this – affords a chance to muse on those alternate stories, the ones the text didn't allow the writer herself to tell. There is a relationship here between *desire* of the body and the desire of the writer to tell the story she wants to tell as she wants to tell it. Lacan may warn that one desires what one does not want, that what one desires will ruin one, but as *The Substance of Forgetting* opens with a face of beauty, not ruin, so too does it try to release the protagonist from her fear of loss: 'Life cracks. Inside the cracks are amazing stories … How not to look behind you. Not to retrace your steps. To let the past be the past and the moment be only the moment' (186).

If *The Substance of Forgetting* presented a lull, then *The Rose Garden: Reading Marcel Proust* is a definitive turn. While *The Prowler, Zero Hour,* and *The Substance of Forgetting* all waver between fiction and autobiography, with lashes and slashes of metacommentary and theory woven in, the subtitle of this book announces that it will metaphorically wear its heart on its sleeve. Though it too has a fictional framework involving a Canadian literary scholar on a research leave in Germany reading all of Proust over the course of one summer, it functions more deeply as an extended essay on the question of the previously mentioned conflict between author, text, and reader. Both the titular rose garden and the subtitular Proust are only the starting points here, as Gunnars calls herself a 'hostile reader or a perverse one.' Only vaguely moved by the scent of the roses, she determines she will not read Proust in any orderly way but only 'dip into those three volumes at random like you would dip a poisoned pen' (201). The author at odds with her text that sought to repress her has now become the reader, betraying the intents of the author with her own practiced engagement with the text.

While she reads, there is a mysterious graffitist at work defacing the churches and other buildings of Trier, Germany. She invokes Artaud in thinking of the language of graffiti, appearing in unlikely places to 'smash' a passerby with their language. 'This must be why Proust is so captivating,' she thinks. 'He knows what he is thinking. He does not dispel your thoughts or blow your thoughts apart like Artaud' (203). Of course, Proust then becomes a symbol of an author who *knows* what he is doing, unlike the writer of *Zero Hour*, necessarily lost in the thicket of her text. But the reader – the reader is meant *to find* the text, isn't it so? 'Perhaps I am not a perverse reader,' she reasons, 'but a possessive one. I am possessive of the text because I know no one can improve on Proust' (207).

Later, a student writes to her about his own experience with one of her books: '[He] told me he read my book on acid. On acid it was a "great book." Then he read it again straight and it was "so different."' In this case the reader's own experience changed the book. Gunnars the writer and Gunnars the reader agree: 'In that sense, the reader should act as terrorist. Should blow things apart. The ideal reader for Marcel Proust, it seems to follow, would have to be Antonin Artaud' (207). It's an exciting idea, the notion of a novel being disordered by a reader, one that corresponds to Barthes' notion of '*plaisir*' (pleasure) or '*jouissance*' (joy or bliss) in a text. Barthes argues that in a 'readerly text' the reader is a passive consumer and may well receive (*receive*: see where this is going?) 'pleasure,' but it is in the 'writerly text' – a text governed by difficulty and shifting modes and codes, where the reader must contend and engage with and even interrogate the text itself – that one can truly find bliss and transformation.

It is possible that such a text is actually narcissistic, suggests critic Linda Hutcheon, though she goes on to say, 'in covertly narcissistic texts the teaching is done by disruption and discontinuity, by disturbing the comfortable habits of the actual act of reading' (Hutcheon, qtd in *Rose Garden*, 210). If it seems like a risky proposition for a writer, it's a worthy one. The 'unsettled reader' (as Hutcheon calls them) has a chance of freeing themselves from old, set notions and calcified imaginations. Neither is misinterpretation the danger one often assumes it to be. Says Gunnars, 'Appropriate understanding is beside the point. So is the fluency of the lie' (211).

Why fiction at all then? *The Rose Garden: Reading Marcel Proust* offers more potential, more narrative possibility, a more grounded exploration in fiction than would be possible in the mere theoretical language of a critical essay. The protagonist's reading of Proust is many times richer because it happens not only against the backdrop of her relationship, but also within the context of the strange nocturnal publications of the anonymous graffitist, as well as amidst theoretical reflections on Artaud, Lispector, Nin, and Kierkegaard. The divergent strands of inquiry and dual structure of theory and narrative actually hold this hybrid book together. 'I am a fickle, unfaithful reader,' confesses the protagonist, commenting on her commitment to Albertine and not to the narrator of Proust's novel. It is this that 'poisons the well of Proust's sincerity. He did not count on the unpredictable reader' (220). But the writer too can be fickle, can approach a subject from many contradictory angles, can swim free of a reader's expectations, can evade a critic's demarcations. Proust, in particular, 'will not be loyal to single thoughts, but allows them all to operate at once' (221).

Once again one finds oneself returning to Gunnars' earliest conundrum, the one she raised in *The Prowler* when she suggested that the text knows 'that what is written is not exactly true' (48) or that the 'text is the writer's prison' (57). Here, after considering her own role as an 'unsettled' or 'fickle' reader, or 'hostile or perverse reader,' she comes to a realization of herself as a writer: 'I am not unaware that I could be telling all this differently. I could be telling a story, the story of my summer in Germany. It would have a beginning, a middle, and an end. A good story, perhaps.' But such a story would come at a cost, a cost too high to pay: 'I would be the protagonist, but not the heroine. I would come out rather vanquished' (*Rose Garden*, 236–237).

This all brings of course to a curious question: is the poetic novel, the novel that includes autobiography and theory and poetry, a particularly feminist form of writing? When one considers the masters of this form, it is difficult indeed to miss their commonality: Virginia Woolf, Marguerite Duras, Anaïs Nin, Marguerite Young, Elizabeth Smart, Anna Kavan, Katherine Mansfield,

Djuna Barnes, Bessie Head, Eva Figes, and among contemporaries one might add Carole Maso, Fanny Howe, Kirsty Gunn, Jenny Offill, Miriam Toews, Rachel Cusk, Ananda Devi, and Eimear McBride. Gunnars makes a case for the theoretical in fiction, especially for women writers: 'There is a certain pressure on women writers, that their work be "moving," emotional, and therefore that it should exclude the intellect' (*Stranger*, 65). The multiplicity and multivalency of fiction that incorporates other genres of thoughts is of particular importance then to the 'hostile reader' who might also be said to be a feminist reader. The novels with plots and Aristotelian dramatic arcs may even favour the male patriarchal reader who does not seek to reconfigure thought but rather seeks reassurance and affirmation that present hierarchies are appropriate, predictable, and safe.

The safely plotted novels actually *confuse*, suggests Gunnars: 'Fictions are false because they provide false endings,' whereas *metafictions* (as we might call them) create openings, avenues, passageways down which a reader could travel' (*Rose Garden*, 241). Metafiction 'shows how it is put together, and that it is an artifice and not reality.' In other words, fiction like Gunnars' does not depict a life of another to be viewed and consumed as spectacle, but rather presents an engaging and engaged text that invites and requires a reader to become an equal in the construction of meaning and impact. On the other hand, the short novel, the one that invites revisiting and rereading, might be thought of as a feminist form, especially the novel in fragments. 'I think of the fragmentary novel itself as a genre with a long history ... that lends itself to the memory and lives of women, because many women struggle with issues of insignificance, of lack of authority, of silencing, all of which break up the authoritative voice of a confident and assertive (in Barthes' words, "militant") speaker' (*KG*, 40).

In such books the woman writer may introduce a new form of 'authorship,' one that disclaims 'authority' and instead can be an open experience, one in which the author can 'know nothing.' As Christl Verduyn explains, Gunnars's writing 'allows a woman access and control over language, writing, and a new cultural expression and re-presentation' (*KG: Essays on the Work*, 185). Gunnars is aware of the radical potential of a 'difficult' book. In discussing her short fiction (collected in the books *The Axe's Edge*, *The Guest House*, and the brilliant *Any Day But This*), Gunnars says, 'That kind of writing, where the narrator addresses someone quite distant and uninvolved makes for a lonelier narrative.' In the novels, on the other hand, she seeks to bring the reader into the text, 'sometimes as intimate, sometimes as magical other' (KG: *Essays on the Work*, 48).

This reach toward the reader as an intimate (or even magical) other governs what would come to be the last novel in this impromptu assemblage of texts, *Night Train to Nykøbing*. The book takes place on a journey – a woman is on a train leaving her lover behind, unsure if she will see him again – and is addressed to a specific, local character, the lover in question, one Jan. Travel has always been important in these books, though normally it is a change in locale and time necessitated by separate strands in the book, the fiction and the metafiction. In the case of *Night Train*, the character herself is *also* in transit, remembering the affair, so one could say there are *three* strands present here. The various travels of Gunnars' narrators might in one sense be said to be a logical reflection of the migrations and trans-migrations of the writer herself, but on the other hand they might be seen as a poetic lens through which to see the instabilities and emotional voyages that govern a life.

The protagonist of *Night Train* enters her compartment at the beginning of the novel and takes the backward-facing seat, because then she can view the station and her lover standing on the platform for as long as possible. She does not want to write the book but she begins writing. 'It is not because I prefer to write about him,' she claims. 'To have him in my words like a ghost in my language ... But because he has to be there. As necessarily as there has to be air ... Without him there, I have no words at all' (269). The space the book takes place in – literally, the train compartment – may be claustrophobic compared to the other novels, but the brain is wider than the sky, as Dickinson says. In one peculiar moment the narrator is remem-bering, an optometrist is examining her eyes and, while she is peering in, the narrator suddenly worries that the optometrist will see the narrator's lover, that she will fall in love with him, that she will want to steal him away. It's a startling moment of the writer of a 'writerly text' being *jealous* of letting the reader in, of being alarmed at what the reader might do.

The anxiety, of course, also stems from a writer being deeply committed to writing this kind of fiction, unable to predict the ending of her own story. 'It had not occurred to me until this moment that I would need to stay until the end,' she writes late in the novel. 'An ending I could not imagine, yet I should wait for it' (308). In that sense too, these seem deeply *Canadian* books, exploring the textures and layers of what it means to live in this multi-ethnic, multi-lingual, multi-historied society. Throughout the books, the narrators experience their own selves as strangers in the landscape, often dangerous or unknown, like the train revealing itself through fog. And what *is* Canada after all? The narrator in *The Substance of Forgetting* thinks about her own lover, the French separatist Jules, 'My English desires his French. It is that simple. Without the other language, my words have no significance' (162–163). The relationship between the two lovers reflect the tension and desire between the different tongues within Canada as well. '*What does English Canada want?*' she wonders. 'English Canada wants the presence of French Canada.' Most often, the narrators know they are not central to their own experience, that the other – whether the Quebecois lover in *The Substance of Forgetting*, or the Indigenous woman in *Zero Hour*, or the mysterious graffitist of *The Rose Garden* – is more central to understanding. The narrator of *Substance* goes on to wonder, '*What does French Canada want? A kiss. A stolen kiss and separation*' (163).

These novels are meant to be experienced, not just in language, but in their rhythms, in their interruptions and silences, in their structures and patterns and shapes of thought. In the shifts between internal and external, between narration and dialogue and philosophical thinking, a reader can immerse themselves and find the flow of thought that every human lives in, a music daily as life. These books do not merely depict life nor tell about lives lived by characters outside the writer or the reader. They are themselves alive. And in them a reader comes to life.

San Diego
Autumn 2021

WORKS CITED

Gunnars, Kristjana. *The Prowler*. Red Deer: Red Deer College Press, 1989.

———. *Night Train to Nykøbing*. Red Deer: Red Deer College Press, 1998.

———. *The Rose Garden: Reading Marcel Proust*. Red Deer: Red Deer College Press, 1996.

———. *The Substance of Forgetting*. Red Deer: Red Deer College Press, 1992.

———. *Stranger at the Door: Writers and the Act of Writing*. Waterloo, ON: Wilfrid Laurier Press, 2004.

———. *Zero Hour*. Red Deer: Red Deer College Press, 1991.

Tschofen, Monique. '"A Moving-On Into the Unknown": Interview with Kristjana Gunnars,' in *Kristjana Gunnars: Essays on Her Works*, edited by Monique Tschofen. Toronto: Guernica Editions, 2004.

———. '"With a Ruse of Heart and Language": The Movement of Thought in Kristjana Gunnars's Writing,' in *Kristjana Gunnars: Essays on Her Works*, edited by Monique Tschofen. Toronto: Guernica Editions, 2004.

Verduyn, Christl. 'Culture and Gender in Kristjana Gunnars's Writing,' in *Kristjana Gunnars: Essays on Her Works*, edited by Monique Tschofen. Toronto: Guernica Editions, 2004.

THE
PROWLER

for Gunnar, my father

The story of my life doesn't exist. Does not exist.
There's never any centre to it. No path, no line.
There are great spaces where you pretend there used to be
someone, but it's not true, there was no one.

– Marguerite Duras, The Lover

1

Perhaps it is not a good book, he said, James Joyce said, *but it is the only book I am able to write.* It is not a book I would ever read from. I would never again stand in front of people, reading my own words, pretending I have something to say, humiliated. It is not writing. Not poetry, not prose. I am not a writer. Yet it is, in my throat, stomach, arms. This book that I am not able to write. There are words that insist on silence. Words that betray me. He does not want me to write this book. The words make me sleep. They keep me awake.

2

We were standing and staring at each other. It was an unexpected meeting. Perhaps because of that no one was able to speak. I was noticing a certain aura, an extraordinary substance without physical properties. Something I had detected before, but I was not sure where.

There are some moments that seem to be live ones. It is not that other moments are dead, but I am not sure what they are. Moments that bring in a host of other moments, those are the live ones.

I was thinking something over.

There must have been something that determined the sudden configuration of thoughts. A shattering experience, perhaps. A card game that did not add up. A game where there were no winners. I was not sure that there would ever be any winners.

3

It is a relief not to be writing a story. Not to be imprisoned by character and setting. By plot, development, nineteenth-century mannerisms. A relief not to be writing a poem, scanning lines, insisting on imagery, handicapped by tone. A relief just to be writing.

4

I do not want be clever. To make myself laugh. I do not feel clever. If I laugh at myself, it is because I have nothing to say and I am full of love. Because nothing I can say says anything. There will be mere words.

It is because I am full of love that my words have no meaning.

5

It is a book marked by its ordinariness. That knows there can be nothing extraordinary in a life, in a language.

6

Yet the story intrudes. Where did it begin? How far back can you take cause and effect until your story starts? I could go back to the day of my birth, but that is too far. Or back to the day my father came out of the airplane that took him far away. He brought in his suitcase Toblerone chocolates and stories of gypsies.

But my father was always going far away in airplanes and bringing home Toblerone chocolates. He did not tell stories of gypsies. My sister and I made up the stories. The gypsies were out on the Hungarian plains, and our father went to see them. He was in love with a gypsy. He stole our mother and brought her back, for she was a gypsy as well.

7

We had visits from Dr. Patel. Dr. Patel was a short East Indian man with a dark complexion, something like cocoa. He smiled a great deal. When he came to dinner, my mother did not know what to cook. Dr. Patel did not eat meat, and there were no vegetables in our country.

My sister and I sat in anticipation at the table and worried about Dr. Patel. He would die of starvation. But he was laughing.

Dr. Patel did not speak our language, and my sister and I did not speak English. But if he asked about the vegetables, What do you then eat? we would say: we are the white Inuit. We eat fish. And in summers we graze like sheep among the mountain grasses.

8

It is true we grazed like sheep in the mountains. I cannot deny it. In the spring it was a preoccupation to hunt for those sour dark green leaves that grew among the grasses in the hills. The ones we called sourdogs. And I ate daisies, carefully picking out the yellow disks. On the shore we gathered wild rhubarb, nibbling as we went.

During the war it was said people scraped up those unappetizing strings of seaweed that lay on the rocks by the water. I thought about it.

In the fall everyone took to the hills, sometimes to the remote interior, to pick berries. It was important. Families took time from work and spent days filling buckets with currant berries and blueberries.

On rare occasions a lemon would appear in our house. It would have come in the cargo of some fishing boat that stopped in Bremerhaven or Hull. I was like a prospector eyeing gold. I was stuck to the lemon, thirstily devouring the juice, the meat, the rind, everything but the seeds.

9

I do not think this is the story of a starving nation. During the Cuban crisis and the Korean war, the decade after World War II, we did have cod roe and cod liver, whale meat and sheep heads. On holidays and Sundays we always had legs of lamb.

My sister was so thin her bones stuck out of her sweater. She had sores on her hands. It was some form of malnutrition. I thought the boats should bring more vegetables, surely.

At school we received CARE packages from the United States. Small boxes were distributed to each child sitting patiently at his desk while the woman went from one to the other. I opened my box. It contained some tiny used toys donated by some American family. I rummaged among these useless objects, looking for a lemon.

10

Since there was no fruit, and there were no vegetables, there were no trees either. If there were trees once on these mountains, they had all been cut away. There was a great campaign to plant trees. At bus stops in shop windows, on postage stamps, there was the slogan: *Let us clothe the land.*

We had very few clothes. I was always cold, and when it rained I was always wet. It was a thought so selfish I hardly dared think it: *I* need clothes. My body needs clothes.

At night I fell asleep shivering. It often took many hours to warm up, curled in a ball under the quilt, and finally sleep came to the exhausted, still shivering.

It was not a country where children spoke to the adults. Only the adults spoke to the children. I could not say: Father, I am cold and need more clothes.

Later, much later, when I had been in America for a long time, my timidity finally collapsed. I had money in my wallet. I went into one of the thousands of stores filled to the brim with clothes and began to buy them. I bought clothes for all kinds of weather and shoes for all kinds of ground. Especially for rain. Never again would I be wet and cold. I bought a carload full of clothes and felt like a criminal.

11

Somewhere in all this, the story begins. It is not *my* story. If there is a God, it is God's story.

12

Sometimes I saw my mother would stop her weaving and look out the window. Perhaps she was remembering a better place than this.

There would be snowflakes coming down.

If it had been a country where children spoke to adults, I would have said: You are lucky that family of yours came up from the Hungarian plains to the Danish peninsula. And you are lucky that my father, the white Inuit, found you there and brought you to this island where there are many seals and where occasionally a polar bear drifts over on the Greenland ice.

I knew this was true because we had a radio. On the radio the woman said there was a revolution in Hungary, and then there was an invasion. Russian tanks went into Budapest.

13

On the bus I met the beautiful black-haired young woman who once lived in my village. She had gone to America, where there were more flowers and trees than could be counted. I said to her: Why on earth are you here? It is raining and cold. She told me the president, President Kennedy, ordered everybody to go home where they came from. Why? I asked. There is a missile crisis in Cuba, you fool, she said. Is there no radio in your house?

I did not know what a missile crisis was, but I knew what a cold war was.

On the street my girlfriend and I met two American soldiers. We must have been fourteen. They wanted us to come into the hotel and smoke cigarettes. That is how I knew about the cold war.

Later I was told the American soldiers had been cordoned off at the American Base. There was a fence around the Base, and the men were not allowed to go out. Even then it was not time to speak, but I would have said: That is the right thing to do. Because American soldiers are interested in children.

14

In the following decade I came to know those American soldiers, as people, in their own country. Some were my friends. They played music, sang ballads, wrote poetry like other people. I knew them before they went to war, naive and happy, and after they came back from war, not so naive and much more cruel. It was no longer a cold war. It was the time when the television showed many pictures of maimed Asian children.

Who are the people looking over my shoulder, writing stories in my name? Is it my great-great-grandfather from the remote north of Thingeyjarsýsla, who had so much to do with the liberation of my father's people from the clutches of my mother's people. Or is it my great-grandfather from the Danish island of Fyn, who gambled away his entire estate? If that man ever wrote a will, there could have been nothing in it.

In my father's country I was known as the dog-day girl, a monarchist, a Dane. Other kids shouted after me: King-rag! Bean!

In my mother's country other kids circled me haughtily on their bicycles. They whispered among each other on the street corners that I was a white Inuit, a shark-eater. The Icelander.

My sister did not care for this injustice. She went on a hunger strike against God.

Perhaps the person telling these stories is a little older. The distinctly lonely girl in Rungsted, Denmark, who had been made to understand that Isak Dinesen lived next door. Perhaps it is someone older still. The girl who lived in the Mosfellssveit hills in Iceland, who was told repeatedly that Halldór Laxness lived on the next farm. That white house you see from your window.

Or it is someone even older, in a small town near the Oregon coast. The one who was made aware that Bernard Malamud lived in her house. He wrote *The Fixer* in your room.

It is someone in the trail of ghosts.

The person writing these words is probably the one who sits beside hospital beds, not knowing what to say. It is an occupation I began at the age of twelve. I sat by my sister, who was older than I. She lay bone-thin on the bed, her cheekbones protruding, her eyes large. Why do you not want to eat? I asked her. People who refuse to eat die. She answered me. I just don't want to be who I am, she said.

19

It is the only consistency in the fragments of what I no longer remember. There have been so many voices, but the one that sits beside hospital beds is always the same. It is no voice at all. It has nothing to say.

Perhaps, I thought, on my way in the train from Rungsted to Copenhagen, walking along the broad boulevard lined with trees, through the gates of the large hospital, perhaps, even though I say nothing, just being there is enough. My sister was putting on weight because they were forcing her to eat. I sat beside her revengefully grim face. No doubt she is planning a revolution, I thought. She is planning to punish everyone for being who she is.

There are things we know long before we know them.

Some of us receive gifts that seem to be open doorways out of dilemmas. It is a kind of CARE package from fate. I was one of the fortunate ones, for at the age of thirteen or fourteen my blond hair turned brown. When that happened everyone thought I was Russian because that is what I looked like. I was called the little Russian girl and was content with that.

20

I helped spread the rumour once it was begun. I studied Pasternak, Yevtushenko, Pushkin. To prove the point I showed my friends the Russian books in my father's bookshelf, the ones with the strange inverted alphabet. If they were incredulous I asked my father to say some words in Russian, which he did. It was my good fortune that Russian was one of my father's languages.

21

Anything that came from far away was good. Life elsewhere was magical. The further away it was, the more magical.

I sometimes stood in front of the mirror in the hall, rehearsing pinched eyes and Japanese words. Life is not enough, I insinuated to the mirror. It has to be magic.

22

In the rubbish of one of my annual CARE packages from the United States, distributed to us at school, I discovered two brown-haired rubber dolls, each the size of my thumb. Around these dolls I built an entire world that was to last for the rest of my childhood. They acquired a house with furniture, names, a language, invisible friends, things to do.

That dollhouse was located in the loft, which could only be reached through a hole in the ceiling, on a makeshift ladder hung by nails to the wall. No one else ever went up there. If all the hours I spent in the loft, under the skylight window in the roof, were counted, they would constitute at least a year of a person's life.

23

But it is not these things I love.

It is a world that never was. Perhaps I love the aspiration. The fantasy. Perhaps it is only the desire that I love.

24

For a story it is enough to find the beginning. Because the end is contained in the beginning. The fulfillment is contained in the desire.

The answer is also contained in the question.

I imagine a story that has no direction. That is like a seed. Once planted, the seed goes nowhere. It stays in one place, yet it grows in itself. It blossoms from inside, imperceptibly. If it is a vegetable, it nourishes.

I have read treatises on male writing. The male line. The masculine story. That men have to be going somewhere. Men are always shooting something somewhere. And that women do not. That women can grow all things in one place. That the female story is an unfolding of layers.

I do not know if this is true. It is incidental.

There were vegetable plots tended by schoolchildren. Every child had an assigned garden patch and was expected to work in it for three or four hours every day. There was a slogan on the radio, in the papers, on the walls of banks and pharmacies: *Work in the school gardens.*

It was a way of bringing vegetables to an undernourished nation.

I had a patch on the south side of our village, just above the shore. Every day I hoed, raked, weeded, or planted in it. There were radishes, cabbages, turnips, potatoes. I planted them and watched them grow, cleaning the patch daily.

I did not like this work. It was tedious. The hours were long. I was tired and those dumb plants bored me. But in the end I could begin to bring them home. The dirty radishes I carried home to my mother's kitchen were something very small I had to give after all.

Perhaps there was some pride contained in this gift. In a country where children were not taught to be proud, and where girls lived under the national suspicion of being potential *American-soldier-whores* there was some pride in this work. But it made me hate gardening.

But is this why, much later in life, I could never take an American lover? Because with a Korean or a Greek or a Hungarian, you can be with a dark and handsome man from a magical place, a man who is difficult, obscure, who plays games with your emotion. But with these understanding Americans, it is understood you are a whore and you do it for money?

It is a relief to be under no obligation. Or to have to balance the books. Not to count the cash at the end of the day. Not to count the pages as they accumulate. Not to think about a climax or a denouement or an introduction. Instead just to watch the egg hatch. It is there and I know it will hatch.

I have often thought, if God were a writer He would write such a curious story. It would take you into many false corners. It would be a maze, and you would not understand it. Repeatedly you would have to backtrack, retrace your steps, acknowledge defeat. Then in the end there would be an ironic twist.

You would not see the irony right away. But it would slowly dawn on you. It would be pure irony.

I waited for the bus on the last day of school. The National Exams were over. We had received our report cards and all been cleared to go into the world. I was waiting in an empty classroom. The late afternoon sun had gone to the other side of the old schoolhouse. From the window I could see the mountains I hiked over every day with my books and notepaper. I observed how cracked the walls of the building were, how run-down, worn. Paint had peeled off in large patches. The desks were riddled with knife markings.

Magnus, the language teacher, came into the room. I looked up. Well, he said, school is over. It took me another twenty-two years to understand that simple statement.

Reading *Morgunbladid*, the Icelandic daily, I saw the population of the island was being reassured. The American Base, it said, is not a nuclear base. Some months later in Canada I happened upon an American military map. Iceland, it showed, is a nuclear base.

Is there any reason to believe that the sense we make of things is good sense?

Some Icelandic novels make no sense. They are not meant to make sense. They go nowhere, refuse to grasp reality, say there is no reality. Potentially there is no reality. My father's people have always known that potentially they do not exist.

3 1

My first story was written at the age of sixteen. It was written out of longing, in a town near the Oregon coast and in that room where *The Fixer* was written. Every night before sleep I wrote a section in my story, in poor English, about a girl who wanted to go home. Somehow she still knew where home was.

It must have been the shore in the fjord below our house. Every stone there was familiar to me. I knew the barnacles and shells and seaweed better than I knew any other place. Our playground was a stranded tanker, rusty throughout from lying on its side on the sand in the shallow water. Sometimes we forgot ourselves on the old wreck and the tide rose, isolating us part way out in the fjord. We could not get back to the shore.

3 2

I went with my father to the black desert sands on the southern coast of the island. They were searching for the submerged wreck of a Spanish ship that had carried gold. The men had metal detectors, and they spread themselves out in all directions, waiting for the signal of gold underground.

I walked out on a sandspit. It was an overcast day. The sand was black, the sea was black, the sky was almost black. As I walked, seals emerged from the water. They stuck their heads out of the sea and followed me as I went. I walked so far and so long that the tide rose behind me, closing access to the mainland. I was out on an island of sand that was preparing to go under.

There was a small shack in that desert. Though it was falling apart in the constant wind, there was still a door to it that could be opened. I went inside. On the shelves were rusty cans of sugar, coffee, flour. For travellers who were lost or stranded.

33

Sometimes there is no door to go through. Schoolchildren were taught by their masters: when that happens, it is necessary to compose poems. When you have composed poems long enough, a door will be granted.

34

I remember the eyes of the seals were distinctly sorrowful.

Because I am full of love, I am full of sorrow.

35

If the winter was not too severe, the horses were allowed to wander freely in the mountains. Sometimes in the mornings I woke and saw a stray horse looking in at me though the window. There were grumpy puffing sounds and impatient lip noises.

On occasion I was allowed to sleep out on the heath. Those times I woke at dawn and found usually one or two sheep who had ventured close staring at me. When I moved they scuffled away as if whispering to each other.

36

Conflicting emotions are silencing.

It was not called a hospital, but a health-preservation centre. A red stone building with a tower, which was only accessible by crossing a wide bridge that led to the entrance. Under the bridge lay a chasm of stones. The centre was built to eradicate tuberculosis, leprosy, scurvy, polio. In that country those diseases were the national inheritance. They moulded the people, their thoughts, their aspirations.

It was my sister's first hospital. Next to the public swimming pool in Reykjavík, where those without baths at home came for their daily shower. I found my way there without difficulty, even as a small girl. I found my sister's bed and could not understand why she was in it. I would have asked her: What on earth are you doing here? but knew there must be a reason.

My mother finally lost her cool. We scrape around in this mud for hours whenever a bit of summer appears to grow a few turnips. We wait for weeks until the herring and cod and haddock come by here so they can be fished out. We pay the price of a house for a few imported Danish apples. Children go about with bleeding gums and adults watch their bones go crooked. And you, she said to my sister, you refuse to eat!

37

My turn came to go to the centre when I was nine. I went there in mortification, alone. The doctor's name was Hannes. He ushered me into the small examining room, sat down, looked at me and said: well? In silence I began to peel off my older sister's hand-me-down clothing. Jacket, mittens, sweater, undershirt. I stood in the middle of his room naked to the waist and extended my arms for him to see. There was nothing to say. He could see for himself. My skin. Something had happened to all of my skin.

Hannes examined me, then helped me put my sweater back on and patted the top of my head sadly. If you live in the Middle East, he said, you can maybe go to the Red Sea and wash in it. That will no doubt cure you. But for us way up here in the North there is no hope.

38

I became aware that for us in the North dreams never did come true. They just remained dreams. I will never be Japanese. My mother will never be a Hungarian gypsy. My father will never be Russian. I began to understand my sister.

Where there is no hope, the dream is all. The end is contained in the aspiration. Dreams are the closed mussels lying among the stones in the fjord. The shells are clamped tightly around a small bit of life.

39

This was the country where people died of starvation. For eleven hundred years sheep collapsed in the mountain passes, horses fell dead in the ash-covered pastures, fishermen were too tired to drag nets out of the sea. Children faded away in the sod huts from malnutrition. Old men ate their skin jackets.

Yet the shores were filled with mussels. All along the water, the black and blue closed shells lay by the thousands. People refused to eat the mussels.

40

I did not like the American serviceman who sometimes came to our house. His name was Chuck. I do not care for the memory. It is a nothing memory. A non-memory.

Chuck knew something about drilling boreholes, so he visited my father. It was a country that needed geothermal energy so there could be industry and growth. Chuck always brought presents. He came to our house with a television, a radio, toys, Disneyland tinsel things, candy in shiny wrappers. I was instructed to thank him for the gifts. I did so. Then I took them outside and secretly put them in the garbage can.

Even at that time I knew you must not keep that which does not belong to you. There are some people who deserve unearned prizes, but those people are all far away.

41

Your sister has done so well in school before you, Ármann the high school principal, said to me in his office, and you have shown such promise that we have decided to let you skip a grade. Also you already speak Danish.

He was grinning warmly. I understood he had just given me the right to speak. So I said bluntly: If I'm so smart, then the question I have must be legitimate. Go ahead, he invited me. I said: In the Bible there are a lot of lepers. But why is this the only place in Northern Europe where there are lepers?

Because this, Ármann explained, pointing to the ground, is where other countries dumped their lepers. They did not think the people on this remote island counted.

What other countries? I asked. Why? But he did not answer me. He just stood in one spot, looking at me with a warm grin on his face. That is the grin I imagine he still had on his face when he died.

42

Our house was in the west end, and the school stood in the east end. The road between took me along the shoreline of the fjord south of town. The water lay blank between the two peninsulas, shining with the silver of the sky. In the bottom of the fjord there was a fenced-off area containing a large white building that had been there for decades. Long before the town was built, this building was there. It was the leprosy sanatorium. Twice a day I walked by it, refusing to look.

43

Somewhere else in town there was a tuberculosis sanatorium. People were taken to these places and imprisoned for life.

Every year they put a band-aid on our bony chests. Every year they took the band-aid off a week later and made notes in big books. We lined up like prisoners awaiting sentence. We called it terror day. The nurse assured us: This is nothing special. It is done all over the world.

44

Also you already speak Danish. He meant I could begin to answer my own questions now.

I had other questions. Such as, why are there no Icelandic dances?

Why has there been such a long history of starvation?

45

Later I read the history of Iceland's involvement in World War II. One morning during the war, I read, people woke up to find they were occupied by the British. This was to pre-empt the possible arrival of the Germans. British soldiers flooded the streets. The radio spoke English. Wartime barracks were constructed on the outskirts of town.

Then just as suddenly the British were gone, and people woke up to find they were occupied by the Americans. Cartoons in the papers showed how the women were the first to know about this change. All of a sudden their British sweethearts were American. Ugly novels appeared, written by Icelandic men, about women who were traitors.

46

Since then, every year Icelandic communists have marched the fifty kilometres from Reykjavík to the American Base in Keflavík. Everywhere there were slogans: *Away with the Base!*

My great-aunt Sirri was the daughter of a statesman whose face is on the fifty-crown note. When I visited the old woman, she always gave me oranges from the Base. Why are they marching? she asked, her skinny hands shaking as she peeled me the precious orange. The Americans have done us nothing but good, she said.

Many years later, in America, there was a broadcast on the nuclear capacity of the United States. I happened to see this, and there was a map of the Nordic countries, Iceland and Greenland. In case of a world war, the announcer said, of course the first target of attack will be Iceland. That will be to pre-empt any possible retaliation by the Americans from their strategic North Atlantic position.

If the Americans go, Sirri assured me, the Russians will come in their place. Sirri also had fine Swiss chocolates in a silver bowl which she offered me when I visited her. She was an aristocrat. An elegant lady.

47

The story is always somewhere else. I imagine a book that pretends to tell an official story. In the margins there is another story. It is incidental, it has little bearing on the official story, but that is where the real book is.

The ideal reader, James Joyce said, *is one who suffers from an ideal insomnia.* The reader is unable to sleep because in the other story there is something wrong. It is a detective story. The reader thinks the enemy must be found. There are clues. They must be pieced together.

The solution is contained in the clue.

Has anyone been murdered?

48

It was not a country where murders took place.

There was development. Geothermal energy had been tapped. Greenhouses were built in the village of Hveragerdi. Fruits and vegetables were cultivated in the greenhouses. Tomatoes, cucumbers, oranges, bananas. There were not enough to go around, and the produce was expensive, but it was a beginning.

I went with my mother and her friend in a jeep to Hveragerdi. She had saved enough money for a bag of tomatoes. We drove for what I thought was a long time, perhaps an hour or two, and went into the greenhouse. There was a sulphuric smell in the air. The scent of the plants was strong and spicy. It was a jungle of plants I had never seen, never known existed.

My mother bought her tomatoes and we drove back. She let me hold the bag as we drove. I sat in the back seat alone while the two women talked in front. I opened the bag and smelled the small dark red tomatoes. It was an overwhelming sweet smell that went into my head and down my throat. Gripped by an irresistible urge to eat one tomato, I surreptitiously swallowed the bites soundlessly. There were many, so I ate another. And another.

When we got home my mother discovered the empty bag. I stole out of the car shamefully. I was afraid she would scold me. Instead she started to cry.

49

Perhaps she thought her life was taking on a hopeless air. It had happened before.

She told me, sometime later, about the strawberries. When she was a young girl, she picked strawberries one summer to earn money. Her family was not wealthy, and she wanted to have a record of some beloved music. It was strenuous work, bending down for many hours, day after day, filling baskets with red berries. In the end she bought her record. On the way home she fell and the record broke.

Many years later I wrote a poem about that pathetic incident. It happened in Denmark, where new strawberries grow every summer.

50

There were records in our house. She must have bought the record again. I imagined it lay stacked among the others.

Sometimes I came home from school and found my father in the living room pretending to work. The table was spread with pieces of paper containing incomprehensible calculations. He was sitting in front of them, pencil in hand, looking at the old record player. There was a heavy record on the turntable, turning, and the loud music filled the whole house. It was always Hungarian gypsy music.

51

If there is a murder it will be somewhere on that American Base, where cumbersome dark green Air Force planes are landing in the fog.

There are stories where everything that is written is a clue.

52

There is nature, which levels all emotions.

When my sister and I slept on the heath, we woke many times during the night, thinking it was dawn. But it was the midnight sun. In the morning we washed our faces in the ice-cold water of the creek. It rushed along its shallow channel bed, over the thick grasses, the water pure and clean. We walked across the heath, jumping over tufts of grass-grown sod, and up the red mountain that loomed over us. It must have been stone that was rich in minerals, for the rocks shone brilliant orange and red as the sun emerged. There were no bushes or grassy patches on the mountain, but on the summit I happened on a few Alpine flowers. Somehow they grew out of cracks in the stone.

I knew only a few flowers by name then. Forget-me-nots, buttercups. Clovers, daisies, dandelions. The common flowers usually considered weeds in other countries. There are times when the English names give no indication of the true nature of these weeds. Or of what I thought was a transcendent quality, given the harsh conditions. The name for buttercup in that country is: island of the sun. Or the sun that never disappears.

Much later in life I contrived a poetics of naming. Only that which is named is able to live in language. But I did not know many names at the time of my earliest discoveries. It was before language.

Words are not what they signify. We confuse the signifier with the signified. Words are only words. They live in an atmosphere of their own.

Words are suitcases crammed with culture. I imagine a story of emptied containers. Bottles drained of their contents. Travel bags overturned, old clothes, medicine bottles, walking shoes falling all over the airport floor. To come to your destination with nothing in hand. To come to no destination at all.

53

All stories are romances. Detective stories, spy thrillers, horror tales are all romances. They are not real. The romance of the threat. The male romance.

I have heard speakers on the female romance. Sentimentality. Emotion. Feelings of love. Fears of rejection.

I imagine a story that is not a romance.

54

You are contained in the things you love, she said, H. D. said.

55

At times I think we have outgrown the story. We are no longer entertained by pretense. There is too much knowledge. Too much self-consciousness. There are always other stories, metastories, about which we have made an industry. Degrees are offered, awards given, livelihoods supported for the deciphering of metastories.

When we recognize that all our stories are pretense, we run out of enemies. When we run out of enemies, all we have left is love. If it is not love, it is a nothingness. A staring at the snowflakes coming down.

A story that does not desire pretense must incorporate its own metastories.

56

In Rungsted, Denmark, we lived on the upper floors of an enormous estate. The park around the building shed itself in layers of all manner of refined flowers and bushes all the way down to the sea. From that shore it was possible to see the lights of Sweden on the other side of the channel. On one side the estate carried a tower from which it was possible to survey the stars. A narrow spiral staircase wound up to the room in the tower where there was a large telescope.

We understood that a prowler was loose in the area. Do not wander too far along the beach. Do not find yourself alone in the park. My sister and I were alone, trying to sleep in the bedroom beside the balcony. Our parents had taken the train into Copenhagen for the evening. We lay in silence in the dark and heard the prowler climbing onto the balcony. His shadow appeared on the wall, flanked by moonlight.

There is nothing in these rooms for a thief to aspire to own. A few tedious objects from the Arctic, carried in a small wooden trunk on a passenger ship. Schoolbooks in another language. Two white Inuit girls, one of them apprehensive.

57

I knew the Rungsted beach very well. It was different from the Fossvogur beach in Iceland, where our stranded tanker lay waiting for us every morning. Here there was a great deal of driftwood. Pale white angelic pieces of wood washed up out of the water, smooth as healthy skin to the touch. The stones were also smooth and round, often so light grey they seemed white. It was a gentle shoreline, where young girls could walk in white frill dresses carrying baskets with flowers in one hand.

Childhood is a time of setting the stage. Later in life you come onto that stage and find it is very hard to change the props.

It was James Joyce who said: *The reader wants to steal from the text.* The reader aspires to be a thief. For that reason the text must not be generous.

It is a relief not to have such rules. To play such games. Hide and seek. Not to have rules perhaps means you are free to steal from yourself. Finally.

In Rungsted I joined the prowler in his imagined activities. I stole downstairs into the rooms on the main floor when I knew the old couple was not home. I fingered the gold door handles. I surveyed the crystal vases. The soft porcelain statuettes. The Persian rugs. The velvet upholstered chairs, where the body sank deep in its own reverie. I sat in all the chairs. I thought: it could be that Goldilocks is the bears. Certainly she is the youngest bear. The one who sleeps in her own bed.

As I sat in the heavy gold-rimmed lounging chair in the elegant living room of that estate, I came upon the greatest surprise. On the wall facing the street there was a stained glass window as large as a doorway. It was green and white, illumined by the light of the afternoon. The picture it portrayed was a map of the North: Greenland, Iceland, and the Polar Cap.

Much later I read in a medieval love sonnet that the lover's eyes are windows to the soul.

Around that time in Hungary, 1956, people were beginning to flee. The Russians had invaded Budapest, and calls for help from the Hungarian revolutionaries, sent in signals to the rest of Europe, went unanswered.

I told him, the one who I think would not want me to write this book, not to be concerned. It is not a book about him. Yet it is a good story, the one he tells. That he was a young boy, the family fled the country separately, one by one. The peasant who was to escort the boy to the Austrian border took him into a large field, pointed in one direction, and said: The border is that way. Then he turned and left, and the boy walked on.

Did he know when there was a border? Can borders be felt? Is there perhaps a change of air, a different climate, when you go from one country to another?

That story has bearing on this book only insofar as one is contained in the things one loves.

61

There are in any case people who flee the Russians in an endeavour to become Americans. There are also people who flee the Americans in an endeavour to become Russians.

62

That was the same boy who was put on a Hungarian children's working crew. Those children were not made to grow vegetables. Instead they weeded railroad tracks.

He pulled weeds from railroad tracks all day. His only food was an onion sandwich, which someone else always stole and ate for him.

For that reason he was very thin.

63

A text that is self-deceiving eventually rejects itself. There is always another author, behind the official author, who censors the text as it appears. The other author writes: that is not what you intended to say.

I think of a book that has left in the censor's words. A book that does not pretend it is not talking about itself. All books talk about themselves.

The novel I at one time intended to write rejected itself. It began to talk about its own genesis instead. The story disappeared. In its place there was another story, an unexpected story. A great surprise.

64

In my mother's country there was a great deal of food. At Christmas there was a large family of aunts and uncles and cousins, a large table where all were sitting and many courses brought in by the house help, one after the other. There were so many courses that my Uncle Hans had to take a break from dinner and smoke a cigarette. I had never seen anyone take a break in the middle of a meal before.

There was also a great deal of music in my mother's country. On the street corners, in the shops, at the train station, people were singing and playing. Families sang before dinner. They sang again after dinner, gathered around the piano.

It was not so happy all the time in Denmark. During the Second World War there were bomb alerts, the lights were out, sirens went off. My mother and father were huddled in the dark along with everyone else. When there were knocks at the door, they were afraid to answer, thinking it would be Germans.

It was during the German occupation of Denmark that Iceland declared its independence. It was known that the Danish army could not easily move in at such a time. However the British army could, so it was a brief moment of independence.

65

The school I went to was in the Sjaelland countryside, a few hours from Copenhagen. It was an old white stone building. I imagined it had been a cloister in the distant past before the Reformation. There was a pond with lilies on the grounds, a number of oaks and willows and birches, and large stretches of manicured lawn.

There were fifty-nine Danish girls in this school and eleven Icelandic ones. The white Inuit girls were not liked because they had packs of dried fish in their rooms and they did not lift their feet properly when they walked. The rumour was that they were too lazy to lift their feet. They bunched up together in the dining room, in the gym, in the halls, and only made friends with each other. They talked about going home again and thought the Danish girls were effete.

The shufflers, as they were sometimes called, did not count me in their group. They thought I was one of the effetes. The effetes did not understand why I was never seen with the shufflers.

The effetes were divided into country and city. The country ones came from farms on Sjaelland. If their farms still had thatched roofs, and if they drew their water from a water pump in the courtyard, they were lower country. If their farms were wealthy country manors, and the house help consisted of more than ten people, they were higher country.

The city effetes were similarly divided into slummers and genteels. The slummers were not as high as high country, but they were above the low country girls. They were city dwellers who came from the poorer districts. Sometimes they had illegitimate pregnancies in the very near past, and this was why they were sent to the country school. Sometimes they were thieves. The slummers were respected for being street wise.

The genteels came from well-to-do homes in Copenhagen's enviable districts. Among them there was a minor division of aristocrats and the nouveau riche, with the aristocrats on top. The nouveau riche were daughters of architects and doctors and politicians, about whom there were stories in the press. The aristocrats were daughters of the gentility, whose fathers collected honorary medals and signatures of the king.

This all took a few weeks to iron out. I was the last to be casted because I fell into no category. It took a bit of deliberation. Through some shortcut of the imagination, perhaps because there was a rumour afoot that I was really a Russian, the verdict came down: I was a genteel.

I became an apologist for shufflers. It is not that the shufflers are lazy, I said to the genteels in the back kitchen. They are just tired of this place. They do not like the trees and all this shaved grass. And besides, they cannot stand your politics. You have too many classes here. They come from a classless society, where there are no kings, no counts, no barons. Only occupying armies.

I suspected that one reason for placing me among the elite had more to do with my one-time appearance on American television than with my uncertain Russian ancestry. Several years back I had appeared on American television as a specimen with braids of what the Americans were protecting. There was no knowing, the genteels reasoned, that I would not appear there again.

Much later I realized they could be right. The man I was eventually to marry had been carried in infancy by fleeing parents from North Korea to South Korea. There were Russians in the North, where there was no milk to be had, and there was an American Base in the South, where there was milk. My future mother-in-law was to say to me: If not for American milk, there would have been no husband for you.

66

While I was enjoying these privileges in Denmark, my sister was taking her Student's Examinations in a gymnasium in the mountains in northern Iceland. It was noted that despite the institutionalization of food services to students she was not putting on weight like the rest.

67

There are some things about this Lord-of-the-flies type of sociology, carried out among girls in a rural Danish boarding school, that are not entirely a lie.

That privileges were not dispensed equally. That certain low country girls sat hunched over on their bunks, staring at their toes, while genteel girls freely sunbathed in the nude, within viewing range of the male gardeners. That some slummers loitered around the grocery down the road, in an effort to shoplift, while high country girls had secretive meetings among the tall wheat stalks with young men on bicycles.

It is not exactly a lie that I was free to partake in the activities of all castes. In doing so I acquired an overview of the situation which enabled me to act as advisor on things about which the headmaster and his teachers remained in the dark.

68

There are theorists who say that all stories are lies. All that is written is a lie. There is no such thing as truth.

There are so many people vying for attention in the telling of any given story that they cancel each other out.

I imagine a story that allows all speakers to speak at once, claiming that none of the versions is exactly a lie.

69

The text desires to be true. It knows that what is written is not exactly true, so the desire goes unsatisfied.

The story repeats the attempt at telling itself. The text tells all other texts: there is only one of me.

70

When we were quite young, and I was growing vegetables in the mud, my sister worked for the Forestry Service. The Service's nurseries were located at the bottom of Fossvogur, the fjord on the northern side of our town. Rows of baby pine trees imported from Alaska and northern Norway were taking root in the shallow soil. Only the hardiest trees were imported, the ones able to withstand deprivation.

After my work in the school gardens, I wandered over to the Forestry Service. The miniature branches, lined with soft pine needles, stood wiggling in the constant breeze.

I would eventually find my sister, crouched out of sight in a corner of the nursery. She worked determinedly and did not talk to me when I sat down beside her. I watched her swollen hands, fingers, so disproportionately large on her tiny frame. They were blue with cold. There were open sores that did not heal. They were digging in the dirt, making space for another undersized tree.

71

There is a disagreement about the nature of this story.

There were two radio stations in my father's country. One was the Icelandic National Radio. On that station there was a news hour at noon followed by an hour of advertisements. They played male choirs singing fatherland songs, deep-voiced women singing about mother's beloved eyes, and Viennese waltzes. On Sundays the Bishop addressed the nation with a sermon, and church choirs sang verses from the Hymns of Passion.

The other station was for American servicemen only, but the populace of the island was able to tune in at will. There announcers with Brenda Lee voices said sweet things in English, and American rock music went on all day. If you were caught listening to the American station, you were thought to have silently deserted the tribe. Rolls of invisible barbed wire circled the American Base across the airwaves.

Because there is an American radio station, which the populace can tune in to at will, it is possible that this is a crime story.

It is also possible that what we have here is social realism.

72

On the other hand it is much more likely that this is a love story.

It is about that Hungarian boy who walked through a border that could not be felt. It must be like walking through a cloud of nuclear dust. The dust cannot be seen, felt, heard, or smelled, but it lodges in you and makes you susceptible to diseases much later in life.

Somehow he made his way to a refugee camp in Austria. There he earned a few coins by helping an old goldsmith translate documents into English. Or was it a violin maker? He did this for a while, or until the old man began to realize that the boy was translating everything wrong.

73

There was no food in Hungary then. His mother was so tired of not having food that she sent the boy to a relative who owned a farm. Certainly there would be food on a farm.

74

There are, I have come to understand, prowlers everywhere. They prowl about, looking for dialogue. They look for threads.

I do not want to shirk the responsibility of joining in the search for threads. I know there are a few, but it is in the nature of things that the threads be kept out of sight. Or be only barely discernible. Yet they are quite obvious.

The text admits: this I how I am sewn together.

75

Few people are as discriminating as prowlers who are thieves. They are exacting and have high standards.

Hansel and Gretel knew they should leave a considered trail of crumbs behind them as they went through the woods so they could steal from themselves on their way back. They were hoping the trail would not be eaten by birds.

76

In another version of the story of Hansel and Gretel, the two children come from opposite directions through the woods. They meet at the house made of sugar and gingerbread, where an old woman is baking things in an oven. Besides sugar and gingerbread, that house has a television, a radio, Disneyland tinsel toys, and candy in shining wrappers.

77

Kjartan was one of the few people on the island in the Arctic who owned a violin. He was also one of the few who knew how to play it. He practiced the instrument in the late afternoons when it was already dark outside. He was in the kitchen, the doors were closed, and the lights were off. When I stayed at his house, I was allowed to sit in the corner of the dark kitchen and listen to him play.

It was not entirely dark. There was light coming in through the window from the outside, and I could see his shadow playing.

When the British soldiers departed from my father's country, they left a number of empty army barracks behind. There were clusters of these barracks that comprised barrack villages east of town, west of town, and also north and south of town.

At that time there was an invasion of rural people into the city. There was no longer food to be had on the farms, and there were too many mouths to feed. These people moved into the empty barracks, where the city allowed them to stay until better solutions could be found. The barrack villages were sorry places, where rats were frequently seen dashing from one iron-clad shack to another.

The white Inuit had no experience of slums before this. They did not know what had come upon them. Whatever it was, barrack dwellers became the social outcasts of the world's first classless society.

At one time we lived close to the barrack village that was located west of town. The slum quarter began only a few houses away, and we were made to understand that those people were segregated from us. As I went about on my street, testing the depth of brown mud puddles, I wondered whether they were lepers. Or perhaps all tubercular.

Inevitably I acquired a friend from the barracks. She took me home to see her house, and I was careful to leave no clues as to where I was going. Inside there was hardly any furniture. It was somehow nondescript. It was an interior not easily remembered. A non-house.

The barrack she lived in contained no bathroom. I asked her: Where do you bathe? In the fjord, she said. I went with her to the shore soon afterwards, and she took me to a secluded spot where the water from the sea was pooled quietly between two boulders. There were no swimsuits then, so we took off our clothes and swam naked in the stilled dark seawater.

80

All the memories gathered in the text are sorry ones.

The text acknowledges its own sorrow. It does not seek an apology for its own transparency.

When we were bathing in the fjord, the barrack-girl and I, an American soldier suddenly appeared behind the rocks. He stood looking at us for a while, and I carefully deliberated what to do next. We were perhaps eleven or twelve then. The young man said to me in American English: I've lost my watch. Would you help me find it?

81

I have sometimes thought: it is possible there is no such thing as chronological time. That the past resembles a deck of cards. Certain scenes are given. They are not scenes the rememberer chooses, but simply a deck that is given. The cards are shuffled whenever a game is played.

The same game may be played several times. Each time the game is played the configurations are different, and a new text emerges.

I imagine a text that refuses to play its own game.

82

There was a conspiracy among the kids in my school to boycott the Danish lessons. The boycott was to consist of a refusal to do the homework. We were all to appear at our desks at the set time, and when the teacher calls us up to recite our homework, no one is able to say the lesson.

I did not know whether the boycott took place because no one liked the Danish teacher or whether it was a political act. If we were no longer a colony of Denmark, it could be reasoned, then Danish should be removed from the curriculum.

The Danish teacher's name was Óli. He called us up to say the lesson, beginning with the first desk. The first offered the excuse that he had not done the homework. The second did the same, and the third and fourth. He went from desk to desk and got the same answer each time.

After a while Óli walked back to his desk slowly, stood with his back to us, spread out his arms and pressed his fingers into the blackboard. He waited for several minutes until he commenced another try. He walked up to my desk, knowing I would be able to say the lesson. After all, I already spoke Danish.

I didn't say a word, but stared him directly in the face. He knew as well as I that it was no longer a language class. It was a kind of cold war. The object of a cold war must be, I thought as we stared each other down, to ascertain who your enemies are.

It was a long silence. At the end of it Óli picked up his briefcase and walked out of the room. I detected a note of triumph in his exit. There are some people, he seemed to insinuate, who are their own enemies.

83

I did not have the proper Tin-Drummish distance required for a story.

Materials for stories came from magical places so far away that people there had never heard of us. The Russian steppes and the Hungarian plains and the Chinese mountains. But for us way up here in the North there never would be a story.

84

There was another boarding school, a small one. This was in the mountains, an hour from Reykjavík, and it contained both boys and girls. It was understood that passing the National Exams was hard work, and it could not be done in an environment where students went on strike in order to change the curriculum.

The headmaster, who had sole authority over twenty still half-incubating souls, took the opportunity to use the dormitory as a training ground for young communists. This was done with directive speeches in the evenings, unswerving discipline, and the availability of instructive books.

There were things about his theories I liked. Such as: in that ideal world it was possible to be what you were, for no one would care. There would be no need for hunger strikes against God.

I was still looking for an argument to present to my sister. There had been many hospital visits, and I was not pleased with the voice that had nothing to say. If only the right argument could be found, I reasoned, she would acquire another view and the cold war between her, my parents, and God would end.

86

The dining room of that school doubled as a library. That was done in order to make the books easily visible. Students would walk by these books at least six times a day, to and from meals. It was hoped they would sometimes stop and read something.

If this was a trap, I was an easy prey. It was a collection of books from and about the places in the world that most fascinated me. Here, I realized, was an opportunity to find out what exactly went on there. No more illusions, no more emotional clap-trap. No more distressed lovers suffering the ironies of fate. No more gypsy fiddlers and women in blue dancing in passionate circles. No more Chinese emperors with fake songbirds that break down at all the wrong moments.

Soon I became a noted prowler in the library. When study hour was strictly enforced, which it was whenever we were not eating or exercising, and young people sat in their rooms bent over their books, checked on every twenty minutes by the headmaster himself making his rounds, I was found in the library, blithely reading. It was a point of pride, I realized, for the headmaster to have caught me his trap. For that reason he did not discipline me. He walked by me on his rounds oblivious to the lack of regimentation I presented him with. Sometimes he stopped to inquire what I was reading, then he patted the top of my head and went away.

I was reading Malraux. *Man's Fate*. The Revolution in China. Here was something worth writing about. That was certainly a story.

I did not know that only one year later I would find myself in an American high school, faced with the ponderously difficult task of pledging allegiance to the American flag.

In the American high school all students were ushered into the auditorium first thing in the mornings. There was an order to stand up, place your right hand over your heart, and recite the pledge. I stood up with hundreds of others, turned to face the flag as it went up, but neglected to cover my heart, and I did not know the litany. I needed, I told the others in poor English, more time to think about it.

There I was free to associate with American soldiers before they became soldiers. There would be no stigma attached to such an association. I was told that if I ever found a Central European in that place, unlikely as it would be, he would certainly be the reactionary kind.

Whatever cardhouses I had been building in my imagination, they tumbled overnight. The voice that was about to press its case to its sister retreated again into a non-voice. At that time I wrote my first story.

The text has a desire to censor the stories it does not love.

Because of that it is impossible that this is a love story.

If I were not full of love there would be no words on the page. There would be no text, no book.

You kill what bothers you, Roland Barthes said.

I imagine a text that does not kill.

There were after all tiny Alpine flowers at the top of the red mountain my sister and I climbed. I did sit down on the stone summit, blown naked by the tireless wind, and look at the flower in the crack. From that vantage point I had a view of the entire heath below, and of a valley of red stone, a thin creek meandering into the sea, and beyond, the sea itself. When I spoke, an echo resounded in the rock face behind me, repeating itself over and over, throwing itself from one wall to the other.

I thought I understood, in a slow dawning of the senses, why it was that my father's people thought stones and water and wind and ocean were alive. Inhabited.

Everything, I told myself, depends on the vantage point.

All that a story is, I thought, is a way of looking at things.

91

It is said that you should not pick those Alpine flowers, for it takes each one twenty-five years to grow. If you pick it you will be snuffing out twenty-five years.

92

My sister, like me, went away for a while to an educational institution. I did not know what it was like there. She told me nothing. At the end of the year, we all came back. It was summer, there were small birds trying to chirp in the homegrown bushes in the small yard. They were starting to spend the night chirping, confused about the midnight sun.

My sister did not walk in, but knocked faintly on the door instead. It was my mother who opened the door. It must have been her, for it was not my father, and I do not remember being the first to see the apparition in the doorway. Whoever it was, my sister stood on the front steps, barely able to stand up. She was no larger than her own skeleton. She was as thin as anyone could get.

Her eyes were large, her lips were blue, and she had trouble holding her head up. There was a crisis in the house. She was carried in, put onto the bed, God's name was called in what must have been vain and someone said, probably my mother: why did not anyone tell us?

The bedside vigils began again. There were doctors, talk of hospitals. I sat down beside her and found I had become afraid of this lonely resistance of hers. There was nothing I could say that would change what was in front of me. Yet I thought there must be something I could say if I knew what it was. It was a matter of outlook. Some pattern into which the story could fall.

Those magic words I did not have. If there are magic words they must all be far away.

93

The writer cannot escape repression. The text represses the writer. The text is the writer's prison.

The words will not take the writer into themselves. The author is therefore locked out of the book.

94

It was not a country where children were asked: What is your name? Instead we were asked: Who owns you? The proper answer for this is: My father owns me.

The kindly cobbler thought I resembled someone he knew. It was in the shop I passed when I took shortcuts home from school and went through the alley. I always stopped at the shoesmith's because I liked the smell of leather. The man in the brown apron said: Who owns you? My father, Gunnar Bodvarsson.

I took these forms of expression literally. I was certain I was my father's property. As property I had the right to speak to him on occasion. Such occasions did not come up with my mother, whom I was less related to.

95

The self-reflective text desires to be a comedy.

In that other version of the Hansel and Gretel story, the birds were awake all night and ate the crumbs lying in the woods. The boy and girl discovered they had lost their trail.

The text desires to laugh at itself. To make the pattern come out happily. Or at least to let the pattern show up in a good light.

The story knows the pattern is given. There are some things it cannot change. It would like to be free to rewrite itself. To surpass itself.

There is a certain acknowledgment in this writing that there is an itinerary. A set. A kind of fidelity is desired.

96

The structure never can close. It is always violated from inside by the writer who is locked in. Before there is a text the writer is imprisoned inside. After the text appears the writer is exiled from it. On both sides there are violations.

There are days when the story deserts me. Usually on overcast days, if the winter is too mild. The idea that the consciousness is free to begin again, to disregard what has gone before, presents itself. I notice an urge to stare the past down. To be haughty toward it, speak to it from a position of strength. The word I have an urge to say is: traitor!

The story is likewise arrogant. It talks back, claiming for itself a certain autonomy. The story tells its exponent: You do not know me.

97

In another version of my childhood, I did not grow up in my parents' house at all. When I was not in school I lived with another family. A childless couple whose house stood by itself in the bottom of the fjord.

In that house I had my own bed. It was an alcove in the wall, in what they called the north-east room, in the loft. From the window of that room it was possible to see the entire fjord as it spread out to the open sea. The stranded tanker lay below, close by, and I could keep an eye on the tide. Above, a large new cemetery was being unearthed.

There were times when I was asked to return to my parents' house. When I was putting on my jacket and shoes, getting ready to go home, I allowed myself to feel that I was being turned out of my home and sent to stay the night with strangers.

In the metatext there is an acknowledgment that the consciousness is *turned out* wherever it desires to settle.

The names of the childless couple I lived with were Hanna and Palli. They painted their house red and their address was: The Red House.

It is a curious story that suppresses its own happiness.

In the Red House I woke in the mornings while it was still dark. It would be winter, and daylight would not begin until just before noon. I crawled out of my alcove among the model ships and oil paintings of sailing vessels. There was a smell of coffee somewhere, and an oil-burning stove.

I went downstairs. There was only one small lamp glowing in the corner of the living room, and most of the house was dark except for the kitchen. When I came down I found Hanna walking about in her underwear, very surprised to see me. She was Danish and said ridiculous things for an adult, crass and funny.

Since they could not have children, they at one time thought they might adopt. So they went to an orphanage to find a child of their own. While they were there, a red-haired boy ran up to Hanna and called: Mom. For some reason they decided against adoption and remained content just being two. But there was always that image of the red-haired boy.

All the stories deliberately collected have notes of regret in them. A touch of wishfulness, that the stories were describing an alternative world.

I looked for red hairs in the mirror. I wanted to occupy the space left open by regret.

It is possible to be so full of love that the voice that is inundated with words is unable to speak.

The simplest words clamour to get out, but all that emerges is silence.

This is the voice that sits beside hospital beds. The voice that cannot see clearly which configuration of words will be the one to remove all the rolls of barbed wire.

Love seeks refuge in figurative language. Love is ashamed of itself, of its own transparency. It is vulnerable territory. A people without its own army, easily occupied by armed forces of other nations.

Love turns itself out.

The problem of Dr. Patel, who came from India, was never resolved. I worried that he might find it offensive watching us eat the meat of a whale. If I had been allowed to speak, I would have said: The white Inuit take what comes in its own season.

There is a reason for the scarcity of stories. Of cards in the deck. Aside from the tendency stories have to repress themselves in their desire to fall in with dogma.

There was much illness. Large patches of months and years were blotched out. A kind of ink stain appeared in the text, where the consciousness became obliterated. It was not exactly unconsciousness that took over, but a state of exhausted ennui. A desire to forget.

The ink stains did not always have names. Often they were called the flu, or they bore the titles of common childhood illnesses. On one occasion it was a form of typhoid fever. On another occasion it was suspected of being polio. But most of them were just there, frequent collapses, a way of life.

104

They were times when I lay semiconscious, vaguely aware that an unknown hand was examining glands or listening to heartbeats with a stethoscope. Voices of the doctor and my mother could be heard above me, coming as if from a great distance. When I opened my eyes there would be faces bent over me, usually bearing an expression of helpless concern.

Times when I found myself on a cold floor in the middle of the night. The familiar ring in my ears, announcing the appearance of some alien force arriving to retrieve me. Slowly I knew I was disappearing. It did not cause me much concern. Everyone else was far too fussy, I thought.

Those who are disappearing are far wiser than those who sit by the bedside. There were times I wanted to reassure the faces that I was simply taking a break. But I was not always able to fetch my voice from that great distance. It seemed like a phenomenally long way to go, down somewhere in an area of wet ocean caverns, where my voice was lodged for a while.

105

That is an area where there is a cessation of stories. If death is another play after the one about life, it must like all good plays have rehearsals. The consciousness rehearses an existence without stories. It is in the nature of writing to contain a note of defiance. To confront its opposite, to stare it down. To make a certain claim for life.

It is also a confrontation that looks in, for what is being defied is located inside writing. A form of cold war, where the ink that is directed into patterns is carefully watched so it will not spill over and spread out, uncontrolled.

106

My mother, who had been brought up in Copenhagen, could not exactly resign herself to her new home on a mountainous island in the North. She had many reasons for taking her two daughters back to her own city and did so frequently. I did not inquire what the reasons were, but let myself be taken back and forth. There was not much to choose between.

There were ocean crossings. The ship that sailed us to and fro was called *Gullfoss* and was an old trusty passenger ship of fairly small proportions. When I lived on it, however, it was as large as any other world I knew.

We lived on the *Gullfoss* so often that I had perpetual sea legs, even after we had been on land for weeks. It was natural that the floor should tilt in different directions. That curtains should extend themselves horizontally. That all loose objects should be securely fastened to the wall. Even on land I watched carefully to make sure that plates and cups would not slide from the table.

The *Gullfoss* was the only place where I loved loneliness. There was the loneliness of the heavy ocean that extended in black billows as far as the eye could see, day after day. The loneliness of having nothing to do and being fascinated by that nothingness. Of being in a world without expectations, where the body was simply being carried forward in an environment where forward and backward did not exist.

Sometimes we saw land. It would be Scotland or the Faroe Islands or Denmark, a thin blue streak in the distance at which people pointed. I resented land when it appeared. I did not want to come near those masses of stone, where people paraded in streets with small paper flags on flimsy sticks. I conceived of a desire to belong to the sea. To have been born on a ship. There were attempts at rewriting history.

I began to understand the addiction of fishermen to the ocean. It became my ambition to be a seaperson. I went about with private convictions.

107

An anonymous person on board had taken an entire table in the lounge to himself, on which a puzzle was in the process of being pieced together. It was not clear what the picture represented exactly. The images resembled an impressionistic painting or some undefined Monet waterlilies.

I never saw the owner at work on his puzzle. We speculated, my sister and I, who it might be and narrowed the candidates down to the First Mate and the Captain. He only worked on it at night, for the puzzle made no progress during the day. But in the mornings we came into the lounge and discovered whole new sections in the picture. The man with the puzzle was a nightwalker. We called him the prowler.

I decided to join the prowler in the compilation of puzzle pieces. During the day I sat over the impossible lack of clarity and affixed a few pieces together after great deliberation. At night the prowler added to what I had done. A kind of communication between us ensued.

We had a joint project at which we took shifts. The project was to clarify the picture. To make the patterns emerge out of a random set.

When the puzzle was almost finished, I saw it must have been a Monet. Something French. But we had rough seas, and one morning I found the tediously arranged picture on the floor, again in shambles. No one had the stamina to begin it again.

Much later in life I found myself in an art school. We were instructed in self-portraiture. Our task was to work from a mirror in oil on canvas. The mirror was affixed to the top of the easel, so the face in the portrait was looking up. A picture emerged of a disinterested face with dark blond hair. I did not like the project. It was beside the point.

It was a long time before I understood that the point is an illusion. That portraits occur without centre. In a puzzle every piece is its own centre, and when compiled the work is either made up entirely of centres or of no centre at all.

In the metastory there are figurative prowlers looking for something. But there is very little for them to find.

On the ship my sister and I amused ourselves with jokes. Where is the best place to put something you don't want a person to find? On top of his own head.

The prowler does not know he already has what is being sought.

The reader is new to being a hero. He is not used to this spotlight, to having books named after him.

I conceived of another sort of self-portrait: the painter paints her own image, but paints it directly on the mirror. The viewer sees not the image of the artist, but his own face through the lines of oil paint. The face looking back at the viewer will have an expression of helpless concern.

In my father's country it was necessary for all people to work. Men worked on the trawlers. Women worked in the fish plants. Children worked in the school gardens. Young boys carried newspapers on the streets, yelling the headlines. Young girls were put in charge of infants while their mothers were in the fish. There were playgrounds where children were confined within concrete walls.

Slogans were written large on the buses that drove by: *Let us build the nation.*

I was in the fish plant and cannery that had been built in the west end of my town. The building was by the water, below the settlement of houses that stood on an incline. My task was to put cans of fish into cardboard boxes. I arranged cans in that square space all day. It was non-work. I did not like it. At the end of the day I did not remember where I had been. The natural world, with its sunsets and blank waters, became an alien place.

It was understood that patience was a great virtue.

My sister was sent up North to a fishing hamlet called Raufarhöfn. There she was to stand on the wharf, wearing an oilskin apron and waterproof gloves, and arrange herring between layers of salt into large barrels. The herring were to be eviscerated and salted as soon as the boats brought them in. An army of workers was required to barrel the herring while still fresh.

There were sixteen-hour days. When she went to her bunk, exhausted, she lay down to sleep, not always bothering to take her shoes off. There would be a few hours of dozing, then the bell would ring again to announce another boat. Everyone went out again and continued barrelling.

114

Those were the summer months. Schools dismissed children early in the spring so they could join the work force. Many went into the country and raked hay in the field.

Children did not play summer games. They went to the places where they were to spend the night, after working during the day, and put their heads on kitchen tables and chair backs. They were found crumpled up in corners and curled up on floors.

Adults did not enter into the picture. Adults were not there. They were doing two, sometimes three, jobs. After one work there was another work, and there were many shifts that came in rows.

Parents turned into rumours. Families became hearsay. Children went about adopting makeshift families and surrogate relatives. The farmer and his wife. The captain on the boat. The shift supervisor in the factory. New parents.

There was an adage that said: *Work as the day is long.* I do not remember there being any night. After all it was summer.

115

Happiness was beside the point.

Happiness could only be found in what you did. It was a non-happiness. An acceptance. A certain sorrow.

Children became cultivators of love. To love the sheep, to love the calves, the horses, the fish. Even as they were consumed. To love the people who were there. A certain longing.

I refused to go home when I came out of the fish plant. It was a silent house. There was no presence in the rooms. The kitchen counter was cleared and blank. The beds were empty. The living room door was closed, and there was no one on the other side of the door. It was a space, but an uninhabited space.

I went to other houses. Wherever there was a person at home. I realized in a slow dawning way that it was a country whose most notable product was love. I loved in a longing and sorry way the person who gave me a bowl of soup. Or a place to sleep. An alcove in the wall. The person who was at home when I walked in unannounced.

116

The question of the murder remained.

In Rungsted, where there were gold door handles and a stargazing tower, there had been a murder recently. A young girl was found on the shore, near the entrance to our garden park that went on up the incline in layers of flowers. It was not known whether the prowler, whose presence had been noted at odd times, was also the murderer, or whether there were actually two criminals wandering about.

There was a hint of *apprehension* in the air, a note of *warning*. Yet I could not resist the beach. I made my way down to the water, careful not to leave any clues as to my whereabouts, and snuck through the gate just above the sand. The sand was white. I was not used to white sand, and it was warm. The water lapped the shore gently, as if trying not to wake the stones and driftwood.

117

When I was in Copenhagen, I stayed with my great-aunt. She lived on a broad and busy street. I slept on her sofa, and all night I heard noises of the city. Cars went by tirelessly. A train passed through distant train yards. There were buses and cable cars. Kids on bicycles. Whistles, horns blowing.

In the morning the house help brought out coffee. It was a young woman whose special domain was the kitchen. It was not considered well mannered for me to go into the kitchen, for it was her area. I observed her from the distance of invisible social barricades.

I was not used to city noises. I was not used to class differences within homes either. It seemed so arbitrary, who worked for whom. I did not love my great-aunt's house. The formality of silver spoons and crystal glasses.

My great-aunt Sirri, in my father's country, imitated those Danish ways. She was, or so it was rumoured, upper crust, so she had house help in the kitchen as well. But that was an elderly Icelandic woman with large breasts and a warm smile. I spent my time on a stool in the kitchen, listening to her talk, watching her wash dishes. She was laughing.

I noticed my father's people could not play the game they were supposed to play without laughing. They made fun of themselves.

119

It was a time when the pattern was not yet clear. Stories had only begun. There had been no development of plots, no interweaving of incidents, no coincidences had meshed. There were no endings in sight.

I could afford a view of the world that was constructed out of simple chance. There was no order to history. Fate took random turns.

The longer you live, I thought much later in life, the more deliberate the pattern that emerges seems to be. If it is God's story, I considered, then it must be waited for. It is a story that is read in time. It is not my story. The author is unknown. I am the reader.

120

The writer is a prowler in a given story that emerges in time. The writer reports on incidents. There are no protagonists in the given story. Any subject is a contrived subject. The point of view is uncertain. The writer is necessarily part of the story.

The writer cannot report on everything. It is not necessary to tell the whole story. There will be just enough to provide a faint sketch of the pattern.

In any case the writer expects rough seas. The entire work may find itself on the floor in the end, again in shambles.

There was an imprint in those early years. I was looking for that imprint already in childhood. It was a face. I did not know whose it was, but someone looked at me and left an imprint.

I have read works on the psychology of early childhood. The face, I read, is usually that of the mother. Or the father. But I do not think the face belonged to my parents. It belonged to another person whose name I have forgotten.

Perhaps it was the First Mate on the *Gullfoss* as we sailed to Copenhagen. The one who dispensed the medicines on board. He came to my cabin. I lay in my bunk, ill, not entirely conscious. The First Mate was speaking with my mother. He said to her: It is possible you have not escaped the polio epidemic in Reykjavík in time. I opened my eyes in time to see his face. He was injecting penicillin into my arm.

There is a first face, and then there is a second face. The second is not the same as the first, but very similar.

It is necessary to undergo the loss of the first face. The consciousness seeks to retrieve the first image in the second. It is a longing that cannot be fulfilled.

The actual fulfillment of such a desire would in any case be a shattering experience. The consciousness is content with the lover's unfulfilled desire.

In literature, I found in later years, the first face is often confused with the face of God.

The writer is given to resorting to differently coloured light bulbs. To placing the story in an inappropriate light. For that reason this is a story about the North Atlantic Treaty Organization.

I had a certain friend in the town between the two fjords who was different from the rest. Her hair was quite black and straight. Her skin was darker, more golden, and her eyes were dark brown. She was not considered pretty. There was a lack of proportion there. She was too short, the nose was too big, her face too narrow. It was a country of intense homogeneity, and any variation was noticeable.

Her father, it was rumoured, was an American soldier. But she did not go to America and she did not speak English, so she escaped the jeers of other kids that were reserved for apparent foreign sympathizers. She lived with her mother and an older brother, who was quite normal. There was no father in the house.

Her name was Álfhildur. Her mother belonged to a religion that was termed Elf-Belief. Elf-Belief consisted of a certain faith in the healing powers of elves. When Álfhildur was dangerously ill, her mother contacted the elves. During the night, while she slept, the elves injected some extraordinary substance into her arm, and she recovered.

Álfhildur claimed she was faintly conscious of the presence of the elves in the night.

I had another friend whose name was Sigrún. There was a curse on Sigrún's family. Among the many children born to the parents, those who did not die suffered from some deformity or other. The rumour was that it had been a marriage of siblings who themselves had perhaps been conceived by siblings.

It was a small country, with a small tribe of people. Repetitions were bound to occur. It was understood.

At last there were only Sigrún and her father left in the house. When her father suddenly died, she locked herself in her room and refused to come out. Some relative had moved in and was making sure she was fed and clothed. No one saw Sigrún for a few weeks. We did not dare guess how she felt.

When she was ready to talk to someone again, she sent for me. I went to her house, feeling uncertain. When I arrived I was ushered into her room by a woman who said: I am so glad you came. Sigrún was on the floor. She grabbed my legs and told me her father had appeared to her in a dream and spoken to her. She was crying.

I sat down on the floor with her. Perhaps, I thought, even though I have nothing to say to her, perhaps just being here is enough.

126

It is possible, I thought as we held on to each other on that floor, that even this has political roots.

At school, as we sat with our open schoolbooks in front of us, there was talk of what was called the Danish trade monopoly. The white Inuit were prevented from leaving the island and prevented from trading with other nations. As a result there was not enough food. The population decreased.

Faces, I was made to understand, began to repeat themselves with greater frequency.

127

When I was twelve I fell in love for the first time. The object of my affection was a twelve-year-old boy with yellow hair that always fell into his eyes. We were the best of friends. He came to fetch me at six in the evenings, and we prowled the streets together until after eleven. We were fond of fences and rooftops, and contrived various ways of climbing over things. We were also fond of open windows, into which well-aimed snowballs could be flung.

His name was Siggi, and we had in common a great love of wooden shoes. At that time we lived in what was called the old town, where the streets bore the names of Nordic gods. There was a street for Thor, for Odin, for Frey, for Loki, and so on. Our house was situated on the one dedicated to Thor. Siggi lived a few houses away, on the same street, in an old wooden building with lace curtains and porcelain statuettes on the windowsill. I had a great desire to see the inside of that house.

The old town had been constructed according to a Danish model. There were several storeys to each building, and they were attached by fences that opened into dome-shaped tunnel entrances. As you entered these openings, you found yourself in a courtyard with several windows looking down at you on all sides. Siggi and I had been passively adopted as the prowlers of these courtyards.

When we moved out of the old town into the village between the two fjords, I lost sight of my friend.

128

Almost four years later there was the annual Independence Day celebration in the city. It was the day before we were to travel to America. I went downtown to join in the dancing. Musicians were playing on the street corners, and people filled the streets, dancing and singing. It was a night in June when it never got dark, and the festivities were attended as usual with a good deal of drink.

Since I had been away at educational institutions, I no longer belonged to a city clique and did not participate in the drinking. I was about to go home when someone grabbed my arm and said: If it isn't you! When I turned around I saw a young fellow with yellow hair still in his eyes.

I had a vague sense of an odd pattern emerging. It is possible, I thought, that such threads, apparently disappeared, reemerge at unexpected moments.

I did therefore get to see the inside of Siggi's house just in time. It was a small home, with aged heavy furniture. Downstairs Siggi had his own room, where there was a fluffy eiderdown quilt on the bed. So I did have a place to sleep on the last night in that country.

129

There are stories that appear as dead ends. They go nowhere. They are knots in the fabric. The text would like to censor the dead-end stories.

Behind this desire lies a tacit acknowledgment that some stories matter and others do not. It is not certain what makes one story more significant than another. Perhaps it is a connection, a hint in the story that there is a relation in it to a broader perspective.

I have noticed in a passive way that in literature, as well as in politics, only that which kills is thought significant. Only murder is taken seriously.

It is because the white Inuit do not murder that they are forgotten. They are the harmless people. The insignificant ones. There is no price on people of peace. It costs nothing to eliminate them.

130

If, as D. H. Lawrence claimed, violence is perverted sex, brought about by unfulfilled desire, then the absence of violence presupposes a certain kind of sexual satiation.

131

Some stories claim significance for themselves without appearing to be correct. The writer tacitly submits to the insistence and fetches the story, usually from some vague preconscious era.

Memories of early childhood do not come easy. There is only a sense of warmth, and all recollections run together. They appear on a kind of drying paper, where the ink seeps out of its channels.

132

When I was five I was allowed to attend a special school that admitted preschool children into the elementary grades. I was in a class of six-year-olds, and we were being taught the alphabet. Large posters with large letters were placed before us. The principal came to fetch me one day and took me into the hall, where he had put two chairs. We sat down on the chairs, he placed a book on my lap and told me to read from it. I read. When I was done he looked at me very calmly and said: Well, what shall we do with you? You already know how to read.

We sat in the hall for what must have been several minutes and just smiled. There was a sense of conspiracy in the air. That he and I shared a trade secret.

Eventually English was added to the curriculum of Icelandic schools. Perhaps it was because of the American Base. Perhaps it was an attempt to connect up with at least one somewhat universal, international trade language.

When English classes started, we were around thirteen. It was discovered, to my own mortification, that I already spoke English. I tried to defend myself. I denied my knowledge of English and said to the others: I don't really know the language, it only seems that way.

I was eyed suspiciously. After some deliberation there was a new name for me. Other kids yelled at me from across the street: American Dane! There were moments of intense humiliation. It was not enough, I thought, for fate to place me in the ranks of our former enemies. Now that the memories of Danish colonization were mellowing out, I was just getting by. But fate has to turn around and join me up with the new colonizers as well.

There was a sense of anger. I studied methods of escape with greater intensity. If familiarity with a language determines a person's identity, I considered, I would learn Russian myself. I unearthed my father's Russian dictionary. I set myself study hours every day.

As time went by an even better idea presented itself. Supposing I were to learn to speak Russian, and then the Russian army would occupy us. It would be digging myself deeper into the hole. The solution was to study more languages. I would learn French and German, Faroese and Inuktitut. I would confuse them all.

It was not exactly a lie that I did not really know English. It was an elementary knowledge, a seven-year-old English, first-grade vocabulary.

It happened when I was seven. My father decided to spend a year in America at the California Institute of Technology and get himself a Ph.D. This was because, I was told, it would enable him to bring the hot water from under the ground more easily into the buildings and the greenhouses. Such an activity requires knowledge, my father assured me, and they know a good deal about it over there.

The whole family went to live for a year in Pasadena, California. There was a lengthy ocean crossing, during which I felt entirely at home. We sailed into New York harbour past the Statue of Liberty. The air was distinctly hazy and rather dirty.

We crossed the continent on a train. There were nights in the bunk in the sleeper when everything rattled ceaselessly. There were meals in the dining car, where it was possible to sit under the glass dome on top and watch while all kinds of landscape flew by.

135

I did not know I was embarking on a year that I would subsequently attempt to erase.

I gained a vague understanding from my year in America that all stories contain a level of under-erasure. A certain urge to blot themselves out. A fear of imprisonment.

136

It was a remarkable year. There was no illness. And there was no work. America turned out to be a country where girls went to school in dresses and where everyone had television that showed Mickey Mouse. There were thirty-one flavours of ice cream in America and a great many palm trees.

137

When we arrived at the house we were to live in, on a broad street in Pasadena, a large number of neighbours suddenly appeared. Ladies brought cookies on paper plates wrapped in cellophane. Men stopped to say hello and show us how the garage door worked. A group of children came to play, but discovered I did not understand them. A conference was held. They disappeared and returned with pictures. We went into the patio. They held up a picture of a cow, and said: cow. I repeated after them.

I could not believe what I was seeing. These incredibly kind people, were they also the ones in the U.S. Air Force trucks that drove by us on the highway in Kópavogur? And the ones in the fighter bombers, rehearsing how to fly overhead? People I had been warned against.

138

For most of that year I remained stubbornly silent. I recognized the English words but did not let on that I understood. At the school I went to, the teacher was concerned that I was not learning the language. A private tutor was called in. Once a day she came to fetch me from the class. We went into the principal's office, and she showed me the basics of English. There was a meeting with the principal. I was not learning.

I understood what they said. I thought they were too nervous about this. I just needed to think about a few things. While I was thinking, people were smiling at me a good deal.

139

It was at this time that my sister discovered she was on a collision course with reality.

I found her on a chair in the garden. The sun was shining. There was a warm smoggy haze in the air. She was pondering and said to me: There are going to be inevitable problems.

140

It was also at this time that I made my appearance on American television, which later so fatefully determined my caste in a Danish boarding school.

A studio in Hollywood was looking for someone like me to put on one of their shows. After negotiations with school authorities, I was chosen for the amazing task of standing in front of a camera, holding a can of peanuts and staring uncomprehendingly.

Some studio people arrived at school and fetched me out of class and drove me into Hollywood. We stopped at the television station, and after going through many doors and being fixed up by various hands, I found myself standing on a stage, in front of an audience, in what was called a live show. There were questions about the white Inuit, who were not called the white Inuit there, and how I liked America. I sometimes nodded. There was not much to say.

I was trying to figure out: if this was a live show, what were the dead shows like?

141

Anything that is written necessarily has a point of view. The text refuses to give in to public demand, which insists it either have no point of view or all points of view at once. This is what is called objective. The text is not objective because it is unable to be so and still be a text.

142

Everything that happened in America seemed trivial and not at all part of the real world.

I recognized even then that it is not possible to sympathize with all sides at once. When you choose your allegiances, I thought, you ally yourself with the one who suffers.

143

My parents had come upon an elderly Russian couple in Pasadena. We visited them. They had, I was told, fled their homeland and made their home in California. There were things to eat and drink on the table, and they were talking. Both of them were kindly looking, with very white hair.

The Russian woman found me staring raptly at a doll she had standing on the mantelpiece. It was a small white-haired doll clothed in a long yellow dress. She came up to me and said: This is a Russian costume. Then, after some silence, she took the doll down, handed it to me, and said I could have it.

I detected that aura, which I have since identified as love, in the elderly woman's silence. It was an ethereal substance, I had noticed, that was oddly charged with warmth, sorrow, and regret. It occurred most often among those who did not speak.

I was to be very fond of that gift and had it with me for thirty years.

144

There are gifts that are gifts and other gifts that are bribes. It later occurred to me that children always know the difference.

145

In my father's country I knew several families where the mother was Danish. It happened because, in the forties, young Icelandic men were still going to Copenhagen for a higher education. There they met beautiful Danish women, married them, and brought them home when the war was over.

My mother and her friends kept the group. They met regularly and laughed a great deal when they did.

Among them there was a Jewish woman who did not laugh as much. She had, I was told, lost her mother and a sister in a concentration camp. When Jews were being rounded up in Copenhagen, one of my father's friends married this woman, giving her the immunity of an Icelandic citizen.

I thought of this often when I was still very young. I was taking cues, gathering evidence, collecting clues on the nature of friendship.

146

The text acknowledges that there is a search. The same game is played several times with different results.

In literature, tradition instructs, there is usually a protagonist. The protagonist is always on a journey. If inquiries are made concerning the stories behind the story, the text yields to the pressure and gives up a form of an answer. The object of the search is, we are told, a kind of holy grail.

The quest in literature is a mirror of the quest in life. It is possible to imagine a story where the protagonist is a reader, who is therefore also the author. It is a story where the boundary between that which is written and that which is lived remains unclear.

There never is a holy grail. Instead it is a quality. An undefined substance without physical properties that is generated in certain instances. It appears at odd unexpected moments. Even while the weaving has stopped and the weaver is looking out the window at the snow coming down.

When we lived in the old town, on the street named after the god Thor, an old couple resided downstairs. They were Björg, who had long thin grey braids and round cheeks, and Magnús, who was tall and thin. Both of them were always smiling.

Magnús had a habit of playing cards with himself in the living room. He displayed the pack of cards on the table according to certain rules and watched how they matched up. Björg had a habit of standing in the kitchen, stirring a large pot. There was always soup in this pot.

I was their most frequent guest. Sometimes I contemplated cards with Magnús, and sometimes I hung about in the kitchen with Björg. On Sundays Björg always put on her Icelandic costume. She appeared in a black skirt, an elaborately embroidered white apron, a white blouse with large loose sleeves, and a tight vest ornately fitted with gold chains in the front. On top of this she bore a black cap, laid flat on her round head, with a tassel hanging down the side next to her braid. Her braids were turned up in the back and tied to the top of her head, under the cap.

In this attire she solemnly sat down in the living room, turned on the radio and listened to the broadcast of the Bishop's Sunday sermon.

148

If this is a detective story, the sleuth has been kept in the dark. The detective is not showing the cards.

Crimes can be hard to solve. Especially when the crime has not been determined in the first place. There is only a suggestion that something is wrong, but the sleuth is unsure which of the stories contains the clue. There must be one card, one piece, that can be used to tip things off.

The sleuth is worried that it is all a misunderstanding.

149

Perhaps the reference to the Hungarian boy is significant after all. He was a perfect boy, as boys go, except for one flaw. It was a speech defect. When he was to speak Hungarian, it was discovered that he could not roll his r's. There must have been some teasing about this, perhaps even yelling at him from across the street, in Budapest. Much later, when he found himself in North America and learned English, his defect came out as an elegant British accent.

North America, it occurred to me, turns out to be a place where major defects go undetected. Clues remain undiscovered. Former ugly ducklings turn out to be beautiful swans.

If there are scars they are all on the inside. Only occasionally do they surface, but when that happens it is a shattering experience.

150

In another version of the ugly duckling story, the duckling discovers that there are no swans.

The text admits that Hans Christian Andersen was a persistent man. He was a hopeful man, who may have spent his time opening clam shells. Somewhere in the longing, he must have felt, lay a certain extraordinary solution.

It was evident to me quite early in the game that it is necessary to make choices.

151

The writer gets a certain amusement out of rewriting old stories.

In yet another version of the ugly duckling story, there are swans, but there are two ugly ducklings. They are sisters, and when the swans appear there is a desire in the plot for the two ducklings to fly off with the swans. The younger one wants to go, but the older one stubbornly refuses.

It is not clear to the youngest duckling why the other wants to stay. All the ducks are gone, and when the swans have left there will be no one there. The younger one knows time is passing, the swans are beginning to take off one by one and it is necessary to make a decision. In the end the younger duckling flies off with the pack of swans, looking back often in a perturbed manner. The older one remains on the mound of earth and continues to get smaller.

The border between Iceland and Denmark is very visible. It is all water, and to cross over it becomes necessary to sail for ten days. In the beginning of the twentieth century, most of the food, the books, and the medicine were still on the Danish side.

My father's parents died long before I was born. My grandmother, I was made to understand, was very beautiful. She became ill while still young, and the necessity of moving her to Copenhagen for medical care arose. But she did not make the crossing in time. Her illness made her blind, and after that she was not considered as beautiful.

At that time she was newly married to a young man who was also beautiful. When his wife became an invalid, whom it was necessary to escort along the streets, life took on a hopeless air to him. In his unhappiness my grandfather died. I was made to understand that sometimes unhappiness is a cause of death.

There was one child. My grandmother's blindness occurred just before my father's birth, and she never saw him.

153

This area of my father's life was never spoken of. It was never allowed to become a story.

All I had were indirect clues. After deliberating for a number of years, I sketched a vague trail through the woods. Perhaps I was thirteen or even fourteen. It is possible, I thought, that if the first face you see cannot see you back, then one of your daughters will refuse to eat.

In the metastory behind the story that was never told, there is a hint of politics. The text allows for certain backdrops. Often the text takes part in its own conspiracies.

154

I was left with the general impression that in the business of crossing borders timing is everything. If you do not cross the border at the right time, you run the risk of blindness. Sometimes you also run the risk of death.

155

On the last day of what I think of as my childhood, we were standing in line at Customs and Immigration in New York. We had an especially long wait since we were applying for immigration. Perhaps we waited several hours. During those tedious moments I was thinking of ways to refute psychoanalysis. My argument was that human psychology is determined by politics. And politics is determined by diet. That is, those who eat best win.

156

The text is determined to act like a demanding lover. The text demands of its author a ruthless honesty, which the author is unwilling to give. The author knows that once a quest for truth is begun it may possibly never end. Truth does not yield itself to its seeker. There is a suspicion that truth may not exist. Yet there is a certainty that what is being told is not a lie.

There is a further suspicion that if the truth were to appear it would be a paltry thing in rags. It would be small and bony, taking off its hand-me-down clothing and exposing its embarrassing skin. There would be a fear there, perhaps of a kind of leprosy, and an aura of hopelessness. It would be a speechless thing.

157

For the white Inuit children at that time, the lesson of patience was driven in like a nail into concrete. At school we were made to stand up and wait in silence until the teacher released us. In the summers we were placed in playgrounds in order to watch over small children. There we waited and watched for hours at a time. After school and during all school breaks, we were given knitting needles and wool. We knitted all through the evening, counting stitches and rows. It was a lesson we learned.

Perhaps for this reason the strongest memory I have of childhood is one of tedium. The slow clock ticking in the hall. The slow progress of wool being tied up into sweaters. The tired vigil over undersized vegetables that would never sprout out of the soil. The tedious arrangement of cans in boxes. The endless tiresomeness of watching small children sitting in sandboxes.

It was not a country where complaints were heard. We steeled ourselves. We clamped our mouths shut.

158

Pleasure, when snatched, was a stolen thing. Prowling was an act of truancy. The more you prowled, the more useless you became. It was possible to work your way down to the bottom of all public estimation simply by prowling.

I made myself guilty of this kind of truancy fairly regularly. For that reason I detected a sense of hopelessness concerning me. A resignation that there was not much potential in me.

For all that, I knew I had learned patience. I was the most patient of all. I could wait for months and even years. All it required was a suitable mental framework. A certain meditative stance. I had the business of waiting down to a science.

159

For some reason there were not many children's books. I had the notion that we were expected to read the books read by adults. Those books abounded. In the loft, where I had my dollhouse and my two rubber CARE dolls, there were numerous boxes filled to the brim with all manner of books. Paperbacks, hardbound, cloth-covered volumes on religion, literature, psychology, philosophy. They came in all languages. English, Danish, German, Spanish. In the living room, shelves on shelves held hefty volumes on mathematics and science. They, too, came in all languages. English, Russian, German.

I waded through these boxes and shelves. Hour after hour was spent silently reading with a total lack of comprehension. I read entire volumes in German, Spanish, Italian, without understanding a single word. They were simply words, with auras of their own, and they presented endless configurations of what seemed to be a very limited alphabet. I discovered that if one read slowly enough there was a peculiar pleasure to be had from meaningless words.

Reading in a language I knew, on the other hand, was a different matter. The added dimension of meaning appeared. *Meaning* was not always evident and always potentially terrifying. An altogether curious world seemed to exist, about which I had ambivalent feelings.

There were two Danish volumes of something called *The Living World*. They presented spectacles of bulging snakes that devoured large animals whole, and Black people with sleeping sickness, who had froth on their lips and were lying on the ground. These were the true stories.

Then there were the false stories that were also true. There was Strewel-peter, who refused to cut his fingernails until they grew so long he could be wrapped up in them. There was the boy who refused to eat, who became smaller and smaller until he turned into a pile of ashes on the floor and the maid swept him up. And grim tales of children who were lost in the woods and then stuffed into an oven. Meanwhile the birds ate the crumbs on their trail. And incredible tales of people who were supposed to be gods and were tied up at a river while poison continued to drip down on them. It was a great relief that the one to whom this happened had a faithful wife, who sat beside him with a bowl and caught the poison in it. When she momentarily emptied the bowl, a drop of poison fell on his head, and there was of course an earthquake.

Of all the false stories that were nonetheless true the worst one was a book called *Palli Was Alone in the World*. Palli was an average boy, perfect as boys go, who wore shorts and a cap. He woke up one morning, and there were no people. He went about town looking for them, but all buildings, streetcars, and shops were emptied. He did what all children would like to do. He walked into the candy store and helped himself. At the bakery he took what he wanted. He even drove a streetcar, and no one was there to mind.

Then he found the candy had no taste, the cakes were not good, and it was no fun after all to drive a streetcar. He loitered about, hands in his pockets, and discovered that he was quite alone. It was not a good feeling. A great gap appeared in the region of the chest. There was sorrow, regret, and a sense of hopelessness.

There was another book like it, which was stranger and even worse. There a little prince with curly yellow hair had an entire planet to himself. And another book written by, I was told, a relative of mine. There a princess, also with yellow hair, whose name was Dimmalimm, had only swans to play with. One day she discovered that her favourite swan was dead. Then she had no swans at all. It was her good fortune that the swan came back in the guise of a young prince, also with yellow hair.

162

There is a tacit acknowledgment in writing that stories that are true and stories that are false mirror each other. That in the business of stories, it is impossible to lie.

Those tales were terrifying because I had the sense that they were all, in their own way, coming true. They were prophetic, and prophetic in an awful way, I thought. None of the voices of reason, usually those belonging to my parents, were able to comfort me with the thin tinsely claim that the stories were not real. All stories were real.

163

Much later in life I seem to have been coming down the stairs of a large North American university building. A kind of gingerbread house in its own right. It had been a long walk. I was tired, and there was a vague sense that I had lost something. When I got to the bottom of the stairs, I saw to my surprise a face I recognized.

Some people have to wait for a long time for stories to come together. For pieces to fit. And there is always a chance, I thought just then, that the entire picture will slide off and shatter before the final pieces are in.

That face belonged to the Hungarian boy much later in life. The surprise was that a rumour had been suggested to me. According to the rumour something had happened along the way, and he was dead. But he was not. Just worn out for a time. It had not been a smooth journey, apparently. A kind of rough seas.

The text conspires in a form of truancy. There are derisive comments between the lines. A sense in the air that there is not much potential in the claims it makes. The text answers back: there are no claims. There is nothing to be fulfilled. Therefore it has nothing to have potential for.

There is an admission that duties have been shirked. That the text has been prowling in the reader's domain. Telling itself and then interpreting itself. Incorporating that which does not belong to a story. Posing itself as a question: it may not be a story. Perhaps it is an essay. Or a poem.

The text is relieved that there are no borders in these matters.

We did not have much to say to each other just then. I cannot deny that. It was a hot day. There were birds in every tree. I was wondering at how all images can suddenly crowd into the mind at once. All memories come tumbling down, scattering at random over the tilting floor. Cardhouses collapse. The Bishop recites his sermon on the radio, and seagulls yap about the ship, looking for slop from the kitchen. All things happen at once.

Behind this, I was thinking in a half-comprehending way, there were somehow guns, perhaps rockets. Fighter bombers flew across the sky, submarines descended into the sea, a couple of low-calibre bombs went off. It must have been in some magical country rather far away.

It must be possible after all to find a beginning to any story. Even if it is arbitrary. I have been thinking that there is an actual beginning to this story and that a story should end with its origins. It is necessary to conceive of time running backwards.

There was a first vessel before all the others that sailed between Copenhagen and Reykjavík. A kind of Noah's Ark of Iceland. Not the longship that journeyed from Norway in 874, full of small-time kings and chieftains looking for an island to settle on. This was the second Ark, after the war.

This ship was named *Esja*. It was 1945. All of the bright young men of the island were studying in Copenhagen when the war broke out. There was no communication with Iceland during the occupation of Denmark. The young people waited, and the *Esja* was the first sailing home. The students boarded with their new wives, their small infants, young children. Many of the young women were pregnant. They crowded into the cabins on board, and the men slept in the hold below.

The seas around Scandinavia were thick with mines that threatened to go off at any moment. The ship sailed slowly, hoping against all odds to miss the mines. It was a tense journey. The crew and passengers huddled on deck, in the cabins, in the ship's lounge counting their last minutes.

167

The captain of the *Esja* had never felt his responsibility so heavily before. He was later to say in public: we were carrying home the cream of our people. These were the educated ones, those who would have to build the nation and take it into the twentieth century. I had on board the future of Iceland, and one mine could shatter that future to pieces.

My parents were on that ship. They had told me that when the blue mountains of Iceland slowly rose out of the sea, on the horizon, the jubilation was unforgettable. Champagne bottles were uncorked, there was laughter, dancing on the wobbly deck. Now they knew for certain they were safe. And when the *Esja* docked in Reykjavík harbour, all the people of the island were there to greet them, with hands waving and voices shouting.

ZERO HOUR

for Tove, my mother

'When the hand of the clock falls, then time is over for me.'
— Goethe's *Doctor Faustus*

To write you this I have come to the Gateway to the West. Not because the West is intriguing. But because it is there: open, dry, with little culture and much politics. And beyond the West there is the ocean. The jungle. The rains. That is a place to long for. To think toward. I think toward the western coastline of this continent, where mist is in the air.

It seems quiet, but that is an illusion. The quiet is in the soul. Out among the elm branches, the wind blows. Cars drive on the streets. Children squeal in yards and on sidewalks. Birds chirp loudly under house gables. Mailbox lids slap in the morning search for letters all along the street. But in my soul there is a great silence.

I have come to that place in life where there is nothing below. There are no lower numbers.

I have heard of *ground zero* writing. I imagine it is a writing in which the author does not know what to do. There are no assumptions to draw on. Nothing is understood. Culture has vanished. Writing is enacted exactly where the bomb fell.

There is only a vague memory of something lost. A hazy recollection that this place was once occupied. There were tears. Laughter. A smile. A forlorn look charged with sorrow.

It is probable that you do not know how you feel when you know the bomb is going to fall and explode where you are standing: when you prepare for it. You get the medicines. You put blankets on beds. You build ramps for wheels. And when the explosion happens, you are running. Helping. You turn. Help is needed and you help. You do all this and you do not know how you feel.

Only later, after, do you know. When it is over. The dead are in the ground. There has been a clean-up. Then you realize there is a feeling in your chest. You are angry. Suddenly you scream, your mouth open. You are surprised at the sound you have made. You did not know this sound was in you. It comes from the deep caverns you have not seen, where forms pass, shadows cross, and you do not know what they are.

Perhaps it seems like a bomb, but that is an illusion. There has been no bomb. Only a loss, as if a world has gone away, and a revelation that sometimes a world goes away and never returns.

When a world disappears, it takes away with it everything you are up to that moment. Your past is erased within a few minutes and you no longer recognize it as your own. Suddenly you stand up and find you have to start over. There is no you. Your personality, culture, knowledge are gone and there is nothing in their place. You have become an alien. A foreigner. You recognize none of the social customs others take for granted. Your priorities are different and you do not know where you got them. They are there, but they are not your own.

I have been present on two such occasions when such a bomb fell and I was changed from one person into another. At the birth of my son and the death of my father. It is like moving into a new home. The old one was familiar. You were comfortable, you had a routine, you recognized the neighbourhood. The new home is an empty shell. The street is unfamiliar, the neighbours are strangers, the smells, sounds, colours are jarring. There is no furniture, no rug, no lamp. The linoleum on the floor is brown and uninviting. The grey wood has white paint spots on it. None of the door handles are on the doors.

I did not know where we were. He did not tell me and I did not ask. It was just north of Victoria on Vancouver Island, in that West which is rainforest and mist. We drove on the highway crowded by pines and alders and then into a dark and spacious park. Here were the cedars that grow for hundreds of years. We came to a river. It was not wide and not very deep, but along the banks on both sides lay hundreds of dead salmon. They had travelled all this way, to the place of their birth, only to beach themselves and lie stinking in decomposing shades of grey and mould, their mouths gaping, their eyes bulging.

I am glad certain souls are meant to travel along the same roads. It is less lonely that way. He was the writer Bill Valgardson, whose path mine has crossed a thousand times. We were hiking under the heavy shadow of enormous pine trees. *The most powerful symbol of our time*, he said, *is the mushroom cloud.*

When I came to the Gateway to the West, I had nothing with me. I arrived in Winnipeg in a very small red car with one red dress in the passenger seat. It was a dress I had never worn. Before this I had never liked the colour red. But that day I was prepared to tolerate it the way I was prepared to tolerate whatever came my way. I was a different person. After the car and the dress, I had only the shirt on my back and very limited funds. Only later did I remember I had a typewriter in the trunk.

When a bomb falls in your life, you can do one of two things. You can glue yourself into your old life, place, routine and repeat to yourself every day that only peripheral things have changed, only marginal things. You are still the same and daily life goes on and soon you will forget that worlds collided a short time ago. Or you can allow yourself to feel as lost as you do feel. You can say to yourself: A world disappeared and took me with it. I will never be the same. l will never get over it. And you can leave it all behind. Go away with nothing and build something new.

I took the second choice.

Or rather the choice took me. It is possible we never choose for ourselves. We are instead swept along on waves of circumstance and emotion. There are very few choices to make. Not much we can do.

There was a Scandinavian Club dinner. This was in the West of my dry, parched memory where all has been left open to the winds: Saskatchewan. I am not a club person who belongs to groups in order to have places to go. But I was writer in residence in Regina city and attended at their invitation so we could meet each other.

There were many tables, much pickled herring, and entertainment: music, speeches, dances, and a comic. A clown. During dinner I found that my dinner companion at my table was the clown.

He was not funny. His name was Kolskog and he was from Swift Current. He spoke seriously at the table, but when he got up to perform he was funny.

His children all did well. He said: *I told them, if you're uncomfortable somewhere, get the hell out.* Right away. This is why they have all done well.

I thought about that long and hard. I was still thinking about it when I drove out of town in the small red car. It must be true, I thought, and I am a fool.

In an essay called 'Against Joie de Vivre,' Joseph Epstein writes that he does not care for the things people do when they are pretending to have fun: dinner parties, picnics on yachts, gallery openings. He does not like 'joie de vivre.' This is because for a brief moment sometime in his early life he thinks he knew real joy. Since then he has been unable to settle for less.

There is something here I recognize. When a bomb falls, you emerge as someone who is not in the game. You seem to realize that everyone is playing a game and you are not in it.

It is surprisingly difficult to tell how you are feeling. You know from some-where how you should feel and you have a sense that you are inadequate because that is not how you feel at all. There is a tacit acknowledgement that human emotions are not all equally pretty.

I find there is a laundering of emotions going around. Certain human experiences are made to come out sentimental. Birth and death are sweetened.

Yet l can sense in the hollow cavity of my chest that birth and death are not sweet. They are awful. They wipe you away, everything you were up to that moment. There is a great loss and a great unknown: an uncertainty the human mind must be unable to cope with. You are disappearing. You want to scream. You know nothing will ever be the same and everything you know is unalterably lost.

The little red car had been used very seldom. Mostly it was in the garage. I was not familiar with it or else I had forgotten my former familiarity.

It was hot and dusty in Saskatchewan when I drove from Regina city to the Gateway to the West. I counted the kilometres on the odometer. Suddenly the odometer was showing an incredible distance covered in a remarkably short time. The numbers rolled around on the meter at breakneck speed. I punched it back to zero and it rolled forward again equally fast. I punched it back to zero again and again.

It may have been at Sintaluta. I stopped at a gas station and asked the attendant if he could fix an odometer gone berserk. He said: *I wouldn't want to touch it.*

I drove on. Later, perhaps at the Manitoba border, I noticed the odometer was quite accurate. I had simply been looking at it wrong. It occurred to me that somewhere near Sintaluta and Moosomin my mind had temporarily left me. Or malfunctioned. I thought of the mysterious disease that grips the people in Marquez's *One Hundred Years of Solitude*: they forget everything. Necessity requires them to pin notes on all their gadgets with instructions on how they work.

When tornadoes blast through in the West, we at the Gateway hear about it. How severe wind tunnels touch down in Prince Albert and Weyburn, roofs are blown off houses, barns collapse, mobile homes are lifted and deposited in ditches. At the Gateway we may see an evening sky turn grey, blue, and maroon, with thick cloud covering the setting sun. We may feel peripheral winds stretching tongues into our streets. There are rumours of summer hail. But for us the day continues to turn into night peacefully. We see the darkening sun rays behind the brown margins of cloud.

This is where the grain that grows in the vast fields between the Shield Country and the Rockies is gathered and stored. From here it is distributed to the East. This is also where the goods manufactured in the East are collected, sometimes assembled, and sent on to the dispersed farm hamlets and colonies, the tiny country communities with one church at the centre of town. This is the city of the warehouses.

When I arrived I found a mansion. An old estate located in a park of such mansions, secluded by three enormous gates through which you pass. I met a thin lady whose name was Jo. She told me I could have one floor of her mansion. It may have been built and owned first by one of the owners of a warehouse during the heyday of the Exchange District.

I accepted. She was tying up yarn ends on a rug. The sun was beaming. She said: I have finished what I was doing here and now I want to go to Mexico. *It's the doing that excites me.*

At the breaking of dawn, five a.m. or so, it is so quiet that the screeching of birds in the trees echoes from empty street to empty street. The early air is flat, grey. Slowly sun rays appear. Streaks of yellow light crawl along the street, filtering through the crowns of high elms. The tops of the trees bathe in the sun. The cool air begins to warm. A jogger appears and runs around the corner. A grey cat looks up from the bottom of the stairs, beady-eyed.

On his deathbed, my father was very quiet. For six weeks he lay on a high bed in a small room. On one wall were shelves lined with baskets of all shapes and sizes. On another wall were shelves full of science books he was no longer able to read. Beside his bed was a small table with medicines. At the foot of his bed stood an easy chair where we could sit and let time pass in his presence. But in that room time did not pass. All times of day and night were the same for him. He lay very still and spoke less and less. By the end he said nothing at all.

That year the beauty of spring in the Willamette Valley was terrifying. Rhododendrons, azaleas, begonias, cherry trees, magnolia trees all stood in bloom along the streets. The air was charged with the perfume of blooming flowers. The blue jays and robins cried and laughed their bird calls in all the bushes and branches. The grass was deep green, the cedar stark rust. The sun shone orange into the valley. The beauty was painful.

I came into my father's room. He looked at me, intensely as always, his blue eyes effervescent. I asked him how he felt. He said: *Here I am like Don Quixote, battling my private windmills.*

Just southwest of Regina city the land is not farmed or irrigated, so it is the kind of desert you find on the high prairie. The soil is caked dry and is fine and dusty if you crumble it. Now and then scrub brush sticks out and gopher holes abound. If you stare at the plateau, over its pale grey, brown, and straw colours, you will see a gopher put its head out of a hole, look around, then emerge altogether. There it will stand on its hind legs, look around again, and dash off. Or it will go down again into the hole. A tumbleweed may blow by on the breeze, circling like a cartwheel across the plain.

I often went across the plateau, breathing air so dry the sinuses felt singed. It was a frequent thought that a place could not be more empty than this and still be a place. Yet I knew it was not true. There was plenty there if one cared to analyze the minutiae of the prairie soil and plains scrub. Plenty of insects, wild plants, particles in the air. But it was a mental emptiness of a kind: as if no one had ever walked here before.

It is an unnamed place, I thought. A landscape without language. Before language.

Then one day I discovered how wrong I was. I went out across the desert on my usual route, expecting nothing. Only parched mud and dead weeds scratching up dust as they are thrown forward in the wind. Suddenly I encountered an assembly of people. One hundred, two hundred or more, gathered in the sun.

I stopped and realized they must all be Cree. Indigenous people from around Saskatchewan must have travelled to this spot for some reason. They had four enormous drums with them. These were positioned at four corners of the assembly, in four directions. Around each drum sat several men holding drumsticks. There were men, women, and children milling about, some sitting on the ground, some standing, some covered in blankets or shawls.

In the crowd I recognized a man I knew. He was an elder from the Navajo tribe from the southern United States. I remembered him for his beautiful voice. When he spoke, the voice sounded so fine I thought the birds would stop singing. He motioned to me that I could join in the proceedings. I went in among them and sat down quietly. I was thinking I must have walked into a powwow in progress.

The Navajo elder stood before them all and explained that a certain woman, Anna, from the Cree tribe, had lost her father. She was in grief. It is a tradition that the grieving one be allowed to dance. *Let her dance away her grief*, he said.

The men around the drums began to beat them slowly and sonorously. Anna went into the circle, a large shawl draped over her shoulders which she held together with her hands. She stepped in rhythm to the drums, placing each foot on the ground twice. Quietly, without expression except for her empty eyes, she paced her way around inside the circle, making large circles of her own.

She danced like this alone for some time. Eventually people began to join her, one by one, and by the end a larger part of the assembly was dancing with her, showing solidarity with the grieving.

If time could be rolled back, I would go into that dance now. It struck me: *they were not talking*. It was pure loss. Loss without commentary.

I think it is time to stop all activity. To make a point of doing nothing. To sit in the sunroom, the huge windows open wide, and listen to the hammering rain fall down. Watch it drop from the sky in torrents, thunder grinding in the clouds, lightning flashing. All is dark and grey. Green leaves droop with the weight of rain. Birds fly furiously overhead in a great hurry, wings flapping desperately.

It is good to do nothing. To sit still and let the thoughts occur in their own time at their own speed. To force nothing. To insist on nothing. Just to be and let living be enough.

I sometimes think life does not pass; it accumulates. You live in a certain way and eventually your surroundings have got you like a puppet. Your obligations, possessions, routines, the expectations of those around you have evolved. Your identity is not you: it is what is expected of you. It is your lifestyle.

It happens that your real loves slip out of your life. You did not notice. They are gone. You have forgotten what they were.

Jo, the thin lady who owned the mansion I found, gave me the key to the second floor. I unlocked the door and went in. There were many rooms in all directions. In each room there were many windows: high and wide, the way they built them eighty years ago, with windowsills. The windows looked out on all sides of the house. The floors were bare, the walls painted white.

All the windows were open. I went from room to room and birds were screeching in the branches at every window. The sun shone into one room, then moved to the next, and on around the house. It was empty and private. A blessedly empty and private place.

l thought: I want to put nothing in here. To let it stay empty. I want to be free.

There are mornings when you have no emotions. You are numb. You see the sun is pouring in through the window. You know it will be a glorious day. You make a cup of coffee. You put your sneakers on and walk to the corner bakery and buy fresh biscuits. You are in the sunroom, all windows open wide, and you listen to the world. But you are numb.

Other people have talked too much. They have not allowed the silence to expand. No sensations have unfolded. There is no understanding in the bones, only intellectual decorations. Commentary that has no meaning. You know if they do not stop talking you will be lost in their words.

And you have gone away to a place where no one can find you. As the warm sunny morning blazes at the world, you notice you are numb. It occurs to you: perhaps I did not get away in time.

My father deteriorated for four years. It was a gradual physical weakening that we all thought was temporary. His left side was not fully functional. Eventually he could not use his left leg much and had to give up running, then walking. Soon he was walking around the yard, dragging his left leg. His condition was occasioned by a benign tumour in the brain.

On occasion he collapsed with an epileptic-like seizure. When he had an extreme seizure in early March, he was sent to the hospital in Portland for further tests. When he went there, I flew in from Canada.

It was not the beginning of the end. It was the end. It was the countdown: five weeks to death. To zero.

The decline and fall of my father is a story. *On the one hand, there is what it is possible to write, and on the other what it is no longer possible to write*, Roland Barthes said. My father's final story is no longer possible to write. It cannot be sentimentalized. It cannot keep its emotive qualities. It cannot be told as a story.

When it comes to my father's death, I fear the violence of my emotions. If the mind were a nuclear reactor with a built-in safety shutdown mechanism, I could say my mind shuts down when thoughts of my father's decline and fall occur. All the meters instantly go down. All the arrows suddenly point to zero. A peculiar quiet grips the rooms where only the blue fluorescent lights linger.

You are left with a story that is not a story. A novel that is not a novel, a poem no longer a poem.

When the plane descended over Portland, the sky was clear. Rafts floated down the Willamette River. A million automobiles went busily around on the highway cloverleaf. The sun was shining. After disembarking, I found my suitcase. It was going around and around on the conveyor belt.

I found a taxi and told the driver to take me to the Good Samaritan Hospital. He drove out along narrow little-travelled side roads. *All the streets into town are blocked*, the driver said. *We have to take a detour.*

I was thinking: it is easy to travel. It is easy to earn money with which to travel. This increased mobility has changed the meaning of the word *goodbye*. In former times, when people moved away, they did not see each other again. They shed tears of farewell. Now we know we will meet again. There are no farewells. A million airplanes fly in the sky on any given day.

When Canadian Airlines was promoting its program for the arts, they issued a poster. On it was a large and colourful picture under the heading *The Art of Flying*. Ballet shoes, typewriters, paint brushes could be seen flying in through the window out of the clear blue sky.

I was never afraid of saying goodbye.

My parents had a garden in a small town in the Willamette Valley. There they had apple trees, pear trees, cherry trees, blackberry bushes, azaleas, magnolia trees, dogwood trees, tulips, rose bushes, begonias, a hundred other flowers and bushes. They had a birdbath, picnic tables with chairs, a brick patio. Towering Ponderosa pines and Douglas firs stood overhead.

My father was always in this garden. He had a small red typewriter which he placed on the picnic table. Next to the typewriter was a large plate onto which he put crumbs. On the other side lay a stack of papers on which he was writing.

It would be a scientific paper in another language, full of calculations involving letters and numbers and mathematical signs in between. Behind his chair stood the trunk of an ancient cedar, half dead and hollow inside.

He had three constant companions on his authorial journeys through his imagined land of mathematics, geophysical explorations worked out on paper, and garden shrubs and flowers. One was a blue jay that hopped from the branch to the table to the typewriter to the plate with crumbs where it stopped its screeching, munched, then hopped onto the back of his chair. All this hopping was accompanied by loud screeching. The other was a grey squirrel with a large bushy tail that ran headlong up the cedar trunk, then down again, inverted, then onto the table where it stole crumbs from the plate, then up the trunk again. A third companion was a Siamese cat that sat peacefully next to his chair with an air of propriety, unmoved by the two divergent members of other species that shared its domain.

I often think this is the century of the countdown. We count down to the blast of the cannon and the opening of the chute on the aircraft that lets the bomb fall on some designated target. A city. A factory. A military base. We count down to the takeoff of the spaceship or rocket. We count down to the hour of Midnight on the Doomsday Clock.

Perhaps we should paginate our books this way. Begin with the last page and count down to the end.

It is good to remember that, before Christ, they were also counting down. Only they did not know it. They did not know what year it was. They could not say: this is 938 BCE. Next year will be 937.

We do not know what happens at Zero. If anything happens. Perhaps it is nothing. A sudden silence will grip the world. Perhaps there will be something: like an explosion in the sky. Bodies of seven astronauts will be scattered like dust over the fields of the high prairies. The farmer will turn them over in his soil unwittingly.

I bought a mug to drink coffee from. Soon I had a huge house with many rooms, lots of light, and one ceramic mug. It was a relief to have nothing, but I suspected it would not last. In my suspicions, chairs, tables, desks, dishes, kettles, forks would begin to float in through the windows one by one. Out of the clear blue sky. It was just a matter of time, I thought.

The Gateway to the West has one long, wide, meandering boulevard that looks like a cross between Beverly Hills of the north and an English Mansion Row. This is called Wellington Crescent. On Sundays and holidays its residents are privileged to have their street closed to all traffic. Those who come in a car find a closed gate blocking access by vehicle. They have to get out and walk down the boulevard like everyone else.

I walk on the sidewalk until I get to the roadblock. From there I walk down the middle of the street. Joggers and runners go by in both directions. Men with babies, old women, middle-aged bachelors are walking both ways in the street. They are happy. Motorists, however, are forced to make a detour.

I was walking down Wellington Crescent on a day it was closed to motorists. An elderly man carrying two Safeway plastic bags, one in each hand, stopped as I passed him. He said to me: *I said to my brother Joe I said don't buy anything cheap it won't last.*

I got out of the taxi in front of the Good Samaritan Hospital, took my suitcase to the receptionist's desk, and asked where my father was located. She told me he had just arrived, Room 362. I left my baggage with her and went up to his room. There I found him in a bed, a forlorn look on his face, and my mother busying herself with cups of water and Kleenexes. When I stepped into the room, he looked at me. No change of expression appeared, as if he thought I had been there all along. His knowing eyes seemed to say: here we are again, caught in a hopeless situation, and this time we won't get out of it. What he did say was: *Hello again, good to have you back.*

I never really left, I told him.

Three solid days of tests followed. X-rays, magnetic resonance tests, blood samples, CAT scans. Morning and afternoon the transport department came in their blue coats with stretchers to take my father to yet another exam room. The doctors promised that at the end of the third day they would appear with an accurate diagnosis and prognosis. Then we could choose among alternative courses of action.

I asked my father how the tests were after waiting. He endured them all in silent patience. He said they put his head in a machine and told him to keep still. *Of course when they say you can't move, your face begins to itch.*

It occurred to me: there will be an effort made to forget. There are things we will want to forget. Memory will become selective.

As my father grew more silent, until all there was were his lustrous light blue eyes, l knew he was thinking about forgetting. I told myself: I will not forget. There will be a book and it will be about forgetting. A book that refuses to forget even as it forgets.

It is precisely because I forget that I read, Roland Barthes said.

Grieving is remembering. Remembering intensifies your sense of loss. When people tell you you will get over your grief, they are saying you will forget. That forgetting is condoned.

So I was thinking. I do not want my grief to go away. My father exists in my memory of him: not a selective memory but a whole remembrance. I want to entrap my grief in a place it will never escape from: here in these words. To remember forever.

Soon after my arrival in the Gateway to the West, it became very hot. It rained heavily for two days, with thunder and lightning in the clouds. Then as suddenly the sun came out and beamed down on the city with a vengeance, producing a mugginess unusual for the high prairies. Instantly five billion mosquitoes poured out of the swamps and attacked every warm-blooded creature within range. City council met in emergency sessions. We cannot get the better of them, they said. In the battle between man and mosquito, the mosquito wins. *They were here before we arrived and they will be here after we go*, a city councillor claimed to the press.

In the heat of the ensuing days, people began to wilt. Limbs were slumped over furniture. Activity slowed to a crawling pace. The concierge, on her way to the vegetable patch, got as far as the lawn chair and dropped into it tiredly. The cat, on its way to the second floor, got as far as the landing halfway up and collapsed in the corner. The song of the birds turned into drawn-out sighs. Even the mosquitoes lumbered heavily through the air, too tired to bite. A dog sat on the porch and wailed pitifully.

There is no winter in this text. I search for signs of winter but in vain. There is no memory of winter.

At the end of the third day the doctors came, as promised, with all the results. On every floor was a pleasant seating area, with comfortable sofas and lounge chairs and coffee tables. The paintings on the walls and plush rugs on the floor were designed to make the environment pleasing. The two neurosurgeons led my mother and me to the lounge area of our floor where we sat down. They delivered the prognosis without decorations: my father had a nearly inoperable brain tumour that had grown to a point where he was incapacitated and only half his brain was currently functioning. He also had a resurgence of a former cancer of the liver, which could not be operated on again. Between his two ailments they reckoned he had one to three months left to live. They could try operating on the brain tumour, but chances were one out of four that he would die on the operating table. Chances were three out of four that he would suffer permanent damage from the operation. They could give him chemotherapy for the liver, but chances were two out of four that it would not work. If it did work, it would only hold the cancer in abeyance for up to a year, at which point he would die anyway. If the operation on the tumour was successful, it would grow back anyway, and within a year he would be back to where he was now. They said they would get the operating room ready and we should let them know in the morning what we intended to do. Then they left.

This is the part of my father's story I want to bury under a thousand trivial words so it will not be noticed. So I myself will read them and forget what I am reading even as I read.

My mother felt sick and glued to her lounge chair. She said: *Would you go in and tell him this, I don't think I can?*

I left her sitting alone in the big chair after a long moment of silence. I had never seen her so small. I walked in the hospital corridors, passing room after room, my feet heavy as lead. In my nerves I sensed there was some purpose to this walking down hospital halls, but in my mind I was already forgetting what the purpose was.

Of all the things in your life that can go down to zero, the most comical is the bank account. I often think banks exist for the sole purpose of avoiding zero.

At the time I took the little red car and drove to the Gateway to the West with nothing but a red dress and a typewriter in the trunk, I had discovered that my bank balance was at zero. All the time I had spent with my father, I made no deposits. The bank immediately put the numbers back onto my balance sheet and made the transaction good by placing minus signs behind them. This way I could owe them money instead of them owing me.

What you do – brain surgery or chemotherapy or nothing, with all the accompanying percentages – becomes a matter of numbers. I pondered how much time could be bought at what cost. How much quality time at how much suffering. I had the sinking feeling that it was becoming necessary for me to think for us all.

I took the elevator down, walked past the receptionist's desk, out the door onto the paved court in front of the hospital. Behind the building on a parallel street was a long avenue of boutiques, restaurants, gift shops, folk shops, bakeries, bookstores. Colourful ice cream vendors rang bells in the sun. Coffee stands were set up on the sidewalks; people in bright cotton clothes were drinking coffee from styrofoam cups, sitting on benches, on doorsteps, leaning against lamp posts.

I bought a cup of coffee, sat down on a bench in the sun, and felt the warmth penetrating my skin. I had a ball-point pen in my pocket and a piece of paper. On the paper I wrote numbers. The numbers went as high as twelve and came in percentages of a hundred. Soon I had a graph.

One year earlier I was visiting my parents in their old farmhouse in the village of the Willamette Valley. The morning sun began to shine on the grass, reflecting flashes of light in the gossamer webs tiny spiders had laid over the green blades during the night. As I came down the stairs, I heard my mother call out in delight. My father was at the window. My mother stood behind him, holding clean cups she was about to lay on the breakfast table. When I came to the window I saw five deer, three of them young, only half grown. The youngsters were jumping several metres into the air, crashing around the huge yard. The adults were gingerly nibbling on the pink roses my mother had so painstakingly put down, eating them up. My father was smiling with a faraway look in his eyes.

I did not know why we were not following a path. Perhaps there was no path, although I had seen a road on the south side of the small mountain. The pale brown dirt road curved as if it would go all the way around the butte in spiral fashion. Instead of taking the road, we were climbing straight up on the western side. The mountain was an infamous dry, hot, and waterless peak called Black Butte in the Oregon desert.

It was when I was still very young. I was hiking with a friend, a Danish American writer who loved the Cascades. It is a low mountain range covered with forest. Occasionally a towering peak rises out of the mass of lower mountains and stands magnificent and snowcapped in its pink isolation. *These are like the great spirits that rise out of humanity*, Erling said. Once in a while. Mount St. Helens. Mount Jefferson. Three Sisters.

Black Butte was so dry that trees could not grow. There were remnants of old forests, and some new forest to spite the conditions, but many of those trees crumbled in early death into the brown dust. Climbing up the mountainside, we had to step over the dead tree trunks that crumbled under our boots. You have to be careful of rattlesnakes here, he warned. *They lie inconspicuously in hiding, usually inside the hollow trunks of dead trees.*

By July sixth, war was declared on the mosquitoes in the Gateway to the West. People were no longer able to stand still because of itching arms and legs. Children showed up in hospital emergency wards with eyes swollen shut. The threat of encephalitis hovered like a cloud over the deceptively beautiful sunshine. The Mayor declared on the radio: *Let's attack the damn buggers with everything we've got. Let's kill them all!*

I have noticed that the mind, like the body, compensates. It is said that when the body experiences sudden extreme pain, the brain instantly produces a substance much like morphine and shoots it through the system. The body does not feel the pain it feels until later. At night, when the lights are off and the house is quiet, the child realizes that the broken arm inside the cast is searingly painful. In the afternoon it had not hurt: when he came in from falling off his bike, his arm dangling in two pieces, it was only a mental shock.

If an impression is too painful, the mind shuts down in the same way. I often think: that is how soldiers can go on with warfare. Yet the impressions have not been erased. Later, much later, when all is quiet, they venture out of their hiding places. Slowly, cautiously, like rattlesnakes testing the conditions, creeping out of the hollow trunks of the past. If you step too close, they strike.

It sometimes pains me to know that nothing can ever be forgotten. No matter how much we desire to forget, it seems to me that *once an impression has been imprinted on the brain, it is there for good.*

It is good to walk about with no destination in mind. In the heat of the day I walked, looking at this prairie city. An Indigenous boy, perhaps three or four years old, sat in the dirt outside the open basement window of a brick apartment building. His feet were stretched straight out in front and his hands were folded in his lap. His back was lightly bent over. He looked up with a sad face at passersby.

I went into my father's hospital room after pondering the situation in the corridors for a while. He lay on his back, looking at the ceiling. He knew we had spoken with the doctors. I could sense a mild anticipation, but his resignation was already so complete that whatever news I had appeared only a matter of curiosity. I sat down on a chair beside his bed. I told him.

Four years earlier I did the same: my father wanted the news from me after surgery for liver cancer. He woke up in the intensive care unit, hooked up to numerous machines and with an oxygen mask over his nose and mouth. Unable to speak, drugged nearly out of consciousness, he still had the force of will that characterized him all his life. I stood at his bed and he signalled that he knew it was me. He made some other sign with his hands. No one present could understand what his fingers were trying to say, but I recognized that with his right hand he was imagining writing on the palm of his left hand. I said: he wants a pen and paper. There was a rush for these items and we gave them to him. From the bottom of his morphine exhaustion, he scribbled almost illegibly: *What did Dr. Moseley say?* I bent over him and said clearly to make sure he could hear every word: *Dr. Moseley said the surgery was successful and all your problems have been removed.* Then he was quiet inside his mask.

I have often thought: our ability to endure suffering is directly proportional to the amount of hope we have for something better.

As I suspected, items began to float into the second-floor window of the mansion I had acquired as my own for a while in the Gateway city. A kettle, fashioned in Holland out of black steel. A white plate, a black saucer, a white cup. A pad to sleep on, two pillows. Two deep blue towels. A garden chair and table, white, began to stand in the sunroom. Here I put my typewriter.

I sometimes think it is not possible to keep an empty life. Life itself is material. It was a comfort of a kind to know that all the items around me were things I had never seen before.

It seemed to happen so suddenly: I discovered I was a stranger in my own life. I do not know when or how it happened, whether it was gradual or not, but I did not recognize anything around me as being of any *significance*. I began to wonder why people were going about their business so *importantly*. It all seemed to me inexplicably absurd. Somewhere along the way there had been a transformation and I came back a different person. Someone no one recognized. Expectations went unanswered.

I could see conflict coming in on the clouds. Like the approach of a thunderstorm. On the prairies you see it from far away: a thick mass of dark purple cloud that reaches to the ground. Streaks of lightning flash out of it in various directions. You watch it move forward. Dark bands stretch over the grasslands: the rain.

That is when I drove away. To let the rain fall down without me.

My father lapsed into total silence on hearing the news I had for him from the doctors and all their tests. I told him they had given us twenty-four hours to decide whether he would have surgery or not.

It was his way: when he had a problem to ponder, he remained silent until the answer presented itself. Like some Viking chieftain who locks himself up to meditate and will not come out until he knows what to do.

I waited with him all night and all next day. He did not speak, but lay staring at the ceiling, then down at his hands on top of the blanket, then out at the window. Day turned to dusk and the lights of the city came on. It was the last room on the corridor, removed from the nurses' station and traffic. The night was quiet. Light from the hall fell aslant into the darkened room. My mother anxiously but patiently rummaged about the room with small paper cups of water, toothbrush, facecloth, whatever she could think of doing for him.

While we waited for him to commune with his own spirit, we did our own thinking. Each in our private way assessed the situation. I now think that everything we have been through since, and every emotion we have encountered, can be boiled down to those twenty-four hours. It occurred to me that to make a decision is to create a reality. An alternate reality. A design of fate that can never be rolled back to the beginning again.

The Oregonian carried an account of a man bitten by a rattlesnake. He was hiking in the Oregon desert. At the bottom of a ravine, he encountered a rattler and was bitten. Panic-stricken, he started to climb out of the ravine furiously. He climbed and ran until, a short time later, he collapsed and died. *His mistake was to run*, the article said.

What you do when bitten by a rattler, Erling told me, *is: sit down*. Stop all motion. The more you run about, the faster the poison spreads through your body and the sooner you die. *If you sit still, chances are you will survive.* Just apply basic first aid.

I conceived of an idea for a book: a man is bitten by a snake. He sits down and waits for help. The book consists of all his thoughts as he waits, the cloud of death hovering over.

When I was fourteen, I was to take the year-end examination in mathematics. It was a national exam, given to all fourteen-year-olds in the country. I had neglected to study over the winter, too busy with other interests: hair spray and high heels. My reasoning was: my father is a mathematician. He can show me in no time how to do these equations. When it comes to numbers, he can work miracles.

For breakfast we had toast and tea. I pushed my plate aside on the red table and put my math book in its place. I said to my father sitting next to me: *Pabbi, can you show me how to do this?* He said: *You mean you don't know any of it?* I shook my head furtively, hoping my mother would not notice. We had half an hour. I pulled at his sleeve pleadingly. He looked at me in astonishment. After showing me the first two problems, he looked at the clock and said: *It simply cannot be done.*

I failed the exam. They must have given me a round zero.

My mother took to my graph, outlined in the Portland sun on that miserable afternoon, with interest and relief. Here was the situation clearly outlined on paper; the numbers were plain to see. It was a kind of cost-benefit analysis of the pros and cons of medical treatment and of no treatment. She showed it to my father and tried to think out loud with him, pointing at the numbers representing months and percentages. He was only halfheartedly following her, persistent in his silence. By the second evening he was not ready to speak yet. I told him we would decide in the morning and he nodded slowly. I informed the doctors they would know in the morning.

We were staying in a small apartment building across the street from the hospital, called Good Samaritan House. It was owned by the hospital and rented out for brief periods to family of patients from out of town. If they had gone out of their way to depress the distraught family members of the ill, they could not have done better. It was an old and worn-down building. Paint was discolouring; rugs and upholstery barely held together. There was not enough ventilation through the building, so the stale air of hospital visitors accumulated and remained.

We had a suite on the second floor. To go in and out of that building, we had to brace ourselves. But it was a bed and a kitchen where we could make morning coffee. One night there was excessive commotion downstairs. We heard people running, doors slamming, a siren outside. In the morning, on my way out, I saw that suite number one was cleared out and all the furniture was out in the hall. I asked the security guard what had happened. *There seems to have been a murder in there last night*, he said matter of factly, chewing gum.

We were wandering through the deep woods of the lower coastal range of Oregon. The rain forest is thick with ferns and ivies and studded with pine trees. It was dark and musty under the cover of the foliage that shielded us from the sun. I did not know where we were exactly, but I was with a friend for whom these forests were home. We emerged from the dank foliage onto an open pasture unexpectedly. There the sun shone golden and inviting on the green grass.

We had only gone a few paces onto this jewelled play of various shades of green, beckoning like a mirage, when we heard gunshots. I could feel a bullet whiz by in the air. My friend grabbed my arm and yelled: *Lie down!* We immediately fell on our stomachs, faces in the grass. Overhead I heard the shots zoom by, some just above our bodies. *It's the deer hunters*, my friend whispered. *They must think we're a couple of deer.*

There is no screen on the windows in the sunroom. When the afternoon sun shines warmly onto the aspen and elm trees, I lean out of the huge window. The breeze blows through the leaves on the branches and the trees shudder with a kind of unearthly delight. There are light green leaves, dark green, orange, brown, yellow leaves wafting up and down and sideways. I often think that green is the most soothing of all colours, the most comforting.

The colour that makes you happy to do nothing except lean out of a window and breathe in the warm dry air.

During the night I stayed up and watched the lights go on and off in windows in other buildings. Noises from the street below floated in: cars passing, bicyclists on whispering tires; a laugh, a call, a heated conversation, a few words looming distinct, the rest barely audible. Perhaps I was not thinking so much as absorbing the time, the place. Rain came down in a few heavy drops toward morning. I could hear them splatter on the street like tiny water-filled balloons.

The small hospital room contained an orange vinyl-clad lounge chair that one could lean back and doze off in. The room was dark except for a night-light at the base of the bed. I could see my father's face in the dim light. He lay staring at the ceiling mostly and sometimes with eyes closed. At six a.m. we were to let each other know our thoughts. There was an invisible cloud of anxious anticipation in the night silence, broken only occasionally by an intruding nurse checking the IV.

Toward morning I went across the street to our flat. My father was asleep. The air was moist from the night rain. The silver hue of daylight was in the horizon behind the roofs of rickety buildings. A conviction had been growing inside me during the night hours: I knew what we should do in my heart and it was nothing any graph could alter. A conviction like faith: it enters you in the form of a revelation and changes you. Its workings cannot be explained.

In the flat my mother was stirring from an uneasy sleep. As soon as I walked in, she called. I told her things were fine, put water on the boil, and freshened up. It was a bitter cup of coffee. Six a.m.

I sat in the front row of the university auditorium along with all the dignitaries and honorary recipients. The President of the country, the Minister for Education, the Minister for Culture, four men who were being awarded honorary doctorate, one of whom I was standing in for. Their families.

Before the convocations began, my father's name was called: Dr. Bödvarsson cannot be here due to ill health, but we would like to call on his daughter to come and receive his honorary degree for him.

I went around to the stairs and up to the stage. Suddenly the stage seemed enormous and walking to the podium in the centre took an eternity. I was to stand facing the podium while my father's accomplishments were listed and his work praised. As I stood there, it felt like the heavy rain clouds over Iceland had descended onto my shoulders and were weighing me down. Finally the Dean of Sciences turned to me and stretched out his hand. I stepped forward, shook it, and took the enormous hard-bound folder containing my father's degree in the other hand. I walked over to where the President of the university stood in his blue cloak, with white trimming down to his shoes, and shook his hand. Then the tremendously long walk to the other end of the stage, down the stairs, and back to my seat along the entire first row, passing personages one could hardly ignore, yet passing them without acknowledgement. Knowing my father could not have taken this walk: he would have stumbled, perhaps fallen. Thousands of people would see him fall. The people of whom he was proud and who were proud of him: he would find himself humiliated.

When l came back to the hospital room, my father was awake. It was time. l sat down next to his bed and said: *What is your answer?* He looked straight forward, at nothing, and said matter of factly: *My answer is what it always has been and you know what it is.* As if it were self-evident. As obvious as that you will fail your math exam if you do not study the material. I waited for him to finish. He had a determined expression on his face even while he focussed on nothing in particular.

I want no more surgery, he said emphatically. Then he turned and looked me straight in the face. In his eyes were mirrored his four years of suffering, the sorrow, the exhaustion. The deep sorrow of it all.

In my mind a hundred dams broke and water flowed furiously out of the cracked reservoirs. I understood. I felt only relief that I did not have to argue my own convictions against anyone else's. I took his hand and he held his steady look into my eyes. I said with all my pent-up emotions at bursting point: *Pabbi, let's get out of here.* The IV bottle hanging overhead, the chart on his door, the clockwork medication, the anaesthetist waiting outside the door to do his preliminary report. My father smiled. *Let's go*

home to the garden and the squirrel and blue jay and Siamese cat and the deer, the azaleas, the dogwood tree. We tried to hold the tears back. But some of them broke through anyway. We were proud. We had a decision. We were in perfect agreement.

My mother walked into the room, tired from lack of sleep. Anxious. When she sat down, we told her. She sat frozen still for a few seconds and then breathed a huge sigh of relief. She said: *It was what I also thought we should do.* She embraced my father, kissed him all over his face, wept, said: *Can't we come out of the horrible room?* We helped him into his wheelchair and rolled him out to the lounge area in the hallways where the comfortable sofas were. There we sat down and hatched our plan of action.

My father announced his intention to pack up and leave that morning. Soon the various doctors were coming up to see him and telephoning in. *You surprise us, Dr. Bödvarsson,* they said. They grouped around his bed: the two neurologists, the internal specialist, the cancer specialist, the nurse. My father said to them, like a professor gently lecturing his students: *You may not understand that I come from a culture where to die in bed is the worst calamity that can befall a man.*

Moments of happiness one forgets, Mikhail Lermontov wrote, *but sorrow never.*

In the Gateway city I had one pot, made in Holland. It soon became clear to me that I no longer remembered how to cook. I had no idea what to put in the pot and how long to heat it. Even though I had cooked meals for many years, the knowledge had somehow left me.

I looked for a cookbook in the bookstore to show me what to do. There is no cookbook in the world called *Cooking for One* so I bought a book called *Cooking for Two.* It is always possible, I thought, that another person will come floating in along with other things. It happens.

As the summer advanced, the heat on the prairies grew more intense. It became necessary to sleep naked, on the floor, all windows open to the mild breeze that wafted in from the night. A welcoming breath of cool air, like a gentle soul blowing on the skin.

I lay in the dark room, empty except for a foam rubber mattress and a navy blue sheet. The room was large, the ceiling high, and the white walls bare except for an unused fireplace. The large old windows were open. Light from the lamp post at the gate that marked the entrance to my street reflected on the wall. Occasionally I heard someone walking below. A dog barking. A car turning the corner. And in between, silence.

I had no thoughts, only a sense of relief that at that moment there was no one and nothing to attend to. That it was pleasant to lie in the dark and allow myself an empty mind.

Soon I noticed a strange odour. It grew stronger: a smell of chemicals, as if I were trying to breathe the Winnipeg International Airport. A yellow light began to flash through the room, sliding from wall to wall around in circles. I awoke out of my half slumber and jumped up. It was as I thought: they were spraying. An enormous truck was crawling along the streets, with a yellow light circling on its roof to warn residents, and a spray of insecticides gushing out of pipes on its side, covering the trees along the street.

When mosquitoes fly into sprayed territory, they fall down dead. Others scramble away and die elsewhere, under leaves or between blades of grass. Every summer Gateway people raise the issue in City Council: how do we know for sure, they ask, that this chemical will not also kill us? There is a long debate until everyone is overcome by insect bites and a tacit agreement to spray is reached.

I closed the windows in all the rooms. It occurred to me that if I had followed the spraying report, I could have closed them earlier.

In the morning a red-breasted robin settled on a huckleberry branch just outside the screen. The sun was shining. He spread his wings and waited. All was still except for the leaves jittering on trees and the tin cones forever turning on rooftops.

Soon there were faint echoes of music in the distance: bells, trumpets, drums, high women's voices. In summer the Gateway city becomes a city of festivals: the Fringe Festival, the Street Festival, the Reggae Festival. In the park, the Folk Festival. In the zoo, pandas. I imagine it is an announcement: there are passions out there. People still have fun, jump, shout. People with dreadlocks, in red tennis shoes, in white T-shirts with pictures of jugglers. Pamphlets lie scattered on corners that say: *just when you thought it was safe to go back to the streets* ... and pictures of one man strangling another.

At noon, when the sky was light blue and clear, I thought: it is wonderful to be alone. To go from room to room in a slightly frayed mansion and think of a book. *A Hero of Our Time.* To come down a street on an overused sidewalk and think of grasshoppers. Unobstructed thoughts that meet no resistance.

But even then I was not quite. alone. A cat resided in the stairway. Whenever I came up the oak staircase, the cat was on the bench under the stained glass window, waiting. When l leaned out the window in the sunroom, the cat was on the roof next door, looking back at me. When I went down to the cool basement to wash something, the cat was on the high windowsill, leaning back relaxed.

So we drove back from Portland to the little town in the Willamette Valley: my mother at the wheel, my father in the passenger seat, and me in the backseat, arms around his shoulders. He made the trip in silence. It was a stretch of 15 he knew he would never see again. The forests of firs on both sides, pastureland newly sown, Luckiamute River, lllahee Xing. Exit 255, 254, 253, going down as you go south. Roadside billboards that read: *Here today, lawn tomorrow.* And a fairy tale amusement park in the woods called Enchanted Forest.

L'homme, c'est style, say the French. My father had a certain style. A certain natural aristocracy. It was important: to be above petty politics. To be above all cynicism, bitterness. To part with your friends *on your feet*. To make sure you have a chance *to say goodbye*. In America it is called: *dying with dignity*.

Because of the heat and dryness, the forests of northern Manitoba began to burn. The Pas, Norway House, Pikwatonei, Nelson House, Pukatawagan, Snow Lake were enveloped in flames. Eighteen thousand refugees fled to the Gateway city in Canadian Air Force planes. The flames jumped over the river *like it's not even there*, a firefighter shouted. Smoke filled the northern regions. Soon rescue flights had to be abandoned because visibility was down to zero.

In the Gateway city, night streets remained quiet and calm, and stars could still be seen behind thin veils of cloud. But if the wind blew in from the north, the air turned to smoke and breathing became painful. Headlines in the *Free Press* read: *The whole north is virtually blowing up on us*.

The name of the town, translated from the Latin, was *Heart of the Valley*. The Willamette Valley is very wide and flat between Coastal and Cascade mountain ranges. Farmland, pastures, small hills, small towns. In summer a still haze fills the air and it is not possible to see the mountains surrounding the valley on the horizons. In winter it fills with rain.

My father was in the habit of hiking up MacDonald Forest. A minor mountain, thick with forest growth, and a gravel road winding to the peak where there was a good view of the valley. Along the roadside, ferns and ivies crowded. Pine trees, fir trees crowded for space in the woods. Whenever he saw a Ponderosa pine, he pulled a handful of needles off one of the branches and held them to his nose, breathing in the sweet perfume they exuded. I followed behind, enchanted by the luscious and strange forest.

It was almost midnight. I stood in line to rent a car in the Portland Airport. Business took me away from my father's bedside for a few days. Between him and Portland stood a two-hour drive. A woman ahead of me got the last available car and took me along as a passenger. She was a graduate student in Forestry, in the valley to do research.

I told her we often hiked in the MacDonald Forest. She said: *That's an experimental forest. The strangest things go on there.* I asked her to name an example. For example, she said, they blow the tops off the trees so the soil below will be nutrified by the falling debris. They plant little bombs at the tips and *blast the tops right off.* Tree debris goes flying in all directions.

The old farmhouse in the *Heart of the Valley* was two-storeyed: downstairs, a living room, family room, dining room, and kitchen. Upstairs, bedrooms. Since my father could not walk, we put a hospital bed into the family room downstairs where he stayed. On one wall, shelves were lined with his science books. On the other wall, shelves were lined with straw baskets of all sizes and shapes. The windows were made of glass prisms leaded together. There was an easy chair, a rocking chair, a television never used. A bright red cabinet of wine glasses with a collection of fifty jade elephants, trunks high in the air, stampeding off the edge: forever perched in furious stillness.

And the one indispensable object: a telephone. From his bed, raised at the back so he could sit up, my father dialled the numbers of all his friends, associates, and relatives around the world. *I have to tell them the news*, he said. To bid them farewell.

My mother and I nursed my father twenty-four hours a day in this last world of his. We brought him his food, helped him wash up, kept him company. We took turns sleeping on the sofa in the living room at night so we could hear when he called. We read to him from books and papers, dialled phone numbers for him, brought him his mail, measured out his medication.

Whenever I walked past his room where the door was always open, I saw him lying there, watching and waiting. His face was always sad, calm, and tinged with a sense of furious desperation. The house was quiet. Hours went by soundlessly. Finally my father said: *I cannot lie here with any greatness of spirit.*

We helped him into his wheelchair and wheeled him out onto the patio in the backyard. The spring sun was shining. Azaleas were in stark bloom. Tulips flowered. He put his red cap on his head and sat in his old place, head leaning slightly to one side. The Siamese cat sat down beside him. The old blue jay hopped and screeched about on the patio furniture. The grey squirrel reappeared and cautiously, nervously approached the wheelchair with the attendant cat.

Suddenly the entire Canadian prairie cooled down. The sky was overcast. A hint of rain was in the air. People waited for drops to fall that never did. The temperature went down by ten degrees Celsius. In the north, firefighters began to have the upper hand. Thirty-six thousand refugees in the Gateway city became hopeful that they could soon go home.

It was at the time of the Street Festival. In Osborne Village, at the Portage Promenade, in Old Market Square, musicians, jugglers, dancers, comedians performed for passersby. They came in groups with street names: dancers who called themselves *The Flaming Idiots*, a magician named *Steve Trash*, jugglers who titled their act *Flying Debris*.

In the cool evening I heard the faint sounds of violin and guitar. People clustered around yellow tents, listening. A bicyclist in black with a bowler hat cycled across the lawn carrying a violin in a black case. A woman from Southeast Asia crossed the street with a bundle wrapped in green cloth on her head. A propeller plane ground through the air above.

I am glad there are such times in life: when you are protected by your solitude. When whoever speaks to you must speak to you on your own terms. Times when you do not give an inch. Because all you had to give has already been given.

It occurred to me: even love runs out when who you love has taken it away from you and is unable to bring it back. Then you have no more.

Except for a treasured space, perhaps, where what is left is something you guard with your life. It is your rope when you scale the cliffs.

I am told my father climbed mountains in Nicaragua, with pick axes and ropes. I did not see him. I am told he climbed in the Montana Rockies and fell in an avalanche. He was assumed dead until he stood up and walked to the road. I did not see this. I am told he careened down an icy path in an automobile in the Coastal Range of Oregon and miraculously came to a halt without damage. I saw nothing. And an airplane he flew in Central America almost crashed. Of that story he said: *When we were about to crash, I* thought *at least I am not perishing in my bed.*

I rounded the corner in the little red car. It was early evening, when the light is deep and colours are stark. The water in the Red River was deep blue, navy. A pleasure boat sailed slowly up the stream and under the bridge. At the edge of the bridge a policeman stopped me. He said: *You can't go across, there's a Folklorama parade and all the streets to downtown are blocked.*

Cats was in the Gateway city from New York. On the stage, cats were sitting, lying down, standing, leaning on precipices, sitting on oil cans, jumping over boxes, floating up on rubber tires. They sang a lot and danced a great deal. As they did, Great West Life ran an ad with a picture of ballet shoes, violin, paint brush, oils, spotlight. Underneath it said: *The arts. The staging of civilization.*

I have seen the blank page referred to as a stage. All that happens on the page is theatre. Writing is a play. Words are actors, props, singers, dancers.

I think of civilization as a great contrivance. A great book.

It occurs to me this is about the ability to start a new life. When you are at Mile Zero. Before you go up in a spotlight.

My father's surgeon knocked on the front door of the house. He was an elderly man of medium height, grey hair, gentle smile. He came into my father's room, sat down beside his bed, asked him how he was doing, assured him it was the right thing, rubbed his back. He said: *I am here as a friend, not as a physician.*

I think it is possible to be many people at once, so long as you announce which person you are before you step in the doorway. Before Dr. Leman came to visit as a friend, my parents were distressed. My father lay in his bed, his face tight with tension, his eyes staring, distraught with guilt, regret, sorrow, uncertainty, longing for the ordeal to end. My mother jumped up at every small sound, unable to sit still, rattling dishes in the kitchen, washing towels a hundred times, driving herself in the possibility that *something else could have been.* When Dr. Leman left, they were both calm, serene, tranquil. *You are doing the right thing,* Dr. Leman said. My father was grateful: I saw it in his look. He was so grateful he could not speak. Even the tears that rushed and gathered behind his eyes were unable to break through.

I thought: someone who can give comfort like that to the dying is not a physician, not even a friend. He was here as an angel. It was an announcement he did not know he could make.

The American people, I began to realize, are preparing themselves to be angels. More and more people will be dying in their homes like this. Of incurable terminal illnesses: AIDS, cancer. And we must all learn to give, I thought.

Two hospice nurses visited. They sat down with my mother and me and discussed what we could expect. They spoke with my father. They said they would come to help whenever needed. Home health nurses came with stethoscopes and blood pressure gauges, inflatable bathing basins, thermometers. One of them, Claudia, sat down with us in the living room. She said: *Is there anything you would like to talk about? You must talk about your feelings. If you don't talk about how you feel, it will come out in other, worse, ways.*

Because I did not take Claudia's advice, when it was all over and my father's story was complete, the world as I knew it fell apart. I found my life in shambles in the dry prairie: papers were strewn all over the floor of my study, my desk, in boxes, in corners. Letters, phone calls, messages remained unanswered. Deadlines passed by. All my nerves seemed to have been clipped and I broke down at the slightest criticism. Wet clothes hung over chair backs in the living room, dining room, hallway; in the sink dishes were piled, on the counter food leftovers, on the floor crumbs, strips of lettuce, bits of bread. On the deck rotting leaves, in the flowerbeds weeds five feet high. In the basement a rock and roll band, five teenagers shaking the walls with amplifiers turned up high, electric guitars, drums, cymbals. There was shouting from one floor to another, telephones ringing at five-minute intervals.

I was shaking, I wept and was unable to handle what was supposed to be the real world. The man I lived with said: *Don't feel sorry for yourself, get on with things.* So I begged: *Can't we have some quiet? I want the world to stop!* When there was no response, I saw that the world had stopped only for me and not for anyone else. It was only *my* father who went to the grave. He was no one else's father.

That was when l took the little red car and drove to the Gateway to the West and the odometer went berserk.

Neither reason nor sense nor greed nor pity nor perspicacity nor worldly wisdom nor expediency nor filial duty gave my hand into yours. No one can say I was carried away in that hour, Elizabeth Smart wrote.

She is talking about love. And she is talking about writing: *in spite of everything so strong in dissuasion, so rampant in disapproval, I saw then that there was nothing else anywhere but this one thing.*

That writing is *a poverty-stricken word against the highly financed world, yet it is not meagre, it is enough. I do not accept it sadly or ruefully or wistfully or in despair. I accept it without tomorrows and without any lilies of promise. It is the enough, the now, and though it comes without anything, it gives me everything.*

I think there is nothing owing to you when you come into the world. And only those you have loved will mourn you when you go.

There was a knocking on the door. It was downstairs at the back door to the concierge's floor. A pounding that would not let up. No one answered. From my sunroom above, through the screens on the open windows, I heard the knocking. It was a cold morning, overcast and windy. Overnight rain had left the streets and grasses wet. It was Sunday and the Gateway city was slowly opening Folklorama Festival pavilions. I opened the only screenless window and looked down. On the steps to the concierge's back door stood a young woman with pitch-black hair. Behind her was a large black German Shepherd dog who looked up at me. We stared at each other.

My mother and I took turns sleeping in the living room where we could attend to my father during the night. One would stay up till ten, the other would do so from ten until six in the morning. Each of us, for this reason, slept only every other night.

It was a large living room and the cot stood next to my mother's large loom containing a wall hanging in the making: wool woven in beautiful gold and brown patterns, but abandoned. A small touch-lamp was lit in the farthest corner so it would not be completely dark. Beside the cot was a small table with a clock radio lighting up the hour and minutes in bright red numbers that went from twelve:zero to twelve:zero. I put my head on the pillow, trying to rest. In the other room I heard my father's uneasy breathing. Then my name and I rose. It would be for a drink. Or a wash. Or company. And at midnight, I counted out nine different kinds of pills in various amounts.

Soon both of us were exhausted from lack of sleep. We were dragging our feet through the days, unable to brighten up. The clouds in our heads grew thicker and darker until the purple hue showed through around our eyes. Finally we hired a woman to stay between ten and six. Her name was Ramona, a Californian of Mexican extraction, slender, small, with pitch-black curly hair. My father called her *the lady from Catalonia*.

Every day my father's friends came to call. They came one at a time and sat by his bed. On good days my father sat in a wheelchair in the living room and visited. His colleagues, friends, former students all came to say goodbye. When a visitor entered and asked: *How are you, Gunnar?* my father said in his heavy accent: *I am sorry you see me here in this miserable condition.*

My father was a Senior Professor of Oceanography at the university in the valley, and later Professor Emeritus. His special field was geophysics, and within that, geothermal heat. He was trained at first in engineering, then geology, mathematics, and physics, and he received his doctorate from the California Institute of Technology under the Nobel Prize winner Richard Feynman.

But it was what he brought from his Nordic culture that set him apart in the academic world. He had many doctoral students under his supervision. He saw them all through: no one who came to him went away without a degree. He never abandoned a student. If they had difficulty, he worked with them until the problem was solved. If office time proved less than enough, they came to his home. He befriended them, opened his home to them, had them over with their families at Christmas, lent them his cottage on the coast. He stood by them and they were grateful.

When we drove into town from the Good Samaritan Hospital in Portland, my father returning to his final hours at home, we rounded the corner of our street. There, in front of our house, stood a cluster of students waiting. They had come to help him into the house. They were silent. They were sad. During his illness, they had come to read to him from academic journals, newspapers, books, for his eyesight was by then too poor. They had helped him into a wheelchair, rolled him into the yard, and sat with him in the sun: no more inclined to abandon him than he them.

In his last days they telephoned from all over the world as the news of his condition spread: from China, Arizona, Texas, Sweden, Iceland, Lebanon. One former student from the Middle East, settled in the U.S., phoned in desperation. Fouad said to my mother in a broken voice: *Please take care of him, he is the best friend I ever had.*

It is because we all admired him. We all took our cues from him: *this is how to be a human being.*

Twice a day I went for a walk. It was good to get fresh air and in April the air in the valley is perfumed with blossoming magnolias, cherry trees, honeysuckle. It was dazzling to see on every side such profusions of flowers, and blossoms hanging overhead from branches dropping their silken petals onto the sidewalk and grass.

Nature was filled with gifts: and that was a mirror of the people in the town. I did not know there was so much love in the world. Every day, neighbours appeared with meals and fruit and bread so my mother and I would not need to spend time cooking. Mary brought lasagna, spaghetti, salads; Joanne brought stews, soups; Jinny brought barbecued ribs; the Smiths brought coffee cakes; Susan left fresh baked breads on our doorstep; Dr. Leman brought fresh strawberries; a barbecued chicken appeared from neighbours we did not know down the street. There were many more: we were overwhelmed with gifts. Flowers came from all directions until the whole house was charmed with the bright colours of blossoming chrysanthemums, azaleas, Persian violets, roses. Even Judy, the cleaning woman, brought flowers every time she came to clean house: flowers that cost her half of her morning's wages.

It occurred to me that I had spent a long time in the scorching prairie where the dust blows up in whorls and the wind eddies on street corners, where the dry air is pierced in spring and autumn by the hoarse calls of geese migrating in formation over the plains. Where the severity of summer, the high altitudes that chisel deep lines into parched faces, harden the soul. I had forgotten what a luscious, mild, damp, gentle climate does to wake up the sleeping soul and give rise to human affection and generosity. I had forgotten how such openness takes away all fear and makes you able to trust again.

Every time I saw a house for sale in the little town in the valley, I had an inclination to phone the realtor and buy it. I thought as I took my daily walk in the still morning, after a sleepless night on the cot and in the kitchen and by the sickbed: *I want to start a different life. To forget about all that has passed up to this day. I want to move here and live here forever as if nothing else existed.*

In spite of festivals, on long weekends the Gateway city becomes deserted. Sidewalks are empty of pedestrians. Very few cars drive up the street. Restaurants are open without customers, waiters loitering empty handed in doorways. Half of the inhabitants of the city have cottages on the lakes in the north. A quarter of the other half go to northwest Ontario or British Columbia or the Rocky Mountains for holidays. Only the sick, injured, and pregnant remain. People either too old or too weak to travel. Those who are healthy and still in the city end up feeling: *There is something wrong with me if I am still here.* They look over their shoulders, worried they will be recognized. They are reluctant to answer their phones. They hide in dark movie theatres showing sleek American films in nearly empty cinemas.

On such empty days the small squirrel I sometimes saw among the branches of the elm trees in front of the house paraded freely along the telephone wire. Whenever I looked out the living room window, the squirrel was either walking on the wire between poles or lying down midway, tail and head hanging down over the wire.

A butterfly with black and yellow wings frequented the flower patch at the side of the mansion where I lived. Whenever I stepped out and walked down the driveway, it flew across my path.

I thought: these are the signs of familiarity. The small notices that we are sharing space in nature, that our homes overlap. When you move into a house, it is not just a house. It is an environment: other species lived there before you and will after you go.

Around the house I lived in was a pretty garden. The front lawn was broken in the middle with a large flower patch and on the sides were other flower beds, all crowded with yellow, orange, pink blooms. Rosebushes girdled the house and huge pots of bright red geraniums stood on both sides of the steps.

It was midnight. The streets were quiet, birds were asleep, lights were off in all windows. In the sunroom the single lightbulb glared unnaturally against the stark black night outside the screens. Electric light seemed just then a rude invasion into nature's gentle show of moonlight and shadow. I heard a whacking and rustling in the leaves outside. Looking out I saw the concierge's teenage grandson on a rampage with a butcher knife: chopping down the flowers in the beds and the leaves from the large green plants that dignified the mansion. Little brown and yellow and pink and red flower heads rolled and lay haplessly on the grass.

We were in the Rocky Mountains where we had gone to hike along one of the many trails. We wanted to take a steep path that would show us a view of the peaks and valleys at the end. We drove to the beginning of the trail as described on our map, parked, and set off.

The path was wide at first, but as it ascended it became narrower until there was almost no trace of a trail in the thick undergrowth. Soon we were deep in the bush of the mountainside forest without a sign of a hiking trail anywhere. Charles said: *This is no hiking path. We've gone up a goat trail.*

The first thing Ramona, the night lady, said to me when I met her was: *Take care of your mother, I see it happen all the time. The wife exhausts herself taking care of her sick husband and becomes the first to go down.*

The sand was warm. I buried my toes in the grey grains of sand at the edge of the water. Lake Winnipeg was unusually calm: the surface was unperturbed by wind. Only very faint ripples wiggled onto the beach. Wind surfers failed at staying afloat. Sailboats further out stood still. Swimmers dived under water and re-emerged elsewhere. On this beach there are no shells or seaweeds or starfish. Only sand and small stones.

I sat in the warm haze through which the sun did not quite emerge. The soft summer colours of the prairie had a soothing effect: pale milky-grey water on the lake, light grey and beige sand, soft green leaves on aspens and birches, pale yellow wheat fields stretching across the plain.

I was thinking about a letter I had received from a friend in Denmark. Hans wrote about my father's passing: *The only consolation I can give you is that you will never get over it.*

In the summer most small towns in the prairie have their own festival. Gimli has an Icelandic Festival. There is a fair; amusement rides are erected in the park; boat races set off from the harbour; foolhardy visitors set themselves up to be dunked in barrels of water. In the park wares are sold: books, sweaters, ceramics. By the pavilion is a large stage, and seats are arranged for hundreds in front. On Monday of the long weekend, speeches are made and music is played and poems are read from that stage.

That summer the Festival was graced by an official delegation from Iceland: the President of the country, the Minister of Culture, the Mayor of Reykjavík, the Ambassador in Washington. Along with them were the Premier of Manitoba, the Minister of Culture for Canada, the Mayor of Winnipeg. The ceremonial stage was crowded.

I took my friend Joan to Gimli. We sat on chairs in the sun and listened to the speeches. The people on the podium were all very familiar to me: *it was so good to be a tourist.*

It was a good friend who presented the toast to Iceland: David Arnason, the writer, stood up in his black suit and imposing grey beard. During the course of his speech, he said: Iceland has produced world-class artists and achievements out of all proportion to its small size. This is because they know that talent is everywhere. *If a country wishes to survive with its culture and integrity intact, it must nurture the creative talents of its own citizens. It must protect its own culture.*

All of a sudden many hundred pairs of hands were clapping madly against the sun-laden blue sky.

It was my father's birthday. When I tried to sleep the sound of the crowd was in my ears and scenes from my father's last moments haunted my mind.

It was in the early days of his confinement, when he often was in his wheelchair in the living room or out on the patio in the back. I helped my father into the chair and rolled him to the fireplace. He asked me to put on the record he had always kept for special occasions: Hans Hotter singing Schubert Lieder in his deep sonorous voice. I did so. Every time he heard this, my father struggled with tears. He sat in the wheeled contraption, head leaning over to one side, and wept from the depths of his sorrow.

When I was small I often went with my father on his geological expeditions around Iceland. We sometimes went to Krísuvik in the south: there was a very small lake in the jutting jagged lava. The water was absolutely turquoise and green, with the smell of sulphur in the air. It was a gem to see: water of such a beautiful hue that I was spellbound. My father told me: *This lake has no bottom, it goes on down forever.*

I had nightmares of falling in: of falling down and sinking in the water forever.

A nursing student from the community nursing school appeared at our door. She asked to be allowed to help sit with my father so my mother and I could rest. Chris said: *Please let me help, it is important to me.* Three hospice nurses were always there when needed. Ramona's daughter was waiting to be allowed to help with the nursing. The physiotherapist made extra visits to chat with my father. Marilyn said: *I want to remember to do the things that are meaningful.* Home Health nurses came and bathed my father, washed his hair, kept a chart of his vital statistics. Every day, women were there, assisting. Volunteers. *It was an army of women.*

It occurred to me to wonder what had marked these women out from the crowd. Why did they come out to help people in need? And soon I detected from words dropped into a sentence or occasional comments that they themselves had suffered some form of loss in the family or illness or crisis. That they reacted to their own suffering by reaching out to others. And somehow, it was a good thing to know.

Literature itself, Roland Barthes wrote, *is never anything but a single text: the one text is not an (inductive) access to a Model, but an entrance into a network with a thousand entrances.*

I allowed myself to imagine that deep within our souls there is something we all share. That each of us is simply an entrance into that common arena.

It was David Arnason's cottage, near Gimli, close to the water of the huge lake. *The world's thirteenth largest freshwater lake*, the plaque in Gimli said. The water was grey and silty, the sky overcast. Small waves threw themselves on the thin strip of sand where green stalks and yellow straws grew out of the ground. Outside, on all the walls of the cottage, covering all the screens on windows and doors, were hordes of dead flies. So many corpses of flies were plastered against the cottage that it was barely possible to make out the colour of the wood underneath.

My father's condition deteriorated rapidly. Soon he was no longer able to get into the wheelchair. Confined to his bed, eventually he could not turn himself. For every move, he needed assistance. For every sip of water, every change in position, every time his forehead needed drying, our help was required. We became his eyes, arms, legs. His extension to the world. The more we took on his being, the deeper that ton of lead inside me sank.

There was something my sister did not understand about this. She was not in the same world somehow. I tried to say to her: *Everything is different. The world has ended: the world we knew.* But to her, things were basically the same as always, only a bit worse.

I could not talk to her: suddenly there was an insurmountable gap between us. l did not want it there but was powerless. I was in her flat stacked with mathematical papers, pictures of sailing ships, astronomical charts. She sat back in her chair, unmoved.

Perhaps I was exhausted. Perhaps the self I knew had already departed from me. I left her place, got in the car to drive back to my parents' house. It was night. Awaiting me at the house was the withering body of my father, the strength of our family. And the fading mind that once charted the scientific world with light and activity. The one person who I knew cared unconditionally, receding into the abyss of timelessness. Driving through the empty night streets of this American small town, I suddenly found myself screaming at the top of my lungs.

I knew then, that night, that I had reached rock bottom. Somewhere in the great depths of the soul that is reputed to go on forever, there is a floor. Ground zero. Where you have gone so far down that the only movement possible is up again. And I knew I would not move from this place for a long time.

I sat with my father and could not keep the tears from falling. He was alarmed when he saw us cry. It was the one thing he did not want to see. He stared at me intensely. It was our sorrow he feared, not his own. Perhaps it was then he decided it was time to go. His eyes were slate blue, like the great Pacific Ocean in the early morning before the sun rises to make it glow.

Soon the big German Shepherd dog I saw on the back steps of the mansion in the Gateway city took up residence in the backyard. Ever time I looked out, the dog was rolling himself over on the grass and scores of flies were busying themselves over the dog food dish.

The cat that had previously been ruler of the roost found itself displaced. Whenever I came out on the stairs, the cat ran crying to me, plastering itself against my feet.

The summer quieted down into early fall. The intense heat went away and instead comfortable temperatures and sunshine blessed the Gateway residents every day. The crabapple tree outside my sunroom windows grew pale yellow. The apples became larger and pink in colour. Berries were suddenly noticeable inside dark green foliage: tiny bright red points of focus.

On the streets long-haired roller skaters with backpacks dashed in between pedestrians. Pregnant women sat lazily on benches waiting for a bus. Beggars became fearless: *You wouldn't have enough for a cup of coffee, thank you, ma'am.*

In that far West I dream of, the Pacific coast, there is a tiny harbour village. Depoe Bay, *the world's smallest harbour,* says the sign in front of The Spouting Horn.

I took my son on a boat, *The Kingfisher. This is the place where they filmed* One Flew Over the Cuckoo's Nest, I informed him. We were taken a few miles out, where no land will appear for weeks. The motor of the boat was stopped and we sat on the water billowing on the undulating ocean. Suddenly a massive grey form rose out of the sea next to the boat: a being so crusty and laden with barnacles that we might have mistaken it for land had it not moved and spouted a stream of water high into the air as it rolled serpent-like before us. *Sometimes they stop and allow us to pat the top of their heads,* the skipper said.

A week after we had returned home; we learned that another such boat had mysteriously capsized in the same place. The passengers were immobilized by cold when they entered the freezing water and perished.

The novelty of being alone in the Gateway city soon faded. Things that were special at first became ordinary: listening to the wind in the leaves in the early morning. Watching the squirrel roll itself over in circles in the elm branches. Seeing bees fly in through the huge open window, take a measure of the sunroom, and then fly out again. Feeling the quiet hours as the sun changes postion without pressure, without intensity, without tears.

The concierge, Jo, was gone. Perhaps to Mexico to find a place to live: the woman who never wanted to see another Manitoba winter. The mansion had a new owner I had never met. A lady from Germany. I could see that my days in that warehouse city, the prism of the West, were drawing to a close.

Many poverty-stricken Indigenous people lived outside the gates of my street. I would see them in groups of twos and threes every time I stepped out for a walk: holding large Coke bottles, carrying children, walking without purpose or pattern, someone always lagging behind.

In front of me were three Cree people: a man, a woman, and a teenage boy. The boy was bare-chested, holding a navy blue T-shirt in his right hand. He walked behind the other two. A small white butterfly fluttered across their path and into the bushes around the hospital wall. The boy jumped after the butterfly into the shrubs and began whacking it with his shirt.

My mother's sister flew in from Copenhagen to be with my parents at the end. She was a soft-spoken woman of fifty, with such a mild manner and gentle demeanour about her that her presence did much to soften the blow of what was happening. In the mornings Birte came down with a bright smile, had her coffee and cigarette in the garden, and then went to work washing and cleaning with constant good cheer.

It occurred to me how wonderful it is to be able to admire one's own family.

It became harder and harder for my father to take his medication. He was sometimes unable to swallow the larger pills. His will to take them began to give.

What is the point of taking these pills? he asked with impeccable logic.

His appetite went away. He slept more and more.

My mother went in to wake him up for lunch. It was noon and time for food and pills. She shook him for a while, but he remained asleep. After trying for about ten minutes, she came upstairs to where I was. *I can't wake him up*, she said, alarmed. I went down and tried to shake him, talk to him, call him. There was no response. We stood for a while, uncertain what to do.

By his bed he had a little hand bell to ring if he needed us and we were out of the room. I took the bell and rang it in front of his face. He opened his eyes instantly. Eventually he was eating and things were normal. I asked him: *Did you hear us when we were trying to wake you up? Yes*, he said. *What were you thinking?* I asked. *I was thinking*, he answered, *now they are going to give me those miserable pills again.*

It occurred to me that people who are comatose *can still follow everything going on around them.* That their *presence* in the room should not be underestimated.

The Dean of Sciences at the University of Iceland said to the crowd: when Dr. Gunnar Bödvarsson was preparing to go to North America, he came to my office. In his hand he carried a book which he handed to me, saying: *I would like you to keep this for me while I am away.* I told him I would take good care of it. Then I saw it was Edward Gibbon's *The Decline and Fall of the Roman Empire.* It has since occurred to me that he left the book with me *so I might read it.*

It was called *Shólahús – The Schoolhouse.* A small but stately building bequeathed to the University of Iceland. It stood on one of the old streets of Reykjavík, overlooking the town pond. After the ceremonies at the university auditorium, a smaller group walked to the *Shólahús* for a reception to honour the four recipients of honorary doctorates. There were hors d'oeuvres and glasses of wine. It was Presidential election day. Among the guests were the President of the University, the Minister of Education, the President of Iceland, the Dean of Sciences, the Dean of Social Sciences.

Soon the other three honorary doctorates had all given a speech to the selected assembly, thanking them for the occasion and adding something thoughtful. It occurred to me that since I was standing in for my father, who was too ill to be there in person, I ought to speak for him. I stood up to do so.

The light was low and I knew it would not get dark. lt was June. Swans swam on the pond below the house, and across the street were the walls of the cemetery where my grandparents were both buried. *It did not even cross my mind that my father would never make it back to join them.*

Since, I have often said to myself: *Be careful where you live for you may die there.*

The light that poured into the Gateway city in the morning and evening was deep and rich. The sky was absolutely blue and clear, so pale blue that the eye is transfigured and hallucinates forms in the utter emptiness that produces such a colour. Blackbirds flew across the bare panorama with confident wing strokes. A small grey airplane showed its underbelly with a drone. Every day seemed to compete in beauty with the day before. The grey squirrel began to free-fall from branch to branch: starting at the top it dropped itself down onto successive branches where it wagged as the branch gave way to the weight.

Yet I thought: it is beautiful, but I am not healed yet. Something is still in me that has not gone away. If I go among people I feel threatened: that whenever someone opens his mouth to speak it will be to say something abusive to me. That my emotions will be held up to ridicule. I will be criticized.

The hospice people left a sheet of paper with us when they visited my father one day. The sheet said: *Symptoms of Grief. Do not be alarmed if the following conditions occur, it is normal when a person experiences grief*: excessive fatigue; inability to cope with noise, severe change in sexual habits, depression, development of the symptoms of the deceased, lethargy, *fear of people*, a desire to hide, excessive weight on symbolism, a need for ritual, bouts of weeping, hot flashes, inability to cope with everyday details. *Do not try to hurry the process. Understand what is happening.*

My father's friends and colleagues, some from the distant past, even childhood school days, were visiting at first. They drove up from California, flew over from Washington, D.C., drove in from the coast. But eventually he was unable to receive them. When Arvid came to chat and sit on the folding chair by the bed, my father fell asleep in mid-sentence. When Don and Jo White came to spend some time in the living room with him, he leaned over in his wheelchair and dropped off to the side in uncontrollable sleep. When Jónas Haralz was there to spend a few days, my father could not keep the train of thought going and lost contact repeatedly with the topic. Friends all went away in sad silence, knowing they were saying goodbye for the last time.

It was one of my father's geological expeditions in the southern Icelandic countryside during my childhood. I walked away from the small group of scientists who were doing a form of surveying I did not understand. Nearby was a small mountain composed almost entirely of barren rock face. I climbed the steep cliffs, ascending higher into the pure blue air of an Icelandic summer. The rock face was whitewashed and the view as I climbed higher was more and more expansive: tundra I did not particularly like. Lava lay round about in old crusted formations, black and jagged. Moss grew over the openings in the hardened rock, disguising traps small people easily fell into.

When I got to the top of the mountain, I was accosted by an Arctic tern. It flew over me close, then away a good distance where it turned around and sailed back at me with incredible speed, like an Air Force bomber on a desperate mission. Wings spread wide, it lowered itself over my head and attacked the top of my head with its beak. I knew I had come too close to a nest. There were other terns preparing to do the same. Only too late did I remember my father's warning: *If you go up there, take a frying pan with you and hold it over your head.*

My son was seventeen years old. During my father's confinement, school released its students for a three-week break. He took the plane from Minneapolis to Portland, carrying his violin in its case.

It was morning. The valley was shrouded in summer haze. The Albany pulp mill issued foul-smelling clouds into the air from its huge chimney. I counted the exits as I drove to the Portland Airport to pick him up: 258, 259, 260. Cushioned in the pine forests I noticed brand new shopping malls and apartment complexes. At the airport I found him: dark jeans, abstract T-shirt, shoulder-length brown hair, violin.

For the next three weeks he gave his grandfather his daily shave with a dose of improvisational jazz thrown in. He became the grocery boy, buying all the groceries and carting them home in a van. He helped lift his grandfather in and out of the wheelchair. For the rest he was off exploring the valley and taping library records onto cassettes.

Often my father asked his grandson to play for him on the violin. It was a Romanian piece, newly learned for a school concert, that became the favourite. Every day there was a tiny concert. My father listened raptly. I thought: now perhaps I finally know *what all those violin lessons were for.*

The three weeks the boy was there, *somehow the picture was lit up with sunshine.*

The way an empty sky can become translucent with light, and though there is nothing there, it is beautiful.

After the boy left, my father no longer called on us. He no longer wanted to know what we were talking about in other rooms. When we came in to him, he looked at us, but his thoughts were far away. Instead of speaking, he held our hands.

The days in the Gateway city became monotonously warm. The only clouds in the sky were thin flimsy ones that stole in on the afternoon but were never substantial enough to block the sun. Air-conditioned charter buses drove slowly through town, a woman with a loudspeaker in front reciting city attractions to tourists: The Forks, Wellington Crescent, Osborne Village, The Zoo. Mosquitoes were still around but had stopped biting. Ticks were gone. Blackflies were bored with the same garbage every day which the garbage truck forgot to pick up.

Instead, dogs went mad. Formerly placid household pet dogs yanked their chains off their collars and followed children down the street for hours. When children stopped and showed fear, the dogs growled and started tearing at their clothes with wet thirsty teeth.

I had to go away for five days. We could not really tell how long my father would remain in his present condition. Meanwhile, all the parking meters in my own life had, so to speak, gone to zero. The yellow disk was down and the red one was up: the one that said *time expired*. So I left my father in the hands of my aunt and my mother with the assurance that if things got worse I would be on the first plane back.

I did a whirlwind rush through six cities: Portland, Minneapolis, Winnipeg, Regina, Calgary, Salt Lake City. Long enough to put new metaphorical quarters into my waiting meters.

Salt Lake City Airport was very hot and stuffy, crowded with people of all descriptions. Young girls dressed up in colour-coordinated outfits with earrings and purses to match. Old fat women who barely fit into the plastic seats. Suntanned hikers striking up conversations across seating aisles, wearing khaki-coloured shorts and Birkenstock sandals. And the Forestry student I was to catch a ride with into the valley from Portland: the one who told me about the oddities of MacDonald Forest.

While I was gone, my father's condition fell into a slump. There were conflicting reports and forecasts did not all agree. He was sleeping nearly all the time, they said on the phone, and no longer eating much. Then, as l turned to come back, he was better. Others said: *You always get a little better just before you go.* I was in a great hurry to get back. The slow-moving line in Salt Lake City was suddenly too exasperating.

When I entered the house I could see something had happened. There was a look of desperation on his face as if it had become hard to breathe: breathing had turned into the focus of all his energies. His eyes darted back and forth restlessly and he was not talking. We were not sure he could recognize everything. My mother said to him the night I arrived: *Do you know who this is?* He said *yes* determinedly but with difficulty. *Who is it?* My mother asked again. My father answered, looking hard at me, as though it were self-evident: This is *Sjana*. But the look on his face seemed to say *pardon me a moment, I seem to be drowning.*

After that he never said anything but *yes*.

In late summer, moving trucks appear with greater frequency on the streets of the Gateway city. Houses that have been up for sale all summer begin to show 'sold' signs on the front lawns. Huge moving vans back onto driveways and block off the streets while men load up furniture. Well-kept lawns are suddenly neglected during the change of owners. Grass turns yellow, flowers droop, ferns die while still upright. Booths that sell lottery tickets are swamped with people checking their numbers: hoping their numbers will match enough to send them to Florida or Hawaii.

Restlessness sets in: the German Shepherd in my backyard no longer lay patiently on the steps between geranium pots. Instead he plodded angrily along the fence, around the yard, through the vegetable patch, stopping at the gate to bark and at the door to look in. The elm tree in the next yard came alive with squirrels. They no longer sat still in the branches. Instead they threw themselves from tree to tree in daring acrobatic feats.

I sat with my father all night. He had begun to breathe rapidly. He did not seem to be asleep, yet he was not awake. Sometimes when I asked him a question, he was able to whisper *yes*, sometimes not. Since he was not awake, he could not drink any water.

I wetted his lips with the hospital sponge we had been given by the hospice nurses. When the small sponge reached his lips, he bit at it with as much eagerness as he could muster.

In the morning he was still hyperventilating but no longer answering. I stayed by his bed. Thinking he could still hear me, I talked to him. I talked to him all morning. I thought: if I do not talk he will not know I am here. It will be less lonely for him that way.

It was a Saturday. A beautiful sunny morning none of us had paid any attention to yet. My aunt came into the room. I noticed the bristles on my father's cheeks. The sweat on his forehead. Some little voice in me said: *he wants a shave and a bath.* For the next hour Birte and I bathed him, shaved him, combed his hair, changed his shirt. I thought: he always wanted to arrive clean shaven wherever he went. He refused to meet guests without shaving first. He would want it this way.

When we were done, I stepped outside into the backyard for the first time that day. The blue jay was at the birdbath. The azaleas were flowering in bright red blooms along the edge of the garden. I was tired and only vaguely absorbing the lush spring that blossomed in defiance of our mood.

As I stood there my sister opened the door and yelled: *Mother is calling for you.*

I ran into my father's room. My mother was bending over the bed. I could see my father's breathing had become erratic: chaotic. He was gasping as if he were awake, but he was not awake. The body itself, as if without the will of the owner, was struggling for air: for control. My mother was desperate, at a loss.

I saw right away what was happening. Birte and my sister came into the room running. Without fully knowing why, I started to give orders: *Birte, grab my mother. Gunna, phone Kathy the hospice nurse.* And I took my father's head in my arms. *Talk to him,* the little voice in me said, *talk to him.*

And I did: I told him it was all right, it was just a little difficult patch and then he would feel so much better. *In a little while you will feel much better, we just have to get through this.*

Then he was not breathing. The body, longing for breath, heaved for air one more time. Then once again. Then nothing.

My mother had her face in her hands. Slowly she came up to my father on the other side of the bed. I wanted to reassure her. I said: *It is finished.*

When I was nine years old, there were graduation ceremonies at the California Institute of Technology. My father was to receive his Doctorate and he had on a floor-length black gown with a cap and tassel. I did not know exactly what a Ph.D. was, but I knew it was something to be very proud of. The ceremonies were on the lawn, outside in the sun. I had a pale purple dress with a black velvet collar and black velvet buttons. It was a beautiful dress of which I also was very proud. And white gloves on my hands, a ponytail, and bangs. l was photographed holding my father's hand: he in his black gown, I in a purple dress. lt was a beautiful spring day. All the flowers were blooming and the palm trees were swaying in the breeze. Perhaps it was the happiest day of my childhood: everyone was so happy that day.

Perhaps because they knew fall was coming, the animals around the mansion became furiously active. They would either have to dig holes for themselves where they could hibernate for the winter or else fly far away to the south for many months. Swallows crowded in the eavestroughs of the house against the garden. A red-breasted robin was settled in the huckleberry bush outside my window, feasting on the small red berries every day. All the elm trees round about were filled with dashing squirrels scurrying between branches and trees at record speed, their long tails flurrying behind them.

I began to look around me as well. My time to leave was coming: I would have to get into the little red car someday soon and drive to a new place. It was moving season. Developers trying to sell newly constructed condominiums placed billboards in front, reading: *If you lived here you would be home now.*

It was a Saturday morning, eleven thirty. I remembered later to look at the numbers. I often wondered about the importance we attach to numbers: how we imbue them with significance at critical times. In his illness my father repeatedly asked: *What time is it?* Even in a completely incapacitated state, as if he needed to go to a meeting or catch an important flight. His favourite poem was Goethe's *Doctor Faustus.* A tiny passage from that grand play had been photocopied many times and lay strewn around in his study for continual reference. The passage said: *When the hand on the clock falls, then time is over for me.* Sometimes in the morning, when I came downstairs to find him awake in his bed, I asked him how he was and he would answer with a small crafty smile: *The hand has not fallen yet.* As if the passage of every hour he could count were a personal triumph. That this was a match of wits between him and the clock.

There is no zero on the clock. To get to zero, you have to step outside of time.

People came and took my father away. Before they removed him, we all went in to say our final goodbyes. I kissed his forehead and I knew he was no longer there. This body we were going to attach such importance to – bury it in the ground and cover it with flowers – was not him. He was gone. I knew for the first time that, despite my confidence all these years that it is easy to catch a flight and return to the people you pretended to say goodbye to before, it sometimes happens that a person goes away and will never return. *You know he will never return.*

They took the hospital bed and the wheelchair away. We cleaned up and put the cot back where it was supposed to be, and the tables and chairs. As if this had been an unhappy play and we were stage hands demolishing the set. The principal actor had already gone home and we had to stay on a little while longer.

Even though it did not make me afraid, I did not have a good feeling: *when I looked around I discovered that all the clocks in the house had stopped.* None of them was working.

Above the town that is called *The Heart of the Valley* is a lilting green landscape where huge ancient oaks grow. Their crooked forms spread out in all directions unhindered, and their crowns hover over the pasture majestically. From there it is possible to see the Cascade Mountains in the east and below them the soft green acres of the valley and the clusters of dark green fir trees in between. It is a peaceful place where birds sing all summer and the sunrise spreads its red wings over the waiting land.

That is where my father is buried. He lies under an oak tree: in the heat of the summer day, there is shelter under the heavy branches. In the downpour rains of the west, there is cover. On his granite headstone is carved an image of his beloved mountains and a Ponderosa pine.

When I saw the beauty of that final resting place, even though I was not inclined to think there was anything good about the story of my father's decline and fall, I somehow felt grateful. Grateful that there had been no pain in his final illness. That it was such a gentle and soft departure, almost like the whispering rain at the window that you hardly know is there. If someone asked, you would not be able to say with certainty that it was raining outside.

Perhaps I had disappointed thoughts: disappointed at being left behind. I always wanted to go with my father on his expeditions: into the heather where loud plovers stand on tufts, crying through the endless summer days of the Arctic. Onto the black sands where heavy ocean waves crawl in from the sea slowly, wearily. To scale the cliffs where seabirds have left their eggs to hatch in the naked sun. To dive under the ribs of the ocean, looking for sunken Turkish sailing ships laden with treasures.

This time you cannot go. That little voice. Perhaps I felt unhappy that I had to turn back and walk tiredly across the huge lawn where the departed lay under gigantic oak trees. I have to go back and busy myself with people and their million deadlines, dates, timetables, charts, machines that circle around zero, threaten, and never get there. Perhaps.

At five in the morning the streets of the Gates in Winnipeg are like a picture someone painted without people. Or a deserted movie set. A slight illumination of dawn has begun, adding an eerie lustre to the darkness of the night. The large houses along the street are touched with a perception of life. All is silent.

I got up. Every time I stepped, the hardwood floors boomed out in the quiet of the night. I boiled water for tea in the black kettle and sat down by the front window. There was a wicker chair and a windowsill for my cup.

From there I could see out of the Gate and into the streets closer to downtown. Occasionally a car drove up to a door out there, someone got out and stumbled inside. One person fell down on the street. Another person came out and helped him in. I could only see the outline of their silhouettes. Then all was empty again.

Somewhat later I saw two figures slowly walking up the street. One was leading his bicycle. They stopped at the corner and talked for a while. Then one walked away up the side lane. The other, pushing his bicycle, continued toward the Gate.

I recognized my son's light, leisurely walk. I heard the familiar clap of his Birkenstock sandals. On his head was the favourite Peruvian hat a friend had given him. Under his arm was the inevitable violin. *He is the one*, I thought, *in whom all my father's hopes are bound.*

The boy turned up the driveway to the house, locked his bike, and came upstairs. I opened the door. He came in, took himself a mug of tea, and sat down cross-legged on the living room floor. He opened his violin case and put the violin on his shoulder.

The city was about to awaken. Soon the first rays of sun would burst in through the curtainless windows. The first notes of a new melody sounded from the violin. I knew soon all the empty rooms would fill with music.

THE
SUBSTANCE OF
FORGETTING

All networks of possible meaning must be exhausted beneath common sense, banal, vulgar, obvious meaning, or cruel, threatening, and aggressive meaning – before we can understand that they are ungraspable, that they adhere to no axis, that they are 'arbitrary' just like the sign, the name, and the utterance, but also pleasure and jouissance.

– Julia Kristeva, Desire and Language

I will arise and go now, and go to Innisfree,
And a small cabin build there, of clay and wattles made;
Nine bean-rows will I have there, a hive for the honey-bee,
And live alone in the bee-loud glade.

And I shall have some peace there, for peace comes dropping slow,
Dropping from the veils of the morning …

– W. B. Yeats, 'The Lake Isle of Innisfree'

I would say I am tired. I thought I could hardly get more tired and then I did. The quiet hours drip. I watch them in the melting snow on the quince plants and juniper bushes. The snow here in the hills above Wood Lake was once four feet deep. The snow was piled up against my windows thick and warm. Then it melted and started dripping into slow puddles clogged in the potholes of the road I call my street. The lethargic drops hang from the balcony railing as if they were translucent pregnant spiders.

There is so much fog in the valley that I cannot see the lake below the house. When I look up the mountain into the pine trees they are bathed in the milk-white dream of the mist. The tops of the trees are lost in cloud.

We have been dreaming too much, the forest and I. When I walk up the old wagon trail toward Mission the woods close in on me. Jack pines push onto the road and the ponderosas stand spread with upward-bending limbs as if conducting the dreams I dream in the mist.

I think I have been mesmerized by the fog. There is nothing to see when you stare into the grey thickness except your own visions.

The lake has been frozen for two months. White ribbons lace the grey surface of the ice. They are the ripples of snow the wind has blown together. By the highway ice fishermen are sitting in lawn chairs beside a hole in the ice. Their fishing lines go down the hole. Thermoses lean against the chair legs. Further out what looks like a heron stands waiting. There will be fish debris when the catch is gutted. Another heron waits down the lake. Their long legs are thin and exposed, their long necks stiff. They follow every movement of the ice fishermen. At the boat launch a puddle has formed on the ice. A duck tries desperately to swim in the shallow water.

When the clouds roll in at the end of autumn they stay snug in the Okanagan Valley for five months. Sometimes the clouds are so low they touch the water. Then they are like a shunned lover lowering for a slight touch of the beautiful earth. Sometimes they rise to the tops of the hills and look down on the forests. Then they are like a captor guarding its prey.

The clouds make me sad. They remind me of what I am not doing, what I am not saying. But I think, *In a short while it will be blossom time.* Then I look forward to blossom time and my mind wanders into dream. In my dream all things are in bloom. Apple blossoms, apricot blossoms, cherry blossoms.

Somehow life has thrown me on this hillside in the receding tide. In this gentlest land possible I only want to desire the hour of clarity in the lake when the forest can see its face in the water. I only want to long for the moment of a break in the clouds when the red sunlight leaks onto the sandy hills and they are luminescent orange in a burst of light.

I have never known such fog. How it creeps onto the valley floor in the late evening. Suddenly the lake is bathed in a thick veil. By morning the valley is filled. The darkness is impenetrable. No light shines anywhere. The hills are nude and asleep, engulfed in a substance of forgetting.

Day crawls over slow day. The frozen water, the crystal-packed soil, the ice-rained jack pines would have us think there is no time. Just a slow succession of light and darkness of concern to no one. There is nowhere to go. No obligations remain. Even the train that whistles as it rounds the corner of Kalamalka's south end is silent and seems not to have any errands in the mountains anymore.

ONE

'You are beautiful, madame.' I would like to begin with that. *You are beautiful, madame.* Just like that. Those words must be spoken in semidarkness. The lights are off. It is night. The curtains are slightly parted and light from a street lamp outside filters into the room. The room is full of dark blue light because the curtains are blue. Perhaps we are breaking all the rules. Perhaps we are together because Jules is a Québec separatist and we are in the United States. Nothing should fit. Nothing should be reasonable. During the day we were going somewhere, walking from one place to another. It is immaterial where we are going except that we had to go. 'What does Québec want?'

Whether I asked that or whether Jules posed a rhetorical question is also unimportant. Someone asked that and the question was in the air. He tightened the collar of his green coat because the cold wind began to blow just then. He answered the question with deliberation. He may even have gesticulated with his right hand in the American air. 'Québec wants a free and independent Québec in a strong and united Canada,' he asserted. There may have been newly fallen snow outside and I was surprised to find his eyes were blue. I said so. Even though his hair was dark his eyes were blue. 'No. My eyes are usually red from reading too much,' he said. I imagined his eyes red. Perhaps we can colour reality the way we want to. Perhaps we can deny what we see with our eyes and substitute what we see with our desire. It was the quiet of the morning and we were about to go somewhere, probably to airports and into airplanes to fly in different directions. There were time restrictions. There was a closed-in feeling. 'Do you really live in the country?' he asked me. I nodded. He would go home to the city thinking I live deep in the mountains, away from urban things. It was not exactly untrue. It was not exactly true. It is the question the writer asks when writing a book: Shall I fill in all the details? Or shall I let the reader imagine them all? Who should write this book, me or my reader? What if I give you dots and numbers and you draw in the lines? Perhaps he would imagine my horse, my German Shepherd, my truck. Chickens and pigs even. Or he would think up my solitary log cabin with nothing but a parrot hanging from the ceiling. No dogs, no animals. Or he would not imagine anything. There would be a blank, never filled in, forgotten tomorrow.

TWO

I have a cottage in the Okanagan. That at least is simple and clear. Not as exotic as having had a farm in Kenya, say, but it is a simpler thing.

First I thought of it as a house. An estate with land. I said I had a house on a mountain with a view. It was true. My cottage is on the mountainside but the mountain is small and hilly. From my windows I see Wood Lake and Kalamalka Lake and the mountains on the other side. There are orchards on the lower part of the hills and pine forests above. Between the pine forests are open stretches of green. As you go further south the open land becomes more frequent. There it is brown and barren.

Then I saw the cedar on the outside wall was warping. There were holes. The front porch was sinking. The windowsills were homemade. The house felt wooden and the wood echoed when I walked on the floor. Then the house became a cottage.

It was my lovely cottage on the old wagon trail to Mission. Nothing surrounds me but a few other houses, all looking at the lake. All of us here have nowhere to go except into our gardens. We sit at our windows, we rake our lawns, we prune our trees, shovel our snow. Here we are. That is all. We enjoy what we see.

At eight in the morning a few schoolchildren run out of a few of the houses and bunch up at the school bus stop. A yellow bus rattles by, stops, and the children are gone. Then some of the restless adults climb into well-built automobiles and drive to town for a job. Sometimes I am one of them. Sometimes I am not.

When I am not, I sit at a wicker table and write a book. As I put words down I watch the sun crawl over the mountain in the east. It rises over the crowns of the pine trees and blares into my cottage rooms. The sun is all around me and I feel warm. I think warm thoughts. I remember warm people.

THREE

Jules was sleeping and I was thinking. His arm was wrapped tightly around me and the light was blue. There was no sound. In American towns like this no one drove their cars at night. The streets were empty. I could tell the streets were empty from the slight parting of the curtains where the light of the street lamp filtered in. I thought about things we say. The more you say about a thing the more you destroy it. The best thing I know is silence. I would like to just read his thoughts. Everything he says is beside the point. There is no point. He says more with his blue eyes than with his words yet his eyes are not expressive. They tell me nothing. I am imagining everything. I am climbing down a ladder. The ladder goes around and around a tower and I am climbing down to the ground. When I am on the ground I know I will look up and on the uppermost balcony of the tower I will see his figure. He will be bending over and looking down at me. He is wearing a dark hat and a large coat that trails almost to the ground. It is so dark that I cannot tell if the coat is green. Only a little moonlight filters through the broken clouds. I can hear a simpering wind in the branches. The branches are barren because it is winter. The branches are naked, wrapped in a sheet of snow. Their arms tightly grip each other. The trees are sleeping until spring. Then there will be little green buds. The green knots will untie and leaves will form. But I do not think about spring. I am aware of the dark figure high overhead observing me from a great distance. I am cold. Snow is everywhere and my feet are wet. The wind penetrates my paltry clothing. The man on the tower has told so many stories and I remember them all. They are enchanting as fairy tales, stricken and tragic as wartime dramas, simple and clear as children's stories. They lead into the woods where I cannot follow. I begin to climb down the ladder. When I stumble he grabs my waist and holds me up. It is only a moment. In the moonlight I see his face for the first time. His face tells me nothing. I know I have to run. If I do not run I will hear too much. The wind will grow louder and the figure above will begin to call. I know I will not like hearing his voice calling. If he calls me back and I try to climb the ladder again the ladder will disappear. There will be no tower. The structure will always be too distant. Like the moon it will follow me when I go away and recede from me when I approach. I think the figure in the green coat will hide his stories from me. I will try to hear them and there will be no telling. Then I will try not to hear them. But when you try not to hear stories they come out all around you anyway. Suddenly you hear things you never wanted to know. You want everyone to stop talking, to take away those words. Everyone is talking too much. I begin to hurry away. There is a path in the snow, a path leading to the hotel. I follow the trail and stumble when it winds. I can see the hotel beyond the naked woods. The massive stone structure towers over the tallest trees. I hear music from the ballroom. Lights are on everywhere. I run into the foyer, knowing the dark figure on the grey tower is still looking down. He could be thinking anything. I cannot tell what he is thinking. I am glad to be back among the many people in their fine clothes with crystal wine glasses in their hands. I greet them elegantly.

As elegantly as I can with my wet feet and paltry clothes. I go into my room and bathe in the warm water I find there. I lie down in the large bed. The night was dark. Through the slight parting in the curtain I saw snow. The snow went around in flurries outside the window. The light of a street lamp filtered into the room. The curtains were blue and the light was blue. Jules was sleeping. His arm was wrapped tightly around me.

FOUR

I know I have wanted to say these things for a long time. Years even. To write letters that would explain everything. Then I see there is nothing to explain. The snow is melting at the edges of my driveway and nothing needs to be explained. When I look I find there is no one to take the words that would set everything right. There is no right and wrong. That is what I was also thinking as the snow flurried in circles in the light of the street lamp. Perhaps we have broken all the rules but it does not matter. Right and wrong do not matter. It does not matter whether the man sleeping is my lover or not. No one cares who he is. Everything is easy, much easier than I thought. Something else matters instead. Jules came to me and said he had no flowers. *I have no flowers.* Apologetic because he was French and should bring flowers but I saw he was not afraid. I was not afraid either. Somehow it matters that we were not afraid. It matters because it will be much easier to take my bags to the city now. I do not even have to bring my bags. I can leave them under the apricot trees in the valley. There are always new bags to be had, new things to put in them. When the snow flurried in circles I saw it is a confused and angry world. I like to think we are not afraid in it. Like the snow we fall where we may. We fall into each other's arms. I wanted to fall like that because it is cold and the snow is coming down and I am in a strange American town. It is a strange town because it is like all other towns. They are all the same and I am confused when I try to find north and south. It does not matter which direction we go in. Knowing that, I take my bag and go home. I see no signs of Jules as I go. He has disappeared into the white air like the flakes of snow. There will never be a sign of him and it does not matter. I can take my bag and watch it come out of a trap door in the wall at the airport. Coming home is easy. I am happy when the airplane lands in the valley. The grass is green and there is no snow between the mountains. I drive along the lakes and see that the ice has melted while I was away. The lights on the hills are reflected in the water that has found a new release in the warm days. I am happy the ice has melted. I like to see the water move in ripples. I like to see if a wind is blowing by looking at the lake from my window. I have learned to read the stories on the surface of the lake and in the colour of the water. What I wanted to be able to say is such a small thing, nothing consequential. How peaceful it is to see. I thought of all the years we wanted to say things and then there was no language for them. Even if we had the language we would not have known how to use it. I must get a dictionary and begin at the beginning, at the first word. There is something in the language I do not understand. I could only say this is a language that is not my own. Now it does not matter.

FIVE

It was August when I first came to my cottage. The sun was shining every day. It was hot. Flowers continuously bloomed. On my land all the apricot trees were covered with fruit. The trees were old and their branches grew in all directions. On every branch were thousands of apricots. The fruit made the branches heavy and they drooped toward the ground. In the morning I went out and stood among my apricot trees. How could I pick all these apricots? If I picked them what could be done with them? Where do they go? As the late-summer days came and went I plucked the small yellow-brown fruit and put them in a blue bucket. Soon there were many buckets full. I washed the apricots, cut them in half, took the pits out and filled freezer bags with halved fruit. Soon the freezer was full of such bags. I put apricot halves in cooking pots and boiled them with sugar. Soon many jars of apricot jam were everywhere. I had never seen so much food coming into my house for free. Soon there were large bottles of apricot chutney. A friend faxed me recipes for apricot wine. When I slept at night I even dreamed apricots. I was not prepared for such a great harvest.

Roberta and Justine came from Vancouver. In the morning they were outside picking apricots. They were laughing. Around them hung the heavy branches. No matter how much we picked, there always seemed to be equally many apricots left on the trees. Roberta and Justine picked and washed and cut and froze apricots until they were silly. At the end of the day they fell into chairs on the balcony, took a glass of cold wine from the Gray Monk cellars further up the hill, and laughed in their exhaustion. Their laughter rang like Indian wedding bells over the water.

My friend Hillary came from Edmonton. She too went out to pick the endless fruit. She brought blue buckets filled to the brim into the kitchen. When I woke in the morning I would find her cooking apricot halves into jam at my stove. She cooked a potful and burned it. She tried again and cooked another potful. The jam burned again. 'I'm not going to quit until I make successful jam,' she insisted. I said she was welcome to make many successful jams. There were apricots enough for a thousand tests. One day I came home from work at five in the afternoon. There she stood proudly with six new jars of successful jam. We celebrated her success with more Gray Monk wine.

My friend David came from Calgary. It was not possible to process more apricots. They were falling from the trees faster than I could pick them. David and I began to shovel the fruit off the ground. We filled garbage bags full of dented and rotting apricots. Every shovelful filled the air with the odour of apricot blossoms, wine, perfume. The bags were heavy. We hauled them up to the road to be picked up. David lifted the bags onto a wheelbarrow and pushed the wheelbarrow strenuously up the steep hill. He breathed hard and exhausted because he was a smoker. 'I came here for a vacation and instead I'm going to die of overwork,' he declared. But he did not die of exhaustion. No matter how many bags we took to the road or how many we filled with fallen fruit, the ground was forever littered with the same number of apricots. Every time one was picked up another fell from the tree to take its place. The fruit lay rotting and fermenting. We gave up. We had more Gray Monk wine and laughed at our failure to make a dent in the piles of fruit all over my land. In the end I sat on my front steps and looked at the mess of fruit on the ground and the thousands still on the trees. The air was filled with the smell of fermenting apricots. I knew I could not even give my fruit away.

Everyone in the valley was faced with the same overload. I could not put a sign on the highway pointing to my house. A sign that said U-PICK.

APRICOTS. FREE. The highway was too far from my house. Not even tourists would come up the hill for them.

Down the road a ways was a honey farm, the Raykar honey farm. When you walked past, the air smelled of penetrating bitter honey. Little beehives dotted the acreages. Across the road bees could be seen blithely searching for nectar.

The bees found my fermenting apricots. As I sat on my steps with my chin in my palm, feeling the heat of the afternoon sun in my bones, I saw the bees discover the fallen fruit. For them it was paradise. Soon there were hundreds of bees. Thousands of bees. They buzzed in the fermenting fruit every day, at all times. I walked among the thousands of bees and they were in no way concerned about me. I knew they would never sting. If I put my hand in the swarm of bees on the ground they simply buzzed irritably in an effort to make me go away so they could drink more nectar. They were happy. When I heard them flying from clump to clump I learned to recognize the sound of bee happiness.

Soon I realized all the bees were drunk. There was alcohol in the fermenting fruit pulp and the bees drank endlessly of the riches of the earth. They flew sideways, without direction, buzzing silly and dazed, droning dizzily, no longer comprehending a thing. My little orchard rang with laughter.

SIX

Justine was bathing in the waters of Kalamalka Lake just below my cottage. She spread her arms and hands over the surface of the water. A cry of delight sounded from her now and then. She called out exclamations in French.

Roberta watched her from a blanket on the grass. She was sitting with her knees in her arms and sunglasses over her eyes. A slight smile was on her lips. She was reflecting on her widowhood, carrying a tinge of sadness with her.

I lay on the grass on my back. I was looking up into the blue sky. I was wondering how it could be. *I am not even on vacation*, I said to myself. *This is my everyday life.*

SEVEN

Times like this the world recedes. I am floating. All is a strange thin haze and I am floating between silk-grey water and down-grey clouds. The clouds are broken. They are torn and strands of their insides lie scattered across the sky. I am looking at the thin leftovers of cloud and I am floating. All is memory and memory deceives. There is nothing to know. Nothing I might know would change anything. There is no reason to change anything. When I breathe, the torn clouds are in my chest. Little fluffs of insulation float in my lungs. I am insulated from the world by my memory. The sweetness, the bitterness, the nothingness of my memory. Now that I am floating in the remnants of clouds I remember everything I have ever done. My actions are strange to me. I do not recognize myself in my actions.

They did not come from me. My life has not been lived by me. It was someone else who did all those things. It was not me Jules lay down with in the snow. The wind was cold and he was there but I was somewhere else. Perhaps I was here between the velvet water and silk clouds. Perhaps I only dreamed him. I dreamed him because he is familiar to me yet I know he is a stranger. Everyone tells me he is a stranger. I no longer remember who is familiar and who is strange. All of them melt into one. In my memory it is so warm that they have all blended into one.

I love my memories like I love a good book. But I do not know who wrote the book. A name is on the cover but the name tells me nothing. Jules is in the book, moving through the pages like a thin haze. Something about his voice or his spirit or his presence moves through the words and lines and pages. I do not know where this presence comes from. He did not ask to be there. I did not ask for him to be there. I think if I see him again I will not recognize him. The man in the book is not Jules. He is someone else. He is a stranger. I know he is stranger. I am a stranger in my own memory. I do not recognize myself either.

EIGHT

I do not sleep because the highway is barren and open. There is nothing to see for hundreds of miles except snow-covered fields. The wind glides across the miles, chilled and snow laden. I can see drifts of snow accumulating. Tongues of loose snow fly onto the road and off into the stricken grass. I do not sleep because of the stricken grass. I know I must cross the empty fields in the new day. It will be a milk-white day and there will be no sun. I will crawl over the land like a crab at sea bottom. The prairie in the loosening ice of early spring is lonely and uninviting. I already feel the tongues of snow crawling under my skin. The ice looks for places to stick in the corners of my bones. In the new day I see empty vinyl seats, old plastic cups, tin ashtrays where no one has been, chrome door handles that have no fingerprints, car seats unwarmed by human heat. All is untouched. The new day waits, crisp and clear. It waits to be invaded. I do not want to go into that cold reality, stark as a dream I cannot escape. I want to pause here in the arms of a stranger in a strange room. He is imprinting himself onto my memory. The imprint cannot be erased. He is making himself irreversible, tattooing his image on my body forever. He has written this text on my body. A text that stops time in its passing. A text that says halt.

NINE

My friend David from Calgary had his first vacation in several years. He is the man who cannot stop working. He came to the Okanagan Valley to put his feet up in view of the lakes and mountains. When he found there were too many apricots to keep from relaxing we drove to the north end of the valley and found a houseboat in Sicamous. We drove the houseboat onto the Shuswap Lake. Here at least there would be no apricots.

We drove the slow boat over the water. Hour after hour went by and the water was grey-blue and the dark green mountains towered on all sides. The water made me glad. The barely perceptible rocking of the boat made me glad. The air was warm. All the world receded into dream. Nothing existed but the tiny rippling waves on the lake and the bulky mountains.

In the dusk we beached the boat and made a fire on the shore. Behind us was thick impenetrable forest. The water slowed in the falling darkness and began to lap the stones lazily. We had fallen silent too. There was no sound except the crackling branches in the flames. It was curious to me that my home in the valley had so many delights around it. I had never lived in so delightful a place before.

David could not stop working. 'We must go out on the lake where there are no distractions and edit your manuscript,' he said. In the early dawn, at four in the morning when the boat was beached at the far end of one of the Shuswap Arms, he was up at the kitchen table working. He was sitting on the bench that was nailed to the wall of the boat kitchen. I got up, made a pot of coffee, and sat down to work as well. It was still dark. All the world was as still as a whisper. The bears were all in the woods. We read the pages and made changes to words every now and then. When we spoke our voices marred the quiet of the morning.

For eight hours we concentrated, not noticing time passing. Dawn turned to morning. The sun rose and shone on the water. Once we stepped out and watched the blank stillness of the water. The thick forests of the mountainsides mirrored themselves in the lake.

We read through to the end. When we were finished David drew a deep breath, the kind smokers take after holding their breath for a while. He packed up the manuscript busily and quickly went outside to stand on the deck. He stood watching the water. I was thinking that the author of the text no longer remembers what was reality and what was dream. What was lived and what written. If I write what I have lived I too will think it is just a story. I will forget where the story came from.

TEN

I told David that the Okanagan is the Napa Valley of Canada. He should drink the wine made from grapes grown here. We have had too much French wine and American wine. 'You should do for Canadian wine what you do for Canadian literature,' I said. David believed Canadian literature was as good as anything in the world and should be supported. Canadian books should be bought and read because they tell us about ourselves the way no one else can. 'But the wine is too bitter,' he said. He would not drink it. 'Canadian wine tastes like diesel fuel,' he declared.

'Today I will convince you that you are wrong,' I announced one Sunday morning. I drove him to the Gray Monk wine cellars. The Gray Monk estate lay on the other side of the hill. We headed west, up the steep inclines, on a road that wound around in sharp turns and sudden corners. Orchards with billowing fruit trees stretched out everywhere before us. Apple, peach, plum, pear orchards. We ascended the top of the hill and headed down the other side. Suddenly we arrived at the winery. There was a white stucco building that resembled the Spanish-style estates one sees in California. We went inside to a large room where products were displayed. In one corner was a wine-tasting bar. Off to the side was the bottling plant. Along the wall were huge windows with a view of Okanagan Lake deep below. We went out on the veranda. On the terrace were picnic tables in the sun where guests could bring their lunch and have wine with it.

All around the estate acres of vineyards lay carefully tended. Grapevines climbed support railings and wound around the strings tied between. Row after row they leaned carefully in the heat of the sun. The view of the vineyards and the lake and mountains beyond was suddenly not real. David forgot we were in Canada. 'You see,' I said, 'you do not have to go to the French Riviera. Everything is right here.'

I could not get him away from the veranda where he stood glued to the view. I went in and joined a group that had been set up for wine tasting. In little glasses the proprietor poured a dash of every type of wine the winery produced. We tasted them all. For the next round I went out and dragged David up to the bar. He tasted all the wines. All the wines with French names. He did not say a word. Every mouthful was swirled about as he appeared intellectually engaged, ignoring everything else. At the end he bought three bottles of some kind of Chardonnay.

We came away from the estate with heads buzzing. The sunshine was sweeter than before, the green was softer than before, and the blue of the sky was hazier. David took a last look over the vineyards.

'I want to be a vintner,' he declared. 'I want to produce exclusive estate wines.'

'Are you sure?' I interrupted. 'Isn't Canadian publishing a good enough occupation?'

'I'm positive of it,' he assured.

He did not say much after that. He was thinking. He said Canadian wines were good after all. He had not known they were so good.

ELEVEN

But why would I forget? What would I want to forget? It would be so useless, so lifeless, not to treasure everything I remember, every moment I spent, even with a stranger. Because some people are close to you even when they are not. There are people whose every movement you are aware of. You do not know why you are so aware of them but you are. When he looks down or up, when he listens, when he does not. When he walks away, rounds a corner, disappears from sight, you follow all his movements even when you are not following them. No one there could say you are following someone's movements but you are. Not with your eyes. You see with your skin, your hair, your ears. You see with all your senses. When he comes and sits down beside you, you do not have to look up. You know it is him. You have waited for him to sit beside you but you did not know you were waiting for him. It seems like an accident. He did not know you had noticed but you did. You were waiting for him and you did not know you were expecting him. You begin to sense he is aware of you. He follows your movements with his eyes and ears. His skin is aware of you, his fingers folded under his elbow are aware of you. Some people are close in spite of all efforts not to be. Why should you deny that? There must be a reason. A chemical reason, a biological reason, a spiritual reason. It could even be a religious reason. A writerly reason, readerly reason. I wanted to know if Jules was a Catholic.

'Are you a Catholic?'

'No.'

'What are you?'

'Nothing. I was a Catholic once but now I am nothing.'

'What are you?'

'Nothing.'

'Nothing?'

'I was not a Lutheran once and now I am a nothing.'

'I saw a picture of Luther when I was a boy in Catholic school. He was, how do you say…?' He raised his shoulders and made a stern face. The face of a grim schoolmaster.

'They would not give you a nice image of Luther in Catholic school.'

'No. Is there a nice image of Luther?'

'The Danish Luther is nice.'

'How is that?'

'Not grim.'

'Do they believe in sin?'

'Yes. It is a sin not to enjoy life.'

'Oh, it is the biggest sin.'

'You think?'

'Oh, yes.'

The morning light was crawling in the window on all fours, damaged by the sudden return of winter overnight. Why would I want to forget the return of winter? It is not fitting that winter should return just then. That people with wildly different spiritual backgrounds should wake up one morning in perfect spiritual agreement. But nothing should fit, nothing is right. All the lectures and scoldings and reprimands poured on the heads of the very young wash off like the baptismal water and are dry before anyone has become aware of them. Under all our differences we are exactly alike. We are mirror images of one another. We follow each other's movements as though they were our own. We are learning with our senses. With our skin, our fingers, our tongues, we are learning to be in perfect spiritual agreement. I do not want to forget we agreed that we cannot regret what we do. We choose to remember. He gave me words. A text. A language not my own. It is a gift I can keep and it will be mine forever and he does not know he gave me this gift. If I tell him what he brought he will be surprised. He did not bring flowers. He was apologetic. But there was a gift and he knew there was a gift. The gift was in his hand. It was lying inside the palm of his hand. When he opened his hand I could feel it there.

TWELVE

Perhaps we already recognized that a million significant perceptions had passed in the air. That we define ourselves in terms of each other. That we cannot exist in a monologue. Yet our dialogue is without words. There is no official agreement, no absolute truth. It is only an outdated morality that says I cannot desire whomever I want. The morality of a world I never saw and never lived in. A remnant of a past my forefathers have told me about but of no concern to me. In this world there is no morality. No truth about human actions. The only truth I find is what is not expected. Not accepted. Not officially correct. My mistakes are the most significant thing about me. My mistakes define me. What I cannot say defines me. What I cannot say to him because he cannot hear defines me. I have known him for a long time and this is our first meeting. What was it that passed in the air before? For this reason perhaps we lagged behind. We were going from one place to another. It is immaterial where we were going except we had to go. It is immaterial who was with us. People. Several people walking ahead of us, going to an elevator to be lifted up. We must have been in the bowels of an institution, deep below ground in the caverns of a building. Jules made us lag behind until all the people had rounded the corners ahead of us and we were alone. He was laughing and I was laughing and I no longer remember why. There is a point at which the interstated dialogue becomes an official story. A point at which others can recognize that something of significance has happened. That is where Jules becomes another. He becomes a man in a green coat whose arm was around me. The man was laughing at something. He was pulling me back so the others would disappear. His arm was around me and he stopped to pull me toward him and he kissed me. He had never kissed me before. There was no reason for it. Then he looked at me as if he had surprised himself. Just as though a blue haze had materialized from the floor and the genie had swung out of Aladdin's lamp. Something extraordinary. Something said without words. A kiss. But a kiss is significant. It tells an official story. It is something identifiable to others. It is where we agreed. It is so much easier now to talk about desire. Perhaps it is just his presence, one spirit desiring another, one language desiring the presence of another. Bilingualism. My English desires his French. It is that simple. Without the other language my words have no significance. His mouth on mine. A meeting of languages. Unofficial bilingualism. We are defined by our desires, by what we want. *What does English Canada want?* No one asked the question but it was in the air. English Canada wants the presence of French Canada. It wants to swirl French words in its mouth like good wine, to taste the words in French. It wants the arm of a handsome man around its shoulder. *What does French Canada want?* A kiss. A stolen kiss and separation.

THIRTEEN

The dance of approach and rejection is stilled in the Okanagan Valley. In the early morning only a mild haze penetrates the air. The water is almost blank. Sometimes the sun that just creeps over the hill shines a mellow band onto the incandescent water. Then ripples can be seen. A tiny breaking of the surface, a ruffling of the tranquility of dawn.

It is a landscape that requires no stance, no answers. No position, no preparations. A landscape that couches those of us who live here in mellow arms and asks nothing of us. A gentle mother who allows us to rest awhile. We can rest just by looking at the hazy green morning of early spring. When all is awakening.

What is a sentence that is at rest? Could I write a sentence that has no tension in it? No elliptical curve from desire to return? A sentence that acknowledges it is tired and wants to rest. The sentence knows what it wants. To rest awhile. A sentence without an Other. Without a lover. Without a desired object. Perhaps even a sentence without a subject. No ego. No narcissistic ego settling its image over the world.

I came to this valley because I wanted all that tension to seep out of the phrases all around me. To uncharge the battery of my language. I was tired. The words were crammed too full. They could not hold the wealth of information and counter-information I had put there. They were so full that it was impossible to recognize what was in them. I wanted to see the disappointments that had accrued fall like fluff from the branches. To see the naked branches.

As the morning lingers the haze melts away. I see the water more clearly. It is blank. There is no wind. The pastures and orchards are reflected in the lake. The sun is behind a thin cloud and the air is soft. So soft. It has the sheen of silk and the texture of cotton.

FOURTEEN

David steered the boat with his feet. He sat on the upper deck in the sun. In one hand he held a can of beer. In the other hand a perpetual cigarette. The boat was crawling forward at eight miles per hour. When another boat went by, the waves created a rocking motion. I lay on the roof of the houseboat, sunbathing. My eyes were closed. The sun was warm and I was melting in the comfort of yellow summer and blue air. The low drone of the boat engine barely reached my ears.

'We still have a job to do,' I heard him say from the deck.

'What's that?' I answered blearily from the roof.

'We have to find a title for your book.'

'I'll think about it.'

'Think hard. How does *Relative Distance* strike you?'

'How about *Point de capiton*,' I said in half dream.

'No.'

'*La où c'était.*'

'No.'

'*Moments féconds.*'

'No.'

I opened my eyes and watched the mountainside glide by slowly. The peaks towered in the distance. The mountain was covered in pine forest. Green and thick, the trees covered the slopes. Then as suddenly as thunder there was a bald patch. A naked area where clear-cutting had taken place. All along the shorelines of the Shuswap Lakes patches of clear-cutting dotted the mountainsides and were alarmingly large and frequent. They were empty areas. Areas made naked for paper. For houses. For pulp.

On the beaches people swam. Children jumped and screamed. Adults lingered slowly, reclining on mattresses, resting in inner tubes. I thought a landscape is like a language. The reason I like to live here is simple. Because this is where people come when they make holes in their lives. Naked patches in busy routines. Holes they can escape through. Inside the life emptied of routine and obligations I hear them laughing. The lakeshore rings with the laughter of those who have escaped their lives. I like best the ellipsis in the sentence. The gap in the construction. The alarming hesitation. It is so dark in the cracked juncture of my sentence. It is a black hole. An area made naked.

FIFTEEN

'I wish I had kissed you on the railroad track,' Jules said.

'Were you thinking of it?'

'Yes.'

We had found an escape. A space in our wildly different lives that somehow made room for us both. Like water that parts when you enter and closes behind you when you depart, this space would fill in again when we were gone. No trace of us would exist. No one coming after us would be able to identify our presence. No one would know where we were. In this alternate space, a double of reality, a negative of reality, things became disproportionately significant. His hands. His lips. The ability to forget. To forget who you are and where you have been and where you are going. To forget that you were ever alone on the mountainside, alone with the ponderosas. That you ever wept because someone corrected you all the time. That you were ever confused because someone redefined you and you no longer recognized yourself. That you were dismissed or rejected or lost. To forget that anything ever happened. Instead his arms, his whole body. A space of pure affection. Nothing but affection that fills the room like water. Every corner, every crack in this space is filled with affection. A soft gentle affection, like the early spring air in the valley, when it is made of cotton, of silk, of incandescence. A laying on of hands. A blessing that says forget. The embrace of a stranger who is no longer a stranger because you have known him a long time. His arms are strong and you can feel the presence of something wildly different. Another world. He carries another world with him like a haze. In his presence you can feel the existence of another world and you are happy. You are glad the world you inhabit is not the only one. If it were the only world you would be dismayed. You would be closed in and unable to get out. But in his arms you remember there are other worlds. It will be much easier now to take my bags to the airport. To fly to another city. To see my bags come out the trapdoor at the airport in another world. There people speak another language. You are so happy to hear another language, to remember you once had another language yourself. A language you had almost forgotten. You recognize you have spent too long with people who think their world is the only world. They have all been solipsistic and you have been listening to one side of a conversation for too long. You recognize you have been living in a place of nothing but Mussolinis and Stalins and Hitlers and you are so tired of dictators. You are so weary of tyrants. They made you weep and your weeping was antisocial and you went away into the mountains just to stop the tears. Jules does not know the gift he has brought. The blessing of his hands that says yes. Yes. There is another world. There are many other worlds. It will be so much easier to travel now. He was speaking another language. It was French. The air of Montréal. The air of Paris. Your own cities are suddenly visible in the light he sheds. Copenhagen, Oslo, Stockholm. Cities whose air you carry with you, an air that makes you antisocial. That makes dictators want to correct you. That drives tyrants to redefine you in terms of a world you do not belong in and the definition is all wrong and you cannot fix it again. But in this space you can feel there are other worlds. Worlds that are gentle. Whose touch is soft as a whisper. The whisper of a barely discernible breeze on an island. The grasses waver so gently there. The highland flowers shudder so imperceptibly there.

SIXTEEN

One morning when I looked out the kitchen window I saw that my biggest apricot tree had fallen. It was the tree just outside the window, the one I enjoyed looking at when I put water on for coffee. Now it lay on the ground, spread across the hillside that made up my front yard. It had fallen over all the juniper bushes growing to keep the soil from eroding and moving down to the cottage. It must have been the fruit. The branches had grown so heavy with fruit that the whole tree fell with a crack and lay spread out on my property.

I called Josef the yardkeeper. He came and sawed the tree into bits of firewood and stacked them in the woodpile behind the cottage. Nothing remained but the broken stump of a formerly magnificent tree laden with golden fruit.

For better or for worse this is where I live. I live in the ellipsis. The break in a continuum. The crack in a line. The juncture in a phrase. The hole in a life. The breathing space. The breathing space they sometimes call a tourist trap. The place we would like to be trapped in but never have time. The vacation spot. The carnival where Ferris wheels roll and whistles blow and laughter can be heard ringing among the bells.

I did not think large trees fell down like that. I thought they were strong and sturdy. I did not think the joy of living would fell them. Because the moments had been too fruitful the apricot tree fell of its own weight. Something about this tree on the ground struck me as absurd. So absurd I laughed.

SEVENTEEN

Perhaps everything I have been thinking runs into pain. Pain and loss. I have been thinking about the early morning sun that beams into my cottage. The silver sheen it casts on the lake. The woods above drowsy in the first notes of forest birds. I have been thinking that under the clouds I have lost my mirror. All surfaces become opaque. I can no longer see myself. I am reflected in nothing. No face looks back at me in recognition. All faces are strangers. I have no memory of my origins. There are only strange American towns. We witness the return of winter in the new daylight. We thought it was spring. We left our coats behind and walked in the spring air. It was warm and the sun shone. But I do not recognize anything I see. Perhaps all stories run into chaos. No matter how well constructed, how well organized, all stories end in chaos. In disaster. Life itself ends in disaster. We are riding the rails of the dead end. The train will have no brakes. The tracks will continue until they stop and there will be no warning of their ending. They might stop at the edge of a cliff. The story will be a cliff-hanger. The train will go over the cliff at full speed. All the cars will disassemble in flight. The ground below will be littered with train wreckage. Attempts at body counts will be made. But the bodies will no longer be recognizable. Identities cannot be certified. Relatives will be warned against visiting the site. Ropes will be strung around the wreckage. Officials will look bewildered. They will claim ignorance. *We did not know it ended there. How could we know the tracks were like that.*

There are no signs. NO THRU ROAD. If there are signs they tell us nothing. We wonder what they mean. A sign that says LAST CHANCE FRUIT STAND. But there is no fruit stand. It is winter. The shacks by the road are boarded up. No fresh fruit arrives in winter. The sign itself is bent over and has been in the rain too long. The painted words are blurred. A sign that says NO U-TURN. But there is no You to turn to. Nothing to forbid. Nothing to warn about. No consequences. Only the mellow drops of rain.

It has been raining all along. The early spring rain is made of satin. It is the evening gown of the beautiful earth. She thinks there will be fruitful moments in the early evening. But there are no fruitful moments, only a light rain falling. The drops have brought down the lightest cloud cover. The clouds drift down the hillside. They penetrate between the trees. All runs into chaos. The sky, the clouds, the woods, the water. Soon they will be indistinguishable. I will be unable to tell them apart. There will be rain on my hands. My hair. My arms and face. I will be unable to see where the tracks are going or whether a train is coming or not. The bright light in front will not be visible until it is too late.

EIGHTEEN

First only an occasional one appeared out of nowhere. It would sit on the cottage wall outside without movement. A large brown insect, larger than a bee and smaller than a bat. It would be impossible to tell where it came from. The creature would crawl very slowly, with difficulty, toward some indefinite goal. It would be easy to smash with a shoe but if attacked it would emit a strong unpleasant odour. Something less incisive than the smell of a skunk but equally distasteful. The cats would refuse to touch it.

Then there were more of them. They crawled across the veranda like languid potatoes. They slithered up the walls. They sat on the steps as if stunned. Only occasionally did one of them fly. It took an extraordinary event to make them fly but when in the air they flew rapidly.

People in the valley called them stink bugs. Some said seeder bugs. The radio broadcast discussions on the infestation of the Rocky Mountain pine bark beetle. The neighbours said the beetles came every fall, sometimes in droves. They soon littered the outside walls of the cottage. When the door was opened they crawled inside or flew through the doorway. Even when no doors or windows were opened the bugs came inside. It was impossible to tell how they found their way indoors.

The neighbours said the bugs like it inside when the sun is too hot. In the heat of the day the stink bugs could not be seen. They hid in the wood, in cracks and grooves of wooden railings and cottage siding. Then in the evening they crawled out again. Sometimes a bug would fall down, apparently from nowhere. Perhaps from flying or a belaboured attempt at crossing from one point to another. A bug would crash with the low humming of an engine gone berserk and out of control. The stink bugs malfunctioned easily. They were too heavy for themselves. They crashed in strange sites. They would crash onto the table on the veranda and lie dazed next to a glass of iced tea. They crashed into the hair of someone bending down to pick a weed. They crashed next to the face of someone lying on a mat sunbathing.

They were the clumsiest bugs ever invented. Yet no matter how clumsy they were their numbers continued to increase.

People said the beetles would disappear when the weather turned cold. But the weather turned cold and the bugs were still there. Snow fell and they crawled out from under snowbanks. Frost came and they crawled in and out of cracks in the wood anyway. They would not stop. They never stopped.

NINETEEN

In the spring, when I first came to the valley to buy a cottage to live in, there were floods. Rain had been falling for weeks. The lakes rose and overflowed their shorelines. Water rolled over the highway. The floating bridge between Kelowna and Westbank was under water. Backyards that faced the water shrank. Some houses flooded.

The hills in the valley are sandy and loose. It is not a rainy country. Unlike the West Coast, the Okanagan Valley sees more heat than water and forests struggle against the odds to stay alive in the dry soil. The hills are barren in places. The mountainsides are parched dry. They glower back at the hot sun in their nakedness. If it suddenly rains too much there is no vegetation to keep the soil together. The hills erode. There are mud avalanches.

When the flood rains fell, avalanches occurred. Houses began to move in the transferral of mud. Trailers sailed down the hill. Houses bent over and cracked. Some houses collapsed entirely. What was left of houses washed away in the rush of water falling downhill. A family sat down to supper and between the salad and chicken stew, the house came down. A mudslide fell from the mountain behind it and landed on the roof of the house.

The premier of British Columbia came in a helicopter to investigate the damage. He looked at washed-away roads, fallen road signs, collapsed walls. He was seen peering over the edge of a cliff at some wooden rubble in the bottom of a canyon. 'Is that someone's home too?' he was heard saying.

But my cottage on the hillside was dry. Forests of jack pines and ponderosa pines were all around it. There was no way for the mountains to move just from a falling rain. From my dry cottage I could watch the disasters below. How some people's lives were running into chaos. I could think about the beautiful rain coming like silver from the sky. How it brings down the clouds. How all things are stirred.

TWENTY

Jules and I were walking on backroads at the edge of that midwestern American town. We did not know where the road led but we followed it out of town. Soon fields were all around us. Fields of early spring, not yet ready for planting. There was almost no snow left on the landscape. A grain elevator broke the continuum of flatness. A railroad track traversed the land, cutting through roads and fields with a dominance all its own. 'Let's walk on the railroad track,' Jules suggested. We went up to the track and followed it into the country. Soon nothing was around us. Our only signpost was the track. He was telling me stories. A story about two men in Québec. They were friends. They were famous friends and they walked on the railroad track together. A train came and they would not leave the tracks. They let themselves be mowed down by the train. Perhaps they did not hear the whistle blow. Perhaps they wanted it that way, to be plowed down together. A final act. A final friendship. I said I knew of only one such incident. A boy walking alone on the tracks in Manitoba. He did not hear the train coming because he had a Walkman on his ears. Fog hung over the fields where we walked, a haze that coloured all things blue. We could not see into the distance very far. All sound was muffled. The wind was blowing when we got to the open fields. We could feel the wind seeping into our hair, our jackets, our fingers. Jules turned the collar of his coat up. We were telling stories, two solitudes. He speculated that the two friends wanted it that way. It was impossible that they did not hear the train. Something must have happened. There must have been a break in their friendship. In their lives. A break just large enough for a train to plow into it. I thought of the story of Elvira Madigan. A man and a woman are in love. They are a carnival woman and a soldier. She is beautiful and has flowing red hair. They cannot have each other. It is forbidden. They run away into the woods together and no one knows where they are. They lie on the ground together. They tell stories to each other while they eat the berries in the woods and drink from the spring. He has a gun on his belt and he shoots the woman. Then he shoots himself. They are gone, just like that. A cold wind was blowing over the American Midwest. Jules turned his collar up and his dark-haired profile faced the wind. We walked slowly because there was nowhere to go to. Loose spikes lay on the tracks, unearthed by the violence of passing trains. There were no people, no cars, no birds, no life. The landscape was empty. Only the two of us. I was thinking I wanted nothing after this. To walk on these tracks endlessly. To follow the wooden bars and spikes as far as they went. This was a break in the continuum of our lives. Unplanned, unofficial. We had escaped and no one knew where we were. He said he was a press clipper for NATO once. He cut out of newspapers articles of interest. I was thinking it must be necessary to know more than one language. If you know only one language you cannot tell which articles are of interest. There was no sound anywhere. His voice telling stories was the only sound and it broke the silence like the tearing of a sheet or the ripping of a curtain. Something that let the bleak daylight into the world. The overcast sky and the cold wind. There was nothing to hear. I was looking out to the horizon. My eyes were following the tracks. In the distance I saw a bright light emerging from the haze. It must be the light of a train approaching.

'I think a train is coming,' I warned.

'No, I do not think it is a train.' He did not see the train. We walked on.

'If it is a train,' I whispered, 'it will mow us down.'

'Yes.'

We would perish together. Like the two friends. There would be press clippings. *Two Canadians perish on railroad tracks.* They had broken away. They were taking a walk and a train unexpectedly crushed them. The train seemed to come from nowhere. The engine was out of control and the loud humming burst across the fields. Perhaps they did it on purpose. It is impossible that they did not hear the train. There would be speculation. We were walking slowly because there was nowhere to get to. In the distance a bright light was blasting out of the fog. There was no sound. The light ripped through the haze. Then he saw the headlight coming at us. 'It looks like a train after all,' he agreed. We stepped off the tracks and stood watching as the train sped by. It was a quiet train. Only a low humming of the engine as it passed. There were many cars. Boxcars. The boxcars had words written on them. They said PILLSBURY. 'Pillsbury,' he read out loud. 'The train is full of cookies!' I was thinking if we had not left the tracks we would have been plowed down by a train full of cookies. There would be strange clippings. *Two solitudes perish under American cookie train.*

TWENTY-ONE

Jules was sleeping. The light of a street lamp outside shone into the dark room through a crack in the curtains. He did not notice the blaring light. Through the crack I could see new snow flurries outside. I was thinking of the other lives. Lives we could have led but did not choose. Choices we did not make. The alternate paths. That what we choose is real only because we choose it. Perhaps what we have not chosen is even more real. Perhaps those lives are being led anyway in some other realm. There are official stories and then there are unofficial stories. Sometimes we break through the official story. We escape into an alternate story. Just for a while. A day, a night. Two days, three. Four nights. However long. We taste the possibilities of other lives. Other stories. We roll them in our mouths like good wine. No one knows where we are. We have dropped out of the picture and we cannot be found. We live behind the scenes for a while. Others are calling from the stage. The audience is waiting. Expectations hang in the air. Two presences are missing. The stage setting is incomplete. Two chairs are empty. Someone is calling and we do not hear. I come into the room late. Hundreds of people are there. They are dressed in nice clothes. They have just put down their wine glasses and are seated in rows. They are smiling. I am late and I greet them as elegantly as I can in my wet shoes and paltry clothing. I have just come in from the snow. I have been walking along a track through the woods and it has been getting dark. I think I am lost but then I see the towering building. I am glad to be inside and find all the people in the large room. There is a stage and a few people sit in chairs on the stage. One chair is empty. I realize it is my chair. I try to hurry so I will not be late but my shoes are heavy. I make belaboured attempts at walking to the stage. I see their faces waiting. Jules is already there. He is in his chair. He has come indoors ahead of me. Somehow he has managed to get there in time. I go up the stairs to the stage and it seems as if I am crawling. I wonder if they notice I am crawling. If I go too fast I might fall. My chair is standing there alone. Empty. Then Jules was awake and he held me. I buried my face in his chest. I did not want to see the light of the street lamp blasting in on us. The light was coming closer and closer and I did not want to look.

TWENTY-TWO

All the things we do not say are filed away somewhere in another realm. Way back in our distant memories. Only we know about them. When we dream they crawl out of the cracks and remind us that we might have said something. We might have done something. Our lives might have turned out differently. If he had kissed me on the railroad track we would have forgotten ourselves in the moment. We would not have heard the train rolling out of the fog. We would not have seen the headlights. The train would have mowed us down at that moment. It might have been the kiss of death. Instead we sat at a table and Jules told stories that made me laugh. I could not stop laughing. Perhaps it was the laughter of relief. A narrow escape. The cliff-hanger.

TWENTY-THREE

Roberta and Justine had picked so many apricots that I invited them for a reward. I told them that for their harvesting work they would be taken for a sailing trip on a paddle wheeler. Justine was touristing from Cologne. To go on a paddle-wheel boat on Okanagan Lake she came out in her cotton summer skirt and blouse with a small sweater hanging on her arm. She was smiling.

I drove them to town and down to the docks where a paddle wheeler lay. People were boarding. The heat of the summer day was still in the air. We went on board. This boat, we were told, used to paddle the lake from end to end. It would carry things from Penticton to Kelowna and back. Then a floating bridge was built across the lake and the boat could not get through. Suddenly there were roads. Highways were built and it became faster to take a load by truck. Now the boat paddles in circles for tourists. It is without direction. Lost in the circles of its own circumference.

There was a buffet of food. Music was playing and people were dancing. We watched the paddle wheel plow the waters, throwing up streams of the lake as it emerged from the depths. It was a festive boat. We began to tour the lake, skirting the edges of the large shoreline. Dusk fell as we watched the hazy green landscape turn maroon in the falling light. After the dinner we walked on the upper deck. All the people came to the upper deck with glasses in their hands and smiles on their faces.

Roberta and Justine were engaged in happy conversation. They marvelled at the lake. They criticized the music. They spoke of memories and laughed at possibilities. I was looking at the increasingly dark water where it parted as the boat furrowed its way forward. Where it gathered behind us as if we had not been there. Only a few remaining ripples signalled that we had plowed our way across. On the hillsides houses were built scenically. Lush gardens surrounded the houses.

I was thinking it is so simple to be happy. It should be so simple yet it is not. Remnants of outdistanced poems went through my mind. *There hath passed a glory from the earth.* Yet it was impossible to tell what the glory was. Where it came from. Where it went to. Whether it might not still be here, hiding, undetected. Showing itself only at certain moments. The moment complete darkness has set in. When the water is black and nothing but darkness can be seen where the hills and mountains were before. And in the darkness, lights glow. The festive lights of town as we sail into harbour again. Strings of light beaded around the dock. They are like golden drops in a sea of darkness. Golden moments.

TWENTY-FOUR

The bedroom of my cottage in the valley has large French doors leading to the veranda overlooking the lake. From there I can see the moonlight on the water. I lie down in the bed and see a broad hand of silver glowing across the water. The moon is large and full. It is pale as a giant pearl in the night sky. I can see how fog rolls in at night, how the air thickens.

I find myself caught on the edges of irresolution. Between happiness and sadness. Confidence and fear. All emotions roll together. Happy memories and unhappy ones. Caught in an inability to distinguish one from the other. The happy moments are the most dangerous. They are dangerous because you want them. You desire what you must not have. You desire your own ruin. *What he desires presents itself to him as what he does not want,* Jacques Lacan said. The permanence of his desire transmitted to an intermittent ego. This way I can pretend that my desire is intermittent. It is a fleeting desire. I do not know what I want.

I would say I am tired. I love the rain. The rain has been falling all night. In the early dawn the wood of my veranda is wet. The branches of the pine trees are wet. The juniper bushes are wet. I love the clouds sleeping between the hills. The clouds were so tired. They lowered themselves into the valley between the hills and went to sleep. They are laden with rain. They are full of sorrow. They are too heavy for themselves.

TWENTY-FIVE

Just as suddenly the morning is brilliant and bright. The sun casts a yellow glow over everything. The pastures are jewel green. The forests are majestic, stretching into the air as if newly awoken. The roofs of barns glow with reflections of light. Shadows fall across open spaces languorously. A solitary boat appears on the lake and meanders its way across the water. A hawk glides smoothly above the trees.

I realize the winter is departing. The cold clouds that covered the valley for many months have lifted and let the sunlight in. I know there will be blossoms any day now. All the world awakens as if from a difficult dream. An unresolvable dream where questions remained unanswered. Where no hope had a foothold. Where faces were tense. It is much easier to be happy now. It occurs to me that being alive to see the brilliant spring morning arrive is enough. Just to be able to tell the story that spring is rounding the corner.

My friend Roger lives in the valley in the British Columbia Interior. He lives in a cottage among the trees across the lake from me. I had forgotten I had a friend across the lake. Perhaps it is the arrival of spring that reminds me.

When it was winter Roger slid down the ice to my cottage. He brought bottles of good wine. They were experiments, he said. We tasted different vintages, rolling the wine in our mouths. He told stories that made me laugh.

About being stoned and listening to Earle Birney read poems. Watching the poet's ego rise from him in a blue cloud and fill the room with a purple haze. I was cooking, squeezing lemon juice over pieces of chicken. The frost outside was deep. Ice clung to the fence posts with a frantic grip.

In the winter Roger brought a pot of yellow flowers to brighten up my cottage. I neglected the flowers. I forgot to give them water. The yellow heads drooped and the green leaves withered because I had forgotten my friend. Perhaps my mind was elsewhere. Perhaps I was of two minds.

When it was first spring we remembered we were friends. We were such good friends that when we crossed the street in Vernon strangers called after us *Newlyweds!* Because we could not stop kissing each other. Because in spring in the valley all things are kissing. The bees kiss each other, the birds, the cats and dogs, the first purple flowers. The trees in the orchard before the blossoms come. The trees reach out their bare arms and beg each other for the last embraces of winter.

Roger said, 'I gotta do a lot of thinking.' He had more than one woman. He was overextended.

I said, 'Like unto like. I have more than one man.'

I came to this valley so I would not have any man. Just to have the golden ripples jittering across the deep maroon water of the lake below my cottage. Just to see the slow rowboat paddling over. Just to be happy there is such a thing as life. Life without belonging, without ownership. Life with memories in it, like unopened buds on trees in the orchard. I know that when spring comes the buds will open and there will be blossoms. Insects will come and kiss the blossoms. There will be fruit hanging from the branches. Heavy fruit laden with gold.

TWENTY-SIX

It occurs to me that I have been dreaming. That Jules's windblown face is a dream. His dark hair ruffled by the chilly winter wind. His collar turned up against the cold. Press clippings flying all over the railroad tracks. Cookies falling out of boxcars and crumbling in the last bit of snow on the ground. A dream we both awoke from. It was a new day. The palm of his hand lay across his forehead. He awoke in a large bed with pillows and sheets. There was an opening between the curtains where the bright light blasted in. He was thinking, his elbow in the air and his hand on his forehead.

'Where are you?' I asked and could barely hear myself asking.

'Have you heard of cloud nine?'

'Yes.'

'I am on cloud twelve. Cloud fourteen.'

All the clouds were rising. It was easy to see the clouds lift lightly into the air. One by one they rose from the sleeping valley. From between the hills where their own weight had pulled them down. The sun was beaming on them and the water that was in them was dissipating. Their sorrow was vanishing. As they grew lighter they floated up. Behind them was blue sky, so azure it was like a gem. The clouds floated into the sky, becoming whiter and lighter as they did so. They were flying home. I could no longer count the clouds, there were so many. But when I looked out the window I saw the angry snow and I knew we were not dreaming. That rising from this bed would be the beginning of a distance. An immense distance we would be unable to close again. Wildly different lives waited to greet us at the ends of that opening. A difference of French and English. Of city and country. A distance of mountains, lakes, rivers, fields, pastures, suburbs. Everything that lay across the country would lie between us. Time itself would lie between us. We would forget each other. Time would place our images in a dream. It is a dream you did not know you had. I was thinking that even though his arms are around me and his body is around me I can feel the unbridgeable gap. The separation is in the moment even while the moment is expanding to contain all time in it. The waters are rushing to the edges of the lake. The lake is rising and overflowing its boundaries. The floating bridge is under water. It is impossible to travel across.

TWENTY-SEVEN

How quickly the clouds dissipate. When I arise in the early morning we are enveloped in thick cloud and fog. It is as though we have been moving during our sleep from our comfortable beds with many duvets and cushions billowing about us into an ethereal sphere high above the earth. A place of nothing but cloud. When I look out the window I can see nothing at all. There is only a thick grey substance, as if the whole cottage had been placed inside the centre of the fog.

Then the day advances and the fog begins to separate. The thick haze over the lake remains, cradling the water. Above, the mist releases itself and turns into billowy white clouds. The fluffy bundles start floating up and between them and the lake the image of mountainsides appears. Soon I can make out the slanting hillsides, the open pastures, the forest. There is still a bit of snow on top of the mountains. Between the trees I can see layers of white dust.

The mist over the lake itself begins to rise. Underneath I see how the water is perfectly blank. In its face I see reflected the rising clouds. The water appears like a giant layer of marble. I know if I went down there and looked in the blank surface of the lake I would see my face clearly. I do not know if it would be the face of a stranger.

It has been raining all night. I could hear the heavy drops falling in the eavestroughs and on the roof. The rain fell straight down because there was no wind. There was just the sheer force of gravity bringing down the water in the clouds. In the morning puddles lie still on the porch. The front steps are wet. Huge drops still hang from the roof, uncertain about letting go. The grass holds up beads of rainwater for the sun to see.

I put on my coat and boots and walk up the wet gravel of the road. The path from my cottage goes through the forest. The forest on such mornings is sombre. The overcast sky keeps the pine trees dark and moody. In the hills above, the trees appear to be waiting for the sun. Like all the world they wait for the warmth of sunshine. I like to walk among the ponderosa pines. Everywhere the gentle ponderosas stand with tufts of needles on their branches.

There was a sudden blast of wind in the night. It came and went so quickly that it was hardly detectable. But it was so strong it tore objects from their places. When I come up on the road I see that a giant jack pine has been ripped out of the earth by the wind. The trunk lies across the road in complete defeat. The branches have splintered off in the violence of the impact. Bits of branches lie everywhere. When I look at the earth where the tree was uprooted I see the roots spreading dizzyingly into the air. I can tell how shallow the roots were. I see it is no wonder the tree fell down. Perhaps this sandy soil is hostile to such trees. Perhaps the whole forest is tottering on the brink of collapse, the tiny root systems just barely holding the heavy trunks steady.

I cannot help wondering if it is so hard to find a foothold in the West. Not even the native trees can do it. A little blast of wind is all it takes. Perhaps this is not true. Perhaps this is not true at all.

TWENTY-EIGHT

These midwestern American towns are so thin and lonely. They lie in a landscape where you can walk in one direction until you perish. Nothing breaks the monotony of the flat plain and sky. In the early spring trucks kick up dust on the highway. They round the corner as the road bends and leave a cloud of dust to settle on the wayside. Jules came to walk with me into the prairie, on the railroad tracks, and I was happy he did. Because we always know who people are long before we know them. That he should be walking beside me in the emptiness of the prairie was unfitting. But nothing should fit. He carried his cities with him but they dissipated in the afternoon air. I was thinking *I remember Montréal*. Coming down Sherbrooke on just this kind of day. Early spring, before winter has departed and summer has begun. The snow piled thick on the streets and sidewalks had begun to melt. Everywhere the slush lay in massive half-crystalline puddles turned brown by passing traffic. I had to stop in a store to buy rubber boots. It was a dingy store that sold cheap things across from the college. I paid for the boots and put them on at the counter. Then I went out again and stepped in the puddles. It was a bright day. Before I got home I stopped in a café. I was gathering my mind. I did not want to be home on the West Side just yet. Where the dog was and the lace curtains and the heavy furniture that came from another era. Where I knocked and entered at the same time, unsure of which to do first. Where I was always knocking in some sense or other, not of the family, not out of it. Neither here nor there. Where the woman I thought of as my mother-in-law was making soup in a pot in the kitchen. It was chicken soup seasoned with chicken bouillon. Where the photographs were, snapshots of lives I did not recognize. Lives I memorized like a foreign language. With a dictionary and a phrase book. I read words in another language in my bed at night. I listened to *Radio Canada. Ici Radio Canada.* Thinking it was an irony that the language of my own country should be foreign to me. I practiced my French on the waitress who brought me café au lait on that cold afternoon. I read the *Gazette*, making time tick forward as I watched the snow turn to slush. My feet were dry in my new rubber boots. I was memorizing the lives of Montréal. People who fought with their fists. Who refused to speak English. I said to my sister-in-law: 'Why not learn to speak English?' But she said, 'No. No more languages, please.' And I eventually left the bistro and rounded the corner to the house. The brick houses stood all in a row. But here in the American Midwest, there it is here again. That particular Montréal. And I remember other Montréals. The theatre where people in costumes sang with high-pitched voices. Where pieces of fruit went into warm chocolate pots. Where dark alleys left you without direction. Dimly lit restaurants whose names were outside the door. Masses of people strolled downtown at night without destination. I remember dancing. Remember listening to strange sounds from a microphone. Remember laughing. Stolen kisses. And it always seemed everything happened at the same time in Montréal. But here in the American Midwest things happen one at a time. One after the other, one step ahead of the other. A chronological progression that somehow seems unnatural. Jules was with me and he was talking and I was thinking it was unnatural that all things should not be happening at once here too. Everything I imagined in the past and will imagine in the future. That it should all be happening as we stepped from tie to tie on the track.

'Do you have a technique for walking on the tracks?' he asked, bemused. 'No.'

I had no technique for anything. I do not think there will be enough repetitions to develop a technique. There are only circles and every circle strikes you as new. You do not remember having done this before. I looked at Jules's windblown profile and did not remember having done this before. Just precisely this. I was thinking it is not possible that this combination will ever crystallize again either. It is a solitary moment. All alone in its immensity.

TWENTY-NINE

I have a cottage in the country. In the country whatever happens, happens in nature. When snow falls. When fog sets in. When trees fall down across the road. When the lake freezes. When it is picking season. The only carnivals here are nature's own. The only festivals, the only holidays, are supplied by the hills and lakes and forests.

A little store sits at the bottom of the hillside. It is in an old house by the highway at the end of Wood Lake. Often I walk down there. When I come in coffee is brewing. The owner gives me cookies. He gives me my mail. Workers in boots and checkered jackets stand around drinking coffee. They are gossiping. I learn about the community at the corner store. The owner named himself Nasty. In the long winter months I hear the gossip about my community at Nasty's.

In the summer the corner store is full of tourists. They are wet from jumping in the lake. They are hot and looking for an ice cream. Young couples in bathing suits will be sitting outside at the picnic tables, licking ice cream. Old couples will be wandering down the gravel road. Perhaps they are coming from the trailer camp.

People who live here are not burdened by poverty. They have come here with their life's savings. They build houses in the hills where they can rest after long tiring lives in Vancouver or Calgary. If they are young they build houses in the hills and struggle to pay for them with odd jobs. They will be carpenters or construction workers or hostesses in restaurants. They are not rich but they have energy. They are possessive. They guard their plots of land and pieces of house with the fury of young ownership. If you offend them they never forgive you. It is a rural culture. Rural cultures are proud. They see their families expanding and their lands increasing and they are proud of themselves. If you come too close they bark like dogs. If you keep your distance they greet you pleasantly on the road.

Sometimes people like me come into the valley. People who want to be left alone. Who want to simply write a book or paint a picture. Grow vegetables, pick fruit, weave tapestries, and watch hawks circling overhead in between. When those people come they move further north in the valley away from the millionaires in the south. You cannot find them unless you have contacts. Directions to their homes can only be had by word of mouth.

THIRTY

My friend Hillary and I drove to the north of the valley. It was a warm summer day. As we drove, the landscape gently changed. The mountains became higher, the forests thicker and greener and darker. The air grew crisper. Instead of orchards with rows of fruit trees there were open pastures with lazy cows standing. It was not hard to sense that the Rocky Mountains were just beyond. We had lunch on a mountaintop. We felt the warmth of the sand at Mara Lake. We were watching everything and thinking everything.

We followed a sign on the road. The sign said ORGANICALLY GROWN CORN. Going down a side road into open fields we found an old house. From the driveway we could see the walls of the house loosening up, the windows rattling, the paint peeling off. It was old and uncared for. A young man with long hair came out. We said we wanted corn. He took us to the corn field and filled a bag for us. He told us he was on welfare for many years. Now he wanted to give something back to society. His wife was weeding the vegetable patch. She was thin. They were both thin. Their clothes were rags. They were poor. They were so poor the wind blew through them.

We paid for the bag of corn and took it home. That evening we boiled the cobs and had a corn dinner. It was especially good corn. There were moments of silence when we ate that supper. Something about the extreme poverty we witnessed put a rupture in the continuum of our thoughts.

I was thinking there are good people here too. I was hoping I would remember. I knew at times I would forget. Sometimes you are weary. You are so tired you think you cannot get any more tired. The water on the lake is grey. The sky is grey. The silence is severe. Then you remember the land gives. That golden gifts come out of the soil. They are meant for you. And you are to give them back to the world that made you.

THIRTY-ONE

'I am sorry I am not in Minneapolis with you tonight. If I were, I would phone you and then … ' Jules said this in his ponderous manner. He spoke English slowly with a heavy French accent. As he spoke he slowly moved small objects from one spot to another on a surface, as though he were playing an important game of chess. I was thinking he would forget he said this. Already in the airplane he would have forgotten his former desire to be somewhere else. By that evening he would be in Montréal and I would be in Minneapolis and all the airplanes would have landed. It was irrevocable. But he was speaking and the words cut into the early morning air like the flight of a crow. Words that escape you rupture reality. They slice through the continuum of your existence and disappear. Your existence goes on. The words are gone. No one has overheard. But the cut the speaking made remains. Perhaps they were illicit words. Unofficial words. But they made a cut that cannot be covered. It is a language that escapes from its organic origins and when all is gone the rupture alone is left. The rupture is the text. I would have liked a text that covers the entire gash like smooth ointment. A wound on the skin. To know it can be healed over. But there is a scar instead. There for all to see. A textual scar perhaps. I was thinking of the crows of late winter in the barren orchards. They seat themselves on the grey pear trees standing stiffly. The crows gawk across the orchard. They are planning strategies. Where to place themselves when the first buds spring out, when the blossoms burst. When the first fruit of summer makes its appearance, how they will be placed at the precise moment. All I could do was smile because he knew I would be waiting if he were in Minneapolis. Perhaps a sad smile since it could not be done and it could not be spoken of and all wishful thoughts are fleeting. They dissipate like morning clouds rising in the heat of the sun. I thought it was just as well. Things are never what they seem. The more you know someone the less he appears like himself. The self you thought he was. People change every day. The things I know about him are not about the man with the eyes that are looking at me. He would not see in my eyes what he knows about me either. He would say no, *impossible*. He would look at me in that alarmed manner. He would hesitate as he scrutinized me again. My face would be calm. He would see nothing there. He would take a step back. There would be an alarmed hesitancy, the way it was when we met on an average afternoon with people all around. We shook hands and he stepped back in alarmed hesitancy. Something ripped. There was a tearing somewhere. 'I will be sorry to separate from you,' I ventured. His arm was around me and the morning was cold and the highway to Minneapolis was covered in tongues of snow and I was not looking forward to crossing the prairies. I would have liked to pause here longer. 'It has to be done,' Jules said slowly. Deliberately, a voice coming from far away, barely audible. And I was thinking it was just as well.

THIRTY-TWO

That night in Minneapolis I spent instead with my friends Jane and William. I drove across the prairie with William and on the way he bought a bottle of Benedictine. It was a large bottle. That evening he and Jane cooked lasagne and we talked. The bottle of Benedictine was opened. We were talking about adopted children. I told them a story about a girl and her three mothers. They told me about their children. They had both adopted children separately and raised them. Then the time came for the birth family to appear.

I thought I would not like to raise a child only to have it separate from me and go to the biological parent. It would be like watching your lover go back to his wife. Wondering in what way you exist. In what way am I real? What determines a real relationship? Is it length of time spent together? Twenty years together can be wiped out in one night. One error can erase twenty years of good family life. Is it official documents? If official documents make reality then emotions do not. Is reality determined by words on paper? If that is true then what I write is real. What I write exists. Unless it is written it does not exist. It never happened.

William's daughter found her biological brother. The incident was taped by the CBC and they met each other on the television screen for the first time. They can play the tape over and over. They can see themselves at the moment of their meeting. The hesitation. The desire to see and the fear to know. The hunger and hate. The love for alternate stories. What might have been. It is only chance that reality unfolded as it did. A piece of paper that says you are mine and not someone else's.

William told of the moment of their meeting. He sat at the table with the Benedictine in front of him. He was a large man with large hair and he wept. 'You see, I can't even talk about it,' he said. His face was weeping. What might have been. What is. My family that is not my family. Home is a place where you knock and enter at the same time. Uncertain of where you belong. A sense that you may be separating at any moment. The erosion of certainty. The wishful thought.

Jane listened to the story I told and exclaimed, 'That's amazing. That's exactly my story.' And I thought of how our stories interlap, overlap. How feelings are always the same. In every house emotions run parallel. How they build up and stay cloistered where you cannot see them. Then one day you meet someone and the shell cracks. There is a break somewhere. A tearing. Life cracks. Inside the cracks are amazing stories.

Stories of what you learn. How not to look behind you. Not to retrace your steps. To let the past be the past and the moment be the only moment. We undergo so many separations on so many levels. It is only because of your love that you notice the break. Only your desire lets you see the discontinuity. The separation has meaning only because you did not want it to take place.

THIRTY-THREE

There were other trees on my property that I knew would bear fruit but I did not know what kind. Below my cottage was an open space ringed with various trees. In the fall, after the apricots that came out first, I inspected the rest of my fruitful holdings. It was a hot day and the weeds and grasses I waded through were dry and brittle.

When the gate was opened the first to appear was a thick bush with bright red berries. They looked like huckleberries or raspberries but were neither. The berries hung wearily from the thin leggings of bush. Farther down, along the northern fence, were grapevines. The grapes were still green and young. They hung firm and healthy, waiting for those magical moments in late September when they could turn purple. When I read up on various grapes I found mine were the kind used in wine making. They were too sour to have as table grapes. I wondered if I would have time to make my own wine.

Below the grapevines stood a fine tall tree. Everywhere on its branches were little translucent yellow bulbs. It occurred to me they might be plums. I took one and ate it. The taste was sweet and succulent. They were yellow plums, hundreds of them. I got the blue buckets and filled them with plums. When they were carried to the house I sat and looked at my crop. It seemed like a miracle that I should have hundreds of plums, better than any I have ever tasted, coming as a gift unbargained for.

I discovered some peach trees below. They were old and had not been tended. Their branches meandered crookedly with awkward joints. The leaves were sometimes eaten through. But the peaches were fine and ripe. When I picked and tasted them I was again overwhelmed by the sweetness. Soon I had buckets of peaches as well. I had no idea what would become of all the fruit. In one corner of my land was an apple tree as well but the apples were beset by some pest that had bored holes in them. I left the tree alone. Later I would decide how to tend to it. Besides, I told myself, what would I do with another ten buckets of apples?

I remembered a time in my life when one could only get such fruit by paying for it with the dearest of savings. All the visions in my memory of signs of malnutrition for lack of fruit were balking at the abundance around me as though my mind were playing tricks on me. Or perhaps reality was. The memories of hunger for this kind of food. Just precisely this. I did not recall ever having prayed for such a thing. But if I had I would have marvelled at how prayers came true. But I never thought it was possible and saw no reason to bother God with the impossible.

THIRTY-FOUR

I was thinking about spiral staircases. How they go around gigantic water tanks or chimneys or towers or lighthouses. How you can go up or down the staircase and it does not matter where you are situated because the staircase goes nowhere and comes from nowhere. It is an empty construct with bars, clinging to nothing, left to totter by itself in the empty air. A railroad track pulled from the ground and made to spiral upward in circles. No train can follow those tracks anymore. The train would go over a cliff and be shattered in many pieces. I am climbing up such a staircase. It is a fire lookout at the top of a dry sandy mountain. There is no water on the mountain and the weeds and grasses and pine trees are brittle and dry. If a tinder were struck here, there would be forest fires, and I am looking out for signs of smoke. I do not know why I am looking. There is no real reason for it. It has been a long climb and I forgot to bring water. I begin to ascend the staircase and feel the thinning air around me. I am struck by vertigo. The world below begins to swim. The brown and pale green hills are swimming. The lakes far below, blue as gems, are swimming. The crows gawking, the hawks circling. They are all floating and I think I will fall from this high place. I do not remember why I did not bring water. There are so many lakes down there and I brought no water. It would have been so easy to dip a flask in the lake and carry it on my back. I no longer remember why I have taken this hike. I do not see a man standing above at the top of the stairs. He is bending over and looking down at me. He may be wondering whether I will go all the way up or turn around. Or perhaps I will fall over and break in pieces on the ground below. Only in recollection do I see a man above. In reality I do not see him there. I do not know who he is or what he is thinking. He seems to come from another country and yet he does not. He is also very familiar but I do not know from where. My memories deceive me. He is wearing a large coat that seems to go down to his ankles. But I cannot see that well since he is above me and I have to strain my neck to look up. Straining my neck gives me vertigo and I am dizzy. I can see the coat is green. A pale mossy green like the pine trees in the early morning haze when the pines will not declare themselves. Yet you cannot deny they are there. If it is very dry they are dangerous. They might catch fire if a tinder is struck among them. I wonder why frost is on the ground. There should not be frost. It is April and the winter should be gone but somehow it has returned. In the mornings I see the heavy veil of cloud among the hills, hovering over the lake. I know the clouds are full of snow. The fine little flakes are floating down effortlessly. The ground becomes dusted with them. The tops of the mountains are powdered with them. They are talking about the return of winter. How we have to traverse the highways through blowing tongues of snow. All the visions are melting in my mind because I am dizzy and I am trying to come down the spiral staircase. I have to report my findings and I do not know to whom to report them. Or for what reason. My report says I see no sign of smoke. There are no traces of anyone having been anywhere. No one would know we were there. Anyone coming after us would not notice we were there. If there are no consequences of us having been there then I can see we were never there. That is what I have in my report. Let us say no one was there.

THIRTY-FIVE

When the morning sun is bright like this I forget it has been a harsh winter. There have been masses of snow. Huge piles of snow have accumulated at my cottage door. The snow was as high as my waist. The veranda around my cottage was weighted down too heavily. The wooden pillars holding up so many tons of snow were about to break. I took a snow shovel and pushed all the snow away. It took many days to get the snow off the veranda. The road was snowed in and I could not drive down to the cottage. I had to park the car above, on the hillside, and wade through the snow in boots that were never tall enough.

Now that the snow has melted it is hard to remember it was ever there. The ice on the lake has melted. The water jiggles nervously in the early sunlight. Millions of tiny dots of light flicker on the surface. It is like the most nervous traffic jam. All the little fireflies are rushing around.

The veil of the morning has been lifted. The clouds have dissipated and become a morning haze. The haze filters everything. The mountainside opposite the lake is bathed in haze. It is hard to tell where the woodland ends and the open pastures begin. Where the orchards end and the lake begins. All melts into one. There is only a change of colour where the mountain meets the sky. A wooded darkness meets a thin lightness.

Then the glitter of the morning is gone. Dogs begin to bark angrily. Women begin to pick gravel on the road. Girls are out gathering pine cones in the forest. Men are hammering together walls. I can hear the hammer blows in the distance. Workers are picking up dead branches littering the orchards.

They were pruning all the trees in the final months of winter and branches lie scattered as though a wind had swept through and all the trees had broken.

I know there is all this work to be done and I know I am tired. I think I can hardly get more tired and then I do. I think the spring will come with blossoms and I will rest in the sun. All my memories will run together and I will be glad they do.

THIRTY-SIX

I am the place from which the voice is heard, Jacques Lacan said. *This place is called Jouissance*. There is nothing here to be seen. It is the empty space where the breath breaks through. It is a wind in a tunnel, strong enough to fell whole trees with shallow root systems. There is no Other for this *jouissance* unless it be through desire. I cannot prove that the Other exists unless it be by loving him.

We are trapped in images not of our choosing. We have come a long way only to find that we went nowhere. We came all this way from the apple tree only to find another apple tree. The apples here are falling before they can be picked. It is because the tree has been neglected and the worms have feasted on the fruit. The apples lying on the ground are riddled with holes. They have been rotting in the grass and the bees have found them.

In the valley where I live the fruit farmers complain about their apple orchards. They say apple trees are the worst. Apple trees attract infestations. They have to be sprayed every season. In the early summer you can see sprayers in the orchards. They are people who appear to have landed in a spaceship. They are outfitted in protective clothing. Their faces covered in masks. They make you think of the war in the Persian Gulf when everyone put gas masks on. In their hands they hold devices from which a hard poisonous spray covers the fruit.

The world has a device it can use to hold me hostage. It is a device of organic symbols where they say words are coming from. In my joy I am illicit. My joy itself is forbidden because no document has sanctioned it. The universe is a defect. I myself am a defect. The cosmos would be purer without me. And that is what I am trying to say. I am trying to say it is the defect that matters. You know you exist because there is a break, a problem. Because something has been forbidden and it is so hard to believe.

Laughter itself is the breath of the mistake. A defection from the rule of tyrants. Because there were iron curtains everywhere and you saw a break in them where the daylight filtered in. In the blue light of dawn you saw clearly the man lying beside you. He was sleeping and you saw with whom you had been. Suddenly there were no tyrants. There were no dictators and the curtain had broken. The veil had been torn and in the tearing of the veil you saw his face imprinted. The face was clearly there. A shadow cast into your world and you were laughing.

Because when you arise in the early dawn you recognize that the unspeakable has laid hands on you. In the unspeakable there has been a blessing. A gift in the palm of his hand. He transferred the gift to you when he placed the palm of his hand on your body. A gift of language. Of accidental joy.

You want to say you are not trapped in these images of valleys and mountains, of canyons and peaks. Of streams and bridges, of towers and ruptures and spiral staircases. That like a circling hawk you can fly beyond them all. They cannot hold you.

It will be much easier now to see the airplane land in the valley. To watch my bags coming out of a trapdoor in the wall, floating forward on a conveyor belt. To drive to my cottage and see that the ice on the lake has melted. The ice fishermen are gone. The ducks are swimming freely. A boat is on the water. The iron hold of winter has loosened. The bars are falling off. Their joints are weakened and they collapse at a touch.

THIRTY-SEVEN

It is a famous saying that parting is such sweet sorrow. As sweet as the plums I accidentally discovered growing on my property. A stately tree holding hundreds of golden plums. They were crisp ripe fruits filled with the golden nectar that was once said to come from the gods. I remember sitting on my veranda wondering what to do with all the plums. How could I keep them from rotting once they had been picked. And how surprised I was that the fruit kept so fresh. Time went on and on and the fruit remained fresh.

There were no words. There could not have been any words. There was nothing to say yet the air was filled with what remained unspoken. Perhaps a clasping of fingers. A touching of elbows. A meeting of lips. Knowing our languages were touching for the last time. A parting.

I went in to get my bag because it was time to go. Someone had left me a basket of fruit. The wicker basket stood there waiting to be taken along. It was filled with grapes, bananas, apples, oranges. I took the basket in my hand and came down to the car that was to take me across the prairies to Minneapolis. I would catch an airplane for my valley in the British Columbia mountains. There was no sign of Jules at the door. He had disappeared into thin air.

When William and I drove across the prairie the wind blew with a certain fury. Tongues of snow flew across our path. It had been snowing overnight and the fields were white again. Winter had returned and it was unexpected. As we approached Minnesota the snow thinned out. We saw it had only been snowing on the Dakota side. We stopped and William bought his bottle of Benedictine.

I was looking south while I waited for him to reemerge with his bottle of golden liquid. The fields were there, which in summer would be blue and yellow with flax and wheat. A railroad track cut through them. Over the tracks, at regular intervals, a long train with many boxcars slid forward with an alarming noise. From a distance the train looked like a slow snake spewing a little smoke as it went. The body of boxes wound itself clumsily around the bend with the tracks. One huge headlight blasted from the front engine. An overcast haze was in the air. Anyone walking on the tracks would find the sound of the train muffled by the falling snow. Would be uncertain what was coming was the headlight of a train or the sun buried in a veil of thin cloud.

Perhaps it has been a sad laughter all along. A sadness infused with the joy of morning.

THIRTY-EIGHT

I have a cottage in the Okanagan Valley. I live here because I can repeat myself as often as I desire. Nothing will come of all my repetitions. Every summer I can watch blossoms come and go on fruit trees. I can see tulips spring out and geraniums grow and corn become tall. I can see beans in a row. Grapevines in a row. Raspberries in a row. Every autumn I can fill buckets with fruit and watch them turn into jam and chutney and pies.

I live here because here I can make all the mistakes I desire. All I will hear will be joyful laughter. There are no censors here. There are only dark blue mornings when the lake water is blank and the mountain tries to find its own vain reflection when the early clouds have lifted. Your mistakes define you. To be censored from your mistakes is to be censored from yourself. I do not want to wander across the cold prairie looking for myself. Trying to catch my vain reflection in the dropping snow.

My cottage is on the mountainside. I can see far and wide from my home. I can see hawks hovering, crows circling, ducks gliding in the water. I can see a solitary rowboat making waves on the lake. See where the prow parts the water and where it closes behind the keel. I can see trucks filled with fruit in autumn on their way to market. The first purple flowers of spring and the falling leaves of autumn.

Because it is my pleasure to live here. Because it is the place of *jouissance* that is censored yet binding. Only your moments of pleasure can stand for the string that holds the grapevines up for the sun to see. It is *pleasure as that which binds incoherent life together*, Jacques Lacan said. All my incoherent years are held up by the pleasure of being here. By the dew on the grasses, the wind in the ponderosas, the grapes on the vine.

Here my thoughts become a pool of water, blank and sleek in the morning sun. Here I can see a host of fruitful moments reflecting themselves. I think warm thoughts. I remember warm people. My reflections will not be torn away from me by Stalinist historians who wish to rewrite my stories. Embarrassed historians, obsessive historians, proper historians. My improper thoughts can be left to themselves. There will be memories of hawks circling in ever-growing spirals, climbing their joy.

THIRTY-NINE

I was glad to see my life come back to me. Glad to see the slow-moving trucks bounce up the potholed gravel road to my cottage. They were bringing all the objects of my discordant life that had been strewn about the continent. Objects from lives I had lent to others in my vain attempts to live properly. To bow to the censor's blue lines and to lose myself in those lines. I thought it would make others happy but it made no one happy. It only created more blue lines. I noticed that the blue lines would never stop being drawn.

I noticed a fear of death. That if you die in the blue line then no one has died because no one was there. A fear of non-being. A non-being that has to be broken. To exist it appeared I had to make myself defective. To make my own mistakes. In my mistakes I can find the pleasure of being.

Brass beds and wicker chairs and oak tables came out of the moving trucks and into my cottage. Objects long forgotten. Pictures of boats and shepherds. Posters of events. Boots and jackets. Hundreds of books came into my cottage library. Plants still blooming in spite of colossal neglect. Records I could still play. Cups and pots and plates with no cracks in spite of all the transportation. Children's books with children's stories and children's memories. A number of things I had forgotten.

I was glad to see my life come back to me. To be able to say I did this. For better or worse I did this. These are my mistakes. The illicit moments. The improper moments. Because I rejoiced in life I bought more objects, read more books, wrote more words. I cleared the leaves of last year away. Cleared the weeds that had grown and hardened into straw. I swept the dust from the veranda and the porch and the driveway. I pruned the apricot trees and weeded the vegetable patch.

It is so much easier now to be in love outside the iron grid and the paper sanctions. To be illicitly in love without a single ripple on the water's surface. To read familiarity in the face of a stranger. To recognize myself in the unknown. To understand another language for the first time.

FORTY

'Whenever I go to a place for the first time, I know I will always come back.' When Jules said that, his jacket was slung over this shoulder in the heat of the day. The Pacific Ocean furrowed itself behind him. I could see freighters sailing toward the deep sea. Buskers on the sidewalk. An old man playing the flute by the harbour. A juggler in a side street casting for pennies. I thought he must be right. There is no end to this chance meeting. Chance meetings continue to occur. They happen all over the country and it is always the same person. It is impossible to be anonymous, to remain strangers. Nothing is ever new. The words we use to speak to each other are loaded. Analysts have looked into the words and found baggage there. They carry our desires, our violence, our love. *All discourse has its effect through the unconscious,* Jacques Lacan said. He was speaking of *the supreme narcissism of the Lost Cause.* I was thinking of Jules's deliberate ponderous way of walking. Of the story of the lost cause. Trying to imagine a story that is not a lost cause. I love the story because it cannot end and it cannot go on. We are suspended in the string of our desire like a spider hanging from its web. The spider is lowering itself from the balcony slowly and it will never reach the ground. There is no ground below. There is only a perpetual descent into an unknown depth. It is night and we are in a beautiful Pacific city and Jules says, 'What we are living now is fiction.' There is a recognition that the body has its own technique. Its own story. Its own fiction. We can try to make sense of the fiction of the body but the thread continues to elude us. The subject vanishes around the corner just as we think we have caught sight of him. A recognition that *we make ourselves the instruments of each other's jouissance.* We cannot do without each other and we do not want each other at the same time. I find I can sit on the grass in the park and listen to a string quartet play Haydn. I forget Jules is standing a few paces away, his jacket slung over his shoulder. This is his country and he is in a foreign country at the same time. No one here speaks French. They refuse to speak French here the way they refuse to speak English to me in Montréal. It is all a refusal. If I lie down on the grass I will bake in the spring sun. There will be hundreds of people around me in the park and I will bake in the sun repetitiously. When my eyes are open I will see Jules standing a few paces away, towering above me.

FORTY-ONE

I would say I am tired. Winter has been long and spring has been slow. I no longer know what I have to do. Work that is made for me piles up. I have confused it with work I want to do.

I have begun to stare at the lights on the mountain at night. On the other side of the lake lights are scattered where people live. The lights are reflected in the lake. All the ice has melted and strings of light can be seen on the water. When the moon is full there is a wide band of moonlight on the water as well. In the country the air is clear and all the stars are visible. The lights of the lake and the lights of the mountain are met by the lights in the sky. Everywhere the world sparkles at night, like the sun sparkling itself in the water during the day.

From my cottage I see shooting stars. They pass overhead at great speed, going from south to north. They are moments flashing across the night sky. Then they are gone.

In the spring, before the leaves are on the trees, the early mornings are noisy. Hundreds of different birds are calling out the daylight hours. I do not know what half of them are. There are more birds than I imagined. They are delighted at the prospect of blossoming orchards and clear blue lake water and tiny red leaves on little plum trees. The grass has become bright green. The blue haze has settled over everything.

I am thinking home is where you choose to forget and choose to remember at the same time. Nothing hinders your choices. Nothing forces you to remember and nothing forces you to forget. There is no reason to repress any memory. There is no reason to hold it up against the daylight either.

And I shall have some peace there, for peace comes dropping slow,
Dropping from the veils of the morning ...
– W. B. Yeats, 'The Lake Isle of Innisfree'

THE
ROSE
GARDEN

READING MARCEL PROUST

… and more than once, as I was reading, it brought to me the scent of a rose which the breeze entering through the open window had spread through the upper room …

– Marcel Proust, 'On Reading' (54)

The only thing I truly remember from my sojourn in Germany during the summer of 1992 was a garden out back. It was a small garden comprised of a tiny lawn, a small cement patio, and a bed for trees and bushes round the corners. Along one side were a few rose bushes. The street behind the garden was one level up, and the houses on that street looked straight down into my garden. I trained myself to ignore the lack of privacy. I had a project for the afternoons while the sun shone. It was to read Proust's *Remembrance of Things Past*. All the while I had the scent of the pink roses and the vague recall of their continuous presence.

Now, I thought, I will not read Proust in an orderly way. I will dip into those three volumes at random like you would dip a poisoned pen. Am I a hostile reader? Or simply a perverse reader? Would Proust have approved of the way I lived with his spirit, even when I was not reading? Even when I was working inside on the dining table in the mornings? Putting notes together on Mavis Gallant? Or at night, reading *The Paris Notebooks* and straining to decode what people were saying on German television? Or in the middle of the day, plowing through shelves at the university library, trying to find out what the Germans were doing with Canadian literature? All that time, dragging Proust around?

Perhaps I was a perverse reader. It was a perverse summer. I had these beautiful hours of solitude with thoughtful texts, yet in the backdrop a crazy drama was going on. The presence of a lover I was working hard to repel. He showed up, we had heated arguments, he left again noisily late at night. Everyone on that street could hear exactly when he came and when he left. All I wanted was to be left alone with meditative texts. Perverse because I refused whatever came easily. I was living in a land full of meat, and I ate no meat. It was the Mosel Valley, flush with wine, and I drank no wine.

I often went to the railway station in the town of Trier, where I was living. Not because I was always going somewhere. Only on occasion did I visit other towns and countries by train. The rest of the time I was driven madly on the Autobahn by the man with whom I argued incessantly. As the discussion heated up, the speedometer arrow rose to frightening numbers.

I visited the railway station because of the trains. The railway station had a strange sense about it, which reminded me of my life. That the reason why I disliked spending the summer in Trier was not because the place was not pleasant, the people accommodating, and everything to my liking. It was because I had no daily life. My state of mind resembled the atmosphere of the train station.

Unhappily, said Proust, *those marvellous places, railway stations, from which one sets out for a remote destination, are tragic places also, for if in them the miracle is accomplished whereby scenes which hitherto have had no existence save in our minds are about to become the scenes among which we shall be living, for that very reason we must, as we emerge from the waiting-room, abandon any thought of presently finding ourselves once more in the familiar room which but a moment ago still housed us. We must lay aside all hope of going home to sleep in our own bed…* (1:694).

The railway station as *mise en scène.* An unpredictable production.

In 'The Umbilicus of Limbo' (1925), Antonin Artaud says, *By your iniquitous law you place in the hands of persons in whom I have no confidence whatsoever* [doctors, druggists, judges, midwives] … *the authority over my anguish* … (70–71). That you have authority over yourself only within certain parameters. Once the intensity of your emotional life becomes too great, you are given over to so-called 'experts.' 'Expert' is simply a euphemism for 'owner.'

I was thinking of Artaud because of the graffiti. Someone went about the town painting curious sayings on walls, stone fences, bus shelters, and on the railway station. They were political statements belonging to no group. Just an individual venting her anguish on the facades of the town. Because she did that, it was understood that she now belonged to the legal system, once they were able to find her. Artaud, it seemed to me, simply wanted some opium to fight off what he termed a 'disease' *called Anguish* (70).

Just because his writing appears on white paper instead of urban murals does not mean Artaud is not a graffitist. His sentences are graffitilike. They smash at you like angry spray paint. Statements like: *All writing is garbage* (85). Or: *The whole literary scene is a pigpen, especially today* (85).

Artaud is also the one who wrote, *I have only one occupation left: to remake myself* (84).

This must be why Proust is so captivating. He knows what he is thinking. He does not dispel your thoughts or blow your thoughts apart, like Artaud. Proust gathers your thoughts together. You calm down. You can sense how one sentence follows another, without strain, without difficulty. Without anguish. Proust is not ragged and frayed and spastic like Artaud. Even though the raggedness of Artaud is powerful, the tranquil rose garden where I found myself reading Proust was more captivating.

Aimé exuded not only a modest distinction but, quite unconsciously of course, that air of romance (II:168). 'That air of romance.' That soft scent in the air. You know it is there, yet you do not notice. A perfume that melds into the air you breathe. You forget it comes from the fragile petals of those flowers on their thorny stalks.

That cohesiveness that says to you the world is a safe place is also the power of romance. Romance is the backside of anguish.

It is, for example, possible to have an agonizing drive from Trier, Germany, to Strasbourg, France, wherein you think any minute you will become road-kill. You argue all the way over things like 'commitment' without knowing what it is, your lover wanting you to 'commit' something you do not have: to him. Then, you have a romantic weekend in Strasbourg. You forgot everything that was said. What did you say?

We were walking hand in hand along the river canal in Strasbourg. It was the dark of night. The last revelers had left the crooked streets of the old town. Lights had been turned off. The water in the canal did not move. Suddenly, unaccountably, I had an idea that we would be surrounded by rats. Then I noticed there were no stairs up to the street. We had become lost in a labyrinth of love talk. Just by a slight turn of the head I noticed my entrapment.

On the other side, speaking of 'the mystical rose,' Julia Kristeva says some curious things about Nerval, 'the Disinherited Poet.' *The 'flower' can be interpreted*, she writes, as *being the flower into which the melancholy Narcissus was changed* ... (*Black Sun*, 154). The Narcissus flower. I cannot help but think of a book by Linda Hutcheon: *Narcissistic Narratives*. Is it because he reflected too much, or because he was too melancholy, that Narcissus became a flower? Kristeva quotes Nerval: '*An answer is heard in a soft foreign tongue … at the same time as it invokes the memory of those who will love the writer ('Forget me not!')* (154). I find these thoughts of hers curious and disjointed. And yet. The 'answer' that is 'heard in a soft foreign tongue' – Can the answer be understood? Does the narrator understand the 'foreign tongue' that whispers back to the melancholy spirit in the garden?

The television was in German; the grocery clerks were in German; the bus driver was in German; the typewriter saleswoman was in German. I thought I understood German, but it is possible I misunderstood German instead. It was not German that spoke in a 'soft foreign tongue.'

Also, when you speak of 'the memory of those who will love,' you are collapsing past and future. It would be a *Remembrance of Things to Come*. This is possible, especially when speaking of love. Love, unlike melancholia, collapses all things together. Melancholia holds all things apart, at a distance. So it is the lover who speaks back to the writer and promises not to forget.

The objects that induced in me the greatest depression were the shutters in my house in Trier. You pushed a button in the wall next to the window and dark brown wooden panels slid down, covering the window and shutting in place. When the shutters were down, it was dark as a tomb in the house. Not a fleck, string, crack of light got in.

Those shutters are my *Madeleines*. They depress me whenever I think of them. I can hear those mahogany panels slide down along the windowsill, a deep humming sound with a snap at the end just as the last flecks of daylight vanish. Those sticks of wood came down like bars on a prison cell.

Proust's Cottard says, '*The Princess must be on the train …* ' *And he led us all off in search of Princess Sherbatoff. He found her in the corner of an empty compartment, reading the* Revue Des Deux Mondes. *She had long ago, from fear of rebuffs, acquired the habit of keeping her place, or remaining in her corner, in life as in trains, and of not offering her hand until the other person had greeted her. She went on reading as the faithful trouped into her carriage* (II:921).

The Princess has learned, 'from fear of rebuffs,' to 'keep her place.' To 'remain in her corner.' I draw the conclusion that only a few moments earlier, Marcel Proust could not decide whether the Princess Sherbatoff was a refined lady of noble birth or the keeper of a brothel.

The conclusion Proust draws is that *Big restaurants, casinos, local trains, are all family portrait galleries of these social enigmas* (II:922). On trains, at casinos, in restaurants, class distinctions are erased. All is theatre. You cannot decide whether she is a lady or a whore, a scholar or a Madame. There is nothing she can say or do to convince you either way, so she simply keeps on reading.

The suggestions Julia Kristeva draws up in *Black Sun*, 'Life and Death of Speech,' are instructive. She speaks of life lived as an experience of *separation without resolution, or unavoidable shocks, or again pursuits without result* (36). Mundane reality offers no solutions: *the child can find a fighting or fleeing solution in psychic representation and in language* (36). An alternative to language is *inactivity or playing dead* (36). Life, as she formulates it, is a *melancholy dilemma*, a condition of *learned helplessness* (36). The child [the adult] *needs a solid implication in the symbolic and imaginary code* (36).

Given the 'melancholy dilemma,' we resort to language. To the symbolic order. People who are depressed, further, do not have this recourse. For the depressed person, language is dead. The symbolic order fails.

For this reason, I was interested in the Trier graffitist. One day a group of professors and lecturers from the university took me to a wine cellar to try the first results of an experiment with Mosel red wine. Since it was a white wine kingdom, producing red wine was nearly irreverent. As we sat around the table, my companions told me the Trier graffitist was actually a woman of about eighty. This information surprised me, for some of her writing was located in places one would have to be an acrobat to reach. Such as the walking bridge over the highway by the campus.

Still, I thought, this woman may be mad, but not depressed. She acted out her condition in language. Could this also be said of the Princess Sherbatoff in Proust's local train? In her 'learned helplessness,' she keeps reading?

Or, for that matter, Antonin Artaud, who speaks of *the terrible inertia of real thought, after verbal memory and vocabulary have disappeared* (189).

Of *the mind living amid the collapse of language* ...

There is also the factor of Catholicism. Unlike most other German towns, the majority of Trierites are Catholics. Trier is the oldest German town. It has Roman ruins. At one time the townspeople voted to be part of France, but they became part of Prussia anyway. This is something they never quite got over.

I never got over the Catholicism of Trier either. When I was given the keys to my townhouse overlooking the vineyards in the narrow valley below, I opened the door and walked into a Catholic tomb. I was rendered speechless and could never explain to my hosts what the problem was. The problem was that in every room were icons of saints staring down at me: from windows, from walls, even from the backs of doors when I closed them. And the walls of the building were so thick you could scream your loudest and no one would hear.

There were also the shutters.

I took refuge in the rose garden because it was outside the reign of the accusing eyes of St. Boniface, St. Paul, the Mother Mary. Those saints gave me the impression I was doing something wrong. I was not supposed to be there.

There was more to this, of course, than simply the icons in my home. It was one reason why I was uncomfortable in Trier: it was impossible to be there and remain innocent. Even if you bother no one and stay home enclosed in your garden, you are doing something wrong. Perhaps it is just the ambiance of the region. Something I had forgotten. Something we have to read Kafka to be reminded of.

It occurred to me that Northrop Frye addressed this in a mythological context in *The Great Code*. Frye writes that the Biblical Job *wishes, like the hero of Kafka's* Trial, *which reads like a kind of 'midrash' on the Book of Job, that his accuser would identify himself, so that Job would at least know the case against him* (195).

Better yet, *He wishes for his accuser to write a book* … (195). By extension, the book that K's accuser has to write is *The History of the World* (195).

What was true so long ago must be true today. If something was true at any time, can it cease to be true later? Or perhaps any truth is a form of art. In 'Within a Budding Grove,' Marcel Proust asserts *that there can be no progress, no discovery in art, but only in the sciences, and that each artist starting afresh on an individual effort cannot be either helped or hindered therein by the efforts of any other* (1:896).

At the same time, as Northrop Frye notices, details of literature *begin to come loose from their moorings* (217). *Epigrammatic comments*, he writes, have been taken out of the literary texts of their origins and copied and memorized out of context (217). It is as if a given text displays itself as an encasement of useful comments one may remove at random. *What is happening here*, Frye explains, *is that the work of literature is acquiring the existential quality of entering into one life and becoming a personal possession* (217).

Perhaps I am not a perverse reader, but a possessive one. I am possessive of the text because I know no one can improve on Proust. Not even Marcel Proust can improve on Marcel Proust.

No matter how far from it we have come, the situation of the reader is explained as exactly as possible by Stanley Fish in *Doing What Comes Naturally* when he talks about modernist aesthetics. What is the reader supposed to do? Given the controversy over interrogation, does the reader interrogate the text, or is it the text that does this to the reader? How do you establish an interpretive community? To Fish, *the rule is that a critic must learn to read in a way that* multiplies *crises, and must never give a remedy in the sense of a single and unequivocal answer to the question* (137).

In other words, there never is an actual answer to the question of the text. There is no single purpose or meaning. In that sense, the reader should act as terrorist. Should blow things apart. The ideal reader for Marcel Proust, it seems to follow, would have to be Antonin Artaud.

A good reader destroys the work read in such a way that it cannot be reassembled. In 'An End to Masterpieces,' Artaud has this to say about the matter: *We must put an end to this idea of masterpieces reserved for a so-called elite* (252). What is the point of a great work? *The masterpieces of the past are good for the past* (252).

I wonder at Artaud's hostility, his sense that great books are just tombs. No spirit sits up wakefully in them. As to reading, *Let us leave textual criticism to academic drudges and formal criticism to aesthetes, and recognize that what has been said need not to be said again; that an expression does not work twice, does not live twice; that all words, once uttered, are dead and are effective only at the moment when they are uttered* (253).

Is it not remarkable, though? How Proust lived his life once, then again when he wrote it, then again when it is read, then again every time it is read. Because he follows each moment into its core. When Marcel is a young boy he longs for the goodnight kiss of his mother, and he is anguished that she leaves again so soon. The reader anticipates and sorrows prematurely with him because *the moment in which I heard her climb the stairs, and then caught the sound of her garden dress of blue muslin, from which hung little tassels of plaited straw, rustling along the double-doored corridor, was for me a moment of the utmost pain; for it heralded the moment which was bound to follow it, when she would have left me and gone downstairs again* (1:13).

At least it seems so to me. Even though all the characters in the scene are gone – the boy, the mother, the guests downstairs have all gone home – somehow their shadow lingers. Here in the boy's text, penned much later in adulthood. A memory even then. An illusion by then, perhaps. I have here the shadow of an illusion at best, dead words at worst.

I suddenly wish to accuse Artaud. The crime is to think in terms of endings. As if anything, whether real or illusory, could actually die. That life occurs only in fleeting moments. I want to return to Northrop Frye because somehow looking at the Bible as another text, just another text, appears illustrative. Frye talks about the word *beginning*: It is the first word in the Bible. That Frye accuses Christianity of *tenaciously clinging to the notion of the finite and gaining little by that emphasis* (108).

But Frye qualifies what is meant by 'beginning,' and by extension, by life and death: *We get a little closer to this question when we realize that the central metaphor underlying 'beginning' is not really birth at all. It is rather the moment of waking up from sleep, when one world disappears and another comes into being* (108).

So Artaud's dead text is only a sleeping text. The sleeping beauty.

But here is the centrepiece of my existence in Trier: that too many thoughts, memories, emotions were triggered simultaneously at every moment. I could hardly look at the vineyards outside, at the stone ruin that once served as a wine press, at the leaden sky hanging over the valley with drops falling, at the facades of ancient buildings in the town centre, without innumerable sensations over which I had no control.

For this reason, the little garden out back with the roses provided me with a setting for sorting out some of my impressions. That I had Proust's great work in my lap as I soaked in the sun was incidental, but incidentally I noticed Marcel Proust had come into the same enigma. He had trouble reading the newspapers because words printed on the newsprint caused too many associations, words like *le Secret, Good Friday, Calvus Mons* caused in him a *violent shock. Some moments after the shock, my intelligence, which like the sound of thunder travels less rapidly, produced the reason for it* (III:553).

At least the thunder of Proust's intelligence travelled faster than mine. I could not discover the reasons for my strong impressions. Proust's explanation for these feelings seemed to me very clear: *After a certain age our memories are so intertwined with one another that what we are thinking of, the book we are reading, scarcely matters any more. We have put something of ourselves everywhere, everything is fertile, everything is dangerous* (III:553–554).

To find yourself in everything, to find all things are fertile with you, must be the reflection that lay in Narcissus's pool. The reason for his melancholia. That the more deeply you read into a book, the more it is your book. That somehow I myself have been scattered all over Germany, and it was the shock of my own discovery that led me to this rose garden. Because I recognized, without any certain recognition, that 'everything is dangerous.'

If it is not here already, here in Proust's *Remembrance*, the move to anti-narrative is not far away. There is a sense in which the reader is burdened by historicity, which makes accusations as it progresses. The progress of history. I am trying to keep in mind accusations levelled at Proust and other early twentieth-century avant-garde writers like Joyce and Musil: that they gave rise to the *neo*-avant-garde, to Robbe-Grillet and Beckett. Instead of the *nouveau roman*, we get the *nouveau nouveau roman*. As Linda Hutcheon explains it, the practitioners of the *nouveau nouveau roman, these poets-turned-novelists saw political implications in their denunciation of the traditional bourgeois normality which formed the optic of the 'old' neorealistic novel.* What constituted the syntax of rebellion and progress at once *became the declaiming of 'fluent lies'* (130–131).

'Fluent lies' such as the ones Proust told. In fact, any fluent narrative presents itself as a lie. Fluency cannot be true. Was it Proust's mistake to think he was writing representationally, instead of simply creating his own heterocosm?

What is the reader to make of the presence of historicity looming all around? In the church towers that ring on Sundays. In the graffiti on the wall of the cemetery that says, *The Pope is an enslaver of Women!* Written by some eighty-year-old woman at night when the town is asleep.

Linda Hutcheon tries to address the position of the reader in relation to what she calls 'self-conscious narratives': narratives that reflect on themselves (unduly, like Narcissus). She writes, *When a person opens any novel, this very act suddenly plunges him into a narrative situation in which he must take part … Overtly narcissistic texts make this act a self-conscious one, integrating the reader* (139). The text has sucked you in, absorbed you. At this moment you are lost in the labyrinth of a 'novelistic code.' However, *In covertly narcissistic texts the teaching is done by disruption and discontinuity, by disturbing the comfortable habits of the actual act of reading* (139). For this reason, I am *absorbed* in Proust: I find myself in a rose garden, faintly conscious of the scent of pink roses nearby. But I am *jarred* by Artaud. I do not know exactly where I am located when I read Artaud. I have a vague recall of the core of an American city, where stray dogs wander with tongues hanging out amid tin cans rolling on the pavement and homeless squatters in a bus shelter, wrapped in dirty blankets.

But Hutcheon says more: *The unsettled reader is forced to scrutinize his concepts of art as well as his life values. Often he must revise his understanding of what he reads so frequently that he comes to question the very possibility of understanding. In doing so he might be freed from enslavement not only to the empirical, but also to his own set patterns of thought and imagination* (139).

They said of John Milton that his writing was so dense it was impossible to understand. They said only Milton could understand Milton. I do not care, actually, whether I understand Milton or not. I do not care whether I have understood Marcel Proust. If my *mis*understanding is good, why should anyone care? Even if my misunderstanding has no value. Appropriate understanding is beside the point. So is the fluency of the lie.

I can see through the window, looking in, that the shutters have not been driven all the way up. A few of the panels cover the top part of the window, shielding the room inside from the starkest sunbeams. Instead, the rays fall heavily on the Persian carpet. I am reminded of those empirical shutters, half closed, half open.

But here I must stop myself. Just as Linda Hutcheon thinks – inevitably? – of the reader as *he*, does it matter that the reader is *she*? What happens to the text when *she* reads it? Does she, as well, 'question' her 'understanding'? I am drawn to the argument of Hélène Cixous and Catherine Clément in *The Newly Born Woman*: *And if we consult literary history, it is the same story. It all comes back to man – to his torment, his desire to be (at) the origin* (65). Now, they write, *it has become rather urgent to question this solidarity ... bringing to light the fate dealt to woman, her burial – to threaten the stability of the masculine structure that passed itself off as eternal-natural, by conjuring up from femininity the reflections and hypotheses that are necessarily ruinous for the stronghold still in possession of authority* (65).

What would happen, they ask, *to logocentrism, to the great philosophical systems, to the order of the world in general if the rock upon which they founded this church should crumble?* (65) What indeed?

What happens to *The Great Code* when she, the woman, sits down in her rose garden to read a book? Can she be an innocent reader? Is the act of reading itself not suspect if she is the reader? If she is the one who gazes, not the one gazed at? The code that, in Frye's words, says, *if the monster that swallows us is metaphorically death, then the hero who comes to deliver us from the body of this death ... has to be absorbed in the world of Death – that is, he has to die* (192). A code that says, in effect, *the Deluge has never receded, and we still live in a submarine world of reality* (192). Someone must pull us out of the dark canals.

But Cixous and Clément have another reading: *So all the history, all the stories would be there to retell differently; the future would be incalculable; the historic forces would and will change hands and change body – another thought which is yet unthinkable – will transform the functioning of all society* (65).

Strangely enough, the mythology changes as they speak: from fish to vermin. *We are living in an age where the conceptual foundation of an ancient culture is in the process of being undermined by millions of a species of mole (Topoi, ground mines) never known before* (65).

Imagine that. Millions of moles. That is, once the reading women open their eyes, *When they wake up from among the dead, from among words, from among laws* (65). Sleeping beauties all. Sleeping in the woods in glass coffins. But wait. *Most women who have awakened remember having slept, having been put to sleep* (66).

It occurred to me, therefore, that I was getting a little closer to the reason for feeling so suspicious. So under suspicion. So under the watchful eyes of the Saints and neighbours. Under scrutiny, it seemed, by all of Germany. Because the watchful eyes were my own. As I had scattered myself over everything, I looked back at myself from everywhere. But the wonder of it was that, in looking, my eyes had to be open. It followed, my eyes were open. Everything appeared to me to be dangerous because, in this position, in the position of the reader, everything is dangerous.

I began to see women readers gnawing away at the foundations of an old order. But they looked so serene. They really did. Deceptively serene. Sometimes in the afternoon, I walked down to the museum. The museum was located in a bright new white building set in a landscaped park. A rectangular pond with water fountain lay in middle, and walkways around it, adorned with tulips, roses, linden trees. There was a café on the verandah overlooking the park. There I sometimes saw a woman reading, a coffee on the garden table, a swan on the water, a slight breath of wind rustling the crowns of the trees above.

Similarly, the code she, the woman reading in the park, is reading against, can be blacker still. 'The monster that swallows us' is perhaps 'metaphorically death,' but also the so-called Western Code itself. The code that is also present in 'alternate mythologies' of the West, as George Steiner outlines them in *Nostalgia for the Absolute*. Steiner writes that after the decline of the great religion(s), other mythologies have taken over: Marxism, Freudian psychoanalysis, and Lévi-Straussian anthropology. All of these 'mythologies' swallow themselves. In 'The Last Garden,' Steiner talks about the vision, the rage, of Lévi-Strauss: *The fall of man did not, at one stroke, eradicate all the vestiges of the Garden of Eden. Great spaces of primeval nature and of animal life did persist. The eighteenth century travellers succumbed to a kind of premeditated illusion when they thought to have found innocent races of men in the paradise of the South Seas or in the great forests of the New World. But their idealizations had a certain validity. Having existed, as it were, outside history, having abided by the primordial social and mental usages, possessing a profound intimacy with plant and with animal, primitive man did embody a more natural condition ... Coming upon these shadows of the remnants of Eden, Western man set out to destroy them. He slaughtered countless guiltless peoples. He clawed down the forests, he charred the savannah. Then his fury of waste turned on the animal species. One after another of these was hounded into extinction or into the factitious survival of the zoo* (31–32).

An elaborate mythology, simplistic and melodramatic at best. Inspired by great – personal? – guilt. Feelings of guilt. Self-accusation. But within this framework, if the innocents in the last garden exist 'outside history,' why not say the woman reading is also an innocent in the garden? Can she be? Does innocence preclude the act of reading?

But these great, totalizing, mythological constructs are phenomenally depressing. They act like those shutters on the German windows: they come down and shut everything off. Shut you out or lock you in. There is no escape.

But then I think: It is only language. In actuality, in separation from phenomenal experience, Lévi-Strauss has spoken of something that does not exist.

Or that only exists nominally. I am trapped in his language, and it encloses because it is unexamined. Heidegger remarks in *On the Way to Language* that *The word alone gives being to the thing* (62). The world does not exist for us outside of language. This can work in reverse. Language alone can give rise to worlds we cannot experience. Fantastic worlds. Imaginative things. The boundary between reality and language continues to blur. *This is why we consider it advisable,* Heidegger writes, *to prepare for a possibility of undergoing an experience with language* (62). It will become clearer that when we speak, we conjure. And unless we speak, unless we name the thing we see, it will not be noticed.

Unless I say there is a woman reading in the park, she is not there. I must also tell you what she is reading. She is reading *Remembrance of Things Past* by Marcel Proust. She is thinking that Proust conjured himself through this text. Brought himself into being because he named his own life, he existed. He exists, in other words, because he is read. It is not an existence in itself, rather a life lived in the reader.

Let us for once refrain from hurried thinking, Heidegger suggests. Let us be still and allow the scent of roses to penetrate. It is a vague scent, only noticeable after you have been in its presence for a while.

In 'The Fugitive,' Proust discovers the world-creation of a word. He is speaking with Saint-Loup about Albertine. Saint-Loup tells him that in order to visit Albertine, he had to go *through a sort of shed*, and into the house where *at the end of a long passage* [he] *was shown into a drawing-room* (III:480). It is a harmless description of the geography of a house. But Proust has never seen the house that Albertine is staying in. He is shocked by the realization that it is a real house with real rooms.

At these words, he writes, *shed, passage, drawing-room, and before he had even finished uttering them, my heart was shattered more instantaneously than by an electric current, for the force that circles the earth most times in a second is not electricity but pain. How I repeated to myself these words* (III:480). It is the words themselves that give him pain. More pain, perhaps, than he would have felt going there himself. The pain of discovering a person who is the object of your imagination also has a phenomenal existence. That existence is proven. There is a witness. Someone who can verify there is a shed, a passage, and a drawing-room in Albertine's house. *In a shed one girl can hide with another, he reflects. And in that drawing-room, who knew what Albertine did when her aunt was not there* (III:480). And now he must imagine the possibility that Albertine could have a secret life of her own. That she, the object of his imagination, could have an imagination of her own. He is shocked: *those words uttered by her concierge had marked in my heart as upon a map the place where I must suffer* (III:481).

The pain inflicted by language: an operation through the surface into a depth we do not understand. The surface of language. The possibility that the surface is all. That the mind is a flat plain without depth. All of psychology would be an illusion. The unconscious, the subconscious: an illusion. Imagine, writes Frederic Jameson in *Postmodernism*, 'Surrealism without the Unconscious,' when describing 'the newer painting,' *in which the most uncontrolled kinds of figuration emerge with a depthlessness that is not even hallucinatory* (174). Imagine *Chagall's folk iconography without Judaism or the peasants, Klee's stick drawings without his peculiar personal project, schizophrenic art without schizophrenia, 'surrealism' without its manifesto or its avant-garde* (174–175).

What Albertine may be doing when her aunt is not there. Creating figurations unconnected to anything. Albertine herself may be a figuration without connection. The pain that there may, in actuality, be no connection between Albertine and the one who feels pain at the thought of her in a drawing-room, where no one can see her. No one is watching. She is uncontrolled. She is disconnected. Imagine, on the other side, Albertine without Albertine. It will be pain felt over nothing. The shock of discovering the object of your pain does not exist. You feel pain for no reason. Just because the electric shock you experience is evoked by language alone.

We were walking through a narrow alleyway in Strasbourg. It was the middle of the afternoon. A dry haze appeared to penetrate the air, but it also seemed the haze was not there. It was Sunday. The old town was deserted at the peripheries and congested in the centre. Where we walked, there were no people. Shop doors were closed. No one's image appeared in any windows. Perhaps everyone was asleep. Taking siestas in midafternoon. We had become lazy. Holding hands lazily, even our talk of love had become lazy. Talk of love was a pleasant diversion suddenly, instead of an intense invitation to self-apprehension. We were privately, each on our own, impressed by the thought that we were talking about something we did not know existed. How do people 'love'? How can you say you 'love' someone when tomorrow it may not be true? That 'love' is a figuration brought about by nothing, by haze in the air. Romantic love is perhaps, at best, what Anthony Burgess in an essay called 'Creativity' calls an *arabesque of smoke from an expensive cigar* (Mariani 269).

The man with whom I often argued, frequently laughed, and now was pointless and lazy with, who was my lover then. We came away from Germany because there was not enough of the *carnivalesque* in our lives there. He was a diplomat: for him Germany was all diplomacy. For me Germany was all serious study. It was tomes of books in libraries. It was the faintly musty halls of great men of the past. Men in frocks. Men with large collars and long hair. It was a private house overlooking an old vineyard that enclosed me like a tomb. Thick walls and dense shutters and interior darkness.

Our steps became slower and slower. We could hear a fly buzz. A bicycle bump over some cobblestones. A geranium stood crooked in a window terrace. We were conscious of how lovers pain one another. The possibility that we have inflicted pain on each other because we are lovers. That is what lovers do.

Suddenly, the narrow alley opened into the city centre. Sunday excursionists were crowded into the small square. Eating ice cream. Sitting on terrace café chairs with beer on the tables. Dominating the square was a carousel: beautiful wooden horses that sailed up and down in circles to tinny music. As if in calling a truce to an eternal warfare, we went on the carousel. Sitting on the wooden horse, holding the pole with my left hand, I found it suddenly absurd: going around in circles in Strasbourg, seeing buildings designed aslant and pointed into street corners sail by as they might in a strange dream. He was on another horse lower down: when I looked down he was laughing. I was laughing. It was the laughter of being caught in the charms of disengaged language.

But how the love life, the life of the emotions of love, has been conveyed by those conscious of their feelings, able to articulate them. The disconnectedness that is conveyed there: Proust, who speaks of her when she is not there. Søren Kierkegaard, who speaks of her when he does not know her. Kierkegaard's narrator in *Either/Or* stands by a house on the Strand, waiting for an unknown woman to reappear. He knows her name is Cordelia. He sees a resemblance between his Cordelia and King Lear's Cordelia: *that remarkable girl whose heart did not dwell upon her lips, whose lips were silent when her heart was full* (277). The beauty of Cordelia is that she does not speak. She does not tell her love: like the Princess Sherbatoff, reading in the railway carriage, who has learned to 'keep her place,' Cordelia is silent.

That I am really in love, Kierkegaard's narrator says, *I can tell among other things by the secrecy, almost even to myself, with which I treat this matter. All love is secretive, even faithless love when it has the necessary aesthetic element* (277). He knows the verity of his own feelings by his reluctance to articulate them. The more he speaks of his feelings, the less real they will be. Love will be spent in the speaking. Transferred out of the nervous system into language, where it will exist in a disembodied form.

But perhaps his trepidation results from the opposite: what he fears is the possibility of bringing his feelings to life by naming them. In language there is self-invention. The fear of creating a relationship where there was none before. Of making a fleeting, evanescent relationship, which like all human affairs drifts in the smoke of time, permanent. By writing something you make it eternal.

Over and over again I discover the diary is an effort against loss, Anaïs Nin writes in her journals of 1944–47; *the passing, the deaths, the uprootings, the witherings, the unrealities. I feel that when I enclose something, I save it. It is alive here. When anyone left, I felt I retained his presence in these pages* (4:142).

An attempt to possess, to hold on to what must necessarily be taken away from you.

For that reason, articulated by a woman, I bought a typewriter in Trier. A simple, white typewriter, which I put on the heavy table in the dining room. I found hidden in a bureau drawer a colourful cloth which I draped over the table. When it rained, I kept the door to the little garden open. From the table where I worked I could hear the heavy drops fall on the porch and leaves. Sometimes I wrote a page: anything that came to mind. I could not understand my own feelings. Perhaps by writing them on the white typewriter, something would be clear to me. I did not want to lose my thoughts. They must be trapped in the net of words.

Or perhaps it was something else still: the fear of being rooted in the suburban feeling my neighbourhood induced in me. I felt as though I had lived in this heavy house for decades. I was familiar with the routes the children took to school. With the way the neighbours came in and out of houses at regular times. The weekly garbage truck. The daily mail. The bus heading up and down the avenue: I knew when it went up, when down. The expectation of a note on my door from a neighbour: 'Your porchlight was on all night.'

I did not want to become part of the plan of this old town. Part of its human geography. I wanted the air: the roses: the rain. In her 1944–47 journals, written during the war, Anaïs Nin one time exclaims: *The conflict in my life is the conflict in my novels: opposition of an ugly reality to a marvelous intuition or dream of other worlds. Not permitting the human to destroy illusion. Opposing the artist to the world of authority, power, and destructiveness* (4:105).

Because a woman can be trapped in a system that denies her. She must always remember the 'marvellous intuition.' She reads not because she wishes to, but because she has to. It is necessary. She either reads or dies.

Through no effort of my own, I stumbled upon a medieval town in the vineyards north of Trier. Somehow I arrived there by bus and got off near the entrance of an ancient monastery. The town was maintained in its original style. No innovations or developments were to interfere with the stucco houses, gabled and beamed wood, or the crooked cobblestone lanes that passed for streets. Roads were too narrow for cars, so people had to leave them outside the town gate.

It was a custom of mine not to memorize any names. I do not remember the name of that town. I did not want to move as a tourist. I was not a tourist. I lived there. I did not carry a map or a dictionary or a notebook or a camera. Like all the other people living in the area, I had come to Bilbert on a Sunday, dressed in Sunday clothes, to saunter through the medieval lanes. No one was in a hurry that day. We all walked slowly and greeted each other politely when we passed. I have christened the town Bilbert: we were all having a Sunday outing in Bilbert.

I was thinking of the Sunday outings with the family in Denmark, where I lived as a child. When Danish life was still genteel and people went in small groups with wicker baskets to the park. We took wicker baskets with bread and apples to the park and watched the deer among the trees. We sat on blankets on the ground and spread plates and utensils, cutting board and wine bottle, on a table cloth. Everyone was lazy in those days. They drank wine and became more lazy.

It was in Bilbert I found myself standing in the book room of the old monastery. It was an abandoned monastery, now used as a residence for the oldest people of the town. The complex still had a study room and book room. They were large, high-ceilinged, stuccoed rooms with deep-set latticed windows overlooking a sunny courtyard. Vines grew about the windows, and trellises stood up along the walls. Inside hung oil-painted portraits of men in deep red frocks, some with pointed hats, others with flat ones. These men were readers. Then they were writers of what they read.

It was also that time I thought of what Jean Cocteau once said. In his *Diary of an Unknown*, he reflects that *all of this would be funny if it weren't sad. One gets that distinct feeling that the more man learns, the more he seeks and believes himself to have attained the mystery, the further away he drifts, for he is down a long slope of errors that he has no choice but to follow, though he supposes himself to be climbing up it* (76). I was looking into the courtyard: so quiet and serene, where one could walk in large circles among flowers and greens, meditating without distraction. I was thinking if it is a slope of errors, what an attractive slope it can be.

On the bizarre and beautiful carousel in Strasbourg's town square, I was on a higher horse than my lover. When I looked down at him on the outside ring, laughing, I saw he was happy. He was not always happy. For the most part he was frustrated, upset, unhappy that I would not acquiesce to a perfect relationship. It occurred to me that I would not yield because I did not want him to be happy. Because I did not love him. It was too simple to be acceptable to him. Like many lovers, he created complicated reasons for our malcontent.

To accept that someone does not love you is complicated. Experience teaches everyone those labyrinths. Some, like Marcel Proust, can articulate them. *When I was in love with Albertine,* he writes, *I had realised very clearly that she did not love me* (III:939). Such a simple statement to make, yet it will not come out. We will say almost anything else: because to claim you are not loved is too final in a world where closures never seem to occur. All endings are temporary, tentative. With a turn of the head, we extract new meaning, better meaning, out of such disappointment. Meanings like: she is too involved in her books. She should read less. She is dragging around *Remembrance of Things Past* to the detriment of real life. Things present. For Proust, however, there is a minor heroism to looking into the face of people's emotions: *I had had to resign myself to the thought that through her I could gain nothing more than the experience of what it is to suffer and to love, and even, at the beginning to be happy* (III:939).

I know I am a fickle unfaithful reader. I take Albertine's part and reject the voice of the narrator. I understand why Albertine might not love the narrator, Marcel. My reading poisons the well of Proust's sincerity. He did not count on the unpredictable reader. And I am not unaware of the danger I am in. If I persist in this demeanour, the demeanour of the one who does not love and yield, I will eventually be rendered invisible and thrown away. Because at the moment, there is no other world.

As soon as we try to reflect on the matter, Martin Heidegger writes, *we have already committed ourselves to a long path of thought. At this point, we shall succeed only in taking just a few steps* (101). Small steps to an unknown destination. You do not know where this thinking will take you. Or when you have gone wrong. Everything you say turns out to be something else. It becomes necessary to follow the logic of a line of thinking, regardless of your fading love for the thought. You no longer care for your argument, yet you must make it, for you are committed to it. There is a love affair between you and your argument.

Perhaps this is why I am able to read Proust and remain in the neighbourhood of his thinking the way I can remain within the perfume of the rose garden. Because the scent is gone when the wind changes; then it is back. Subtle, barely noticeable, it is a poetry of breathing. And Proust himself wafts his thoughts, so nothing quite sticks. There is always another angle. Proust, it appears, is a fickle unfaithful writer. He will not be loyal to single thoughts, but allows them all to operate at once. Or to disappear if it seems better to be gone.

As a matter of fact, Heidegger himself admits that *Thinking is not a means to gain knowledge. Thinking cuts farrows into the soil of Being* (70). It has not become necessary to reflect seriously on the subject after all. The only requirement made of the reader is that she allow herself to remain in the neighbourhood. To be there and notice the peculiar fragrance.

Is it, then, that literature takes over from life? That reading and its consequence, writing, take away from Being? And love: can love only occur at the expense of literature? On the 27th of July 1867, Gustave Flaubert wrote to George Sand, *I was not so 'submerged' in work as not to want to see you. I have already made enough sacrifices to literature without adding this one* (81). To sacrifice yourself, as though on an altar, to a certain deity. How can literature have such power? Yet it does. That the writer is always unfaithful to the lover: because literature is a greater love, more demanding. The writer's lover is always jealous.

Or is it, rather, as Antonin Artaud supposes, a war between life and death? That written texts are not life? But something else. *We must put an end to this superstition of texts and of written poetry*, he writes in his essay 'An End to Masterpieces.' *Written poetry is valuable once, and after that it should be destroyed* (255). What is that once, when a text is valuable? Is it to the writer of the text, at the moment of writing? Can there be any value for the reader? *Enough of personal poems which benefit those who write them much more than those who read them,* he says (256).

Artaud's answer to the malaise of the written text, which intervenes in the act of living, is simple. He writes, *This is why I propose a theatre of cruelty* (256). To merge literature into life, so what we have is theatre. And in this arena, there is cruelty: *a theatre that is difficult and cruel first of all for myself,* he adds (256). So it is not a matter of a writer falling into Narcissus's pool, but of the writer participating in the difficulty of life and calling it theatre.

When I looked at the pile of books building up in the living room in Trier – on the sofa where I read them when it rained, on the dining table where I puzzled over them and sometimes wrote back to them, in the deep windowsill where they ended up after lying on the garden table outside – I thought they are more than books. These volumes are objects. They are symbols, icons, like the saints overlooking me in every room in the house. Antonin Artaud, George Sand, Anaïs Nin, Søren Kierkegaard, Gustave Flaubert, Marcel Proust – above all Marcel Proust. They were not just writers. Their job was to be representations of themselves: so the rest of us can be reassured it is possible to be something other than framed within the bourgeoisie. Their job is to separate themselves from people at large. From society, so we may be attracted to the idea that individual thought is possible. *We are attracted by any life,* Proust wrote, *which represents for us something unknown and strange, by a last illusion still unshattered* (II:589). It is not that we love an illusion: it is that illusion is all we know. Reality is much harder to get hold of. If a writer suddenly breaks the spell, we may feel betrayed.

The lure of bohemia. Coffee stains. Abandoned ashes. Illicit sex in small wooden rooms. The sound of an accordion outside. If you turn into a bureaucrat, the magic is gone. I will not read you.

It was in those long afternoons, which grew longer it seemed as summer progressed, when I had these thoughts. In the small rose garden, which I understood to be my private courtyard. I could not walk in meditative circles like the former monks of Bilbert monastery, but I was able to meander from rose to rose, like a bumblebee or a hornet, whenever I wished to stop reading. The thick volumes of Proust's *Remembrance* weighted down the flimsy garden table by my chair, which was getting rusty from being left out in the rain. Sometimes you may read several pages of Proust and at the end of it be surprised you were not there yourself. It is a talent for recreation.

I took the liberty of fingering the petals of the large rose blossoms. The white ones began to singe into brown with time. The cherry-coloured ones retained their dangerous hue and freshness longer. I stood there and looked over at the little table, the book left open and upside down on top of another volume. I recognized that everything went on aslant this summer. I was in Germany to consider the writing of Mavis Gallant, specifically. Yet I had taken the time to involve myself in Proust. My book on Gallant would turn into a book on Proust. Yet it would not be a book on Proust at all. *Remembrance of Things Past* is only an opportunity. A site. A gathering place.

When Martin Heidegger wanted to discuss 'Language in the Poem,' he used the poetic work of George Trakl as an opportunity. It was not Trakl he wished to discuss: it was language and poetry. Something too general to float on its own. The specific work under discussion becomes the barge on which more general notions float. *We use the word 'discuss' here to mean, first, to point out the place or site of something, to situate it, and second, to heed that place or site* (159). To Heidegger, the literary work is a compass. A campsite in a moist jungle. The kind of jungle where you may go for a walk, get lost, and die. Perhaps you die of a pre-existing condition, or else a new case of hypothermia, or even the emergence of a brown bear, fresh from hibernation. Such conditions as one might find in Canada.

Our discussion speaks of George Trakl only in that it thinks about the site of his poetic work, Heidegger writes (159). I not only want to remember this notation. I want to repeat it: so I do not end up feeling as negligent as I do feel. Marcel Proust's work is my site. For now. Heidegger writes that *Originally the word 'site' suggests a place in which everything comes together, is concentrated. The site gathers unto itself, supremely and in the extreme. Its gathering power penetrates and pervades everything. The site, the gathering power, gathers in and preserves all it has gathered, not like an encapsulating shell but rather by penetrating with its light all it has gathered, and only thus releasing it into its own nature* (159–60).

I am glad it can be that way. I recognize that the garden itself, with its roses and rose leaves, its encompassing wall no one can climb over, its out-of-control grass, its clumsy brick patio, is the actual site. The garden that takes all things into itself and keeps them. Preserves occurrences in its embrace and emits them again in the fragrance of the rose.

Even though I could see over the vineyard from the gables in the upstairs bedroom, my townhouse lay in a middle-class neighbourhood. In spite of the tomb-like ambiance suggested by the thick walls and unforgiving wooden shutters and a front door so large, thick, and heavy it could not be opened easily, the house reminded most of the structured middle-class life of the *Bürger*. The sheltered life of the *Bürgerin*. Above all, the house suggested containment and shelter. Even the garden, with its high rock walls, was a place of protection and shelter. The saints in their robes. The crosses with the tortured man on them. The predictability of the mail wagon and the schoolchildren.

I could not explain the discomfort I felt. It would sound foolish if I told of it, but I began to fear the house and the life I was meant to lead there. An extreme discomfort I could not pin down. There was a shower in the stone-walled bathroom which was loud and harsh, and no shower curtain. I would stand under the furious waterfall, soaking my hair, face, shoulders, all of me hoping the sheer force of the shower would wash away my apprehension. But it did not. I had begun to recognize the separation between me and continental Europe: that in my Danish mind there were only light birch trees and ash forests and galloping deer and straw-thatched roofs. Nothing prepared me for the stone walls of this Roman tradition that encloses its prison house around you. The world of the gothic, this one I was in, was something I did not understand. I found myself standing in the shower one evening, surprised to discover I had burst into tears. And once begun, I could not stop crying.

Having recognized the nature of my emotion, fear, and found a name for the stage setting of my personal theatre, gothic, I wanted to understand what it was. Fredric Jameson, in *Postmoderism, or, The Cultural Logic of Late Capitalism*, calls the gothic a *boring and exhausted paradigm* (289). But his explanation of what it is is not so boring: *on an individualized level – a sheltered woman of some kind is terrorized and victimized by an 'evil' male* (289). He focuses on the idea of the shelter, shelteredness, as the central feature of the gothic: *Gothics are indeed ultimately a class fantasy (or nightmare) in which the dialectic of privilege and shelter is exercised: your privileges seal you off from other people but by the same token they constitute a protective wall through which you cannot see and behind which therefore all kinds of envious forces may be imagined in the process of assembling, plotting, preparing to give assault; it is, if you like, the shower-curtain syndrome (alluding to Hitchcock's* Psycho*)* (289).

The lure of bohemia turns out to be more than an attraction. The purpose of the artist is to lead the observer out of her prison house. It is the prison house imposed on women: the one that makes a woman reject the advances of a lover. Because the lover represents middle-class marriage. Jameson explains that the gothic's *classical form turns on the privileged content of the situation of middle-class women – the isolation, but also the domestic idleness, imposed on them by newer forms of middle-class marriage* (289).

I cannot help remembering Anaïs Nin's description of the pictures of Janko Varda: *In his landscape of joy women became staminated flowers, and flowers women. They were as fragrant as if he had painted them with thyme, saffron, and curry. They were translucent and airy, carrying their Arabian Nights cities like nebulous scarves around their Lucite necks* (4:242).

It remains no less obvious, writes Jean Cocteau in 'The Justification for Injustice,' *that there are those capable of giving offence, and those who must swallow it* (111). I was aware that I would rather be the offensive one. My body knew something I did not: by bursting into tears, I had to acknowledge I was being spoken to. I dried off and picked up the telephone. It was so easy to dial my lover's number. When he answered I said, 'Take me away from here.'

But it was more than the intimation of the gothic which was foreign to me. More than the barrier of language, so even watching a movie on television became an intellectual effort, an exercise in translation and retranslation. More, even, than the frustrating aggressiveness of a lover who drives up to the door in the evenings with noise. It was my work. Even though Mavis Gallant had my mornings, and frequently evenings, she did not become clear to me. On the hard, Victorian sofa I read through her *Paris Notebooks* and recognized the large distance between Paris in the sixties and Trier in the nineties. The difference was not time. It was the urban environment in Gallant's writing. So I was drawn to Proust instead, whose narrative, while further removed, was closer. Perhaps it was simply a space of mind.

When I read all the commentary on Gallant in the library, and there was a fair amount of it, I noticed none of her commentators and critics had understood her either. An essence was not coming through. It is, perhaps, an essence of doubt. What makes a work of art go from being good to great: the presence of doubt. It is not something directly spoken in the narrative; it is a thing you feel when you are in the presence of the text. Like a vague scent of blossom somewhere. The sorrow of knowing at the last moment you have failed. For this reason, photographs frequently show writers as pensive and sad. They know something you do not: that the work you admire is really a failure. Because language itself fails. There may not be words for the ambition of what you wish to utter. Susan Howe, in *My Emily Dickinson*, calls language *mutilated*. In speaking of Robert Browning and Emily Dickinson, she explains how they felt about their own writing: *Driven by enormous intellectual ambition into the vicinity of the mutilated message of all poetry, they fear the failure of their own energy* (84). Perhaps it is that sense of 'mutilation' I cannot see in Gallant.

That, after all, one is in the vicinity of sorrow. Someone like Dostoevsky, about whom Julia Kristeva writes in *Black Sun*: *Biographers point out that Dostoevsky preferred the company of those who were prone to sorrow. He cultivated it in himself and exalted it in both his texts and his correspondence* (176). That if you have spent a long time with such people, with their writing, you pick it up like a disease. The diseased reader.

It is about the Trier graffitist. A woman in her eighties who writes sentences on walls, murals, bridges, fences. Not sorrowful, but angry. I recognize what I am doing is inside a European tradition: I read within the classical arena. There are precedents, forerunners, a line of thought that can be traced. I am tracing that line, as I would the string in a cobweb a spider created between the leg of the garden chair and the table. I am finding my feet inside the tradition: the foot of a woman reading the classical score.

That the graffitist belongs to something called 'outsider art.' Even though there is no such thing as 'outsider,' she is among the artists and writers who belong to no tradition at all. Or perhaps they do, but their tradition is not codified. Naïf writing. Naïf because there is no consciousness in it of artistic value. In an essay called 'Toward an Outsider Aesthetic,' Roger Cardinal writes that the Outsider is *one who often has no conception of his or her work as art* (33). He believes that *creativity alters its character once the creator is made aware of the expectations or aesthetic standards of other people* (33). For this reason, her writing was necessarily of interest. I noticed that graffiti writing is not transmitted as a disease, but rather enforces a certain power in the reader.

On occasion, Marcel Proust disguises the word *love*. He says 'love' but means a kind of addiction. When the boy Marcel is in love with Gilberte, he is addicted to the chance of seeing her once a day in the Champs-Elysées. He watches the weather intensely to see if it is a day Gilberte will be out. He writes: *I no longer thought of anything save not to let a single day pass without seeing Gilberte* (1:433). This syndrome, this addiction that persists with people throughout life, is something the reader instinctively recognizes. That mental framework is also a site, a region of hysteria and terror that parades under the banner of love. The site of domestic abuse. The one thing contemplatives avoid: addiction to an individual other. It is a sensibility capable of cruelty. Even when so young, Proust recognizes the discord. He says his addiction to his meetings with Gilberte was so strong *that once, when my grandmother had not come home by dinnertime, I could not resist the instinctive reflection that if she had been run over in the street and killed, I should not for some time be allowed to play in the Champs-Elysées* (1:433).

I wonder how often one can be reminded of this and still not know it. *When one is in love, one has no love left for anyone,* he says (1:433). It is about the cruelty of lovers. The monomaniacal lover stalking his prey.

I was not in love, so I was free. In the train station, I changed money. I bought a copy of *Der Spiegel*. I had a cup of strong coffee. Travellers went from one place to another in the station, and I noticed they were not in a hurry. The platforms where we stood waiting for the arrival of the train were a passive place. People stood there in an oddly contented way. When the train arrived, I boarded and seated myself in an empty carriage next to the window. The only other passenger was seated on the other side, next to the window. The train moved out of town and into the rolling countryside toward Luxembourg. We struck up a conversation because we were alone in the carriage. The other passenger was a gentleman from Israel, in Germany for the first time.

It occurred to me to wonder how we misrepresent ourselves to each other. Often this is done without our knowledge. We assume to know what we do not know. I could tell, for example, that my colleagues in Trier thought the graffitist was comical. They were not laughing, but simply dismissive. I could not help thinking of a story Jean Cocteau tells in his diary about a priest in a hotel *who takes a dying man's groans for erotic ones, and raps on the wall instead of coming to his aid* (91).

Yet I find it odd that Cocteau should use that story to illustrate our distance from one another. We commonly say we need to understand one another. Misunderstanding is negative. But such an idea assumes we are capable of empathy. Perhaps we are not. Perhaps each of us lives in a world no one else can be privy to. How else can one explain history? The history of the world: the book that K's accuser has to write. If Job wishes to know the case against him, perhaps it is here. It was all a misunderstanding. The suggestion is that God misunderstood our intentions.

It has often been pointed out that misrepresentation is erotic. Our ability to participate erotically depends on our capacity for play. For drama: theatre. That we wish to be someone else at that moment or to be seen as someone else. It is the conversation with the *other*. We not only need an other, we wish to be that other. At least, one would think so from reading. In *Either/Or*, Søren Kierkegaard's narrator, Johannes, corresponds with Cordelia, his fiancée. He thinks she is getting bored with the engagement. He agrees and concedes that a formal engagement is really a partition between them. *Only in opposition is there freedom*, he writes. *Only when no outsider suspects it does the love acquire meaning. Only when every stranger believes the lovers hate each other is love happy* (358).

That the resting point for erotic love is in opposition. So lovers argue.

One would think lovers were poets. That poets hold up the play of oppositions that exists in lovers' relationships and bring it into language itself. I had a vague sense that what was missing in the life of the *Bürgerin* I had taken on in Trier was the resolute boredom of life along rigid lines. The boredom of daily existence, which glared at me every morning. The predictability of small-town life: you know what day the gardener will cut your grass. You know at what hour the neighbour's door opens and closes. You hear the sound before it occurs.

That this lifestyle subsists on the exclusion of poetic language. The marginalization of Bohemia, of 'outsider art' remaining 'outsider.' In her essay 'The Ethics of Linguistics' in *Desire in Language*, Julia Kristeva talks about this juncture between society and language, society and its books. She critiques Roman Jakobson's reading of poets in 1930s Russia: his essay 'The Generation That Wasted Its Poets.' The article was read as *an indictment of a society founded on the murder of its poets* (*Desire*, 31). But she expands on Jakobson: one may say this about all societies rigidly bourgeois. *Consequently*, Kristeva writes, *we have this Platonistic acknowledgment on the eve of Stalinism and fascism: a (any) society may be stabilized only if it excludes poetic language* (31).

She also acknowledges that *poetic language alone carries on the struggle against such a death, and so harries, exorcises, and invokes it* (31). Poetic language flirts with its nemesis: social order. *The question is unavoidable*, she asserts: *if we are not on the side of those whom society wastes in order to reproduce itself, where are we?* (31)

It occurs to me the 'wasted poets' are the outsiders that cannot be let in: not because they are mad, like Artaud and van Gogh. The myth of the mad artist. But because they see more clearly. The social order is not clarity of vision; it is just social order. If you let an artist in, the clarity of seeing that occurs can only break the spell of the middle class and leave the helpless Bürgers stranded in the blinding light. *This is the torrid truth of the sun at two o'clock in the afternoon* (499), Artaud says of van Gogh. *There are no ghosts in the paintings of van Gogh, no visions, no hallucinations* (499). It is a world so clear you cannot be held captive in myth and paranoia: there is nothing gothic, no terror except in what is unblinkingly clear. You are free to enter the nightmare of reality. *A slow generative nightmare gradually becoming clear* (499). Seeing this way, you are in no one's power but your own. So the vision of clarity needs to be wasted or society cannot be controlled.

The discomfort I felt in my townhouse – in the library, in the streets of the town, everywhere except the rose garden itself – must, I thought, be part of this picture. I did not find myself weeping in the shower for no reason. Instead, I had intimations of that 'slow generative nightmare' that tells you the way society is organized has nothing to do with reality. And reality is largely unknown.

I did not think about this any further. The morning after I called my lover on the telephone, he picked me up and drove me to Frankfurt. Before I knew it, I was home: in another country, in my own house, buried in my own work in the office. It took another three years to turn the pages of that book back to where I was.

It was at a picnic with a friend of a friend of mine. We went to a park by the oceanside. There was a table close to the water. It was evening and golden sunshine gleamed on the lightly rippling surface, where a few children were jumping and swimming. Their calls and shouts could be heard, coming from what seemed like a great distance. There were not many people in the park.

It was the end of a hot day. All was still; not a single gust of wind stirred in the tall fir trees towering over us. I spread a red-checkered table cloth over the table, napkins, plates, and wine glasses. My friend's friend took out a bottle of white wine. She poured the glasses full and I looked at the bottle. It was Mosel wine. From Bernkastel.

In a flash, the entire summer, in all its details, its smells and sounds and texture, welled back into my mind. It was of course at Bernkastel that I walked, intrigued, into the courtyard of the old monastery, thinking of enclosures for classical thought. What both Cocteau and Heidegger might describe as a slippery slope of errors you cannot escape, once you are on it. I have misnamed the town on purpose: in an attempt to turn real experience into fiction. I have named the mythical village Bilbert. But it was not mythical at all. It was Bernkastel, situated on the slopes of the Mosel River, flanked by the sticks and stilts and trellises of vineyards. So real, in fact, that I could sit at a picnic table half a world away, a red-checkered table cloth and a plate of salad and glass of white wine, and at the first taste be instantly transported back.

At that moment I was watching the sunset behind the hills on the other side of the inlet. We were now two women in a park, after being one woman in a garden. The evening grew more peaceful. The families seated in small groups round about packed up and moved on. Soon we were the last picnickers except for a small group that had set their lawn chairs on the sand and were dragging on the evening languorously. I thought again, after having thought it so many times before, how pleasant it is to be lifted out of the squirming discomforts of social life as we know it. Of culture as we know it: all cultures. Codes that impose their rigidity on you and keep you from being free. The enforcers of these codes: the company of men. How much more gentle, airy, light, free, and empowering is the company of women. No arguments, no manipulations, no veiled criticisms and damaging innuendoes. Just a good time: a joke, a laugh, a good story.

All of history, the book that K's accuser needs to write, attests to the truth of Heidegger's slope of errors. Errors build on one another. The classical tradition feeds on itself and produces more classical works. Classical because presumably valid for all times. It is called culture and becomes something worth waging war over. That culture is conditioned by notions of theology: that tell us we are guilty at birth. We look around and do not know what it was we did. What our punishment is. Everything appears to be a strange circus. What would happen if the woman, the audience for all this, left? As Hélène Cixous and Catherine Clément say in 'The Guilty One,' if she just *Quits the show? Ends the circus in which too many women are crushed to death* (56). They dream in their text *The Newly Born Woman: She has loosed herself from the looks fixed upon her … she has loosed herself from the ties that bound her to those showmen … all the masters* (57).

But I am not alone: the woman I speak of is not alone in wishing to 'loose herself' from history. After being 'crushed to death' for so long, how does she re-emerge? Find the garden that releases her? It is a symptom of the present to wish for this release.

Frederic Jameson thinks the word for this is 'postmodernism,' which he explains. In *Postmodernism, or, The Cultural Logic of Late Capitalism*, he points out the empowering effect of this new scheme of thought. He writes, *I think we now have to talk about the relief of the postmodern generally, a thunderous unblocking of logjams and a release of new productivity that was somehow tensed up and frozen, locked like cramped muscles, at the latter end of the modern period* (313). And what was the modern, then? In the eyes of the postmodern, the modern represents *a long period of ossification and dwelling among dead monuments* (313).

But when you look again, the monuments of the past are not so dead after all. We write the obituaries too soon. We bury them alive. We are jolted out of the newly contented present: the pleasant supper in a park, shaded by tall trees, free of innuendoes, by the sudden appearance of a bottle of wine. It is a bottle your friend's friend innocently brought. Wine so good only because it took a long time to perfect. Centuries, even. And the taste of the wine itself brings back memories you did not think about in your effort to be free.

It is a condition re-enacted in the life of every individual. It is something Marcel Proust is famous for having noticed. When he speaks of literature, he thinks he cannot see what is important, and therefore has no gift for literature. *Always I was incapable of seeing anything for which a desire had not already been roused in me by something I had read* (II:139), he writes. Had he not read it, he would not have noticed. Therefore he thinks he would make a poor writer. *How often*, he continues, *have I remained incapable of bestowing my attention upon things or people that later, once their image has been presented to me in solitude by an artist, I would have travelled many miles, risked death to find again!* (II:737) That it takes the presence of the artist, even when the artist is a vintner and his art is wine, to remind you: there was something there you left behind.

That what was highlighted throughout the summer in Germany and France was the continuous need for escape. When I was at home, encompassed by thick walls and the complete absence of erudition, I could escape into the rose garden and hear Proust's easily flowing sentences. As though he had been talking on those pages for countless decades, and like an eternally revolving wheel was unable to stop. No matter what the subject – trivial chatter at a social gathering, or morose thoughts in his solitary bedroom, or a silly conversation on the telephone – all was absorbed in his easy language and transmitted onto the endless page. Chimes that continued to ring, even here in my garden, so late in the century. Then I could also escape the town I lived in and go to another, where l was still a stranger and could wander in happy anonymity. Or I could escape to another country: to Luxembourg or France, and pretend it was all a vacation. There was nothing serious. Nothing hinged on whether I came or went.

The tug-of-war between enclosure and escape became objectively interesting to me. This phenomenon actually kept me awake at night. It was a curious feature of that whole summer that I did not sleep. I followed the routine of all other people in town and shut my lights off at eleven or sometimes twelve at night. The shutters were down and the streets were quiet. The bedroom was upstairs, and like many European houses, the room followed the pattern of the roof. The ceilings leaned inward toward their apex at the centre, which meant one could stand straight only in the centre of the room. The bed was tucked in under the leaning walls, so it was necessary to crouch low in order to crawl into bed. I lay in the wooden box that passed for a bed, with an uneven, lumpy straw mattress, looking at the window set in the gable. Eventually, I got up again. I put on my robe and went downstairs. All was very quiet. It became a habit to cut myself a piece of thick nutty rye bread, butter it, and have a midnight snack at the small kitchen table. I thought of a comment made by Stanley Fish at the end of his chapter on 'Critical Self-Consciousness' in *Doing What Comes Naturally*. He reflects that *It is because history is inescapable that every historical moment – that is, every moment – feels so much like an escape* (467).

That I was fooling myself thinking I was doing the escaping. To feel like you got away: that was simply an inescapable feeling brought on by an inescapable fact that one lives in history. Fish goes on at length about another inescapable condition: that *change cannot be engineered, neither can it be stopped* (463).

It is at night, when one is further enclosed by darkness and entrapment seems complete, that the mind plays freely. What plays is everything one has heard and read. There is apparently no limit to how much the mind takes in. There is a limit to how much of it becomes conscious, at any given moment, but beneath what we can recognize is there, a thousand other thoughts are lurking. It is a condition the so-called postmodernists have not only noticed, but made much of, that we are not so original in our thoughts. In that mental cage, which is not a cage but a freely open universe, there are all the texts we have come across and imprinted there. The mind is a perfect scanner, scanning page after page. What we see and hear is permanently imprinted there. *And I have never encountered a logic that seemed to me anything but borrowed* (144), says Artaud in his essay 'In Total Darkness' as early as 1927.

There were two rooms in the small upstairs floor of my townhouse. One was the bedroom, where it was necessary to crawl into bed. The other was a study. Unlike the bedroom, the study had high ceilings except for the extreme edges, where the room sloped inward. It was truly a garret, the kind depicted in drawings of nineteenth-century poets dying of tuberculosis, etching out their last heartfelt laments. There was a desk in one corner, facing the window in the attic gable. The window was in the ceiling above the desk, leaning with the wall, so on looking out one could detect the red roof of the house opposite, higher on the hill.

Sometimes I went into the study and wondered what I should use it for. As it was, the whole house had become my study and I did not need a separate room. But it had the feel of a private place, so it became a correspondence room. When I walked in there, it felt like I should have a private conversation with an intimate. I wrote letters to my friends at the desk. The act of writing these letters became important, as though serious events hinged on the missives I produced. I had to articulate my daily life. It was becoming noticeable to me that, for all practical purposes, I was not there. No one knew I was there. If I did not say so, put my life into words, it would somehow not exist. I would not exist. I was afraid of my nonexistence without exactly knowing that was how I felt. That writing it would make it happen was not a new idea. The need to articulate has been speculated on richly in European thought. I knew that. I respected that, and so, I did not mock myself. *Language is the house of Being*, wrote Heidegger (63). *Something is only where the appropriate and therefore competent word names a thing as being ...* (63). Or, *The being of anything that is resides in the word* (63).

When it rained, the window over my head filled with raindrops. I could hear them splattering on the pane in my small garret.

In *Either/Or*, Søren Kierkegaard has a peculiar passage about the art of forgetting and the art of remembering. I returned to that page several times in order to reflect on how I thought about my life in Germany. Everything there was so vividly remembered, yet I could not say I remembered anything in particular. It was a situation, a place, and a time I both wanted to remember and forget. It was the idea I wanted to remember, perhaps. Life in Germany should have been better than it was. Romance in France should have been more intense than it was. I suspected myself of fictionalizing for the sake of my own memory.

The small, unexpected moments are what I remember with pleasure. I remember sitting in a courtyard café in the evening with my lover. We were putting an end to a hot day. Our table was in the shade of a leafy tree, and the white Mosel wine in our big glasses was cold. We were waiting for the closest thing to a salad the German chef could make. I remember the moment because my friend was too tired to be intense and romantic. For once, he was calm, slightly absent, not on my case. He was just a friend at that moment, something I suspected he should have been all along. Just a friend. It seemed I had to go through so much fury in order to get to such soothing spaces with him.

I remember setting eyes on the secret garden of the monks at Bernkastel. It was just a fleeting moment, full of shade on a warm day. Those seconds are like floodgates. You open them and a thousand other waters rush in. I thought of all secret gardens. Places where you go deeply into thought, not just your own, but the thought of your whole community. Here it was the Christian Fathers. I remembered my rose garden. Not just the blooming roses and their vague perfume. But the books. I remember the stack of books and how I dipped into them like a pool in the afternoon shade.

Kierkegaard writes that *The more poetically one remembers, the more easily one forgets, for remembering poetically is really just an expression of forgetfulness. In remembering poetically, what was experienced has already undergone a change in which it has lost all that was painful* (234). Perhaps I have singled out those moments for their poetic value and have changed them to soothe an otherwise discordant summer. That I find small pools of tranquility because everything else was confusing and a bit painful. But to Kierkegaard, there is a lesson in that observation. He says that *To remember in this way one must be careful how one lives, especially how one enjoys* (234). I do not know if I was careful. I do not know if it is possible to be careful in that way.

This leads me to the thought of what was, in fact, painful. Because I am not unaware that I could be telling all this differently. I could be telling a story, the story of my summer in Germany. It would have a beginning, a middle, and an end. A good story, perhaps. I would be the protagonist, but not the heroine. I would come out rather vanquished. Because something happens to a telling when it becomes a story. Suddenly, there must be opposition. Hélène Cixous and Catherine Clément state emphatically that *Thought has always worked through opposition* (63). Like He/She or Father/Mother or High/Low. *Through dual, hierarchical oppositions. Superior/Inferior* (64). *Everywhere (where) ordering intervenes* (64).

A woman alone can come out a 'victor' in a story only when the reader concedes to poetic language. Otherwise, what happens in a plotted narrative works to the advantage of the male character. This is because, as Cixous and Clément say, *We see that 'victory' always comes down to the same thing: things get hierarchical. Organization by hierarchy makes all conceptual organizations subject to man* (64). I mention this only because I found myself at a disadvantage. I was a woman alone. I was a guest in another country. I was at the mercy of my hosts.

In a few short words, I have discovered a set of experiences that always occur to women in the position I have said I was in. These experiences include: she is set up; she is presumed upon; she is foisted upon others; she is approached as if she were a battleground, assaulted either for love or for victory. Meanwhile, she says nothing. She does nothing to undermine her assailant. Instead, she quietly goes home and lets stories go whichever way they please. Because she knows she cannot control the stories men tell each other. Nor does she wish to.

She does not exist, write Cixous and Clément, *she can not-be; but there has to be something of her. He keeps, then, of the woman on whom he is no longer dependent, only this space, always virginal, as matter to be subjected to the desire he wishes to impart* (65). In retrospect, I think those are fine words. But I also know, in retrospect, the world will never think so. It will never occur to anyone, seriously, that our very logocentrism ousts the woman from the central story. She must be there as the opposition, or as the margin that frames the picture.

For this reason, my friends are the poets. I am loyal to the poets because they see outside the story. They vie for credibility in a world where poetry is not credible. Readers may presume on the poet, may suspect his or her integrity. May freely slander the poet because of the language used. So Antonin Artaud wrote in a letter to George Soulié de Morant on February 17, 1932, a Thursday morning, that *nothing is so odious and painful, nothing so agonizing for me as doubt cast on the reality and nature of the phenomena I describe* (287). There is good reason to fear what has come to be known among women as 'crazy-making.' Above all, she must be sane, reasonable, cool, and comforting.

Speaking of Emily Dickinson, Susan Howe suggests that *In the Theatre of the Human Heart, necessity of poetic vocation can turn creator to corruptor* (108). 'Poetic vocation' is not simply the act of writing poetry. It is also the act of reading. Of finding poetic language in the midst of 'mechanical empiricism.' The vocation of responding to another language when it appears. There is a suggestion that the woman reading is the woman corrupting. Wherever she goes, intentionally or not, she disturbs, corrupts, the comfortable logos that was there before.

All she did was sit and study. Why was there so much commotion in her wake? *Dickinson was expert in standing in corners,* Susan Howe says, *expert in secret listening and silent understanding* (116).

After being deeply embroiled in social life for three oversized volumes, Marcel Proust, the narrator of *Remembrance of Things Past,* decides to withdraw from society in order to attend to his writing. It is an uncharacteristic move and one which his friends and acquaintances are unlikely to sympathize with. He has to make strong resolutions. He tells himself, *Certainly it was my intention to resume next day, but this time with a purpose, a solitary life. So far from going into society, I would not even permit people to come and see me at home during my hours of work, for the duty of writing my book took precedence now over that of being polite or even kind* (III:1035). Like the lover, the writer has no time for anyone. He has gone from lover to writer, and the configurations are the same. His book has been with him all this time, like an intimation, but he did not recognize it. The way you are with a person with whom you are not yet in love. And why should friends and acquaintances sympathize with the writer? It is not a particularly sympathetic undertaking. Also one that is hard to explain. Marcel resolves to explain as accurately as possible. He says, *But I should have the courage to reply to those who came to see me or tried to get me to visit them that I had, for necessary business which required my immediate attention, an urgent, a supremely important appointment with myself* (III:1035).

He concludes this will look like egotism to other people. But he does not say what the more far-reaching conclusion will be. It is only an appointment with himself while he is writing. Later, it is an appointment with the reader. On the other side, the reader will behave like the writer. She will not have time for anyone else. Suddenly, she will have a pressing appointment with a book, while her lover argues about loyalties. The argument will fall on deaf ears.

The reader will then be infected with the disease of the book being read. As with all infectious illnesses, she will be caught in its bonds unconsciously. She does not know she has a disease. But she goes on to write a consequent text, borne of the text she has read. But it will not be another auto-representational novel. It will be what Linda Hutcheon, in 'The Metafictional Paradox,' calls *anti-representation* (137). It will be a text that remains outside the novel genre. And outside the critical genre. It will be unidentifiable: because it was a disease to begin with. A new virus, something like AIDS.

Speaking of the *nouveau nouveau roman*, that French invention Proust has been accused of generating, Hutcheon writes that there are *very serious implications of this particular mode of metafiction for the novel genre itself. And it would appear that it is not so much a matter of intense textual self-consciousness being self-destructive, or leading to the death of the novel; it is rather a case of its suggesting a further but different stage – anti-representation – which, usually for ideological reasons, would deny mimesis and even diegesis* (136–137). The writer of such metafiction, who was the reader of fiction, does not want her text to resemble anything from real life. What must the reader of the reader's text then do? Hutcheon says that *When this stage is reached, one requires the extra-textual aid of the author* (137).

ॐ

The town of Trier was frequently crowded. Especially in the downtown area, where the tourists congregated and marched and sauntered. The locals joined the tourists on their rounds, probably out of curiosity. Every sidewalk, courtyard, and plaza was given over to sidewalk and terrace cafés. The chairs and tables were always full, coffees and beers on all the tables. To walk through the downtown streets was a matter of wading past thousands of eaters and drinkers. The university area, where I went every day, was also crowded. But there it was full of cotton-clad students in wool sweaters and large, sensible, leather walking shoes. The busses were always full. The town parks were filled with people relaxing. There were no vacant parking spaces.

There were times when I allowed myself to get lost in the crowds. Perhaps downtown, among books at the book stalls, or striking up a conversation with someone at a terrace café. But the scene never seemed quite real. It was not real life going on there, the daily necessities and routines acted out by the populace. Instead, it was Americans with cameras or Italians with loud voices marauding about as if the town were a playground. And the old buildings had been renovated to appear more worthy as time pieces. One Canadian writer, a friend who happened to be there one week, expressed the opinion that downtown Trier looked like a Disney scam. I often found it strange, like wearing clothes that do not quite fit, that I would not be going 'home' with my friends when they appeared. 'Home' for me was up that hill, just above the valley, just as you leave the downtown area in the direction of the university.

I preferred to be away from the confusing crowds. In retrospect, I do not think I was 'anti-social' so much as I was getting slightly perverse. Moribund. Saying 'no' to most things, just when there was this plenty around. I would find myself in my small garden, staring transfixed at a rose. It would be off-white, fading at the edges, singed by age to a dirty brown.

Perhaps, as Proust says, I had a kind of appointment with myself. But it was a meeting of a different nature. I was not engaged in the act of writing a book. There was just a question I needed to ask myself. The question was so unfocused, I did not exactly know what it was. I wondered, for example, about the woman who wishes to be alone. Is it different from when the man wishes to be so? The idea of solitude has been dignified for men by the great thinkers. But I could not escape the suspicion that the women who choose solitude in our literature come out of it a little odd. Perhaps I was imagining things. I found solace of a kind in what people like Kierkegaard – whose solitude does in fact appear odd, whose whole narrative titled *Either/Or* is surprisingly cruel and manipulative, even when it is brilliant – have written. Kierkegaard's narrator asserts in a letter to a friend, that *When around me all has become still, solemn as a starlit night, when the soul is all alone in the world, there appears before it not a distinguished person, but the eternal power itself. It is as though the heaven parted, and the I chooses itself – or, more correctly, it accepts itself* (491).

To accept oneself: perhaps that is a taller order than it seems. Paradoxically, the reader may encounter herself in so many books which, on the surface, appear to have nothing in common with her.

What I am writing here is an account of something that may strike the observer as non-narrative. Because there is no discernible progress from one event to another. This observer was expecting story, perhaps. But already by the advent of the *nouveau roman*, we could see the possibility of the internal story. A character may be doing nothing, outwardly: she may be sitting in a rose garden reading. The only movement in the scene might be a bee flying among the flowers. Or a gentle breeze suddenly brushing the corner of the page. Everything that happens does so in the mind of the reader. That, in itself, might constitute a story. In his chapter on rhetoric, for example, Stanley Fish wishes to say *that something is always happening to the way we think* (501). It is perhaps impossible to exist without something taking place. To be outside of story would be to not exist.

What confuses is that stories never end. Fictions are false because they provide false endings. There is always a next day: just as the idea of the end of the universe can never gain currency, since it is forever trailed by the question of what is behind the end of the universe. In fiction, we strive for a last word of some kind. The same happens in theory and philosophy. It is, Stanley Fish wishes to say, *a tug-of-war between two views of human life and its possibilities, no one of which can ever gain complete and lasting ascendancy because in the very moment of its triumphant articulation each turns back in the direction of the other* (501).

In saying this much, he proceeds to discount reader-response criticism, feminism, Marxism, and Freudianism. *Here one might speak of the return of the repressed,* Fish writes. *Were it not that the repressed – whether it be the fact of difference or the desire for its elimination – is always so close to the surface that it hardly need be unearthed* (501). It would seem he wishes to eliminate all dialogue and give the last word to himself. He writes: *What we seem to have is a tale full of sound and fury, and signifying itself signifying a durability rooted in inconclusiveness, in the impossibility of there being a last word* (501). It occurs to me Fish might think of the Trier graffitist as a bag of hot air. So, too, is Marcel Proust. From opposite sides of our dialogism comes a 'tale full of sound and fury.' But empty at the core. This view strikes me as profoundly unsympathetic to human experience. Fish's remarks have the flavour of the atom bomb: since no one can win, we simply eliminate them all.

In this context, I am reminded of Antonin Artaud's comments about a new 'tragedy' he had just written. In a letter to André Gide on February 10, 1935, he invites Gide to a reading of the text of his play. He explains that *The dialogue of this tragedy is, if I may say so, of the most extreme violence. And there is nothing among the traditional notions of Society, order, Justice, Religion, family and Country, that is not attacked* (340).

Then he adds, when considering audience response: *There must be no incidents* (340).

On the eve of the 'shower-curtain syndrome,' when I phoned my lover in Bonn and asked him to take me away from Germany, I was awake all night. There were brilliant stars in the sky, for it was a clear night. The silhouette of tall-gabled houses and the spires of churches stood out against the moonlight. When I went into the rose garden in the dark, the brilliance of bright green leaves shot through with sunlight, and starkly coloured flowers that cheered up the afternoon so vividly, had dampened. The small garden now looked like a small garden enclosed by high stone walls. It was no longer a place of repose, but a kind of enclosure. I began to think of the rose in its prison, how in one day my perception had changed.

My sense of oppositions had come to haunt me as being purely symbolic. That there was an argument at all was now, in the unexpectedly final night in my house, doubtful. The books I had been reading, which I presumed to presume a male reader, and which I therefore did not read but 'dipped into' the way a bee dips into a flower, did not presume such things at all. I thought of a remark made by Northrop Frye concerning the Bible. In *The Great Code* he suggests that *Wherever we have love we have the possibility of sexual symbolism. The kerygma, or proclaiming rhetoric, of the Bible is a welcoming and approaching rhetoric, addressed by a symbolically male God to a symbolically female body of readers* (231).

Next morning my friend arrived. My suitcase was packed and I was ready to go even before I opened the door. During the night, I had discharged all my social duties. I paid the rent for the rest of the summer, paid the telephone bill, handed the key over to my neighbour. In case I decided not to return. We drove from Trier to Frankfurt, and for once I was glad of the lightning speed at which my friend drove on the Autobahn. I listened to him talk all the way, like the humming of the engine of the car. Perhaps he was disappointed. If he was, he put a good face on it. He said I did not have him on a silver platter now like I did before. He would play harder to get. In fact, he would ask for a transfer to the other side of the Iron Curtain, which was no longer an Iron Curtain, where no one, and certainly not I, would ever go.

Paradoxically, in this light we were friendlier than before. My plane did not leave till the following morning, so he took me to a restaurant in Frankfurt. He ordered meals we would have to cook ourselves on cooking stones brought to the table. But he did the cooking. He stood up, rolled up his sleeves, and began flipping prawns, scallops, bits of cod into the air with more dexterity than a Japanese sushi chef. He put on a show and made me laugh. There were no arguments anymore, just a good time. The irony was not lost on me – that I had to actually leave for him to wake up to a relationship I suddenly really liked.

Perhaps it is, when you think back over a period of time, whether three months or three years, that retrospective gives you a chance to fictionalize. That does not mean you alter the reality of what took place, if anything. Your ability to fictionalize the past has more to do with narrative time than with story. This is suggested nicely by Fredric Jameson in his chapter on 'Video.' In arguing why experimental video does not work with fictions, he defines fictions in terms of 'fictive time' rather than story. *We all know*, he writes, *but always forget, that the fictive scenes and conversations on the movie screen radically foreshorten reality as the clock ticks and are never – owing to the now codified mysteries of the various techniques of film narrative – coterminous with the putative length of such moments in real life, or in 'real time'* (74). We find videotapes that do not 'foreshorten' 'real time' irritating to watch. We go through the experience like the subject of daguerreotype. The photographer had a clamp to hold the subject's head in place for the ten minutes or so it took for the exposure.

Jameson writes: *Is it possible, then, that 'fiction' is what is in question here and that it can be defined essentially as the construction of just such fictive and foreshortened temporalities (whether of film or reading), which are then substituted for a real time we are thereby enabled momentarily to forget?* (74) In that way, when you loop out of your 'real life,' into another existence, where things happen in reverse order, or happen too fast, or suddenly stand still like a bower of transcendence halting the universe in its course, you enter a world of fiction. Suddenly you are Alice in Wonderland. Or Dorothy in Oz. Everything is disproportionate and you become homesick for 'real time.'

But to Jameson, the consequence of his observation is theoretical. *The question of fiction and the fictive would thereby find itself radically dissociated from questions of narrative and storytelling as such*, he says (74). It seemed to me just then, on the eve of my departure, that we use fiction to escape the ennui of 'real time,' a condition so explored by the moderns. We also use the act of travel for the same purpose. Compared to fictive time, the time of our lives seems heavy and slow and monotonous.

It had occurred to me on a walk through the vineyard below my townhouse in Trier that it might be true, what Virginia Woolf confessed to be the usefulness of women. Women are mirrors, she says. *Whatever may be their use in*

civilised societies, mirrors are essential to all violent and heroic action. That is why Napoleon and Mussolini both insist so emphatically upon the inferiority of women, for if they were not inferior, they would cease to enlarge (36). As we walked there, on the winding path to the ruins of the old wine press, I realized I was my lover's mirror. That was why he talked so much and I listened so much. It must become infuriating for him when I cease to listen.

But more, I suspected myself of acting as the mirror for the texts I read. In the stillness of the garden, under a blanket of sun, the narratives of Proust and Kierkegaard and Artaud, and also Nin and Kristeva, found a reflection in me which, like a mirror left under the glare of the sunbeam, must eventually ignite. In the meantime, the language of them all became enlarged.

For this reason, also, Frye's Bible might be assumed to exist before a body of female readership. It is a big surprise for the classical culture, which has absorbed its own protestations, when the mirror cracks and splits the text in two. Much of the material of the texts has leaked into the crack and been absorbed by the body that reposes there.

But all readers act as mirrors to words. It is an inevitable outcome. Words are not people. Heidegger suggests that words are more than words. In *On the Way to Language*, Heidegger says the gods appear to human beings through words, the way the gods appear to you in Nordic mythology only through an oak tree. *The approach of the god took place in Saying itself* (139), he writes. Further, *Saying was in itself the allowing to appear of that which the saying ones saw because it had already looked at them* (139). You can utter words because a god has looked at you. The word, the poetic word, is the gods looking at you, having looked at you.

However this may be meant, there is a transcendent element to language which appears to exist outside both form and content. It may be in voice itself. But when a thought is well articulated, there is a spark that does not escape the reader. That is why the texts are so mesmerizing. Certain texts become more important than the reader's immediate surroundings. Daily life goes into the shadows for a while, and the sun shines on some other reality the reader has begun to glimpse. That other reality has little if anything to do with the subject matter of the text.

On the poet's side, *Is anything more exciting and more dangerous for the poet than his relation to words?* asks Heidegger (141). Is writing not analogous to working with fissionable material? Something radioactive, for which you need gloves?

For this reason lovers give each other words. It is the best gift a lover can receive. The most generous gift. So they write each other letters. The recipient keeps the letters, envelopes and all, and ties them together in a red ribbon. Love letters become precious. They are hidden in special places, like talismans: something with magic powers.

Letters to friends are pale imitations of the love letter. But I clung to those imitations because I missed my friends. In the silence of the southern German evening, when the town had quieted down to television and chocolate desserts, I turned on the lamp in the garret and phrased yet another letter. It is one of the difficult things about being away from home for a whole season: you make a life without your friends and family. You try to go about your daily business in the ensuing emptiness. The only loving face you see is the face of the rose. Even if you have a lover who is frequently at your side. He sits beside you on the sofa in the overstuffed German living room. He sits across from you at your kitchen table, eating your vegetarian soup. He lies beside you on the wooden bed with the straw mattresses at night, and you are aware of the sharply vaulted ceiling like a dagger over your head. Even with a companion such as this, you miss your friends.

So I felt sorry for the old age Proust describes in 'Within a Budding Grove,' a time of life when not even words can give pleasure. Proust's narrator says of himself: *I returned home. I had just spent the New Year's Day of old men, who differ on that day from their juniors, not because people have ceased to give them presents but because they themselves have ceased to believe in the New Year* (1:526). Presents: words. Old people who have lost the pleasure of receiving gifts. *Presents I had received,* he says, *but not that present which alone could bring me pleasure, namely a line from Gilberte* (1:526).

That to live outside of love is a form of 'old age.' But it is not actual old age, only symbolic. To be without the spark that gives its bearer joy is to live in anticipation of death. But to exist in the hopes of 'a line' from a loved one, that is to anticipate life. Perhaps that summer in Germany, it was my sorrow to not be in love. In spite of that, I was in love. It was a condition not directed at a specific person, but something that found its central existence in the rose garden and which was transmitted in the words of innumerable writers.

The same rural people came every day into the town square of Trier and set up their stalls. There they sold vegetables grown on their farms: potatoes, beets, carrots, cabbage. Fresh eggs. Honey. The open-air stalls were integrated into the shopping sector of the town, and the faces behind them became familiar to those whose daily rounds went through the town centre. These merchants existed outside the system of commerce otherwise sanctioned. They did not pay rent on their shops. They did not buy goods wholesale. They simply brought in what was on their property and took money in return. It occurred to me to view the farmers' market merchants as one would other artists operating outside the corporate system. Because in the arts, mainstream works are incorporated: absorbed, distributed, sold by corporations that profit by the exchange. So-called 'outsider art' does not profit and there is often no exchange. Yet the 'goods' are the same, and not infrequently 'outsider' goods are the fresher.

I had come to view the Trier graffitist as a kind of 'farmers' market' of literature. When I rode on the bus, usually packed with those going shopping between the downtown and the suburbs, and with students going to and from school, and twice a day with workers going to and from work, I would end up reading her lines without exactly being aware I was reading them. 'The Pope is a murderer of women!' 'The Catholic church kills!' On occasion there were long paragraphs that took up a whole wall. 'If you think you have escaped Fascism, you are wrong. Fascism is all around us. In your home. In your school, in your church …' When I sat down on a bench in the town centre, tired of walking for so long, I would find myself looking at one of her sentences, perhaps inscribed on the base of a beautiful water fountain, with angels pouring water out of celestial jars.

When I wished to know something more about what I was looking at, I picked up an essay titled 'From Domination to Desire' by Eugene W. Metcalf, Jr. There I came on the following warning: *the designation of the art of certain* people as 'outsider' can be a result (and even, perhaps, a cause) of their social disempowerment. Touristically seeking authentic experience beyond the boundaries of social convention through confrontation with the antimodern Other, some supporters of Outsider Art, it can be argued, transform the mentally disturbed, impoverished, or simply isolated and unusual people into willful, antisocial heroes (218). Even when sympathetic, the interested reader needs to guard against presuming on the object of her interest and thereby misrepresenting her. The only possibility left is to let the quotation, the graph, the song, stand on its own. Without commentary. Metcalf also states the consequence of unintended appropriation: To the extent that they symbolically celebrate the very people they have, by implication, socially disempowered by defining them as deviant, many supporters of Outsider Art romanticize and trivialize the marginalization of these people (218).

There was one thing that held an enchantment for me beyond others. That was the sound of the bells of the great cathedral in central Strasbourg. The cathedral is in itself extremely ornate and gothic, and did not relate to the filigree Catholicism of the building. It was enough for me to say it was magnificent, but not particularly welcoming. The sound of the bells was something else. When the Protestant churches removed the decorations of Catholicism, they left the bells alone. For this reason, I awoke to the ringing of a thousand memories I had not heard since childhood.

The place we stayed in while in Strasbourg was close to the cathedral, and the sounds from the cathedral square could be heard clearly. It was a small apartment in a building at least three hundred years old. The furniture was large for the small space. I opened the tall window looking into the tops of trees and birds vying for space there. Below, the foot traffic of the narrow street bustled. The sun blared into the room. The bells of the great cathedral rang. I could not help remembering the village of my childhood. On Sundays, the bells in all the steeples rang all around town. First one began slowly, sonorously. Then another in another church rang in a tenor clang. A third joined in from the west end, piping an undeclared melody. A fourth church steeple, this one from the Protestant cathedral on the hilltop, bonged over all the others. I listened to this as a child in the window, indefinite feelings welling up in my chest. I looked forward to the ringing of the village churches. Now, so many years later, this magnificent cathedral could not anticipate the thoughts of Protestantism its bells engendered.

I recalled something Proust had written about his recollection of the garden bell at Combray, at the end of his *Remembrance*. It was about how one could create a vantage point out of specific events for one's whole life. Speaking of his life and his memories of it all, he writes that *In this vast dimension which I had not known myself to possess, the date on which I had heard the noise of the garden bell at Combray – that jar-distant noise which nevertheless was within me – was a point from which I might start to make measurements* (III:1106). An artificial point of origin. A theoretical True North in the compass of a 'vast dimension' in which life takes place.

Even while writing his memoirs, Jean Cocteau declares he could never write his memoirs. *If the contents of our memory were able to materialize and roam about,* he writes, *they would clutter up the entire world. How amazing, then, that such a clutter can fit into our brain* (149). Memory were better left as memory. As a kind of dream. As the fictions memories are. Like textual fiction, there are medieval memories, surreal memories, romantic memories, existential ones, dada ones. There are even postmodernist memories. They come in all genres.

Cocteau has categorized the memories of Marcel Proust as dream literature. His explanation is that *The instantaneous nature of dream is such that one can dream in the space of a second the equivalent of Marcel Proust's entire work. For that matter, Proust's work is closer to dream than what is commonly passed off as dream narrative. It has the innumerable cast, the shifting plots, the lack of chronological sequence, the cruelty, the dread, the comical, the precise set design, even the 'all's-well-that-ends-badly'* (149).

Shifting plots, a large cast, lack of chronology, a surreal setting with every item accurately and weirdly in place, a bad ending. These must constitute a dream for Cocteau. It is a tragedy, this Proustian dream. Yet the reader does not realize it is a tragedy until too late.

It is possible that Cocteau's dream narrative is something more sinister. Proust's narrative is a tragedy because it is not a dream, but a hallucination. A waking dream. An episode under the influence of something else. There is a discussion of the relationship between (written) art and magic in Northrop Frye's *The Great Code*. Frye contends that there is a *long-standing connection between the written book and the arts of magic, and the way that the poetic impulse seems to begin in the renunciation of magic, or at least, of its practical aims* (227). The writer takes over from the magician. Perhaps because of the nature of the word – the power of language, as Heidegger might say. The written word, says Frye, *re-creates the past in the present, and gives us, not the familiar remembered thing, but the glittering intensity of the summoned-up hallucination* (227).

Perhaps if one were to see the text as an opiate, the question of the reader as mirror might be answered. Now I understand, the reader might say, why the sun seems so extraordinarily bright, why the roses have such an iridescent hue, why the perfume in the air is so pervasive. Why the whole garden has taken on an air of brilliance under the influence of those voices. Those words. But on such trips, as trips go, there is no guarantee the beautiful dream will not turn into a horrible hallucination. I was reminded of the bad acid trip experienced by an acquaintance in my youth. He saw a beautiful sunflower. The sunflower came closer and closer, and he basked in its fragrance until it started to eat him.

In this context, Frye mentions the phrase *ut pictura poesis*, which came ultimately from Horace: *that poetry is a speaking picture, refers primarily to this quality of voluntary fantasy in writing and reading* (227).

The garden as a trope has come to stand for many things. The rose garden could as easily be a magic garden, the lotus land of the mind, the couch grass on which one meditates. The garden could be the bower of bliss or the den of errors. It could be the room of one's own. It has not escaped my notice that landscape designers speak of outdoor spaces as if they were indoor spaces. The garden is to be landscaped as if it were a house and divided into rooms. In this context, my rose garden was a room of my own. In Virginia Woolf's essay on that room, she allows for many unspeakable moments of imagination. *One goes into the room,* she says, *but the resources of the English language would be much put to the stretch, and whole flights of words would need to wing their way illegitimately into existence before a woman could say what happens when she goes into a room* (91).

Hélène Cixous has echoes in her writing of what Woolf is saying. There is not the language just now to describe the fantasy, the dream, or the hallucination of the woman reading. Instead of being the opportunity to bring the world into being, as Heidegger suggests, language for the woman reading may be a halter. So what goes on in that room is bound to be, as Woolf says, 'illegitimate.' It may be nearest to simply speak of the secret garden.

You too are in the business of eulogizing love (467), Søren Kierkegaard writes in 'The Aesthetic Validity of Marriage,' to a 'friend.' He is defending marriage, perhaps as a kind of garden where human aesthetics may flourish. Yet the spouse as well as the lover are not what they appear to be. All they have done is imitate the true lover: the poet. It is only in verse, in poetry, in poetic language that actual love may be found. *I will not deprive you of what,* he goes on, *indeed, is not yours to own since it belongs to the poet, but of what you have nevertheless appropriated; yet since I, too, have appropriated it, let us be sharers – you get the whole verse, I the last word* (467).

A hierarchy is established: the poet is the source; the philosopher is the perpetrator; the lover is the imitator. In that order.

In light of Kierkegaard's hierarchy, the features of my emotions appeared to me to be sanctioned. It was no longer an aberration that I should prefer the company of my books to that of my lover on certain occasions. Mostly in the mornings, when my papers were spread over the dining table and I was stooped over them, trying to make sense of someone's lost argument. And in the afternoons, when I left all that and retired to the garden. There I could hear birds piping and see butterflies wafting about. There the roses blossomed in red and yellow, and bushes crowded themselves about the stone wall. In that place I had set out to read all of Proust. And at midday, when I went to the campus and did things like sit and chat, photocopy articles, search the library shelves. Daily life had become routine. Only at night, after all that, did I look up and discover something missing. When it was dark and the streets seemed to close in on the house. But that was also when he would appear, as if by magic. He would be driving off the highway at two hundred miles an hour, spinning wheels at the corner and careening up to my door in his diplomatically immune automobile.

That was after the poetry. And after the philosophy. *And then, too, innocence,* says Kierkegaard (467).

But when these three are all combined: what ecstasy.

On October 25, 1871, George Sand wrote in a letter from Nohant to Gustave Flaubert: *Your letters fall on me like a good shower of rain, making all the seeds in the ground start to sprout* (248).

On June 4, 1872, Gustave Flaubert wrote in a letter from Croisset to George Sand: *'How much time can I spare you?' Chère maître! But all my time! Now, then, and ever* (274).

But of course, nothing is as it seems.

In April of 1946, Anaïs Nin wrote a surprising entry in her diary: *Writing for me is not an art. There is no separation between my life and my craft, my work. The form of art is the form of art of my life, and my life is the form of the art* (159). She is her own art.

I suspected it was this thought that lay behind the lure of bohemia. The distress that surrounds middle-class life. The ennui of the *Bürgerin.* The shower-curtain syndrome. That you know you have come so far from the source of your feelings. So far from poetry. You have to make restitution to yourself. You have to perform a ritual that will give you back to yourself. That will remove you from the bureaucracy you are in. *I refuse artificial patterns,* Nin goes on. *Stories do not end. A point of view changes every moment. Reality changes. It is relative* (159). You wish to be free to change your mind. To provide no conclusions.

I had been to a reception in Bonn. It was a party in honour of Indigenous Canadian culture. Like all such occasions in Germany, there was a great deal of formality. The social hierarchy in the air was thick. As usual on such occasions I went through the affair in a kind of out-of-body way. I was not registering things exactly; only fleeting impressions occurred to me, which I might recollect later at greater peace. Receptions are scatter-brained affairs, and it is hard to talk to ten people at once. I vaguely remember posing for a photograph with a university president and a museum curator. I posed for a photo with Tony Hunt since we were the only two Canadians present. It was not my place just then to correct them. Tony Hunt was reaping the benefits of the unending fascination Germans have for the Indigenous people of North America. I was feeling absurd. I guessed Tony felt even more absurd. But he was enjoying himself, and I was only appearing to enjoy myself. That was the difference.

At a party in the evening, Tony was the celebrity of the season. It was a garden party. Food was spread on tables on the grass and wine flowed freely. People had congregated not just in the garden, but on all floors of the house. In every room, another intrigue. Eventually, the inevitable happened. Tony was adjured to play his drums and lead a Kwakwaka'wakw dance. He did. He proceeded to instruct the Germans in the dance. Soon the various guests had covered themselves with blankets and were dancing in a circle.

I looked on with curiosity. This sort of thing could never happen in Canada, could it? Tony was laughing. I think both he and I were as fascinated with the Germans as they were with him.

The party would go on till morning. By the time of the dance, I knew things would get increasingly bizarre. A social orgy would eventually take place. People would be walking around in one another's clothes. They would be paired and tripled up in rooms. I quietly removed myself. I went out the front door and closed the heavy contraption behind me.

I wanted to look at the Rhine River in the moonlight. I found my way to the riverbank by taxi. It was past midnight. The town of Bonn was closed for the night. Streets were empty. I went past the main building of the university and into the adjacent park. There was the water, flowing softly like a silken ribbon. Not as large a river as I always imagined it to be.

The errand I had to the Rhine was private. Something lodged in family memory. Like hundreds of other Scandinavians, my father went to Germany to study. He supported his university career by taking stand-on roles in the German Opera. While the melodramatic tragedies of the European imagination acted themselves out hyper-realistically on the German stage, my father stood in the background, holding a spear.

I sat down on a riverside bench. It was at a conjunction of street, park, and river. There was an indeterminacy about the setting. It was hard to tell where one began and the other ended. Facing one way, there was the river. Facing another, there was a street crossing. An empty street. The light of a street lamp shone on the intersection the way the moon shone on the water. So much of northern culture was bound up in that river. Over the centuries, the Rhine has taken on a heavy load of human emotion: tragedy, nostalgia, horror, sentiment. The water was thick with it all. By now, the Rhine was so polluted with the past that it was unsafe for use.

On the other side, the empty street at night lay there, still wet from an earlier rain. I thought of a comment by Frederic Jameson in *Postmodernism*. In the chapter on 'Video,' he writes that *The urban street crossing, to begin with, is a kind of degraded space* (92). A place, perhaps, where establishment culture, washing past at my feet, may begin to 'come loose from its moorings.' To Jameson, the urban street *begins faintly to project the abstraction of an empty stage, a place of the Event, a bounded space in which something may happen and before which one waits in formal anticipation* (92).

For that reason, you find yourself transfixed by the window at night. You are looking at the street. Any moment now, the play may start. It will be a dark production. Sordid, perhaps. Inevitably, *the event fails to materialize and neither of the lovers appears at the rendezvous* (92).

It occurred to me in this summer of reading that the whole idea of 'reading' is suspect. We think that to read is to sit down with a book, scan its pages word for word, finish it, and put it away. That is a consumer model of reading, and that is the one we have. Then we make an industry of the commentaries we produce about the book we have consumed. The market economy relies on this idea of the reader as consumer, in order that we may go and purchase another book, and then another. So we can say 'I have read that book,' and it will be equivalent to saying ' I have been to the Andes' or 'I have seen India.' The reader as tourist.

But if you care about a book, you will be 'reading' it in a very different way. I have known people to smell their books. A new book, just off the press, smells glossy, fresh. An old book, taken off a used bookshop shelf, has the smell of previous readers on it. The smell of the rooms it has been in. I have known people to get emotionally involved in the size and shape of the print, the size of the pages, the colour of the pages and nature of the binding. It is a personal matter. I have known people to carry a book with them wherever they go. They cannot leave the book behind: it is too meaningful a possession. There is too much of themselves in the volume to let it stay behind. I knew a woman who carried a book of poems in her purse always. When she felt depressed, which happened often, she took out the little book and read a poem for consolation. The book as best friend. I knew a man who spent his life reading one work. He spent ten or fifteen minutes every night before sleep reading a bit of Robert Musil. It was like a companion through his life, one whom he would not give up. At least here, he seemed to say, is a soul mate, an intelligent man on whom I can rely. The book that holds the world together. People will give a book to a child or a friend. It is more than gift: it is an inspiration. A gesture. The gift of soil, something that grows with time and does not get used up. This carrying a book around, this sleeping with a book, giving a book to another, finding solace in a book: these are all ways of reading. It is not in a publishing company's best interests to publish lasting classics. For such a book will be too satisfying and the reader will not rush back for another hit immediately.

For me, the summer I spent in Trier was intimately wound up with my reading of Marcel Proust. In retrospect I can see why. In the three volumes of *Remembrance of Things Past*, I had, in fact, a full summer's reading. There was so much there. I knew the summer would be confusing and discordant. I knew I would be treading the minefields of a difficult love relationship. I knew the work I was doing would be frustrating. I knew my life would be disrupted socially and emotionally. I would be without family and friends.

Without a comforting person to turn to. Proust's narrative would then provide me with a consistency I could string the discordant days on, and it would feel like I had a place from which to measure all other activity.

So I cannot think of my little rose garden without those volumes there. The heavily peopled world of an era gone by. The configurations of a ''high society' that no longer existed. The 'war' between that society and 'bohemians' of the day. The voice that runs through a thousand social situations and holds them in place. Then, this narrative becomes a pool into which other narratives are cast and their reflections are clear.

The relationship, it seemed to me, between writer and reader is reciprocated when the reader is not simply a consumer. At the end of the third volume of *Remembrance*, Marcel Proust, the narrator, has determined that he will now write the book that has, at the point of reading, already been written. He has a fully formed sense of this 'book' he will write, which he has been preparing for all his life. He has a clear sense of the reader as well. *It would be inaccurate,* he writes, *even to say I thought of those who would read it as 'my' readers. For it seemed to me that they would not be 'my' readers but the readers of their own selves, my book being merely a sort of magnifying glass like those which the optician at Combray used to offer his customers* (III:1089).

If the reader can be a mirror, the book may very well be a magnifying glass.

Proust explains: *it would be my book, but with its help I would furnish them with the means of reading what lay inside themselves* (III:1089). The writer does not need to construct a how-to book or a narrative on psychology or sociology or therapy. The writer just needs to write, and the reader, if she is a good reader, will find herself in it. The text will be the land of Oz.

On the writer's side, Proust is not at pains to describe his realizations. Why the writer becomes so involved with the task of writing that all of society fades in importance. He says he sometimes had thought life worth living as he went about in society. But now that he had determined to write his book, it was different. *How much more worth living did it appear to me now, now that I seemed to see that this life that we live in half-darkness can be illumined, this life that at every moment we distort can be restored to its true pristine shape, that a*

life, in short, can be realized within the confines of a book! (III:1088) He has not lived until he has written about his life. *How happy would he be, I thought, the man who had the power to write such a book!* (III:1088) For while you may be happy in your life, your happiness cannot compare with the happiness of the writer who manages to execute his work.

As I sat in the sun, the summer having grown late and the sun a bit lower in the sky, I would see this is only one half of the story. Proust is iterating a classical notion: the elevation of the classical genius. The *Übermensch*, in a sense, for the artist rises above the commonality of human life and renders it all godlike. The artist is able to lend meaning to the life of the reader the way god makes the believer's life meaningful. But this is a romantic idea.

If a woman were to talk about her relationship to her creativity, I wondered, would it be different? What would a woman writer say about this? Would she be intoxicated with the realization that she had the power to dignify her reader's life? To put a magnifying glass to existence and allow us to see it for what it 'really is'? I thought of Anaïs Nin, whose journals are quite articulate on this subject. And in fact, what she says is surprising. In a letter to Leo Lerman, in December of 1946, she writes in response to Lerman's request for a short autobiography: *I see myself and my life each day differently. What can I say?*

The facts lie. I have been Don Quixote, always creating a world of my own. I am all the women in the novels, yet still another not in the novels.

It took me more than sixty diary volumes until now to tell about my life. Like Oscar Wilde I put only my art into my work and my genius into my life. My life is not possible to tell. I change every day, change my patterns, my concepts, my interpretations. I am a series of moods and sensations. I play a thousand roles. I weep when I find others play them for me. My real self is unknown. My work is merely an essence of this vast and deep adventure. I create a myth and a legend, a lie, a fairy tale, a magical world, and one that collapses every day and makes me feel like going the way of Virginia Woolf. I have tried to be not neurotic, not romantic, not destructive, but may be all of these disguises (198).

Nin knows what a chimera a piece of writing may be. What a changeable thing a life is. How subject to fluctuations of mood and temperament. What an illusory thing personal identity can be. How unattainable meaning is. What inaccuracies lurk in every portrait, especially self-portrait.

It is impossible to make my portrait because of my mobility, she writes. *I am not photogenic because of my mobility. Peace, serenity, and integration are unknown to me. My familiar climate is anxiety* (198). No rose garden here. No rest.

I write as I breathe, naturally, flowingly, spontaneously, of an overflow, not as a substitute for life. I am more interested in human beings than in writing, more interested in lovemaking than in writing, more interested in living than in writing. More interested in becoming a work of art than in creating one. I am more interesting than what I write (198–199).

How text and life become integrated. How one cannot exist without the other. And how does Proust end his great narrative? He is afraid he will have become too weak for the task: that he will have described human beings as though they were giants. *Like giants plunged into the years* (III:1107). The writer as distortionist.

And what does Antonin Artaud say on the subject? *I would like to write a Book which would drive men mad, which would be like an open door leading them where they would never have consented to go, in short, a door that opens into reality* (59). The arena in which we conduct our lives is not reality. It is a fabrication of our insanities. And even though *all writing is garbage* and all writers are pigs (85), the text is still more real than life.

When I knew I was leaving Germany, and I would not be seeing my lover again for a long time, if ever, I reflected on the haphazard and crazy time we had just spent. Our inconclusive and tense discussions. Evenings in the living room, talking, the lights low, the streets silent. The shutters down. Nights in the cramped bedroom, when I would look over, thinking he was asleep, and I would see his eyes open, staring into the room. The few amicable, if not joyful, hours in Strasbourg. Walking down the street, finding ourselves in the midst of a street parade. Clowns and jesters jumping onto one another's shoulders, yelling at the populace. Stopping every few feet to put on a show. Crowds gathering. Gypsies with beggar bowls and half-naked children.

We would go back to the long-distance phone calls. The hurried visits from him when he could squeeze a few days into his schedule on a mission of diplomacy to North America. The off-hours ringing he would succumb to, when he had too much to drink after a social event for the embassy and came home feeling alone. It was a routine we had become accustomed to. Every morning at nine, my phone rang. For him it was the end of the day. The embassy was closed up for the day and he was the last to leave. My day was just starting. But I knew that after the summer it would not take too long before those communications would grow scarce. No doubt he had seen enough. He could not move me more than this. Such matters are not in our control. He knew that. We both knew that.

He left me at the airport when I went in to catch my plane. I do not remember anything about our parting. I was concerned to get away, to make my date with the airplane.

On the return flight, I happened to be on the same airplane as Tony Hunt, the Haida artist from Vancouver Island who played his drums for the guests at the party in Bonn. When we got to Vancouver, we stopped at the bar and clinked a glass of beer together before heading on. We had a laugh. This Indigenous man was no mere drum player. This was a man of several residences and automobiles, who travelled with his cellular phone, who had offices in Victoria and Qualicum Beach, who was fully technologized and on the Information Superhighway.

Welcome back, we said.

I wanted to leave her, because I knew that by carrying on I should gain nothing (III:400), says Marcel about Albertine. He finds himself pitched between boredom and pain. The pain of jealousy and the boredom of the bourgeoisie. I thought it is impossible to know what might be gained by staying or leaving. Before he left, on our last night in Frankfurt, my lover looked at me and I saw the uncertainty there. His dark eyes were neither sad nor happy, furious nor relieved. They were all those at once. He just sat and looked at me for a long time. The city quieted down outside the window behind him. The noise of automobiles and airplanes lessened. I was trying to read his face as though it were a book. It had been a good evening. We were close. The tension usually there, an expression I was used to, was gone. I thought of the books I had been reading one last time. My lover's face. A line by Marcel Proust: *If there had been any happiness in it, it could not last* (III:400).

WORKS CITED

Artaud, Antonin. *Antonin Artaud, Selected Writings*. Ed. Susan Sontag. Trans. Helen Weaver. Los Angeles: University of California Press, 1988.

Cardinal, Roger: 'Toward an Outsider Aesthetic,' in *The Artist Outsider: Creativity and the Boundaries Of Culture*. Ed. Michael D. Hall and Eugene W. Metcalf, Jr. London: Smithsonian Institution Press, 1994. 20–44.

Cixous, Hélène and Catherine Clément. *The Newly Born Woman*. Trans. Betsy Wing. *Theory and History of Literature*, Vol. 24. Minneapolis: University of Minnesota Press, 1986.

Cocteau, Jean. *Diary of an Unknown*. Trans. Jesse Browner. New York: Paragon House, 1991.

Fish, Stanley. *Doing What Comes Naturally: Change, Rhetoric and the Practice of Theory in Literary and Legal Studies*. London: Duke University Press, 1989.

Frye, Northrop. *The Great Code: The Bible and Literature*. Toronto: Academic Press Canada, 1983.

Heidegger, Martin. *On the Way to Language*. Trans. Peter D. Hertz. San Francisco: Harper Collins, 1982.

Howe, Susan. *My Emily Dickinson*. Berkeley: North Atlantic Books, 1985.

Hutcheon, Linda. *Narcissistic Narrative: The Metafictional Paradox*. London: Methuen, 1984.

Jameson, Fredric. *Postmodernism, or, The Cultural Logic of Late Capitalism*. Durham: Duke University Press, 1993.

Kierkegaard, Søren. *Either/Or: A Fragment of Life*. Ed. Victor Eremita. Trans. Alastair Hannay. London: Penguin Books, 1992.

Kristeva, Julia. *Black Sun, Depression and Melancholia*. Trans. Leon S. Roudiez. New York: Columbia University Press, 1989.

———. *Desire in Language: A Semiotic Approach to Literature and Art*. Ed. Leon S. Roudiez. Trans. Thomas Gora, Alice Jardine, and Leon S. Roudiez. New York: Columbia University Press, 1980 .

Mariani, Philomena, ed. *Critical Fictions: The Politics of Imaginative Writing*. Dia Center for the Arts, Discussions in Contemporary Culture, Number 7. Seattle: Bay Press, 1991.

Metcalf Jr., Eugene W. 'From Domination to Desire: Insiders and Outsider Art.' In *The Artist Outsider: Creativity and the Boundaries of Culture*. Ed. Michael D. Hall and Eugene W. Metcalfe, Jr. London: Smithsonian Institution Press, 1994. 212–228.

Nin, Anaïs. *The Journals of Anaïs Nin, 1944–1947*. Vol. 4. Ed. Gunther Stuhlmann. London: Quartet Books, 1979 .

Proust, Marcel. 'On Reading.' Trans. John Sturrock. London: Penguin/Syrens, 1994.

———. *Remembrance of Things Past*. 3 Vols. Trans. C. K. Scott Moncrieff, Terence Kilmartin, and Andreas Mayor. London: Penguin Books, 1989.

Sand, George and Gustave Flaubert. *Flaubert–Sand: The Correspondence*. Trans. Francis Steegmuller and Barbara Bray. Based on the edition by Alphonse Jacobs. London: Harper Collins, 1993.

Steiner, George. *Nostalgia for the Absolute*. Toronto: House of Anansi, 1997.

Woolf, Virginia. *A Room of One's Own*. London: Harcourt Brace Jovanovich, 1957.

NIGHT TRAIN
TO NYKØBING

Dear Dear Jan. But this is not the greeting that says what I want to say. Inside every greeting there is also a farewell. I try to wrest the good-bye out of the words that mean to greet him. Fully, without reservation. But the word will not go. The farewell inside is waiting to spring out.

Like a cougar. The cougars here have become many. They lurk in the trees. People who pass underneath are suddenly pounced on, taken by surprise. *The Globe and Mail* yesterday listed every cougar attack in British Columbia in the last ten years. They say attacks are becoming more common. The cougar is not friendly. They say you must look it in the eye. You must fight back because the cougar has only one goal. To kill.

Every single household cat in my neighbourhood has been killed by a cougar or a bobcat or a lynx. The wild cats prowl the bush behind us and crouch in empty lots still wooded. They prey on the small cats that wander out of doors. At least sixty cats are gone, a kind of ethnic cleansing performed by wild cats on domestic cats.

When I lived in the Okanagan Valley, I had two white cats named Winnie and Pooh. Pooh was eaten by a coyote, or so I thought. Now I think it may have been a cougar. Later I sold Winnie for a hundred and ten thousand dollars to some Kabalarians who had a belief in numbers.

I changed my seat in the first-class compartment so the station would not go out of view when we left. Riding backward, I could see the red brick platform elongate itself as we pulled away. He stood there still as a statue, the man I had just recently risen out of bed with. Hands in pockets, face of stone. The touch of his fingers was still on my breasts. The taste of his kiss. And yet the train was heading out of Skovshoved Station, severing us. Soon I would see nothing but wheat fields and straw-thatched farms.

My aunt Bodil stood in the hallway in her transparent nylon underpants and white brassiere. She was applying cream to her face in front of the mirror. Her bare feet on the cool parquet floor by the front door. I told her I was coming home again. I was moving back to Copenhagen from Vancouver.

The long sojourn was over now that Quebec was going. I said I had come to identify with the Québecois, and when they seceded, I would be without a country again. It was folly to go from one small country to just another small country. To exchange all of Europe, with the European Union, for a paltry bit of the Canada I used to know. I said it was madness to make such a bad exchange.

The heat rises from the ground like an old saying we no longer want to hear. Sunshine fills the air to bursting. I want to drown in that yellow heat. Lie on my deck naked, exposing myself to the harmful rays. I wonder how the day will pass. Why time has become so slow. Nothing stirs. The birds are strangely silent. This morning when I flung open the door to the garden, no birdsong greeted me. Only once did I hear an eagle call from a treetop in the nearby wood. An announcement of carrion, perhaps. A carrion call.

Alain Robbe-Grillet, in *For a New Novel,* says the world has only *one certain quality: the simple fact that it is there. An explanation, whatever it may be, can only be in excess…* That we imagine everything. That *Drowned in the depth of things, man ultimately no longer even perceives them.* How we colour the world with our own desires and aspirations. Everything is contaminated with our longings. Our fears. We invest ourselves in everything we see. *It is, quite simply.*

I think of how I have coloured the man at Skovshoved Station, who waited while my train pulled out, with everything I wanted to find in him. That it is impossible to know someone for who he really is. He is always an image of my desire.

Bodil had a small device for rolling her own Prince cigarettes. She pressed the tobacco into a tiny ditch in the mechanism and attached an empty roll of cigarette paper to the end of it. The lid would close and she pushed the tobacco into the empty cylinder of paper. She sat down in the morning with a small tray on her lap, containing tobacco, empty cigarette paper rolls, and the red plastic shuttle. There she sat filling cigarette after cigarette, the day's supply, while the coffee went cold in her cup. I sat down opposite her and watched.

It was her meditative moment. With these scraps of tobacco, she contemplated her family and how she had lost them one by one. How few of us were left. I think she wanted to burn up her sad thoughts. To smoke them out.

From her small apartment in Vanløse, I could hear the noisemakers at eight. The trucks and cleaners and garbage collectors and sidewalk scrapers. A man in a blue cotton uniform that resembled a Maoist pyjama set, with a cap on his head, stood across the street with an assortment of brooms and pans. He was cleaning the sidewalk. Down the street the bicycles had begun.

Martin Andersen Nexø was a Danish writer who died in the 1950s. He wrote the novel *Pelle Erobreren*, which was made into the movie *Pelle the Conqueror*. Nexø was a communist. He moved from Denmark to East Germany and lived out his days there. When I came back, he was posthumously made honorary citizen of his birth town, which celebrated its six hundred and fiftieth birthday. It took the Danish authorities over thirty years to get over their author's politics. Or was it just the very idea of preferring East Germany to little Denmark?

In time, I thought, the oddest absurdities may be forgiven. Time always seems to be the conqueror.

Above the brown leather sofa in Bodil's flat was an oil painting. The picture showed an old Danish farmstead on the island of Fyn. There was a courtyard of cobblestone. The stuccoed walls were braced by wooden beams. The straw on the roof was held down by crossbeams at the top. The houses were small and low. This was my great-great-grandfather's farm, when he was a landowner, she said. The old man had a penchant for gambling, but he was not good at it. Because of his gambling, our family lost the farm and went from landowning class to labour class in one generation.

I said we would buy it back. Now that I had returned from Canada, we would go and buy the old farm back and return it to the family. Then we could also say time had conquered that adversity. She looked skeptical. I think she did not believe me. She took some deep, slow drags from her cigarette, and her eyes were fast on me, languorous, almost dreaming.

Yet I had not actually returned, for that was still only a plan. Something in the cards. Written in the tea leaves. Something I saw in the face of the man at Skovshoved Station. His was a beautiful face and in it I could read a volume. Several volumes. Something that said I was about to return. They were penetrating eyes. It was the man who waited with me for the train. The one who held me and I him. The one I would not let go of.

I still had to go back to British Columbia. The house I had constructed was still there. Everything I desired to keep from my life was there, where I left it. A few memories. Pictures, wood carvings, photographs. Piano. Guitar, dulcimer. Fireplace, iron bedstead, empty. They were all there, the roses and hydrangeas, azaleas, and rhododendrons. The hemlocks and maples and cedars still wafted in the breeze off the sea. But somehow the taste of it all was not there. The flavour that kept me happy before was lost. I could not find it.

It occurred to me to wonder if you can lose a happiness because another, greater happiness has supplanted it. Can we not have two happinesses at the same time? Is joy such a jealous emotion that it will not be shared? If so, then the man at the station – whose hair was just beginning to turn white, whose eyes crinkled when he smiled, whose arm I still felt around me – that man had taken too much with him. I did not know what I was leaving behind as I watched him recede farther and farther away on the platform, the hum of the train engine in my ears, the scratch of the steel rails underneath.

No doubt after the death of my mother, I became depressed. Nothing deep or profound, but enough to take away my joys. The little things that make us happy in a day. A carnation in a blue vase, perhaps. Watching *Citizen Kane* again. Or dressing up in red silk so loud that heads turn. Or even a flute sonata or a night at the jazz club. Whatever might have put a happy edge on me before was suddenly gone. Then the man at the station, the one I left there, walked into my life and the colour of things altered.

Perhaps it was a thought in the back of my mind as I changed my seat and put a bottle of water on the table in front of me. That he too was dangerous. If losing him meant losing more than what I had already lost. I was led to wonder how deep a depression needs to get before that is no longer what loss is called. And did we both know this about each other?

But even then, I remembered in an unclear way, like you vaguely recall a dream you had, that the home I constructed in British Columbia was the one thing that did give me happiness. A quiet happiness, a whisper without agitation. The sound of a finch or kingfisher or an eagle. The sight of a seal. The flowering of a rose. The sun in the morning. That gave me a very quiet joy, so silent I almost missed it. And then it would all still be there.

So dearest Jan, I begin a hundred times. The beginning is everywhere, like his image. His voice. Annie Dillard says in her book *The Writing Life* that *A writer looking for subjects inquires not after what he loves best, but after what he alone loves at all.* That is how I know he will be standing there for as long as I am writing this. I will continue to see his sad face through the murky train window as we wait to depart. He will walk up to the window and put his hand against the glass where I put mine. Our palms will touch through the glass, as they did that day. The feel of the cold glass will remain on my hand long after.

It is not because I prefer to write about him. To have him in my words like a ghost in my language. A spirit in my alphabet. Not because I choose to. But because he has to be there. As necessarily as there has to be air. As I have to breathe. Without him there, I have no words at all.

My beautiful cousin Kari looked at me across the table. Her long, dark hair spread out from her shoulders. Her hazel-brown eyes focused intently, wide, on me. Yet not on me, but through me. As if I had become the site for surprising sorrows. Her suntanned arms and neck, her long, slender limbs alternately stood and sat restlessly. Around us were scores of posters and prints and objects from the Copenhagen underground. Her garret apartment looked out over other garret apartments, a line of them holding up the horizon.

She showed me her picture. When her daughter Asa was born, the picture she ordered taken. Kari's body lay naked on the floor, spread to the two midwives bending over her. Her face turned sideways in a pain that resembled ecstasy. Her daughter Asa's new head had just emerged in the birthing process. A woman with two heads, one of which was her little daughter's.

I pace the floor. I cannot help the thoughts that lie in the pit of my chest. That I can tell I am going. Like a nomad, I pick up my blanket one more time and head for the sky. The blanket is an old Navajo blanket my mother left me. She had it nailed up on her living room wall. Two square human figures surrounded by a bed of red, ochre, and pale violet stripes. A large rug that covered the whole wall. This is the one I take with me now. When I return to him, the one I cannot let go of. I will be there with my mother's Navajo blanket. I have come back home with my only possession.

When the telephone rings at three in the morning, it is as if I am expecting it. Even while asleep, I expect the ring that comes unexpectedly. And he is in a phone booth in Oslo, Norway. I can hear the din of traffic, the city noise. It is noon and I cannot tell what the weather is. I cannot hear any rain. He tells me his love. I hear his words reverberate across the wires. And I am tongue-tied in my bed, wishing to speak, unable to. When the call is over, the silence of the night opens its large mouth. And he, if it is raining, is walking away from the booth, his white trench coat flapping in the wet gust.

Morten, my aunt Trine's husband, stands barefoot in the water of Roskildefjord. He has rolled up his loose, black pants with old suspenders to keep them up. His small, shaggy dog wades in and immerses its stomach in the cold sea. Roskilde-fjord beach goes on in a stretch of grey sand and pebbles, laced with the pale green brush of the fields. The water is the colour of pewter, glinting like chrome where the sun hits it. Small waves shiver in the fjord, sliced occasionally by a slow sailboat. Morten stands still in the water, facing the outer sea. His long, curved pipe still in his mouth, his left hand supporting the bowl, his now old face still in contemplation. Perhaps he is thinking of himself as suddenly adrift. That when the railroad for which he worked for the last thirty-five years suddenly laid him off, he was without his moorings. He was set adrift. His wife, Trine, stands on the beach in her brown sandals, her navy skirt and blouse, arms on each side, and watches him. She knows he has come loose from his anchor.

The Canadian dawn continues its russet flavour into the morning, the white morning. Tall cedars stand still as if petrified. As if waiting. Not a shred of wind. All seems locked in anticipation. We hardly dare breathe.

I think of him at the station. As he looked back at me through the glass, feet firmly planted on the red brick. His face was clear, but had an edge of something sad. He too was still, as if turned to stone. I wonder now, did we know this about each other? What we know now.

Because of my travelling, I was not on the same schedule as my Aunt Bodil. I woke up at five, the streets outside still dark. I got out of the small, single bed she set up for me in the spare room, out from between the two duvets she lent me. The morning air came in through the open window. I put my slippers on and went into her kitchen. She was asleep in the outer room. I could hear her deep breathing. I quietly scrounged around for filters and coffee beans, made a pot of coffee, and sat down on a stool in the corner to drink it. A community newspaper lay on the side tray. I read the community news. Letters from the neighbourhood youths. *We teenagers in Vanløse*, said the letter, *are bored to tears.*

He and I engaged ourselves to each other over the telephone. After. As if we had not realized what lay inside us. It was like the sound of thunder that comes after a flash of lightning. A sound that carries enormous distances.

That we had been caught in a current we could not get out of. That we were bound to spiral forward and come to an abrupt resting place. A crash of some kind. An explosion. He spoke calmly on the phone, but he was not calm. *If we do this,* he warned me, *I will be branded a criminal.*

My cousin Kari lived in the artists' quarter of Copenhagen. Rows of brick apartments with tight, sharp gables and high roofs lined the neighbourhood. From one gable, you had a view of the next, in succession, one after another. Kari's partner, Anders, had moved to a roof apartment across the street on one side. Her eighteen-year-old son, Njord, had moved to a gable flat on the other side. It was the quarter where all the streets bore Icelandic names. *Gunløgsgade. Njalsgade. Islandsbrygge.* When she looked at me across the room, her big eyes had something wild in them. *Why do they leave you like that?* she was asking. Her son and husband. The three of them were able to see one another through the windows of their three apartments, Kari in the middle.

I insist writers should expose themselves to contradictions, Christa Wolf says in *The Fourth Dimension.* I think it is impossible not to. The way time itself is contradictory. Whenever I look at my watch in British Columbia, I calculate what time it is in Oslo, Norway. What time it is in Copenhagen, Denmark. I live in more than one time zone. They contradict each other. It is both day and night for me. Morning and evening. I am going to work and coming home from work at the same time. My feet trace the fall dust on the street, tiny stones exploding into my shoes as I walk. My feet can feel the pain of glass like shards pressing against them, my toes facing opposite directions at once.

The red brick of the *perron* had long since receded from view. Perhaps he was now ascending the stairs to the street. Perhaps he was now in the garden, seated in the sun. *I am going to go to the garden,* he told me, *once you are gone. I am going to go there and just sit.*

Because it was a first-class compartment on the train, there was free coffee, mineral water, and Tuborg beer in the corner. We could take a drink to our tables. A brown-haired woman in a flowered, cotton dress came into the compartment. She took a beer, a glass, sat down at a table and lit a cigarette. She smoked and drank for ten minutes or so, looking angrily out the window at the landscape of Fyn. Then she stood up and came over to me. *I left my husband at Skovshoved and am meeting my blind mother in Nykøbing*, she said to me. *I seem to be ten crowns short for my fare. Could you give me ten crowns?*

I could see she was riding the rails. One of the destitute who had taken up sponging in first class. Perhaps she rode back and forth all night. *No*, I told her. *I just ran out of everything myself.*

The red-haired doctor had already written the woman's schedule. She sat in his office restlessly, then asked if she could phone her husband. Ten minutes later she returned sobbing. *I'm not going to have an abortion after all*, she wept, gathered her purse and jacket, and went out. The red-haired doctor went out slowly after her. She was standing by the elevator, waiting to go out again into the sooty streets outside Copenhagen Hospital. He went up to her. *Listen*, he said gently, *you are always welcome back here. There is no stigma to your coming back.*

I moved to Edmonton for the winter months to teach classes at the university. Since there was no work to be had in the mountains of British Columbia, it was necessary to go. I had a small flat in the university district that was more like a thoroughfare than a home. People came and went in my apartment. Mealtimes were chaotic and my daily schedule fluctuated wildly.

With my last bit of cash, I bought an essay by Clarice Lispector called *The Stream of Life* at my friend Jodey's bookstore. It was a Tuesday afternoon, warm and windy. The grit off the streets blew in my face when I walked to the bookstore. The air was penetrated by petroleum fumes, car exhaust, and very dry, cream-coloured dust. I took the small book home and began to read it. I saw that Clarice Lispector was using the language of ecstasy to talk about being free from love. No longer in love. To fill herself with her own life instead.

I come from the hell of love, but now I am free of you, she writes. The sunshine filled the small room of my flat, and the day was slowly ending. I found suddenly I envied Lispector. I envied her for her freedom. I who was captive.

My Aunt Bodil and I walked back from the Vanløse train station. It was dark already. Lights were on in the small brick houses. The narrow streets were deserted. Only the thoroughfare of Jernbanevej was busy, buses, cyclists, last-minute pedestrians heading home. We came to the yellow brick apartment buildings where she lived. Across the street from her door, we could hear shouting from an open window. A man and a woman argued at the top of their lungs. They were hitting each other, shouting in pain. There were crashing sounds, things breaking.

We stopped on the sidewalk. All about, people had come out onto their balconies to see what was going on. People stuck their heads out of open windows, craning their necks in the direction of the shouting. Some had come outside and stood on the sidewalk in front of the building, smoking cigarettes. As if they were all waiting for something.

We don't have much time, Bodil said to me with quiet determination, *so let's get straight to the point. Tell me about your love life now.* We were sitting on her small balcony facing the park. Below us was the green grass a gardener tended daily in his dark blue, cotton, Maoist uniform. The flower beds were fresh and colourful. Swing sets and picnic tables and a barbecue pit were there, but no one was using them. Farther away, a neat row of clotheslines with clothes hanging to dry. The view of the small park was framed by a series of potted geraniums on the handrail of her balcony. Between us we had a small table, where she had put rye bread and shrimp and Carlsberg beer. It was afternoon.

Her question came as a surprise. I was trying to slake my thirst with a Danish beer. It was very hot. I was seated in the sun, and I could feel a tired drop of sweat forming on my forehead.

In an essay called 'On Writing,' Eudora Welty says that *We do need to bring to our writing, over and over again, all the abundance we possess.* The excess of our lives. That which flows over. That *jouissance.* I could not help thinking that the abundance of my life was circling him. The one at the station. That bringing my own abundance up in what I write was to bring him into the writing. And it was such a quiet excess. The way he stood so still, as if being pulled by a distant question. A question he could hardly hear, but was trying to listen to beyond the din of squealing train engines and conductors' whistles.

He imposed a silence on us. He said we must not be seen to talk until it was all over. We must leave no voice prints, no fingerprints, no electronic trail. Until it was over.

We had spoken daily for weeks. Mailed each other letters daily, twice a day, three times. *This conversation is really hard to end*, he said on the telephone. It was the last time we talked before our silence. Five in the morning. The streets were wet and glistened in the yellow light of street lamps in the dark. Lights of the city pinpointed everywhere.

I hung up the phone and looked around the messy room in my flat. I had been too preoccupied to put things away. Papers, magazines, letters, briefcases, and shoes everywhere. A dark, empty feeling had descended. I thought I would have tears, but there was nothing. A stony silence in my chest. And anger. I discovered I was angry.

The image of Thérèse Raquin kept appearing in my mind. At odd moments, in the mornings as dawn broke, in the afternoons as the sun baked the room. Not the face of Thérèse Raquin, which does not exist, but of some actress who played the part in a movie adaptation. Émile Zola's story of two lovers who commit a crime in order to be able to be together. She knows when her lover is committing the crime, when he is drowning her husband. She does not want it to happen, but she does not stop him. She sees it happen and is upset, but she is paralyzed. When it is over, she tries to save the drowned man. When she cannot she becomes hysterical. Her lover is pleased with her reaction. He finds it a convincing performance. But it is not a performance. She has agreed to something she does not want to see happen. She wants something to happen she knows she cannot live with once it has taken place. Her terrified, paralyzed eyes and hands are what I keep seeing. The hands that instinctively move toward the eyes but never succeed in covering them.

I went back to the town I lived in as a child. The town of Rungsted, north of Copenhagen on the coast. I took my Aunt Bodil with me so I could show her the house. The one we lived in, with the tower on it where I found myself dreaming about my future, looking over the steep roofs of the village. We took the forty-minute train ride and got off at Rungsted Station. When we emerged from the red brick *perron* and found ourselves on the street, I discovered I no longer remembered which direction my old neighbourhood was.

We wandered the streets for a while, hoping to run into the house by accident. Whenever we passed a big white stone house, she pointed at it and asked if this might be it. I always had to say no, the tower is missing or the balcony is wrong or the front door was not like that. And always the stained glass window was missing, the big green glass map of Greenland. It was hot. Our feet were tired and sore. We were getting lethargic from the heat. In the end we gave up the search. We made our way to Rungsted Kro, a tavern that had been there for over a hundred years, and sat down in the shade outside. We had a cold beer and a sandwich. It occurred to me that maybe one should not retrace one's steps anyway. That time can only move forward. Time is an arrow. Once it is launched, it cannot turn and go back. An arrow cannot change its destined direction. All it can do is helplessly strike its target.

Let us do something instead that I could not do when we lived here, I suggested. *Let us visit Rungstedlund.* The home of Karen Blixen, which was just around the corner. Because when I was her neighbour, Isak Dinesen was still alive. I could not go and knock on her door then. Now that she was dead, the house was open to the public. In death, she was finally accessible.

Dear Jan. All the aborted letters I can no longer send him. They pile up in my mind like abandoned infants on an island. Suddenly there is no reader. I write into a void where there is no gaze. The milky fog piles in over the town of Edmonton, and I can see nothing but white outside my window. Any sound I might make will be muffled and unheard.

Staring into the fog, I understood I was experiencing our silence in a way we had not intended. As willful cruelty. I found myself wanting my revenge on him. That because I was in love, I wanted revenge.

At that Danish school I attended, all the girls were rounded up into the auditorium. We were told to sit quietly and listen. The village doctor came in to talk to us. He said we must be realistic. It would do us no good to have our heads in the clouds. We must have our wits about us. He took out some rubber contraptions and a diagram of the female reproductive system. He proceeded to show us how to insert a female condom. I was fifteen years old then. I remember paying very close attention. I was not sure exactly how the sheet of rubber was meant to fit, but I memorized every word he said. It seemed very important just then. A matter of life and death to understand what he was saying. *You know perfectly well,* the doctor was telling us, *that men will be men. Men will always be men. Your job is to look after yourselves.*

I knew what I would do in the loneliness of his disappearance. I would take the airplane back to British Columbia. Go to my home in the hills above the water. Build a fire and listen to the rain fall on the roof and the windows. Feel the warmth of the fire spreading all over the room while water poured from the sky outside.

If I thought your affection for me was waning, I would be wild with jealousy, he said. *I would go wild.*

The department I worked for at the university in Edmonton was large. There were over sixty faculty members, and although there was a concerted effort to hire women, two thirds of the department still consisted of men.

There was a party for everyone the day after my last conversation with my lover. I did not know what to do with my newly realized anger. There was no one to send it to. Instead I found myself acting it out. I dressed for the party. I discovered I had put my mind to a certain appearance. A short, black dress, shiny and sleek as leather but soft as mohair. Black stockings and black shoes with heels. I put gentle perfume on my whole body, just enough to be detected without anyone realizing what was being detected. Something in the air.

A colleague sat down on the easy chair armrest beside me. He had come back from the summer looking tanned and spectacular. I asked him what he had done. *Roller blading*, he said. *But I took the wrong turn and fell down.* He showed me his two broken fingers.

We talked about how quickly everyone grows old in this job. How people come to the university youthful and vigorous, and five years later they are old and tired. We agreed the process had to be reversed. Later, when I had my coat on and was leaving, he came up to me in the front hall. *Let's go and get young together*, he said.

I had my party smile. The one I learned after coming to America. I smiled. In my mind I found myself calculating how many times I could go out and hurt my lover. Revenge was so easy. I did not recognize myself. My own thoughts were strangers to me. They appeared like automatized calculations, like numerical problems computing themselves on a screen. Numbers gone insane.

I was thinking of a poster that hung in the mailroom at work. A black and white photo of an attractive woman's face. The bold headlines underneath said, *If you are dressed to kill, make sure he is dressed not to.*

A Slovenian scholar, Slavoj Žižek, was giving lectures at our university. I attended them. The auditorium was packed. He spoke with unusual animation. His arms gesticulated, often with hands spread flat, as if steadying a wobbly person in front of him. Or reaching out to someone with both arms. He often pulled at the left side of his shirt. He told us about a children's book in his country. It was about an island inhabited only by children. On this mythical island, the children sat around discussing all the reasons they were aborted. Why their parents did not want them. It was the island of the aborted.

In my mind you are already my wife, my lover said to me. He spoke with emphasis. Seriousness. As if I needed to understand this or we would be ruined. It was so early still that everything was dark. I was on the sofa in my living room in British Columbia. The many windows glared their blackness at me. The rain pelted down. As he spoke, a storm flared up and the rain beat itself down with extraordinary force. It sounded like war. Like bombs and gunfire and warplanes and explosions. I could hardly hear him. The voice in the receiver was so small.

The worst thing that can happen to a woman, Simone de Beauvoir once said in a radio interview, *is to be in love.* An interview my mother taped and sent me in the mail. I listened to it as I drove in a small red sports car across the Canadian divide. I was pulling up stakes to go and live with my fiancé. When Simone de Beauvoir said that, somewhere close to the Saskatchewan–Manitoba border, I almost turned around. Instinctively my hands turned the wheel toward the shoulder of the road.

She did not have to elaborate. I understood what she was saying. The many ways a woman is taken from herself when she is in love. She accedes. She gives herself over. Her own life has paled and the life of her lover has overtaken her. She pulls up stakes. She forgets.

As it happened, I did turn around. It took a full year, but I did make that U-turn. That was several years ago. Now I look out over the lightening southern horizon. I am keenly aware of the silence of the telephone. There has been no conversation with my lover. I feel the silence like a hole in my chest. Paralyzed by the quiet, with the sound of the city's first cars rushing down the road like a rhythmic accompaniment. I recognize I have been caught again. I hear the voice from the tape again, in memory, exactly the way I first heard it.

On that same road trip, a police car came up behind me, flared its light and sounded its siren, and pulled me over. I could not understand where it had come from. There was no one on that deserted road for a hundred miles in either direction. A young police officer stepped out of the car with a small notepad in his hand. He walked up to my window and looked at me with a smile. I remember thinking he had materialized out of nothing. He told me I was speeding. He fined me seventy-five dollars and said I should slow down.

It occurs to me I should have listened to him. I look for such emissaries now, but there are none. This time I am alone.

During professional meetings in Hamilton, Ontario, I was put up in a new hotel by the highway. After a full day of meetings, I was tired and went downstairs to a restaurant for dinner. A man I did not notice came in behind me and was also waiting to be seated. The hostess assumed we were together and showed us both the same table. We were about to correct her, but on the spur of the moment decided we might as well keep each other company.

His name was Philippe and he was from Brittany, France. A professor of political science, he was unusually handsome, except for his arms, which had been ruined in the war. We had a conversation that lasted four hours. We did not notice the restaurant had emptied, the place was closed, and the staff was waiting for us to leave.

He told me his wife had recently died. He was in grief. In his inconsolable sorrow, he found himself taking risks he had never taken before. He walked into a street full of heavy traffic. He leaned too far over high balconies. He was careless with his health. *It was not conscious*, he said. *Somewhere inside me*, he confessed, *I think I must have wanted to die.*

It occurs to me now that I am having the same experience. That I am experiencing my lover's absence as a form of grief. The bare walls, the quiet dawn, the empty hum of an electric gadget still plugged in. That I do not sleep and I do not eat. I go out for a walk in the dry breeze and five hours later, I am still walking. As if I could walk away his absence.

As day followed day and we did not speak, I understood I was also becoming free. That even if his reasons were good, and I had agreed to his silence, I could only experience that silence as hurtful. Because I was hurt, I could only love him less. *I'm almost free of my mistakes*, writes Clarice Lispector. *I let myself happen.*

On the day I was to leave Copenhagen for Vancouver, I woke up angry. It was a morning flight, and Bodil and I had to get an early start. I did not know why I was angry. I barely touched the breakfast of toasted crumpets and marmalade she gave me. The coffee tasted bad to me. Our conversation was brusque. I answered her questions in monosyllables. That morning I got dressed as though I were dressing for an execution. My blouse went on grumpily, without care. I pushed everything into my suitcase without folding or straightening, and dumped the bag in the front hall.

My Aunt Bodil did not notice my bad temper. She was admiring my dress, the one I bought on an impulse in Vancouver. She put her hand on the smooth fabric with the white lilies patterned into it. *You can get so many nice things over there*, she said wistfully. Over there, in America.

Slavoj Žižek, the Slovenian lecturer at our university, peppered his talks on Lacanian psychoanalysis with anecdotes from daily life and popular culture. One example he used had to do with the telephone ringing. *Whenever the telephone rings*, he told us, *I am always worried I will not pick it up in time. I always think that maybe this is The Call. I do not know what this call ought to be, but I am always expecting The Call.*

My dear Jan. There was a time when at least once every morning I would curl up somewhere and weep uncontrollably. I wept without reservation, without self-consciousness, without the guilt that says I am weak and small. I wept because he did not call. Then suddenly one day I had no inclination to break down. I was unmoved. It was a Thursday morning. The cold rain and wind had stopped. It was possible to go out without an umbrella again. I discovered that by some miracle, I had become cold inside.

Even in her fifties, my other aunt, Trine, still behaved like a tomboy. When she walked, her arms were held elbow-out at her side, as though she carried a heavy weight in each hand. She took big steps and her head bent in rhythm with each footfall. She smiled to one side of the mouth, one eye closed, as if in mischief. She said things in a guttural way, making rasping sounds as if it was all too much.

I understood Trine's tomboy behaviour was a defence mechanism. I did not know what she thought she was protecting herself against. Perhaps the suspicion that she was weak. Underneath her bluster, she was the least able to cope with distress in the family. When we sat around her wooden table on the deck of her log cabin in the country, she offered us a pile of food. As though riches and generosity were self-evident. She encouraged us to eat aggressively, as though we needed to prepare for a long journey. Mackerel, shrimp, tuna, liver paté, pickled cucumbers, cheeses, all types of rye bread. Wine, coffee.

When we returned to Copenhagen, I said to Bodil that I thought Trine's husband, Morten, was in for a hard time. The one who was retired from the railroad against his will. The one who sat in silence and smoked his crooked pipe while the rest of us chatted. What will happen to Trine if her husband becomes ill? I asked. Men often become ill when they retire. *Oh,* my Aunt Bodil said almost matter-of-factly, without having to give it a moment's thought, *Oh, Trine will not at all be able to cope with that. She will simply fall apart.*

I thought of a French film I had recently seen. About a novelist whose love life is extremely complicated. Her husband has children with another woman. Her lover is married and has children. She herself maintains a childless independence and reserves her privacy for writing. But she cannot help being in love. She has to ask her two men, when they both leave her for the weaker woman, the one with the children, *what is it about love that makes women weak?*

Six-thirty in the morning and it is still pitch dark outside. The town of Edmonton is so far north that I know as the weeks progress it will be later and later before dawn breaks. Soon it will be eight, nine, ten, and still dark. But the blackness allows me to reflect. It seems to me every morning is a new junction in life. What will become of me? It is such an easy question. That I have somehow set things in motion I cannot stop.

On a Saturday I went to my office at work to pick up a student's thesis. I noticed a colleague of mine in another office, bent over a mess of books and papers, sorting them out. I stopped for a chat. He said he could not relax, so he came to work. He had given up his marriage for a woman in Ontario. He accepted early retirement so he could be with her. Now they were having trouble. He did not think the relationship would survive. After all that.

I sat on the chair in his office, my books on my lap, and found I could offer him nothing. No consolation. No cheerful words. He had just described the kind of cruel irony that seems to make up our lives. And fears. He had described my silent fears. The ones that keep me awake at night. What if you miscalculate? What if you design your life in a certain way and then find you have forgotten to factor something in? You were too certain. Your mathematics were not good enough.

It sometimes seems to me that a pestilence has struck the human race in its most distinctive faculty – that is, the use of words, says Italo Calvino in his book *Six Memos for the Next Millennium.* That we flaunt words cheaply. We throw them about for effect until they lose their meaning. *It is a plague afflicting language, revealing itself as a loss of cognition and immediacy, an automatism that tends to level out all expression into the most generic, anonymous, and abstract formulas, to dilute meanings, to blunt the edge of expressiveness …*

I find myself wondering why Italo Calvino is so angry. That he should think we do not know what we mean when we speak. Because inside every word there is another word lurking. A word that has the opposite meaning. That points in the opposite direction. I think it is true, what he says. Yet I cannot help feeling I have never been more sure of the meaning of my words. The words that say I am in love. That I know both meanings are inside what I say, many meanings, opposing each other. It is a full word, *love.* Full of everything we could not say, dared not say, desired to say.

So dear, dear Jan. It is not true that I was angry. That I am angry. That I take my revenge on him. That is not it at all. What is true is that I miss him. Such a simple logic.

My beautiful cousin Kari, with the rich, dark, flowing hair, was a midwife. She went to the Rigshospital every day and talked to pregnant women about birth. She told them birthing is natural. *It is not a disease,* she said. That they should trust their bodies. She helped women deliver naturally. Then one day she came home and was midwife to her cat. Four kittens in a row. After she had rubbed the cat's stomach and all the kittens were out, the mother cat was very attached to her. Whenever Kari came home, the mother cat put its head affectionately in her lap.

She was hula-hooping in the middle of the floor for the benefit of her young daughter, Asa. She stopped and said to me, *Women in our family have an easy time giving birth. Wasn't it easy for you?*

I am certain of so many things, he wrote, my lover wrote me, *except the one thing: what this is going to do to us.*

We had a date for our return to each other. It was on the calendar, marked by a name for a month and a number for a day. An exact day. There was going to be a precise time on the clock when we would step out of anonymity and into each other's arms. Now I discovered I no longer had the patience I so carefully cultivated before. Time had slowed massively. Time did not seem to pass at all. When I looked at the clock, it was 10:00 a.m. I looked at it again later, and it was still 10:00 a.m.

When this is over I may not be worth having, he wrote.

The train drove onto the ferry, and the massive steel doors shut behind it. I went upstairs to the observation deck. I wanted to see the rain-coloured water. The low, pencil line of the island receding. To chart our passage across the water by imprinting it on my visual memory. To see us approach the island of Fyn, where I had told my aunt we would resettle.

But the view was not there. Before us was only a blank sheet of white. As if a mist from the clouds had overtaken the world. I could see nothing.

It was not yet dark. The sun was low in the sky, and everything had a deep glow. A tangerine aura. The train raced through Fyn at high speed. Farmstead after manor after cottage washed by. Long ivory-coloured roads stretched through the countryside. A rare automobile, a bicyclist. Fields of wheat, straw-coloured and lime green. Homesteads with straw-thatched roofs and crossbeams on top to hold them down. Old farms with courtyards and water pumps, handles protruding into the air. *One of these,* I said to myself, *one of these is ours.*

I knew already then, on the train, that I was being diverted. There was a debate inside my head, but I could not make out the details. The problem of seeing clearly because the familiar face, the quiet, thoughtful expression, the tone of patience in the atmosphere, his pale eyes, superimposed themselves on all the farms of Fyn.

He told me he had many priorities in his life before this, and love was not among them. That now he understood his error. That love was the most important thing. *It is the most important,* he said with emphasis. With finality.

Paula Gunn Allen, a Laguna Pueblo from New Mexico and professor at UCLA, came to our university to give a course and lecture. I attended the lecture in a massive auditorium packed with people from all over. When Paula Gunn Allen spoke, her whole body participated. She gesticulated with her shoulders, her hips, she raised one leg behind the other, she walked across the stage. She gave a holistic talk somehow, involving not only the intellect, but our emotions, our sensibilities. In her colourful print dress and curly black hair.

She told us about a certain Indigenous writer who had told a story in a novel that should not have been told. A sacred trust of the community was violated when that story was told outside. When you violate that trust,

Paula Gunn Allen told us, something very unfortunate is likely to happen to you.

I was thinking perhaps all communities have such codes. Stories that must not be told. That we have to be able to recognize sacred material and not trivialize it. I searched my memory. Have I ever done such a thing? I could not help wondering. Violated an unarticulated code? Walked through it as if it were a translucent cobweb?

At the end of Toni Morrison's novel *Beloved*, the narrator turns the whole world around. After telling so much, she stops. She attests: *It was not a story to pass on*. Since the protagonist's story was best not remembered, *They forgot her like a bad dream*.

It was black night by the time the train neared the end of its journey. While still in the country, there was nothing to see outside the cabin window except my own face. Trying to make out the contours of my ancestral country yielded only the image of myself. It was a tired face. Sad, even. A face filled with the image of a man left behind in Skovshoved. When we came to the city, there were large apartment buildings with lit windows. There were embankments and bridges, rail crossings and highways with headlighted automobiles scuttling about. There were underpasses with lights in them. When we rolled through, black and red and navy graffiti rushed out of the concrete walls with torrid images and desperate words.

The graffiti continued along the walls of the station after I left the train. We all marched through a long corridor to the steps that would take us up to the street and the night life there. An occasional youth could be seen flopped onto the floor, drugged out by something. Coming through the glass doors and out to the pavement, I saw a horde of parked bicycles knotting the passage to the street. People grabbed various bicycles and headed off in all directions.

I walked slowly to Bodil's apartment. I wanted to savour the night air after the long ride in a closed compartment. It was not clear to me how tired I had become. Passing the small brick houses with little gardens around, I could see people settled into their evenings with books or tea or newspapers. Through windows domestic lives became visible. Lights were on inside. Pictures on the walls. Plush furniture. Antiques, decorative plates, even model ships on shelves. There was no one on the street except me. I was thinking of the small bed Bodil had set up for me in the side room. About the pillows and duvets and how I wanted to bury myself in all that eiderdown and forget what had just passed.

But when I walked into my aunt's apartment, I found it was full of people. The living room, the hallway, the bedroom, even. Every chair was taken. On the tables were plates with dinner on them. Meatballs and red cabbage and cucumbers in vinegar. Almond cakes and marzipan chocolates, espresso coffee and liqueur. They were engaged in loud conversation. The whole family. They were all there. Cousins and children of cousins, people's former husbands, aunts. All except for those who were dead. Assembled to greet me.

I stood for a moment by the door and tried to collect energy I knew I did not have. It was something I had asked my Aunt Bodil not to do: gather up everybody at once. I said I could not talk to everyone at the same time. But I understood it was like an ocean wave. Something that could not be controlled. If one person knew I was coming, another person would know, and another, until the idea spread, independently of everything else, that someone should be there to greet me. In the end, no one wished to be left out.

Because I was losing my vision, I found an optometry clinic in my university city and had my eyes examined. An attractive young woman in high heels came out and told me she was my new optometrist. In the examination room, she leaned my head back and suddenly stood over me with an eyedropper. *I want to put this dye in your eyes*, she said, *then I can apply this blue light and see what's inside.* She held up an instrument with a blue light at the end of its handle. She told me the dye would freeze the eye and she would be able to see everything inside it.

The yellow dye felt cold and covered both eyes instantly. She put the instrument against her face and peered into my eyeballs with it. I could see the blue light travelling everywhere inside my vision. I could not help worrying about my optometrist. That she would see what I saw. The image I had there all the time would become visible to her with the blue light. She would see my beautiful lover and fall helplessly in love. Because she could not have him, perhaps she would want to throw herself off the bridge. The Highlevel Bridge that lay across the North Saskatchewan River.

The idea that this thought would occur to my optometrist only appeared because it had occurred to me. Since he plunged us into a silence that stipulated we not speak or write or send electronic messages to each other, I did not know what to do. I realized too late it was more than I could bear. But I could not send him a message to say so. This was something I had to endure alone. This silence. This emptiness, where nothing but blank whiteness can be seen through the window.

I took a long walk that led across the high bridge over the river. At the middle, I stopped and looked at the flowing water below. It was not yet icy. The trees along the banks were still lush and green. They had not turned their fall colours yet. I leaned against the railing. I imagined myself dropping the long distance. It had occurred to me that I could not take my revenge on him. I could not hurt him. The only person I could hurt was myself.

Karen Blixen's manor in the town of Rungsted, Rungstedlund, turned out to be a bit like the human brain. Very little of it was in use at any given time. Only a few rooms were available for viewing. The rest was corded off, left untouched, and what had remained of the manor burned down long ago.

We discovered all this on our visit the afternoon I tried to find my old home and failed. Bodil and I arrived at the wrong time. There were no tours through the house just then. But the hostess unlocked the door anyway and told us just to walk through on our own. We took the cotton bags provided to cover our shoes and rambled from room to room. For a large, well-to-do manor, this was a small place. The furniture was frayed and sorry-looking. It was not easy to picture the famous author working there. I imagined she did not write in those rooms.

The door to the courtyard at the end faced south. I knew about this door. About the windows of her study. That Karen Blixen lived her whole life without the man she loved. He was dead. Buried on a hill in Africa. That every evening at sunset, Blixen opened the window facing south and stood silent for fifteen minutes.

I found time had begun to stand still altogether. Time was trapped in the month of September. The end of the month was forever approaching but never arrived. The wind became cold. Frost was in the air. We stepped out and turned our collars up. Everyone expected snow. *Any minute now*, they all said. In this expanded minute that stretched itself for weeks, I had gone from desperation to acceptance to desperation again. I knew what went on inside my days. What I could not bear was not knowing what was happening on the other side. The possibility that something was going wrong. Someone was dead. The possibility of anything.

As for the unforeseeable, Clarice Lispector writes, *the next sentence is unforeseeable*. She does not know what the next word is. The next event. Yet she wishes to live inside that darkness. *I don't ask questions*, she says.

I welcome the darkness where the two eyes of that soft panther glow. The darkness is my cultural broth.

But dear, dear Jan. No two words are the same. Lispector writes to the one she is now free of, *I write you because I do not understand myself.* I do not think that is why I write him. These letters that cannot go anywhere. They live and die in the palms of my hands. I write them because I know something about myself. I know how I react to sorrow. The way you begin to understand the actions of a wild animal under stress. A panther, perhaps. How the panther balks once, then again. You know it will draw back every time. It will close down its senses.

Paula Gunn Allen, who was visiting our university, was treated to a departmental dinner after her public lecture. As it happened, I sat beside her at the meal. We talked about our children. She said both her grown children were musicians. When she visited them, she stayed in a hotel. It took too much time, she explained, to clean their places so she could stay there. She saved herself the trouble with a hotel.

It occurred to me we might be miles apart culturally, she and I. She of New Mexico, Pueblo, immersed in what she called the Oral Tradition. And I, of Denmark, with nothing but texts. Written texts. Yet there was this one point on which we were in complete agreement. Our children. We understood each other perfectly as the mothers of our sons and daughters.

Do you want children? he asked out of the blue. For some reason he had left the bed where we lay and was returning again. Coming toward me. It was a hot night. I had thrown the covers off, the blanket and sheet onto the floor, and hoped the breeze from the open window would cool down my naked skin. It was an unexpected question. Out of context. His question so surprised me that I forgot he was coming toward me. There were still people out on the streets. I could hear them through the open window. Streets of this Danish town that, for some reason, did not sleep.

The woman had no feelings going into this. She bunched up the pillow under her head to make herself comfortable. Everyone had gone away. She was alone in the small, white-walled room. The husband went home to breakfast. The mother-in-law was already back at the house, cooking. The nurses took their break. The doctor went home for breakfast too. She took a book out of her bag and started to read. John Steinbeck, *The Grapes of Wrath*. Everywhere in the opening scene, red dust filled all nooks and crannies. Red dust lay in people's eyelids, in their shoes, on the potatoes they ate for dinner. The air was red with dust.

There was no pain, no labour, nothing. They said it would take hours. But when a nurse walked by accidentally, she noticed what was happening. Suddenly everyone was summoned. People in green shirts came and rolled her into the delivery room, her novel still hanging from her fingers, pages flying as they rushed down the hall. The woman did not understand everyone's panic. Nothing was happening. But oddly enough, even though she felt nothing, there was a baby. The doctor rushed into the room in time to receive it. He held the infant high up in the air where she could see it. Like a grail of some sort. He called to her, *Look what you got.*

The woman looked at this infant, whom she had not exactly expected. Almost instantly she was overcome by some invisible cloud. She began to cry. Once begun, she could not stop.

My cousin Kari's son, Njord, was now a handsome and tall young man of eighteen. He was slim and tanned, his light brown hair tied in a pony tail. I sat down beside him the night I returned to Bodil's flat from the train station and found everyone gathered there. I took a few bites of food and listened to them talk.

Njord's impulsive mother once took off to New York without warning or planning. She took her young son along. Kari insisted she simply wanted to see New York with her own eyes. It was Njord's only visit to America. Since I had just come from there, he wanted to tell me his personal impression of America. *In New York*, he told me with grave enthusiasm, *everyone was shooting everyone else left and right.*

Jeremy, my roller-blading colleague, who had asked me if we could go and get young together, was leaning against an espresso stand on campus. He was wearing a three-piece suit in grey-green and appeared very official. As I walked by, I stopped and asked him why he was dressed up. He was serene-looking that day. It occurred to me he always did look serene. In control. *Because I'm going to a funeral*, he answered without a touch of emotion.

Send me your picture, my lover asked me on the phone, *just to have with me while this is going on.* I promised him I would. But a month went by and I had not yet done it. The picture I had of him, the one I took myself under a tree in Denmark that caught him unawares, was on my nightstand. But after he imposed silence on us, I banished his photograph. I took the picture in its frame and placed it upside down in my desk drawer. Then I refused to indulge him by sending him mine.

It occurred to me if words were not allowed, I could use other signs. My friend Mikel, who was a photographer, came to my flat with her camera and we mapped out a strategy. We went to the room with the swimming pool. On the blue-tiled poolroom wall there hung a bright red lifesaver ring. The kind you throw out to people who are drowning. I positioned myself next to the rescue device. A red circle leaping out of the blue wall. Mikel took the pictures. Will he understand? I asked her. She could not know. I knew she had no way of knowing.

But it was my colleague Jeremy who offered to come to my rescue first. Because I had stopped by the espresso stand on a day when I found it hard to conceal the despair I felt. He asked how I was. A rhetorical question we ask each other, to which we do not expect an answer. So I gave him no answer. But that day I had been holding back tears in the middle of all my duties. Before a class of forty-two students, I held back tears. During consultations with thesis writers. During a committee meeting, my reticence almost noticeable. My colleague noticed. *Look*, he said by way of answer for me, *I have just the solution for you.*

My mother requested, before she died, that we not have a memorial service for her. Instead we should have a party at her house. On the afternoon of her burial, we opened the big, old house up to the people of the town. There was plenty of food and drink. The house was packed with people. They came from all directions. From faraway cities. We played the music she loved on the piano. We read the poems she cherished. Carl Nielsen and Rabindranath Tagore. We tried to do what she asked of us: to have a good time.

But I could see we were a sad bunch. There was a cloud of wrath over the whole house. Underneath the sweet and consoling demeanour, everyone there was in shock. This was not supposed to happen, we seemed to say when we looked at one another. This could not have been in the cards. Reality took a wrong turn, we insinuated. It was evident to me, even at that early moment, that what we had in the passing of my mother was a genuine loss. We looked around and realized we did not know what to do without her now.

In the middle of the celebration, I fell into the arms of a big woman who had helped with the care-giving. I sobbed uncontrollably and deeply. Never in my life had I sobbed like that before. Not even as a baby.

It was my son who suddenly stood there like the only strong pillar the family had left. He suggested a solution for me. He said we should go and see the Dalai Lama.

One day in Copenhagen, I woke up unusually late. It was already daylight and the grey walls of the room looked matte and clean. Through the gauze curtain draped against the open window, street noises sounded. A delivery truck. The scraping of a street broom. The swishing of bicycle tires. I could tell it was overcast. The voice of a radio announcer could be heard through the closed door. Bodil was no doubt up, listening to the morning program on Radio Copenhagen. The peculiar city accent of the announcer sounded striking just then. I crawled out from under the duvet and put on a robe my aunt had left hanging on the front door hook. When I walked into the foyer and looked down into the living room, she was there. Bodil, seated in her black leather chair, head cocked slightly to the right as if to hear better. Rolling her cigarettes.

The Dalai Lama did not just come into the hall. He arrived preceded by a number of monks and followed by a number of monks. All of the devotees wore maroon-coloured robes. They had their beads and strings. The teacher himself wore ochre yellow and maroon, one shoulder left naked. He sat on a low chair in the centre of the podium, all his disciples settled around him. My son had found me a good seat close by. I could follow every move the teacher made. His every breath. It occurred to me then, as it had often before, as he prayed and chanted before speaking, that if Jesus Christ were back now, he would be very much like the Dalai Lama.

The teacher spoke in a deep, sonorous voice. Everything he said was crystal clear. He summarized over two thousand years of complex Buddhist teachings into phrases that rang pure as spring water. *Once it has begun,* he was telling us, *it is very difficult to alter the course a certain Karma has taken.*

Dear, dear Jan. I want to tell him I am not here. That I have left my body and am spinning in the spheres somewhere. I have turned into a vibration of sound and cannot be found. I am everywhere at once. My feet do not come down anywhere because there are no feet. Love did this. I want to tell him about this transformation, but he cannot hear. He is unable to hear because I am no longer human. The sound I make cannot reach the human ear.

All of a sudden a door was thrown open through which life came in, says the Steppenwolf in Hermann Hesse's novel *Steppenwolf.*

You have a dimension too many, Hermine says to him. *Whoever wants music instead of noise, joy instead of pleasure, soul instead of gold, creative work instead of business, passion instead of foolery, finds no home in this trivial world of ours.*

One late afternoon at my Aunt Trine's log cabin in northern Sjælland, I became tired. We had wandered along the Roskildefjord coast for hours, through the wheat fields, the woods, along the beach. We had stood in front of the pale ocean and sat on the white rocks. But when we returned to the house, I realized the last days were weighing me down.

I lay down for a nap in the extra bedroom. This was where Trine's son, my cousin Niels Eric, lived when he was home. Lying on the hard wooden bed that had no mattress, I looked at the bare log walls of the room. The wooden cabinet against the wall, unpainted. Not a sign of my cousin was in the room. Not a single memento, personal object, item of clothing that might be his. It was as if he did not exist. It occurred to me to wonder where his place was. He was the cousin I had never met. Not once, even though we had both been alive for over thirty years. He was a rumour to me. A story told of a tall, blond fellow in wooden shoes who gardened for a living and hiked through the countryside on weekends and managed to pay his parents a visit on occasion. When he did, it was rumoured he lay down on their sofa and slept the visit through.

In his novel *Snow Falling on Cedars*, David Guterson calls *the art of waiting over an extended period of time – a deliberately controlled hysteria …*

But as the days progressed from cold to warm again, to summer and back, I found there were cracks in that control. That the hysteria peculiar to lovers, to lovers who have to wait, began to leak. The seeping of one world into another suddenly showed up in my work, my thoughts, my body. I became disorganized. Forgot to answer letters, reply to messages. Forgot to think thoughts to the end. Subsisted on fractured, fragmented conversation. Then I found my private hysteria had invaded my body like a disease I could not prevent. All my nerves were buzzing. My muscles were on edge. I was shaking. Even my bones were shaking.

I realized something had to be done. But I did not know what I should be doing.

I stood in the mail room at work, facing the mailboxes. My back was to the room. Something in my mailbox attracted my attention, so I stood reading it. I did not turn around, but I could sense the presence of someone behind me. Someone in the room. When I did turn around, I saw it was my colleague Jeremy. The one with the solution, he said, to my problems, whatever they were. He was standing very still by the door. His clear face showed no expression. Glasses shielded his eyes. He wore an immaculately pressed suit and a very slight, overconfident smile.

The slowness of time became harder to take. The days lumbered forward. When the weather was good, the whole town was out on the streets. People walking, sauntering, sitting on terrace cafés on Whyte Avenue. Hiking briskly through the river valley parkways. Bicycling with helmets on. It seemed everyone but me was engaged in the day. I had found myself out of focus. Somehow I was not there. Out to dinner with friends, out walking with friends, in the middle of conversations with friends, I discovered I was somewhere else. Disengaged.

In this core I have the strange impression that I don't belong to the human race, Clarice Lispector writes.

Hovedbanegaarden, the main train terminal in Copenhagen, was larger, busier, and dirtier than what I was used to. People rushed forward on both sides of the station, milling through like water. Some just sauntered, often foreigners looking for something. People filed through the kiosks, the magazine stands and cigarette stands, piling up the newspapers for journeys ahead. *Berlingske Tiderne. Aftenavisen.* A couple of cafes were enclosed behind glass partitions to give the illusion they were separate spaces. People had coffee there in the middle of a thoroughfare, the tables still full of napkins and used cups from former customers. In the very clean public toilets below, the purple lights were so low it was almost impossible to see. The attendant sat on guard behind a glass window, dispensing soaps, tampons, underwear. It was to discourage the use of drugs that people had to tend their affairs in darkness.

The whole station, it seemed to me, was a terminal for much more than trains. It was an exchange centre for the underground. The nether world that milled about on the surface, disintegrating itself in the illusion of invisibility. I had come in on the Skovshoved connection. I bought a ticket at the wicket in the terminal and found the *perron* with the number for Nykøbing. Track number fifteen.

The Call came unexpectedly at five-thirty on a Thursday morning. I was up reading *Snow Falling on Cedars*. Often I lost concentration and looked out the big window. It was still dark. The lights of the city sparkled like waves on water caught by sun. City lights went on as far into the south and east as I could see. There was the constant pain in my heart I had become used to. The hollow place in my chest. The need to pray this time would end – and the inability to do so. The sense of futility.

His voice was clear but the surroundings were noisy. Crowds could be heard milling, shouting. The sound of loud motors. A loudspeaker blared into the receiver, crowding out his voice. *I will run out of time in three minutes,* he said. He had to speak. Had to call. He was in the airport in Trondheim. A brand new terminal, glinting with the clatter of travel. He had found a phone in a corner. He sat with his back to the world, his forehead pressed against the glass and his hand covering one ear.

Anything you do not give freely and abundantly becomes lost to you, Annie Dillard says in *The Writing Life. You open your safe and find ashes.*

It occurred to me this giving had become my life. Something so unnoticeable I could hardly tell it was there. A transferral of my energy to him, the one who received whatever I had to give. Just so this part of me would not be lost, but instead inhabit him where he went. Across the street, into the store, at a meeting, in front of his desk. Everywhere he went, there was that which I had given him.

Something I could not tell him during that hurried phone call from the Trondheim airport. That on some level, a space hardly discernible, he called too late. Something had passed from the scene. That I answered with only the remnants of myself. That I was no longer in my own possession.

I returned to my home in the mountains of British Columbia to think things over. It was important to take the time, the space, to find out what had happened. In what sense I was lost from myself. I flew over the Rocky Mountains and found it was raining in Vancouver. The long bus ride had standing room only. People packed themselves into the bus, crowded into the back and dozens more filed in through the front door. Finally the driver had to deny waiting passengers access. He told them to wait half an hour for the next bus. The ferry plowed through Howe Sound, made choppy by wind and misty by rain. We could not see the coast on the other side. The islands along the way were half hidden from view. On the other side, there was no bus and stranded passengers stood looking helpless in the terminal.

Clarice Lispector writes about a dream she had. In the dream, many people obeyed a soft drink advertisement. The ad was stronger than they were. She says it was a dream about *automatic people acutely and solemnly aware that they are automatic and there's no escape.*

I put the book down on the ottoman and looked out the window. There was a full moon sliding over the skyscrapers in the southwest. I thought I knew exactly what I was afraid of. That I too was in the process of becoming automatic. Going to work, to the office, obeying orders, filling in my evenings with small entertainments, getting by. Reducing the flow of emotions, so I would not recoil over feelings like Lispector's oysters do when lemon juice is squeezed on them.

On our meeting in the mail room, my colleague Jeremy invited me to come home with him for tea. It was the hour between the workday and dinner. Late afternoon. The sun is low in the sky. The light has paled and become flat. He said his invitation was not an advance on my person. Just a friendly tea and a solution. I relented. It was not difficult. We closed up our offices and drove away in his newly purchased grey Toyota. The car still had that new smell.

Jeremy's flat was in a high-rise on the corner of 100th Street and Saskatchewan Drive, by the river. He had the place furnished in black and chrome, modernist objects of leather and glass. It seemed in character, the place and the man. He actually did make tea, a kind of Earl Grey mixed with fennel. The hour between four and five in the day stretches and slows. I watched the view from his window and could feel the time lengthening while lights began to come on in the downtown tall buildings. One by one, small squares of light suddenly turned on.

Jeremy was talking, but I was not listening. I heard the words, but nothing really registered. He could tell but kept talking anyway. I heard him say he understood something difficult was going on. He would not ask the details. He knew it was personal. But there is something that is preferrable to jumping in the river, he said. I did not know what he meant. I looked at him quizzically. It was then I noticed him unwrapping a diabetic kit. A small, plastic box that contained a device for reading blood sugar levels, something to prick the finger with, a small bottle of insulin, and disposable hypodermic needles.

I telephoned my Aunt Bodil to let her know when I was coming back. The airplane ticket was already in my purse. She was happy to hear the date was set. Her voice was sweet. She told me she was having trouble with her daughter, my cousin Kari. For months, Kari had been scolding her mother, angry with her for things Bodil did not understand. For things done in the past she did not remember. *I think she is fictionalizing all this,* Bodil said to me. *She is making it all up.* I did not know what to say.

Why do your children all of a sudden turn against you? she asked in genuine confusion.

My dear Jan. We began to speak again. But not like before. What was deprivation became excess. Every chance we had, at any hour, every day. Often at night. At work. At home. Between us lay half a century of things we did not know. Or if we knew them, they were things we had to learn again.

The first snow fell in my university city. The roads were iced over. Snowflakes mixed with hail fell harshly on the windowpane, the railing, the branches of naked trees. I was oblivious to this new winter. The wind blew corns of ice into my face, and I did not notice. I did not know how to make the time pass faster, so the day would arrive when I was in his arms again. I looked at the white light of noon, and the universe seemed frozen in place. A world of cold days that refused to give my lover to me.

I miss you something awful, he said on the telephone. There was an echo on the line.

The Norwegian writer Sissel Lie was touring Canada. When she came to my city, I was her host. I took her to dinner, to lunch, to see the town, to a friend's house. We went for tea at the Highlevel Diner. She read from her books with dramatic intonation. With her short, grey hair, her grey jacket and black slacks, she presented an androgynous profile. Her left hand was often in her pants pocket while she held the book up with her right.

I read her first novel before we met. The book was charged with sexuality and eroticism. *Lion's Heart* it was called. In the novel, two women have an erotic relationship. A man and a woman also do. A wife and her faithless husband do, but separately. A man and two women do, in a Renaissance bed, limbs and tongues intertwining, bodies sliding over other bodies. I asked her why she inundated her novel with so much sexuality. She was unhesitant. *Sex is the most important thing in life*, she said, her cup of Earl Grey tea halfway in the air.

Why is it that an instant before things happen they seem to have already happened? asks Clarice Lispector. In a flash, you see your fate laid out before you. You hear the door slam before it does. You hear the phone ring before it rings. You see your lover reach for you before he is your lover. I recognized what Lispector was saying. It was not a surprise to me that this man, who the day before was unknown to me, today put his arm around me. This evening reached over and kissed me on the lips.

How everything that happened afterward was already known to me. His movements, people he spoke to, what he had for supper. Everything he did was as familiar to me as what I did myself. At the same time, I knew nothing, and I knew I knew nothing.

In my own life, the one I led before, I had bought a house in the country. A place far away from where I worked and where I carried on social and professional obligations. In this other home, my real home I called it, there was nothing to press me in any direction. Just silver beaches glinting like chrome and mountains of ochre and rust-coloured maple leaves on the ground in the fall. This home existed for me so I would not lose myself. I never want to lose myself again, I decided when I moved there.

On the Remembrance Day weekend, I went back to British Columbia. The ferry was just leaving when I drove my Jeep down the hill and was the last vehicle on board. The rain clouds over Vancouver parted when we reached the Sunshine Coast, and I drove home with streams of sunlight falling on the green trees and grass. Back at my university city, the ground was covered in snow and patches of ice, and the wind blew flurries of snow dust on street corners.

When I came home, I turned the heat on, read my mail, opened the curtains to let the sun in, and put his photograph on my desk. It was disconcerting. I felt dislocated. Coming home was not the same any more. My delight in the sea and mountains around was not there. My relief at being home was gone. The telephone rang ten minutes after I arrived. It was my lover, wishing me a welcome back to my house. But I did not like what had happened. For the first time, I did not want to talk to him. I realized that in spite of all my efforts not to, I had lost myself.

That I had lost my head. I was compromised when I had committed to a lifestyle where I would not be. My own life, my own decisions, my own schedule. But now I found myself at the mercy of another's. His life, his decisions, his schedule. The clock went from four to five to six. By seven the dawn was in. A pastel white and crimson light lay over the hills. Clouds hovered low, touching the white water. The branches of tall cedars spread perfectly still in the morning calm. Yellow and brown leaves of maple trees. Withering leaves of alders, half eaten by autumn rains. I knew as I once again watched the splendour of the country morning that with everything my lover and I had set in motion, I was nonetheless planning to do something I could not do. He would in the end be waiting in some premeditated location, and I would not be there.

The Danish writer Michael Larsen came to give talks and readings at our university. Since my schedule conflicted and I could not attend, I agreed to take him to lunch instead. We went to a Korean restaurant on campus. He had a beer and lentil soup. He chain-smoked and gave off the air of having lived hard. His straw-blond hair was cut short, his cheeks ruddy. He told about being a film critic covering the festival at Cannes. How he and the photographer sent with him drank and partied all night, slept it off on the beach, and woke up in the sunshine with people all around, children playing, balls bouncing by.

He said he lived alone with his dog in a country house in northern Sjælland, near Gilleleje. I confessed I had in mind the same situation and had been looking on Fyn. As I told him this, I wondered why some writers absent themselves from society like that. Why it becomes so important to go away, into the countryside by yourself, when what you do in life is write. It dawned on me at that moment that I did not know anymore whether I was moving back there because I wanted to go home or because I was following my lover and leaving myself.

Michael Larsen was on a reading tour of Canada. He did not know the country and had been given a schedule of events by the Danish embassy in Ottawa. He came to my office and we studied his schedule. I told him the itinerary was crazy. It was trips like that, concocted by bureaucrats in Ottawa who did not have to go on them, that killed authors. I said I had a schedule like that once, and it was the last time I did a reading tour. Forever after, I said no to tours. He looked at me slightly alarmed. His ocean-blue eyes were obviously lost in reflection. *I will never do this again either*, he said, shaking his head, holding his lit cigarette in his left hand.

In the late afternoon, when the sun was low and the maple leaves became coral red, I sat down at the big grey pinewood table that served as a dining table. The chairs were large pinewood stools with high backs, painted dark, moss green. They were hard to sit on, and the table had lines and grooves chiselled into the top. On the table I placed a blank sheet of paper. I pulled out a ball-point pen from the pencil container, a ceramic mug I once bought in the city where I work. I traced a line down the middle of the paper. On one side I wrote 'what's right'; on the other side, 'what's wrong.' This way, I thought, I could systematically figure out what to do in my life.

I found many things wrong with the relationship between me and the man I was addicted to. The one I spoke to every day on the telephone. Whom I wrote to. Whose letters and phone calls came in once, twice, three times daily. Often. I discovered there were more things wrong than there were right. I had to weigh one item against another and I could not. I tried to establish a list of priorities. I soon realized that the difference between one priority and another may only be one of degree. There were some things that could not be balanced. Or compared. How could I compare the act of writing with my child? My own happiness with his? Risk against certainty?

I searched for something ultimate. In an essay by Hélène Cixous on Clarice Lispector, titled 'Clarice Lispector: The Approach,' I found something I thought I could hang on to. Cixous wrote: *We have only to love, be on the lookout for love, and all the riches are entrusted to us. Attention is the key.* I could not help wondering where Cixous, and even Lispector, got this certainty from. How could they be so sure? And what should I pay attention to in that case? Everything? Love itself? Would I know it if I saw it?

I did not think I would recognize love. Even if it called me at four in the afternoon and declared itself.

The blue upholstered seats in the general compartment of the night train were comfortable. There were not many people in my car. The table between seats was large and useful. I had evening coffee and looked at what had become darkness outside. Nothing to see except the occasional farmstead lights.

I was joined by a young woman and her child, who seated themselves opposite me. A boy of about two years who walked in the aisle on short, stubby legs and crawled up and down the double seat that contained his mother. The woman was a picture from a fairy tale. Her long blond curls went in every direction. Her long cotton dress suggested romantic domesticity. She had a perpetual smile and an air of gentleness about her. The child spent most of the ride eating. Every time his mother put a bite of food on the table, an apple or a sandwich, the boy ate it up. Carrots, crackers, cheese. After an hour of this, I began to wonder. Was there room in that small body for all that food? The child was an eating machine.

The woman woke up in a roadside motel in Red Deer, Alberta. It was 6:00 a.m. The brown and orange fifties-style furniture stood dark and depressing around the room. Outside on the highway, huge oil trucks and cargo vans rumbled past. The woman was on a lecture tour and was scheduled to speak to a college audience at 9:00 a.m.

She discovered she had awoken to severe abdominal pain. Her body was cramped up and she could not move. The only thing she had ever experienced that resembled this pain was being in labour. Labour pains. She tried to stand up but could not. She ended up crouched on the floor by the bed, where she tried to put her feet. There was a telephone on the nightstand. From the heap she was in, she reached for the receiver and managed to dial the number of her friend Arnold. When he answered, she only managed to blurt out that he should come and take her to the hospital. *Hurry*, she said.

Arnold arrived after what seemed like an eternity. The woman managed to put her jeans and shirt on, and they went to his car. He had to hold her up while one wave of cramping after another shot through her.

At the emergency ward, the receptionist's desk stood imposing and large. The intention was for patients to sit down and register themselves, give their names and health care numbers. Instead, the woman threw herself on the counter in front of the receptionist. *Help me*, she whispered. Then she blacked out and came to on a stretcher in an examination room. There she lay for four hours, the pain that most resembled labour holding on to her.

The woman was examined by three different doctors. She was wheeled into the ultrasound room, and two doctors rolled a little ball over her abdomen. After being back in the examination room for what seemed like a long time, in and out of consciousness, miraculously the pain left her. She lay like a ruin after the flames have been put out. In the end they told her they could not find the fetus she had apparently miscarried.

Ours is the century of unreason, the stamp of our behavior is violence or isolation, writes Eudora Welty in an essay on Jane Austen. *Non-meaning is looked upon with some solemnity.*

It occurs to me Eudora Welty has described my life. The inevitable twentieth-century life. Life at the end of the millennium. Whatever the next century may bring, I cannot but wonder if this combination of violence and isolation can be surpassed.

That I find myself in a tower above the city in the dead of night. The lights outside seem to blink as the currents of cold air pass between me and them. Street lamps glow yellow all along the main avenue that stretches from my window to the horizon in the south. Behind me is the blank telephone. The memory of ringing the night before. That the voice on the other end was a voice of desperate ecstasy. And the knowledge that around him and me, whole worlds were crumbling.

I'm making myself, writes Clarice Lispector. *I'll make myself until I reach the core.*

As if there were a core in us. Up to now it seemed to me I had only experienced the self as a fluctuating puff of steam. The kind that blows off the train as it sets out from the station.

We stood in each other's arms on the platform, waiting for the train. It was a last good-bye. A solitude lay around each of us, shielding us from what would have been sorrow. It was not sorrow. His arms tight around my waist, my back. My arms enveloped his shoulders, his neck. His cheek rested against mine. I could feel the cheekbone, the forehead, as though they were my own. He was thoughtful. As if there were something more to think about. I was not. I was simply taking the evening train. It was my intention to travel into the night and into my life.

In the middle of November I found myself in Normandy, France. At the Castle in Caen, as part of a small group of Nordic writers in town to talk about Nordic writing. It was alternately rainy and sunny. The narrow streets crisscrossed one another, packed tightly with boutiques selling lingerie, coffee, pastries, books, and high fashion. Antique stores crammed the sidewalks, and cafés stayed open. Inside people sat alone at small tables, smoking and lingering, in what appeared to be serious thought.

At the banquet in the Castle on a Saturday night, my companion was the Icelandic writer Gudbergur Bergsson. His latest novel, *The Swan*, was attracting much attention in France. Milan Kundera had recently written a glowing article on the book. It was said Bergsson had written the book of the decade.

Gudbergur was a tall, handsome man with slightly greying hair and a modest, if not shy, demeanour. He was overly reserved, and absented himself from most occasions. Over dinner he told me he had seen me cross the street of Tjarnargata in Reykjavík nine years ago. He told me what I had been wearing, whom I had been with, and exactly how I had moved around the corner. I said he seemed to have an extraordinary memory. *Yes*, he told me, *at that time I was so sensitive, I remembered everything I ever saw.* When he looked at me across the table, his eyes were large and sad. The expression on his face was intense and seemed to say he had reason to be overly sensitive. I could not help thinking this must be how you look at a dinner companion you have decided to trust, if you have been abused earlier in life.

After our stay at the Castle in Caen, I took the 8:00 p.m. train to St. Lazarre. My cousin Thorir rode back with me. Thorir was such a good-looking man that people stopped what they were doing when he appeared. His perpetual smile drew people to him like a magnet. His casual demeanour made him seem comfortable in the world.

On the ride home we shared a first-class compartment. He bought us each a Heineken, and we sat down to catch up on family history. We told each other what had happened over the years. His brother was an actor in Paris. His sister, he said, disappeared. She was nineteen. It was ten years ago. She was depressed and her counsellor advised she go to school in Norway, near Sognefjorden. She went, but during the winter she wrote a good-bye note and then disappeared. Eventually the whole family was in Sognefjorden looking for her. They never found her. In the end it was assumed she had drowned herself.

I asked Thorir what could have made her do that. He sat with his elbows on his knees and looked at the floor. Then he looked me straight in the eye. *She was in love with a boy*, he said, *and he rejected her.*

My dear dear Jan. Missives that do not reach him. Thoughts that contain everything I know about him. How they cannot travel. Like orphans, they return to me. To my own fingers.

What he wanted from me. To reach into me and find something he did not have. As if my body contained the missing ruby. His naked body tightly against mine. His ardent love. The way he whispered my name to me as he loved me. As if my name were a revelation. *You are a revelation,* he said.

It was nearly eleven at night when we reached St. Lazarre. The wind was blowing rain-filled gusts in circles at the station. Thorir stood in the taxi line with me for a while. We parted with a handshake. It had been a topic of conversation in Caen, how different cultures construe different modes of parting. In France it is a kiss on each cheek. In Norway it is a warm hug. In Iceland it is a handshake. I got in a cab and made my way to a tiny hotel in the rue de l'Annonciation.

The hotel room was cold and barren. No pictures on the wall, no decoration. Just two single beds next to each other, a desk, and a telephone on the wall. When I took the receiver off the phone, the whole machine came loose and almost fell off the wall. I turned the heaters on. While I waited for the room to warm up, I tried to call my lover in Oslo. The lines to Norway were busy. I tried several times. I still had my coat and boots on, for the room was chilly. I could feel a certain anxiety crawling up my spine every time I heard the busy signal.

Outside were the rooftops and courtyards of central Paris. Flower beds hung in unlikely places along backyard walls. Chimneys stood up like sentinels.

About the city that night, diesel-fuelled trucks were parked everywhere, blocking traffic in and out of town. Truck drivers were on strike. They parked their trucks across the road, turned the lights off, and left them there as roadblocks all night. The news reached me that just a bit earlier, a sedan full of teenage boys tore into the roadblock. The boys wanted to get home. They were impatient. They took down the wooden barricades on the highway, got back into the car and sped down the road into Paris. They did not see the truck parked across the road. There were no lights. In the fury of their driving, they crashed into the truck. All the boys died.

He told me we could not meet again till it was over. That I had to wait. I did not know exactly what I was waiting on. I had to trust him. Put faith in what I did not know. Except that someone would be harmed, and I did not know who it was.

I counted the days till I would see him. Every morning I resumed the count as if for the first time. How many days left. I looked at the calendar once again, as if it were a stranger, and I had to decipher its hieroglyphics. Even now, alone in a cold hotel room in Paris, my black laced boots on my feet, still wearing the brown, knee-length velvet jacket I bought in Caen. Sitting on the edge of the thin bed with a telephone receiver in my hand. I could hear the beeps of the busy overseas line. I was counting days. The sense of isolation and helplessness seemed to emanate from the white walls of the room. I tried to keep the involuntary tears inside my eyes. Then I thought it did not matter. No one would care whether or not I wept in a small room in the rue de l'Annonciation.

The terrible duty, writes Clarice Lispector, *is that of going all the way to the end.*

It had not occurred to me until this moment that I would need to stay till the end. An ending I could not imagine, yet I should wait for it.

By the end of the school term I found everything in a strange kind of shambles. By seven in the evening, I collapsed with fatigue and slept until two. I got up in the middle of the night as if it were morning. Much of the city was still up. The last cars were plowing the roads with people getting home from parties. I made a pot of coffee and wondered again what was happening to me. There were all my projects lying about the apartment in pieces. Unfinished. It was clear to me that something valuable was gone. The ability to carry on uninterrupted. To finish what I started. To see things through. Where did it go?

In the beauty salon on Whyte Avenue, a very young woman cut my hair. Young men wearing costume jewelry and young women in black ran back and forth. While I waited I fingered a magazine. The kind of magazine put out for the young and the restless. Inside there was an advertisement for a

Champs Élysées perfume. There was a black and white photograph of the Champs Élysées in Paris. It was night and it was raining. The picture was blurry. Many cars were heading down the avenue with lights on. The caption said, *If you let your spirit free, where would it go?*

It was while I was in Paris that André Malraux was interred in the Parthenon. The ceremony was at night. The Parthenon was lit up to blaze magnificently in the black drizzle. People thronged the sides of the avenue and crowded around the square. Plexiglas covers had been constructed so the dignitaries would not get wet.

Six uniformed soldiers carried the remains of André Malraux on their shoulders. They marched in step down the square with the heavy coffin. Inside the box there must have been only bones. The corpse had been exhumed for this moment.

The term ended and I went back to my home in British Columbia. In the Vancouver airport I was picked up by my friend Imogen. She was there in her black and white checkered coat and curly brown hair. We took my suit-cases to the car. It was my own Jeep, which Imogen kept for me in Vancouver. As we drove to her house, she told me she had just read a book by Joseph H. Berke titled *The Tyranny of Malice*. She wanted me to borrow the book. It was about envy. About malice.

We had pasta with pesto sauce and a little wine. After, I took the book and the Jeep and headed out to Horseshoe Bay. It was the last ferry. Very few people waited to board. On the way across the sound, I fell asleep. When I arrived at my house, the place was cold. It was so evident no one had been there for at least six weeks. A lonely feeling.

I knew then that I loved my home and I did not love it. My reasons for moving into the country, away from everything, were still unclear to me. I did not know what I was trying to avoid by being so out of reach. Out of curiosity, I began to read Imogen's book. In it, Berke claims that envy, once aroused, is sadistic and malicious. The envied person is affected by the begrudging of the envier. The envier can actually alter the victim's responses to the world. He cites the case of Othello and Iago. How Iago alters not only Othello's perception but his whole psychology by his envious actions.

The envied one knows this. There is an attempt to escape. *The wish to escape from the envier*, Berke writes, *whether real or imagined, external or internal, leads the envied person to have an extreme sensitivity to the malevolent intentions of others. All his senses may be constantly attuned to detecting shafts of hatred and misfortune emanating from inanimate as well as human sources.*

It is this phenomenon that explains what is known as a fear of success. The fear of rousing envy. The fear of receiving compliments. Because it is dangerous.

The worst thing that can happen, he said to me on the phone, *is that someone dies from this*. I was looking out into the empty space that should have been the water of the fjord. Instead the falling snow shrouded the view. Nothing was visible except the dark air and the golf-ball-sized snowflakes lightly sailing down.

I was snowed in. The snow was wet and slippery. It was not possible to drive down the hillside and make the turn at the bottom without ending up in the forest below. Among the tall cedars, perhaps upside down in the Jeep. So I waited at home. Perhaps the weather would warm and the snow turn to rain. But the snow fell all day and all night. In the morning I saw the paw prints of some large animal, a cougar perhaps, threading its way from one end of my yard to the other. The path of the cougar cut a straight line just below my bedroom window.

I watched my colleague Jeremy unpack his diabetic kit. He took out a small vial of clear liquid, a wad of gauze, and one of the disposable needles. His slightly balding head, I noticed, actually suited him. His straight nose and clear eyes made him look focused. His face betrayed no expression. *I didn't know you were diabetic*, I said to him. He did not look up. *I'm not*, he countered. *Then what's this stuff?* I asked. *Isn't it insulin?*

He shook his head slightly. With his glasses on, he was filling the plastic compartment on the needle with the transparent solution. *And this isn't for me*, he corrected me. *This is my solution for you.*

My dear Jan. There was so much I could not have told him anyway. Imposing silence and secrecy made no difference after all. It was obvious to me that when two people communicate, most of what they wish to say is lost in the transaction.

There were not many ways to avoid feeling pain. Just a few. From my reading, I could tell how some release their pain by transferring it to others. Some internalize the pain and suffer immensely. For me there was a way after all. Just numb it. I found it did not hurt at all. Just a moment, while the needle went through.

It was not something I would have wanted to tell him anyway. How I simply let it happen. The way I had let everything happen this time. Let my life wash over me without trying to control it. At first it seemed of no consequence. Jeremy and I continued to talk about work, colleagues, the weather. About ourselves and the books we read. I stood up to go home. It was getting late.

On my way to the front door, I stopped. Standing in the middle of the floor, I noticed the room was going through changes.

How do you translate the silence of the real encounter between the two of us? asks Clarice Lispector.

It's so hard to speak and say things that cannot be said. So we let it go. We do not try to translate. There is no meaning to find here except in the light beating of the heart and the sweet tinge of nerves that will not go away. To read our encounter as a poem. To try not to impose meaning, but simply let it wash over.

At Christmas I went back to Copenhagen. While I was gone, my Aunt Bodil had made peace with her daughter Kari. She, in turn, had made peace with her son, Njord. My two aunts, Trine and Bodil, who had never been close, had made peace with each other and begun to socialize together. The two sisters, Kari and Gitte, had made peace with each other as well. It was almost a shock to me when I walked into the house. I came back to a happy family.

My cousin Niels Eric was a tall, slender fellow with yellow hair. He was a gardener by trade and wanted to show me the gardens at Frederiksborg Castle. We drove through the tiny Danish villages with crooked roads meandering through straw-thatched houses made of stone, bracketed by wooden borders. There was a thin layer of frost everywhere and haze in the air. When Niels Eric spoke, his voice was subdued and he seemed to mumble. It was the dialect of inner Copenhagen and I was not used to it. He had a scar on his chin from an accident at work and wide open, blue eyes.

We parked at a village roadside and walked onto the castle grounds. The sun was low in the sky and the haze shrouded the light. The castle towers stood in silhouette against the orange sun. Around the towering building was a wide moat, and the water in it was lead grey. In December, when the leaves were gone, the pruned linden trees stood crooked and knobbly like sentinels from death. The walks along those denuded trunks were eerie. Something out of a dangerous tale.

After a while I found myself freezing cold. The black leather boots and brown felt coat that somehow kept me warm on the Canadian prairie at thirty below were suddenly far too thin and flimsy in the Danish winter frost. The climate was much milder in Denmark, but strangely much colder. The cold penetrated my bones and my feet ached.

We went into the castle, thinking perhaps we could warm up inside. The fortress was a labyrinth of rooms. We repeatedly got lost wandering from room to room. Each room had several doors in all directions and there were no hallways. The building was very cold, and I did not get rid of the chill in my bones. I wandered around inside the labyrinthine castle, shivering. Everywhere overhead hung portraits in oil of Danish aristocrats. They all wore wigs and were overweight and ugly. They must have been short people because the beds looked like they were meant for children. Later I learned they slept sitting up in them.

Niels Eric told me that Frederiksborg Castle had once been gutted by fire and had to be rebuilt inside. It happened because the king was so cold that he ordered fires to be lit in all the fireplaces. In every room the fires were going, and the whole castle burned down. When they rebuilt, radiators were installed. A mild warmth issued from them where they stood under the huge windows. I went up to one of the radiators to get warmed up. With my cold hands on the heater, I stood and looked out the window at the grounds we had just come through. The surreal linden trees towered beyond. The tiny village beside the grounds could be seen between the huge trunks. Yellow stuccoed farmhouses and silver-frosted grass. I felt at home.

Fantasy is a place where it rains, asserts Italo Calvino in *Six Memos for the Next Millennium*. He is talking about Dante's *Purgatorio*. The poet is in the circle of the Wrathful and has a myriad of images form in his mind. *He realizes that these images rain down from the heavens.*

I was trying to remember what freedom was like. The personal freedom that had taken so many years to perfect. How I had thrown it all away because of love. Not mild or gentle, but mad. A mad and violent love that made me desperate. How I lost myself.

In the early morning, the sky still black over my university city, I looked at the lights glinting in the distance. The occasional spot of yellow that moved in the sky to say an airplane was coming in or leaving. The cold frost on the streets. Eddies of old snow fanning in circles at corners.

I was thinking about spring. My home in the hills above the Pacific Ocean. About going home and closing the door. Secure in myself.

In the centre of Oslo there was a high fashion boutique by the name of Désirée. The haute couture shop was on the corner of a slick part of downtown. Cars drove past on the avenue and slowed down at Désirée's corner. The windows displayed a row of full-sized mannequins in elegant attire. It was December. All the mannequins were garbed in shiny, ruby red dresses. Some had black vests or black shoes or little black jackets, but all the dresses were bright red.

It was rumoured in Oslo that the owner of Désirée was the king's mistress. That sometimes at night, a limousine pulled up to her door and then drove her to the palace at the end of Karl Johan Street. There, Norway's solitary king waited.

It's time now, he said to me over the phone. *We can't put it off any longer. We need to be together.*

I picked up my airplane ticket at the post office in Caen, in France. A pleasant man behind the counter rolled a cylinder into the wall, and after a minute the cylinder rolled back with my ticket inside. On the way back from the post office, the streets of Caen became congested around the stadium. A hockey game was about to start. The taxi driver picked up his wife on the way. She seated herself in the front beside him. Her hair was newly shaped and lacquered. Her face was painted and her nails were stark red.

We crawled through the tight Normandy streets. I was thinking to myself in the back seat. Who was this man in Oslo who could tell me to wait and I waited? Who told me to come to him and I went? As I sat quietly in the back, looking at the passing antique shops and lingerie boutiques and cafés, it seemed to me I was hypnotized.

I sent a black velvet dress ahead of me in the post. It was a simple, ankle-length affair, with long sleeves and high collar. It was not clear to me the occasion would ever arise when I would wear the dress. But he kept it for me. In the end I did put it on. It was to see Puccini's *Tosca* at the old Oslo Opera House.

In the first act of *Tosca*, the two lovers are introduced and flirt their way through to the end. In the second act, he is tortured and then she is tortured. The torture lasts to the end. In the third act, he is jailed, she commits murder, he is executed, and then she is executed.

When I arrived at the train station in St. Lazarre in Paris, it was already dark. A heavy rain fell and an icy wind blew. The damp chill penetrated my brown felt coat. I tried to figure out which train went to Caen. It was not obvious to me.

The station was dark and damp. Debris lay about the concrete floor. Some mad people wandered aimlessly, mumbling. The entrance to the tracks was open to the wind that welled through. People stood in stony silence, faces intense, shoulders hunched forward. They crowded around the board that displayed track numbers. As soon as a new number appeared, they raced madly to the train. The sound they made rushing forward was thick and furry. Overhead, heavy pigeons flapped across the open spaces under the ceiling.

The family was assembled for a late holiday dinner. We were in my Aunt Trine's log house in the countryside, near the village of Kregme in northern Sjælland. The long table stretched from the dining room into the kitchen. Food went around and wine was poured. All my aunts and uncles and cousins and cousins' children were talking like a happy family. I had been so cold when we were out walking earlier in the day, and the food warmed me up.

It seemed to me they were beginning to understand that I was returning. That I would be a presence at these gatherings from this year on. They were not sure what to make of it. They did not ask many questions. Niels Eric sat opposite me across the wooden table. He kept returning his attention to me, as if there was something he was about to say.

I told them I was going to Norway to see my lover. That he had sent me this ticket when I was in France. Niels Eric's sport was hiking, and he said he often went to Norway to wander in the mountains. He had a mischievous look on his face. His short yellow hair appeared matte in the low light of the room. *You know*, he said, *if you put a roof over Norway, it would be one long church.*

When we walked into his house in Oslo, he presented me with a gift. It was a gold chain with a gold pendant on it. Two loose ends were connected around a small, bright ruby.

When I was fourteen, I was confirmed in a small, wooden church. My family banded together and gave me a gold cross on a gold chain. I put the cross on around my neck and never took it off again.

Now I took the cross off for the first time. I put the small, red ruby around my neck instead. *I have a new mythology*, I said to him.

The rose is the feminine flower, writes Clarice Lispector, *that gives of itself all and so completely that the only joy left to it is to have given itself.*

All day I tried to understand. How I removed myself from my life and then longed for my life back. I knew I could take it back any time. Nothing went away. My work, my friends, my home, my family. They were all there. It was I who was no longer there. Everything was up to me.

The days passed slowly. I did not go to the office. Instead I took my work home. The afternoon lingered, sunshine coming in the window. The weather warmed. Small drops fell from the balcony above. I tried to concentrate, but my mind was elsewhere. I could not help thinking that if you give yourself away, you want to know you have not thrown yourself away.

Through the window of the small airplane, the floodplain that is Denmark receded on the left while the jagged edges of the Scandinavian peninsula appeared on the right. So close. I left my cousin Gitte's husband, Harry, at the airport in Kastrup, Copenhagen, and boarded the flight for Fornebu at Oslo. Harry could not help carry my bag because of a bad back. But somehow we got it to the check-in. Now I was taking the last leg of a long journey. My lover was in Fornebu airport waiting behind those glass doors.

I could tell I was nervous. I had not seen him for months. Months of silence and desperation. Always the promise this day would come, and the fear it never would. The counting of days. The staring at the silent telephone. The days of doubt, when I had given him up for lost. The way you do with relatives gone to war, whom you do not hear from anymore. The sense that something unsayable has happened. Someone has died. And yet the day came. Inexplicably the airplane began its descent over Oslofjorden.

The department I worked in was divided between two factions: the conservatives and the radicals. The conservatives wanted traditional teaching and traditional texts. The radicals wanted innovative teaching and nontraditional texts. The conservatives wanted to strictly safeguard the field. The radicals wanted to involve all sorts of other disciplines.

My colleague Jeremy was in the forefront of the conservatives. He was in a gang that called themselves merit only, which meant they were against affirmative action. I was grouped among the radicals. One of the post-modernists, which meant I knew no bounds. These two factions were not on speaking terms. Hateful polemics sometimes appeared in the university and city media, one side pitted against the other and townspeople generally siding with the conservatives. Some arguments between members of the different factions ended up in a call for lawyers or in resignations. There was always character assassination involved.

For this reason it was highly unorthodox that I should find myself in Jeremy's apartment. Theoretically we should never be friends. For us to be together was like crossing over from the West side to the East side, or from the East side to the West side. A sense of betrayal was in the air.

It occurred to me I should be careful with my Karma. That my Karma remained much the same as it was ten years ago. Something always interfered with my plans to abdicate my own life. It was never in the books that I should be allowed to give myself over and try to live on another's agenda. I was forced back to my own track. It seemed to me an ominous record, and I would be a fool to disregard the evidence. That the only way to prevent the chaos of taking a wrong turn was to realize my fate and stick to it.

Or perhaps that was what my Karma was actually made of. My sense of doom when it came to my own happiness. That I would not forge ahead because I thought I should have to pay for it. Pay for my own happiness. That happiness was not something I could expect. It would never come to me. I could not help wondering how it was possible to know these things. What was the truth about fate?

There is a suspicion that the world unfolds according to your own expectations.

My dear Jan. In every greeting there is a hidden farewell. Because we have been apart long enough to require a greeting, there is the understanding we will be apart again.

Something in his story did not wash. No matter how hard I tried to reason out the circumstances, the story could not come clean. I became weary of taking his side. Of blaming others for what was happening to him. The idea that we are responsible for ourselves took hold of me.

It was the first time I had ever been upset at him. Before this, my blinding love clouded all perspective. Perhaps this was a sign that I was awakening. That he was losing his power over me. That I wanted to awaken. The dreams that beset me had become bad dreams.

But the daylight I woke to was bitter and cold. The radio announced it was minus thirty-four. However, there was a wind, so the effective temperature was minus seventy-two. They said your skin would freeze in one minute if it was exposed.

I trudged to work in the extreme cold. We had a thesis defence scheduled, something I had supervised. The examination took place in a room with big windows through which the arctic air penetrated. I had two extra sweaters with me and a box of Kleenex with which to nurse a cold. The candidate answered all the questions. He proved himself intellectually competent and well read. So I took him and the committee to the Highlevel Diner for lunch when it was over. My colleague Doug sat across from me over leek soup and told us about a friend of his in Siberia. In Siberia it got to be sixty below. When people walked along the road, you could see the trail of the swath they cut in the air. The groove in the sliced air behind them remained visible for several minutes after they were gone.

I had been back from Oslo for a week when I fell ill. It was something I might have expected. The intensity of our meeting, the sense of expectation, and then returning. Then nothing. The sky over my university city was bleak and cold. The streets were slick and frosty. I battled my condition for a week, continuing to go to work, until I gave up. Cancelled everything and took myself in hand. It was a self-destructive attitude to care nothing for my health. I could not understand where this disposition came from.

For the weekend I returned to British Columbia to finish what appeared to be a good recovery. It was warm in Vancouver. The sun was shining. People were out in their shirt sleeves. The smell of wet cedar and salt sea air reminded me I was glad to be back. I knew somehow in my bones that I had been very upset. But I did not know exactly why. What about. Whatever it was, the toll was being taken.

It occurred to me only too late that I might have been wrong. I was expecting something to happen. A casualty. That we could not come to the end of our story without someone falling by the wayside. Now, when I looked around me, I could see the table, the lamp, the Kelim rug. I knew the room was spinning. I knew it was because I had allowed Jeremy to put that needle in my arm. But it had not occurred to me till that moment that the casualty was me. It would be me.

That I had walked into a trap I could not get out of. The walls were moving toward me. The floor was rising at me. I could see the door from where I stood. It was the door I was heading toward. A large, brown door without a threshold. On the other side was a hallway and an elevator. I would go down the lift and out to the sidewalk. The early night air would be crisp. The river on my left. I could go down to the river along the walking trail. The snow would be crusty and old under my shoes. But my feet were not moving.

In those few moments of what seemed like extreme clarity, all of Oslo returned itself to me. I remembered clearly that Oslo did not have many faces. It was the dark time of year. Daylight came late and night arrived early. In between, the sky was overcast and the clouds were tin-coloured. The air was humid. In the winter cold, hoarfrost settled everywhere. The barren trees were layered in a coat of rime. In the park in Bygdøy there was a sculpture of a nude, life-sized man. He was lying down on his right side in the snow. With a white coat of hoarfrost patched on him everywhere, it was hard to tell this was not the corpse of an unfortunate wanderer.

In the building that had been erected to house all of Edvard Munch's paintings, pride of place was given to a canvas titled *The Sick Child*. It was a painting of a young girl sitting on the edge of a bed and a woman administering to her. The girl had yellow hair and a pale face. Her expression, looking up in profile, was angelic. The painter had written about the picture, *This is not just a painting of my dying sister. This is everyone I have ever lost.*

Almost everyone in Edvard Munch's family died before the age of thirty. Those who were not dead yet were coughing. It was the inheritance of tuberculosis. A ghost that would not vanish.

Munch's most famous painting, *The Scream*, was stolen. The news flash went out all over the world. *The Scream* had been stolen.

South of Oslo is a series of small villages. One of them is called Berger, once a factory village. The industry was shut down now. The large, red brick factory in the centre of the village, where they used to make blankets, was abandoned. Artists had moved in. Outside the door was a life-sized sculpture by a local sculptor, Marit Wiklund, of a nude man standing, gesticulating. His body was dented all over, as if he had been severely beaten.

Below were streets lined with rows of identical wooden shacks. Small, white row houses, which were factory workers' quarters before, were now lived in by others. It was dark and the streetlights were few and dim. The streets at night were empty corridors. No one was about. It seemed to me just then that it was easy to imagine being poor.

It had been so long. I was afraid my memory deceived me. That the man I remembered, the one I had written to, spoken with, waited with, waited for, was different. That the one I cancelled myself for was not the one I remembered.

I had on the brown velvet jacket from France. I told him he should look for the jacket in case I too was different. It had been so long. While I waited for the baggage to come out onto the conveyor belt, I could sense that strange, vacant feeling that comes when a flood of emotions proves too much for the limited brain. One feeling cancelled out the other. Instead of a weakness in the knees, I had the kind of energy that is peculiar to soldiers heading for the front lines. I took my blue bag and walked toward the glass doors. I knew he was there on the other side of the glass. I went through.

Oslo is the world's largest village, my cousin Niels Eric claimed during dinner at my Aunt Trine's cabin near Kregme. He was joking. Everyone around the long, wooden table laughed. I disregarded his remark. The Scandinavians, I knew, were always making fun of one another. But when I came to Oslo and began living there, I discovered Niels Eric's joke had a ring of truth. That with the exception of the downtown core, all the Oslo neighbourhoods were like villages. There were village streets, village corner groceries, village houses made of wood, and village neighbours.

The basement apartment that was to be my home was very small. It was the bottom floor of a single-storey house. There were only two rooms, both overheated, condensation forming along the windows. The kitchen was only a corner of the single room where everything went on. Old and faded furniture lined the place. We did not notice. We spent our days and nights in each other's arms.

It was something I had not thought myself capable of. That I would exchange my life of luxury, an estate by the sea in British Columbia, a desirable university job, for a life of poverty among the hills of southern Norway. Where the water in the fjord froze every winter. Where the damp cold penetrated the wooden walls. Where we had to search the lining of our coat pockets to find loose change so we could get a bit of herring. It had appeared to me finally, after all this time, that love was the only thing that counted. After love, the love you have for another, everything else falls away. Everything else is unimportant.

The night was dark. Almost no streetlights could be seen. We slept in each other's arms in the small bedroom. Tightly together, we would not let each other go.

I awoke to the sound of his voice. He was asleep but his lips were parted. It was a nightmare. He screamed. He was trying to wake himself up from the horrible dream, so he screamed.

Dear, dear Jan. We came to a place where my words could finally reach him. We could send our words over the wire. We could talk on the telephone. The white phone in my living room showed signs of use. A darker band where my hand gripped the receiver. The sweat of my palm because there was always some level of agitation. That we were always too far away from each other. Being together only made the later, inevitable separation worse.

And yet I wanted my freedom. My desire to be free lingered, like the remnants of a disease you cannot quite recover from. *And that's why I sense we shall soon separate,* writes Clarice Lispector. *My astonishing truth is that I was always alone, separate from you, and I didn't know it. Now I know; I'm alone. I and my freedom.*

It was a winter that would not go away. In the middle of March, it was still twenty-one below. Snow was still falling. Roofs of houses had snow piled high. Streets remained impassable. On election day in Alberta, there was a blizzard. City streets had not been cleared because of government spending cutbacks. People risked their lives behind the wheel. Only fifty-seven percent of the populace made it to the polls, and they re-elected the Tories. This way we could be sure the streets would remain unsafe for the next four years.

I did not tell my lover directly what I was thinking, but he knew. It was apparent to him across the distance between us that I was withdrawing. It was a psychic withdrawal. An emotional fading. He said he could hear it in the tone of my voice. That I had begun to whisper. That he was determined to persuade me to stay with him. To return to him.

Two days later he was on a British Airways flight that landed in Vancouver at five in the evening. I promised to be there and to take him to my home in the mountains. The home I wanted to keep for my own life. As I waited in the new wing of the Vancouver Airport, I thought of the words of Clarice Lispector. What she said about the life I wanted for myself. *Yes, life is very oriental,* she wrote. She talked about *the elusive and delicate freedom of life. It's like knowing how to arrange flowers in a vase; an almost useless skill.*

Because I went home, to my retreat in British Columbia, to think. To ask myself the important questions. The big questions. As it happened, it was Valentine's Day. At ten in the morning on the fourteenth of February, a dark-haired woman knocked on my door. She was holding a bouquet of flowers. She delivered the flowers to me and said she was from Anne Lynn's flower shop in the village. I took the bouquet and read the card. It was from my lover. He was trying to win me over again.

I did not have a vase, so I took down an old pewter coffee pot. The pot had belonged to my mother, who got it from her father, who got it from his ancestors. The pot originated on the Jylland peninsula. Now it stood on the railing of the landing in my house. Out of this small ancestral inheritance, my lover's live spray of tiger lilies, carnations, roses, and daisies burst open.

I began to gather strength. This time I could tell I was much more successful. I altered my thinking. Put on men's clothes. Jeans and men's shirts, striped suits and ties. I invited my friend Linda to come to my house in the mountains for three days. Linda was getting a divorce. I said to her we should celebrate her divorce, which happened to fall on Valentine's Day. Three days before my lover flew in from London.

The only restaurant with a free table on February fourteenth was Lord Jim's Resort, sixty kilometres north on the coast. Linda and I drove through the black rain, turned off the highway, and wound our way to the resort through the dense forest. It was a log cabin by the sea. We walked in, my black suit five sizes too large, so the sleeves hung out over my hands and the pants bunched up at the bottom. But I was feeling careless.

Linda and I turned out to be the only same-sex couple in the place. They were trying to serve haute cuisine that evening. Nouveau cuisine at Lord Jim's consisted of simply putting very little food on the plate. During dinner a woman in high heels went around to all the tables offering a long-stemmed rose to the lady. When she came to our table, she stood there lost, holding the bright red rose. She looked from one to the other and did not know which one of us to give the flower to.

So I think that once we are no longer little children, it is really up to us to show a certain poise, and stride out into the space provided for us, Christa Wolf said in an interview. Now it seemed to me that it was useless to do anything else. To be courageous, to face what there was. Not to flinch. Not to complain. And I had made my decisions. To stand on my ground. Not to give myself away.

So I stood at the Vancouver International Airport. It was the new terminal with the green sculpture by Bill Reid. Of a canoe full of creatures. The sculpture said we are all packed in the same canoe together. We cannot escape. In my long, navy, pinstriped suit jacket, I paced the gleaming floors. I sat down and read the *Globe and Mail* cover to cover. Then the *Vancouver Sun*. A kind of peace had descended on me.

Eventually they let the passengers out of the British Airways flight from London. One by one they came through the glass doors and strode down the long passageway.

The unseasonable cold lay over all of Canada. It was at that time that I went on a business trip to Saskatoon. From cold city to cold city. At the Ramada Inn, where I was put, the American rooms were large with big beds in them. Downstairs in the huge foyer, people in jeans and cowboy hats and big winter parkas ran in and out energetically. I unpacked in the room and went out for a walk. There was a brisk wind. Snow was everywhere. I chanced into a shop that was selling everything at nearly a hundred percent discount, so I bought a red shirt. It was blood red.

Next morning I made coffee in the room with the machine provided. It was a pale, icy morning. I put on the blood-red shirt and drank the coffee. Settled in to read a book of interviews with Christa Wolf. It occurred to me that I was strangely happy. Even though it was only yesterday I was so agitated. Yesterday I wept over what lay between me and my lover. Today I was strangely happy. I did not understand my own happiness.

The poet Tim Lilburn picked me up at the Saskatoon airport. He was a little rounder than I remembered him. He had on a white jacket and white trousers, padded on the inside, and a fur hat. We went out to lunch. Tim had a glass of Australian Shiraz and we talked about wine. About living in rural Saskatchewan in houses that cost only a thousand dollars.

In the evening several of us were gathered in a Vietnamese restaurant where we spent a long time talking and sampling what appeared to be an endless number of dishes continually appearing. Afterward we all went in different directions. As I got into my friends' car, I looked down the street where Tim was walking away by himself. It was a lonely, white-clad figure that walked away from us in the snow.

The floor in Jeremy's apartment rose to meet me. I knew what was going on. It was clear to me I had allowed this to happen. It was also obvious to me that what I had done would have to take its course. I could not turn the clock back. We could not even go back the twenty minutes or so since my colleague Jeremy had put the needle into my arm. He said I would feel better. He said I would forget my pain. The illness of uncertainty and fear my lover had caused. The apprehension someone was being harmed. And that person must be me. It rang like a siren in my ear that it must be me. The light in the distant darkness that signaled an oncoming train.

It was the dead of night. The sky was pitch black. The ocean water below the floor was coal black. Our house was made of wood and shaped like an octagon. It was a houseboat because it floated on the water, tied lightly to the pier. He and I, my lover and I, were inside. We were seated at a small, round table. Perhaps we were having dinner. There was a child with us. I did not remember if the child was his, or mine, or one we had together.

We looked out the window into the south. Just then a train sped into view. I said happily to the child, 'Look, a water-train.' Because it was a sleek, yellow train that ran on the water like a hydrofoil. The train went very fast. Just outside our houseboat, the water-train made a sharp turn. All the wagons behind the engine ended up banging sideways into the platform of our house. We felt the reverberations like heavy earthquakes. The whole house veered and jolted with each wagon that hit. The house came loose from its moorings.

Just when I thought it was over and the train would continue, the engine turned toward us. The front light shone starkly into the dark interior of the house. A big clip in front of the train took hold of the deck of the house and began to push us. It dawned on me, only too late, that the train was taking us away. The whole house and everything in it. The three of us, surprised inside. The yellow water-train sped off into the darkest night, carrying us three in its mouth.

Clarice Lispector I have been reading all along. *The Stream of Life*. It is a short book, only seventy pages. It is chaotic and formless. There is no pattern or development. She says her writing is *a night passed entirely on a back road where no one is*. She says her story is *of roots dormant in their strength*.

It is that strength I find myself drawing from. I wonder at her, that other woman, who gave something of herself I could take, so long after. It was something she wrote in between. While sitting on a warm verandah, a cigarette smoking itself in the ashtray. She had moments of happiness. *I'm being happy*, she wrote, *because I refuse to be vanquished*. But more: *therefore I love*, she says. *That's happiness: even love that doesn't work out, even love that ends.*

To be free, says Toni Morrison in her short book *Playing in the Dark*, is also the freedom *to narrate the world*. To say what is. To be in my own story and not someone else's. That is what I saw in Clarice Lispector's book. She seized her own story and held it. The way a tiny Rufous Hummingbird holds on to the naked branch below. The branch stands straight into the sky without leaves, and on the very tip is a red-throated hummingbird, ticking for a new aerial display. It is his desire to fling straight up and then throw himself down at breakneck speed.

I know it is not an easy flight he is about to make. But he will. I know he will.

WORKS CITED

Berke, Joseph H. *The Tyranny of Malice.* New York: Summit Books, 1988.

Calvino, Italo. *Six Memos for the Next Millennium.* New York: Vintage, 1988.

Cixous, Hélène. *Coming to Writing and Other Essays.* London: Harvard University Press, 1991.

Dillard, Annie. *The Writing Life.* New York: Harper Collins, 1990.

Guterson, David. *Snow Falling on Cedars.* New York: Vintage, 1995.

Hesse, Hermann. *Steppenwolf.* Trans. Basil Creighton. New York: Henry Holt, 1963.

Lispector, Clarice. *The Stream of Life.* Trans. Elizabeth Lowe and Earl Fitz. Minneapolis: University of Minnesota Press, 1989.

Morrison, Toni. *Beloved.* New York: Signet, 1991.

———. *Playing in the Dark.* New York: Vintage, 1992.

Robbe-Grillet, Alain. *For a New Novel.* Trans. Richard Howard. Evanston: Northwestern University Press, 1965.

Welty, Eudora. *The Eye of the Story.* New York: Vintage, 1990.

Wolf, Christa. *The Fourth Dimension: Interviews with Christa Wolf.* Trans. Hilary Pilkington. London: Verso, 1988.

NOTES AND ACKNOWLEDGEMENTS

The five books contained in this volume were written and published separately over a decade. I wrote them slowly, and the writing ended up becoming a kind of ritual. I was more engaged with the act of writing than what would become of the text once done. At the time I took seriously the Bakhtinian thought that books do not exist in isolation: the books that appear over time talk to each other and they generate each other like a different species of life. I wanted to be transparent about the books that influenced my writing so I could feel I was engaging in an international conversation not bounded by time.

I was, throughout, aware of the requirement in our time to be 'authentic' and 'original,' and yet that was not how I experienced writing: not as a monologue, but as a dialogue. I was aware of the reality that this kind of text cannot end, so there is always a new one so long as you are able to write. This actuality creates a tension within the text that needs to end but does not want to end. Nor do any of these texts have an obvious beginning. When they are all joined together in one long work, they have found their true format: they can now be read as the long journey from innocence to experience that they are.

In coming together like this, the five books constitute a long work in sections, each of which has its own theme: Remembering; Grief and Loss; Dreaming and Lingering; Reading; and Relationships. These themes are rendered in a blend of essay, both creative and academic; fiction, in that the stories here are fictional and not 'true'; and poetic reflection, in that the narratives often operate as poetry would, with the same associative leaps and symbolic or metaphoric layering. In some cases, there is also the input of a kind of 'memoir' writing. There are inevitably 'ghost books' behind each of these texts in terms of temperament: Marguerite Duras's *The Lover*; *Njáls saga*; Clarice Lispector's *The Stream of Life*; Marcel Proust's *Remembrance of Things Past*; and Hermann Hesse's *Steppenwolf*.

I am indebted to the late Dennis Johnson, publisher of Red Deer College Press, for being a great supporter and for being willing to bring each one of these books out. He had the creative energy to make them happen, which I was grateful for. Now I am indebted to Kazim Ali, who has been equally supportive and has motivated the present publication. I have a lot to thank him for, including the essay contained here. I would finally like to thank Alana Wilcox and the team at Coach House Books for their positive and enthusiastic willingness to take this on.

One learns over time that not only do books not get written in isolation, they do not appear as published volumes without the input of a large group of literary people who make literary history unfold.

Kristjana Gunnars is a writer and painter, author of several books of various genres, and she frequently exhibits her artwork in Canada. She has participated in Buddhist groups and retreats with Tibetan teachers in years past. She lives in British Columbia, Canada. She is currently Visiting Professor in Languages and Literature at the University of Iceland in Reykjavík.

Typeset in Arno and Domaine.

Printed at the Coach House on bpNichol Lane in Toronto, Ontario, Lynx Cream paper, which was manufactured in Saint-Jérôme, Quebec. This book was printed with vegetable-based ink on a 1973 Heidelberg KORD offset litho press. Its pages were folded on a Baumfolder, gathered by hand, bound on a Sulby Auto-Minabinda, and trimmed on a Polar single-knife cutter.

Coach House is on the traditional territory of many nations, including the Mississaugas of the Credit, the Anishnabeg, the Chippewa, the Haudenosaunee, and the Wendat peoples, and is now home to many diverse First Nations, Inuit, and Métis peoples. We acknowledge that Toronto is covered by Treaty 13 with the Mississaugas of the Credit. We are grateful to live and work on this land.

Cover design by Natalie Olsen, Kisscut Design
Interior design by Crystal Sikma
Author photo by Charles Marxer

Coach House Books
80 bpNichol Lane
Toronto ON M5S 3J4
Canada

416 979 2217
800 367 6360

mail@chbooks.com
www.chbooks.com